Mirrors of the Past

Mirrors
of the
Past

KIRSTY FERRY

Cornish Secrets Book 5

Choc Lit
A JOFFE BOOKS COMPANY

Choc Lit
A Joffe Books company
www.choc-lit.com

First published in Great Britain in 2024

Cover art by Alexandra Allden

ISBN: 978-1781898017

To my family, with love.

CHAPTER ONE

Present

When Tegan Burton arrived at Pencradoc, the first thing she did was to drop her well-travelled suitcase on the ground and stare up at the old building.

'Hello, Pencradoc,' she said. 'Where are all your ghosts, then?'

The grand old house, which stood on the very edge of Bodmin Moor in Cornwall, didn't respond.

Tegan hadn't really expected it to. It was just a step too far to believe in the Pencradoc ghosts. Her sister, Merryn, swore the place was swarming with them, but Tegan wasn't convinced. Tegan had, she liked to think, both feet too firmly on the ground for any spectral visitors to whoosh up to her and go "Boo!"

'Nobody there? Nope? Okay.' She shrugged and picked up her case. 'I guess this is the point where I need to go and meet my new boss. Last call for any ghosts!' She raised her voice and looked around. Still nothing. Unsurprising. 'Right. Coren Penhaligon, here I come.' She walked up the steps into the grey building, which perhaps should have felt foreboding but definitely didn't.

Pencradoc was an arts centre — it was populated by artists and creatives who taught and learned from one another. Visitors and families enjoyed looking at the galleries and wandering through the centre and gardens — perhaps stopping by the Tower Tearoom for a coffee and a cake — and, if Merryn was to believed, all the while being supervised by ancient members of the Pencradoc family who had lived and loved there years before. Merryn's husband, Kit, and her brother-in-law, Coren, had inherited the place a few years ago from their Great-Aunt Loveday and turned it into what it was now — not only a highly respected place for the arts, but a beloved local community hub and a place that attracted visitors from all over the country.

And that place, Tegan thought as she looked around the hallway, was the location of her new job.

'Little Elsie!' she cried, momentarily forgetting she was trying to find her new boss and hurrying towards a marble bust of a little girl at the bottom of the stairs. 'Well, I've heard all about *you*, that's for sure.' The girl was beautiful, all wild hair, mischievous eyes and a big smile. She was the famous Lady Elsie Pencradoc, an ancestor of Kit and Coren, and someone who had, if all accounts were to be believed, tilted Edwardian society on its axis by her surprisingly modern outlook for the world she'd lived in as an adult.

Patting the marble curls and taking a moment to appreciate the sculpture, Tegan continued through the hallway. Merryn had given her directions to find Coren's office and Tegan walked confidently towards it.

Starting a new job was exciting and something new, and she always looked forward to the challenges and excitement it brought. Tegan had a very varied CV, it had to be said: hospitality and tourism expertise, barista work, waitressing, a chalet girl in Switzerland. She'd worked in a gift shop. She'd been a tour guide. She'd done nannying and event planning. She had a raft of qualifications in all sorts of things, but she hadn't yet found her niche.

That was the one thing she envied her sister for. Merryn was the eldest, settled and sensible, working for an art dealer in London, then she'd come here, to Pencradoc. Met Kit. And the rest, as they said, was history. History that was about to become even more settled and sensible with the imminent arrival of Merryn's first child.

Tegan shuddered. She didn't envy *that*. She had too much of the world to see and too much of her life to live yet.

Oh. And lemon-picking in Sicily. That had been Tegan's most recent adventure. But she was ready for a change of scenery, ready to sort some things out in her head, and this post at Pencradoc — as Merryn's maternity leave, no less — was the ideal solution. She'd do Merryn's job for the year, as agreed. Decide what she wanted to do with her life in the meantime. And move on.

* * *

Ryan knew there was a logical order to the boxes and boxes of "stuff" in the family archives at Wheal Mount. It just wasn't *his* logical order. That was all.

Tammy, the archivist at Wheal Mount, and the woman who seemingly guarded the archives with fire and brimstone, had worked with a placement student last year to get some of it organised. The student, Bryony, had left, and Ryan had made the mistake one day of mentioning that it sounded like quite an interesting task.

Tammy had reported back to Sybill, the manager of Wheal Mount Arts Centre, and almost straight away he'd been called into Sybill's office and welcomed with a big smile. Which had scared him a lot. Usually intent and efficient, Sybill had loosened up over the last few weeks and then she and Coren Penhaligon at Pencradoc had announced their pregnancy news, so she'd been smiling much more.

But it had still been pretty scary to stand in her office and be — well — smiled at.

'Ryan.' Her smile had grown wider. 'Tammy's been telling me a few things.'

'Sure . . .' He blinked, confused. He talked to Tammy a lot; the pair of them had been at Wheal Mount the longest out of all the staff and had formed a friendly relationship, so he wondered which "thing" Sybill was referring to.

'So, the thing I'm interested in,' Sybill continued, as if reading his mind, 'was your interest in the archives.'

'Oh! Yeah. I just said that it seemed there was still a lot of work to do, but the things they'd found had been good. Especially since you've got Pencradoc's stores too.'

'Yes. We all decided the Pencradoc items were safer here.' Pencradoc and Wheal Mount had been owned by the same family, and everyone at Pencradoc knew that Sybill had more experience and more staff to deal with them. 'But, our placement student could only do so much. And Tammy is fantastic, but I'm going to be working more closely with her on the day-to-day management of the centre, because she'll be covering my maternity leave. It makes a lot of sense.'

'Yes — it does. Tammy will be great in that role.' Ryan smiled, genuinely delighted for his friend.

'She will. But it means there'll be a big gap to fill in the archives and stores management. Which is where, Ryan, you come in.' And there was that smile again. Yep. Still scary. 'Because you've been with us a while, I'd like to give you more responsibility at Wheal Mount Arts Centre, and I think that's a perfect place to start.'

'Oh! Well — yeah. Thanks. That's great. But I'm not sure how long I'll be staying. I'm going to have to start thinking about a career. A proper career.' He caught Sybill's horrified look and quickly back-tracked. 'I mean, I love it here, I really do — and, yeah, it's a great career for you and Tammy and such like—' hell, she looked even *more* cross with him — 'but do you really want me here on a more permanent basis?' Yes. Good. That was a good thing to say. 'What I'm trying to say, is that I've worked here for years, through my course and everything—'

4

'Just like I did,' replied Sybill, a little coldly. 'I started by sitting on a seat and welcoming visitors too, you know.'

'Yes, I know. But what if — what if . . .' He took a deep breath. 'What if I decide to go back to Glasgow or something?' Ryan thought back to the summer job he'd had during his course at a gallery in the west of Glasgow. He loved the vibe up there and he fully intended going back at some point.

'Your point being?' asked Sybill. She blinked at him and a chill ran across his shoulder blades.

'My point is,' he said uncomfortably, 'is that I haven't really decided where I want to settle yet.'

'But you have no imminent plans to go to Glasgow?'

'No.'

That was a small white lie. He had, just this morning, sent off an application to a new gallery in that very city, where he would be working closely with art deco items and artefacts relating to the Glasgow Boys group of artists. And while it wasn't *imminent*, exactly—

'Any imminent plans to go anywhere else?' Sybill's words made him jump.

'No.'

'Any imminent plans to leave Wheal Mount, or indeed Cornwall?'

'None.'

He felt the heat rise in his cheeks and hoped Sybill's razor-sharp mind was elsewhere today and she didn't actually pick up on his blushes.

'So, for the sake of argument, you're here now. You will more than likely be here for a little while.'

Perhaps.

'And this whole arrangement we're talking about here is temporary.' Sybill leaned back in her seat. She knew she was winning. Ryan could see the little triumphant expression on her face, even though she was doing her best to hide it.

'I guess.' He gave up. To be fair, the fact he was here, right here, right now, was true. He loved it here and it fitted his art history background to a T. But there was always that sneaky suspicion that he wasn't really meant to be there — that one day Sybill would go, "Hmm, you did good handing out tickets, mate, but you're not that great and Wheal Mount is not where you should be. Bye bye."

Or that one day, he'd get that next opportunity and decide to up and go.

That was why he wanted the Glasgow gallery job. Most of his memories of that city were fantastic — except for one particularly irritating girl that he'd worked with — and the chance was too good to miss. If he was successful, he knew he would feel awful about leaving the little team at Wheal Mount in the lurch. It wasn't so hard to replace a ticket seller, or a meet-and-greeter, or even someone who could sit in the galleries or the museum and talk about the place. Or someone who could make a mean cappuccino in the tearoom.

But it would be bad if he left something like the archives out of kilter. Because then that would mean Tammy was tidying up after him, as well as Bryony. And that made him feel a bit guilty.

But he was being rather stupid. There was no guarantee he'd even be invited to an interview in Glasgow and he didn't want to give up a chance like this at Wheal Mount for, well, possibly nothing at the end of the day. He didn't really know why he felt he was always competing with some invisible enemy or making something out of nothing. He shook his head. He would be making a huge mistake if he said no to Sybill.

'Sorry, Sybill. I'm being stupid. It's not like I think the universe has any plans for me at present or anything like that.'

He looked at her and her face softened. 'You *are* being stupid. Can't you just accept that we want you here and we're going to do everything in our power to keep you here? We actually *don't* want you to bugger off to Glasgow.' Her eyes glinted. 'Even if it's something you might be considering.'

Ryan shivered. Sybill was, he knew, named after a witch — it was something even Sybill joked about — and the suspicion she was aware of his actions this morning niggled at him.

However, she grinned and he relaxed a little. But still — his specialist subject wasn't archives and what if he messed up? 'But I don't want to let you down either — miss something that's important in your archives, sort of thing.'

Sybill pulled a face. 'Trust me, Ryan. If there's anything important enough for you to find up there, you'll find it. The universe and all that.'

He couldn't argue with the logic — it was his logic as well, wasn't it? 'Okay then.' He nodded. 'I'll do it. Thanks for the opportunity.'

'Great!' Sybill sat back. 'That sounded awfully formal, by the way.'

Ryan felt his cheeks grow hot. 'Yeah. Sorry about that. It's just a responsible sort of job and I'd hate to spoil things after everyone's hard work.'

Sybill laughed. 'Don't worry about it. I'll let Tammy know and she can set you off. You can pick up from where Bryony left off. I'm sure there's a ton of stuff that needs mining up there. We'll be talking to Merryn's replacement at Pencradoc soon about what sort of things they want us to look out for, but I think if we can just create order out of chaos for now, that would be most useful.'

And now Ryan was up here in the attics, amid all that chaos. He could certainly see why they needed someone to take over from Bryony. Sybill had told him she was setting up a meeting with Merryn's replacement this week and that they wanted to toss some ideas around for another exhibition, but with the state of the archives he hoped it would be something easily accessible and already listed . . . which might well be the coward's way out, but, hell, it *would* be easy.

CHAPTER TWO

1911

Nobody had quite expected it to blow up like it had done the week after Pearl and Ernie's midsummer costume ball.

Laurie, however, had not been surprised. He'd been as shocked as the rest of the family — understandably, as his elder sister, Elsie, had suddenly announced that she had a three-year-old daughter — but he'd not been *surprised*. It was unlike Elsie to do anything without an element of drama. And, as he understood it, the champagne Elsie had consumed that night had contributed to the announcement as much as Elsie's dramatic personality had. Especially when she'd called out Louis, the man she had "loved forever" apparently, as the father, just as he'd been on the verge of, it was said, offering marriage to the appalling Margaret Corrington.

Louis was one of Laurie's friends, although Louis was a few years older than him, but he'd always liked and respected the man. And he was utterly glad Louis wasn't going to marry Margaret now: she was — so Laurie's younger sisters, Isolde and Medora, said — a singularly

8

dreadful woman who didn't really have a good word for Laurie's family anyway.

Laurie was selfishly glad. Because, just after the announcement, Elsie and Louis had buried whatever ridiculous hatchet they'd had between them for the last few years, and had returned to London and their daughter, Marigold, and he, Laurie, knew that he would be gaining a brother rather than losing a friend.

Well — that was entirely dependent on whether Louis and Elsie decided to marry. So far, they hadn't mentioned that at all. And Margaret Corrington's mother had wasted no time in the few days since the ball, poisoning Louis' and Elsie's reputations amongst the local families.

The story had spread like wildfire and the day after Louis and Elsie had left for London, Medora had gleefully shared the fact that Louis' Great-Aunt Hortense had driven up in a carriage and threatened to disinherit him. Hortense had called little Marigold all kinds of terrible names and Hortense's daughter, Priscilla — Louis' spinster aunt — had been with her, and *she'd* sworn that she would never speak to any member of the Ashby family ever again, "at all". Louis' mother and father had apparently stood their ground and said good. They didn't particularly want to speak to Priscilla ever again anyway.

Laurie thought it best not to speculate on where Medora had got her information from, but now it was four days after the midsummer ball and to his mind the situation was what it was. Elsie was . . . Elsie. Scandal would follow her wherever she went and whatever she did.

He, on the other hand, was in Bodmin, peering in the window of a toy shop, wondering if he should buy his niece a gift. He'd never had a niece before and it was an odd feeling.

He turned away from the window, deciding to think about it a little more, and wondering if he should head to the bookshop instead — or even the stationery shop, because he could really do with a new notebook for his scribblings. Just then, he bumped into a petite, fair-haired girl with an armful of parcels.

And he really did bump into her. He walked right into her and she fell backwards into a muddy puddle that had collected on the pavement from a recent summer storm. All the parcels she'd been carrying tumbled to the floor — Laurie didn't know what was in them, but some of them made a dreadful, tinny noise when they landed on the pavement and they scattered around her like nine-pins.

The girl herself looked startled, with splashes of mud all over her perfect, oval face and globs of brown mud sticking to her fair hair.

He opened his mouth to apologise and automatically held his hand out to help her up, when she began shouting at him. And not just shouting, yelling about how careless he was and had he not seen her?

'Jeepers!' The girl scrambled inelegantly to her feet. 'Do you English guys not *look* where you're going?' She wiped her hands angrily down her skirt, which seemed to make her even more cross as she looked at the ugly marks smeared all over the fine lawn material.

Laurie stared at her in surprise. Although he came from a relatively liberal, bohemian family and had three sisters, and four female cousins, he was fairly sure that none of them — except maybe Elsie — would shout at a stranger in the street.

'It was an accident!' he said indignantly. 'Look, I'll help you pick them up . . .' He bent down and picked up the parcel nearest to him. However, it too had fallen into a puddle and the brown-paper wrapper unravelled itself, and a host of marbles tumbled right back down to the ground, rolling around in a most annoying fashion.

'Oh, sorry. Here. Let me get this one instead.' He picked up another one. It made a sickening sort of rattle and he had the horrible feeling that whatever had been in it was broken beyond repair . . .

The girl almost growled at him. 'Leave them! Just leave them! You'll break everything if you touch any more.' She flapped him away and bent down herself to gather up the remaining parcels. As Laurie tried to gather up as many marbles as possible, he became aware of a pair of polished leather shoes coming into his line of vision. Oh, God, this was the girl's husband or father, and he was going to get severely reprimanded. And what a way to be discovered, grubbing around on the wet pavement, marbles rolling into the muddy road . . .

'Lost your marbles, have you, Laurie Teague?' said a familiar voice, which contained, it had to be said, a hint of amusement.

The fair-haired girl frowned. 'Ernie! You *know* this juggins?' From his vantage point on the ground, Laurie noticed that the hem of her pale-pink dress was also soaking wet and her smart, black shoes were disgustingly muddy. But *juggins*? What the hell did *that* mean? He had a feeling it wasn't complimentary.

'I sure do, Viola,' said the owner of the polished shoes. 'Come on, Laurie, enough grubbing already.'

Laurie stood up, dusted his own knees down and faced his friend Ernie — Ernie from Elton Lacy, who had hosted the infamous midsummer costume ball four days ago.

'Ernie. Good morning,' Laurie said stiffly. 'You sound more American every day.' He cast a glance at the scowling girl — Viola, apparently. 'That's not a good thing. Doesn't seem that some Americans speak the same language as us.'

Ernie just laughed. 'Sorry, old man. I've lived with Pearl a long time now. And we have Viola staying with us too at the moment. And Sam was here for a few days as well, so I fear I am, and *have been*, outnumbered by Americans. The lingo can't help rubbing off on one.'

'Quite.' Laurie's voice was stiff and suddenly very, very English.

11

'You sound more like Elsie every day,' said Ernie. 'I say, how is she doing?' He looked a little concerned. 'And Louis, of course.'

'Well, they went to London together,' said Laurie. 'And neither one of them has come back spewing fire and brimstone yet, so I suspect they're jolly good.'

'Wonderful.' Ernie nodded and smiled.

A female voice chipped in. 'What's wunnerful? Oh, Laurie! I see you've met my sister. Viola, has Ernie introduced you properly? Oh, but, *Viola*! What happened, honey? You sure are *miry*. Say, how much mud can actually stick to one person?'

Viola flushed bright red and slapped her sister's well-meaning hand away as Pearl started trying to rub the mud off the gown with a tiny lace handkerchief — possibly thinking that Viola needed treating in a similar fashion as Pearl's four small children.

Then Viola and Laurie stared angrily at one another as Pearl continued ineptly clucking at her sister, and Laurie had the feeling that Viola wanted to get as far away from him as he wanted to get away from her. The escapade had been embarrassing and annoying, and he desperately wished he had never come to Bodmin today at all.

Then Viola slowly shook her head and pasted a fake smile on her perfect, mud-splattered face. 'Oh, no. That's all right, Pearl. I don't think we need to be introduced. I have no intention of seeing this man again. He's an absolute *fool*. And, besides, he doesn't look where he's going.'

'I echo that sentiment,' said Laurie. He didn't particularly want to see Viola again either. He bowed politely and dismissively. 'Good day, Pearl, Ernie. I hope your sister returns to America very soon and we never have to cross paths again.'

Then, without waiting for an answer, he stalked away up the high street and wished himself a million miles away — yes, perhaps even in America itself.

Because if he was there, he'd at least be in a different country to that woman right now, and be unlikely to bump into her again for quite some time!

* * *

'This country!' Raging, Viola fruitlessly wiped her hands down her frock again. 'Jeepers! You sure have some odd friends, Pearl.'

'My friends are wunnerful,' replied Pearl with a grin. 'You like Holly, right?'

'Well, yes. But *he* is something else.' She pointed angrily in the direction of the tall, dark-haired young man who was striding, it seemed equally angrily, away from them.

'That's Laurie.' Pearl smiled affectionately after him. 'Elsie's brother. He's *corking*. Honestly, he's just *so* delightful.'

'Oh! So he's related to that crazy girl from your party?' Viola had really liked Elsie. The fact she deemed her "crazy" was, in Viola's world, a compliment.

'Yes. Oh, I *do* hope Elsie and Louis are settling in with that glorious little girl. I must write soon.'

Pearl's eyes went all misty and Viola hoped beyond hope that her sister wasn't getting broody again. Four children was quite, *quite* enough. Which reminded her . . .

'Oh my gosh! Pearl, I am so, *so* sorry.' Viola indicated the mess of soggy packages and escaped marbles on the pavement. 'These were gifts for the children. Until *he* wrecked the surprise.' She hunkered down and started collecting more marbles from the roadside, and, to her surprise, Pearl hunkered down next to her — a lot more elegantly, though.

'Don't worry about it. Nothing's spoiled.'

Ernie joined them, gathering up packages. 'Ah. This one might be spoiled.' He rattled one, the same one that Laurie had picked up and shook with that look of dawning horror on his face.

Viola looked at the package and then laughed. 'Hey. No, that's not a problem. Honestly. It's a jigsaw. It's *meant* to be in pieces. Otherwise, where's the fun in that?'

'Oh!' Ernie stared at the parcel. 'Gosh, don't you think we need to tell Laurie? I'm sure he'll feel dreadful.'

'No.' Viola shook her head. 'I'm sure he won't be giving it a second thought. Thank you, Ernie. Thank you, Pearl.' She stood up and waited for the others to join her, then the three of them split the parcels between them to take back to the motor car. Ernie very kindly put some in his overcoat pocket, and she and Pearl filled their reticules with them.

'I'm sure the children will adore the gifts,' Pearl told her. She smiled affectionately in the direction Laurie had gone. 'I suspect that's what Laurie was doing — finding a gift for Marigold. Oh, I say. Will you be here at Halloween, Viola?'

Viola pulled a face. 'I don't know. I do intend to go visit Sam in London.' Sam was Viola and Pearl's brother. The trip to Cornwall had originally been planned as simply a stopover on their way home to New York from Paris, but Sam had decided to make the most of their time in England and travelled to London two days after the ball. 'But, you know, it's the end of June. That would mean me staying here for four more months.'

'And?' Pearl looked curious. She obviously couldn't see a reason for Viola to *not* remain in England until the end of October. It was all right for her, for Pearl. She was happy and settled now. She'd found her Prince Charming and had never really been like her younger sister. Viola had always wanted to travel and see the world, see what was over that next hill, that next river . . .

'I don't know. We'll have to see, I guess. We'll just have to see.' But Viola was at least certain of one thing — she was in no hurry to see that Laurie person again.

14

CHAPTER THREE

Present

Tegan found the door she assumed — no, she *knew* — was to Coren's office. She allowed herself a small smile. There was no ethereal, otherworldly feeling about that; none of this walking straight towards a doorway one had never encountered before and knowing what lay behind it. This door had a modern sign on it which said: *Estate Office, Coren Penhaligon, Manager.*

She rapped on the door and looked around curiously. This place was well hidden away, though. Right at the back of the hallway as per Merryn's instructions. It was quiet at this end of the building, Merryn had said. The visitors tended to use the front half of the building and flow into the rooms there. This part was for staff only, and Merryn had told her there was a main office just along the corridor from Coren's domain, which Tegan would work in. There was a photograph on the wall just opposite Coren's office. It seemed to be a wedding photograph. The man had fair hair and the woman was dark, a froth of veil and bouquet surrounding her. Tegan peered at the label: *Louis and Elsie*, apparently. Ahh — Little Elsie all grown up, perhaps? She looked more closely and she

15

could definitely detect the look of mischief in the woman's eyes, mirrored in Little Elsie's marble bust. Tegan smiled to think of that little girl growing up into such a beautiful, happy-looking bride.

'Come in!' called a voice from within the office, and Tegan moved away from the photograph and pushed open the door. A man was sitting at a desk staring at her very intently and for a split second, her stomach turned over. He was the image of the man in the picture.

'Um . . .' she said, quite unusually thrown off track.

'Tegan?' The man's face changed and softened as he stood up and smiled at her. Holding his hand out, he continued. 'I'm right, aren't I? You look a lot like Merryn.'

Tegan wanted to disagree. Yes, they both had similar hair, but hers was strawberry-blonde, bleached a pale rose-gold by the Sicilian summer, whereas Merryn's was, in her opinion, dirty blonde. Well, it had been when she'd been in London. Now, Tegan conceded, Merryn's hair might be lighter because she lived in Cornwall. She hadn't seen her sister since last Christmas, although they'd been in touch via email and text message, the way busy people like Tegan managed their lives and commitments.

The Burton eyes, though, were definitely the same in the sisters; that dark, mermaid-green that ran in the family. But where Merryn had curves, Tegan had nothing. She was, to be perfectly honest, quite flat-chested and narrow-hipped. It was a figure many women envied and Tegan did appreciate it, but, sometimes, especially when she'd been younger, she'd bought push-up bras and stuffed tissue down them to give her that little extra shape. She would, a well-meaning friend had told her, look good in a flapper dress or a 1960s minidress. As flapper dresses and original 1960s minidresses cost more than Tegan could afford in the vintage clothing stores, Tegan hadn't rated that advice as very helpful really.

Tegan shifted her attention back to the moment in hand and the man standing in front of her. 'Yes. I'm Tegan. You're Coren, I guess? You look like the chap in the photo outside

16

the room.' She nodded back towards the door and held her hand out to shake Coren's. 'But it can't be you, because you're obviously not called Louis.'

Coren smiled. 'Yes. That's Louis and Elsie's wedding photograph. They're relatives of mine. We thought it would be nice to take a copy of it and put it up there. This used to be Louis' study and, well . . .' He shrugged, seemingly reluctant to continue.

'And if he comes to visit his study, he can see the photo outside, without coming in and bothering you,' said Tegan smartly.

Coren looked a little taken aback and she reminded herself this was her new boss and that had probably been completely the wrong thing to say to him. *Strike One.*

'Oh. Sorry. Merryn mentioned Pencradoc might be haunted . . .'

Ugh. She really needed a filter . . .

But then he surprised her by laughing. 'Yes. That's one way of looking at it. Please. Sit down.' He indicated the chair at the desk and Tegan obediently sat. She'd got away with that one, but she really needed to be more careful. 'I have to say,' continued Coren as he sat down too, 'that I wasn't expecting you until tomorrow.'

Crap.

Strike Two.

'Ah. Yes. I got an earlier flight,' replied Tegan. 'I kind of thought I'd come and show willing. You know.' She smiled brightly. 'I'm keen to get started.'

She didn't think it was worth letting him know she had thought it so much easier to just head here, than head down to Marazion to spend the night with Merryn. It just seemed a long way to Marazion and she was very tired, and she'd been promised accommodation at Pencradoc for the term of her contract.

'Well, I'm not going to start you in a new job at three in the afternoon,' said Coren. 'But your suite's all ready. Merryn did have an inkling you'd rock up early.'

'Did she?' Tegan was surprised.

'Yes. She said you'd seemed anxious to leave Sicily and all her recent messages to you were undelivered, so she assumed you'd hopped on a plane.'

'I must be more predictable than I thought,' Tegan said wryly.

'Maybe your sister just knows you well. Anyway. I'll show you up to your rooms and tell you where you can go for food and drink in the village — there's a really nice pizza place, we like to go there — or you can try the Tower Tearoom if you don't want to go too far. And we'll start properly tomorrow. Do you need some help with your bags?'

'The village is fine. I like pizza. And I don't have much luggage, so I'll be *totally* fine. This is it.' She indicated the case she had with her. 'I'm used to travelling light. I'll go home at the weekend, see Mum and Dad and grab anything else I need.' It was the back-end of September after all and this was England, so she didn't think she'd need much in the way of summer clothes. Cornwall, however, still seemed to think it was the height of summer. Tegan had noticed the gardens were looking green and lush, the flowers still blooming, a profusion of roses and summer flowers had greeted her on the way in, and there was that unmistakeable scent of moss and earth and distant moorland on the soft breeze.

Maybe she *should* retrieve some of her summer clothes this weekend — just in case.

'Anyway. I've just got the essentials here today. And thank you. I do mean it. For the job here and for letting me stay, and for not getting cross because I'm a day early.'

'Our pleasure. It makes things a bit easier to cover Merryn's leave if she's happy with the person in the job.'

'And can tell them what to do!' She said it with a smile, though.

'Yes. Like I said, so much easier.' Coren grinned.

'I'm looking forward to it.'

'Us too. I have to warn you, though, I think she's coming in tomorrow to see you. Something about a handover?' His eyes twinkled a little mischievously and he stood up. 'She said if you didn't go to her house, she'd catch you here instead.'

'That sounds like Merryn.' Tegan stood too.

'Oh, and we're arranging a meeting later in the week with Sybill and someone from her team at Wheal Mount. We work so closely that it makes sense to introduce you.' Coren indicated she should leave the office and offered to take her case. Tegan, however, shook her head and walked out, pulling it behind her. 'I can manage, thanks,' she said. 'Just lead the way to the room and I'll be forever grateful.'

The stairs seemed to go up and up and up. Tegan bounced her case along in her wake and followed Coren upwards and along a corridor. She had a feeling they had just travelled up the servants' staircase and wondered if she could get to her accommodation via the Grand Staircase she'd spotted when she walked in — the one with Little Elsie at the bottom and the beautiful painting of that old-fashioned lady hanging on the staircase wall. Ruby? Rachel? Rebecca? It was an "R" name — she remembered that. Merryn had mentioned it when she'd been telling Tegan about the artworks in Pencradoc and how excited she'd been when she'd discovered it with Kit.

Regardless of who the lady was, Tegan did have a longing to flounce down those stairs herself, maybe in that flapper dress her friend had mentioned. Maybe even *dancing* her way down, like in those old Hollywood movies she loved. Now *that* would be fun! The opening bars to "New York, New York" came into her mind, and she bit her lip and ducked her head to hide her smile. *Doo, do, doo dodo, do do do doo do doo do . . . .* Entirely inappropriate to start humming that now.

And also, Coren was talking.

'It's the flat Merryn and Kit sometimes stay in,' he was saying. 'So it's pretty comfortable. Here we go.' He opened the door and stood back, and Tegan walked into a light, airy kitchen area. Beyond that, was a lounge with a big picture window overlooking the grounds and a small dining table in the window with two chairs. A door led off on one side of the lounge to the bedroom, and a door on the other side led to a bathroom.

'It's really nice!' said Tegan. She meant it. She'd been in some dodgy accommodation before, and to be honest had stayed in worse AirBnBs.

'It seemed madness for you to rent somewhere when this place was available,' Coren said. 'Merryn won't be using it for a while if she's off work and Kit will be more than happy to drive home if he's up here.' Marazion, where Merryn and Kit lived, was a pretty coastal town full of artists in the south-west of the county. You could see St Michael's Mount from Kit and Merryn's little cottage, and the soft, golden sands of the beach were a hop, skip and a jump away from their blue-painted front door. 'So you might as well make use of it,' continued Coren. 'I'm along the other end of the house, a couple of floors down — basically just break all the rules and walk through any door marked "Private" and you'll eventually find me.

'So it might seem like you're rattling around in Pencradoc on your own, but you're not. My number's on the business card there if you need anything.' He nodded to a bowl on the dining table, which was probably supposed to hold fruit but looked to be the receptacle for keys, phone numbers and other useful bits and bobs. 'And if ever I'm going to be away overnight, I'll let you know.'

Tegan was tempted to ask if there were meant to be any ghosts on that side of the house who could keep her company, but she bit her tongue and thought better of it. She suspected there wouldn't be — she definitely didn't feel a spooky vibe here — and she didn't want to run into a potential *Strike Three* within her first hour or so of being here.

'That's all great. Thank you so much. What time do you want me down in the morning?'

'Nine o'clock will be fine,' replied Coren. 'I'm usually around earlier, but won't have had enough coffee before nine.

So you're safest to come then. Just head back down to the office.'

'And . . . can I go down the main staircase to get there?' She had to ask.

'Oh, of course. It's that way. A little longer travel time, but do whatever suits you best.'

'Thanks. Right, I'll get unpacked, have a shower and head out for food.'

'Great. We'll see you tomorrow, then. Have a good evening and of course don't forget to call me if you need anything.'

'I won't.'

Coren nodded and headed out of the room, and Tegan followed him, shutting the door behind him. She turned around and looked at the room. Yes. This was nice. This would do.

And it may not have had spooky vibes, but it had *good* vibes and that was awesome.

* * *

Ryan felt he'd made a good start with the boxes and papers in the Wheal Mount archives. Bryony had set up a database and once he'd had a play around with that, things started to make more sense. It was okay recording things — that was the easy part. It was thinking of the wider picture and remembering the items, making the database searchable and knowing what related to what that could pose a problem.

Nothing for it though but to roll up one's metaphorical sleeves and get on with it.

'It'll fall into place,' Tammy told him as she brought a mid-morning coffee up to the attics for him. 'And Sybill's very much of the opinion that the most important stuff will make itself known to you.'

Ryan looked at her and pulled a face, even as he accepted the hot drink gratefully. 'Not sure I believe that one, Tammy.'

Tammy grinned and sat down, perching herself on the edge of a trunk.

21

Her bright dungarees, rainbow paint-spattered Doc Martens and colourful hairband were incongruous in the dusty, cluttered room. The glint in the top of her ear piercing caught the light and Ryan thought back to when they'd first met. He had started at the place as a student when he'd been going through some weird, emo/goth art student phase, and Tammy had been the first to compliment him on the industrial-sized piercing in the middle of his ear.

'Daith piercing. Cool,' she'd said. 'I was thinking about getting mine done but I don't like pain that much, so I think I'll just go with a helix instead.' Ryan had been impressed with Tammy's knowledge, admired the piercing high up on her outer ear when she'd finally been for the procedure, and they'd formed a friendly relationship.

'There's never been anything that jumped out at me, I must confess,' said Tammy today, 'But I have a mind like a machine and a very good memory so I'm pretty good at knowing where things are. Problem is, if I ever leave, nobody will know that. Hence Bryony coming and now you taking over.' She leaned over and punched him lightly on the arm. 'Thanks, by the way. There're not many people I'd trust up here. It's my treasure trove.'

'You'll be too important to come up here before long,' Ryan said, teasing his friend. 'I'll have to book an appointment to see you in the boss's office.'

'Hmmm.' Tammy laughed. 'I'll let you in any time if you bring biscuits.'

'Done.'

'Great. So, where are you working at the minute?' Tammy looked around curiously.

'Here.' Ryan indicated a box of paperwork. 'I'm not getting far. I keep getting distracted and reading the papers.'

'Hazard of the job. What are they?'

'Letters between Elsie and her brother, Laurie.'

'Oh! Yes, I think he was the one that fought in World War One.'

'Did he?' Ryan didn't know much about Elsie and her family. He'd worked at Wheal Mount a long time and knew a lot about Elsie's Uncle Jago and Aunt Alys, the Duke and Duchess of Trecarrow. He knew about Lady Elsie's professional status of course — the fact that she was a brilliant artist, photographer and all the rest. But he didn't know much about her private life. 'These letters were from well before the war, though.' Ryan pulled one out of the trunk at random and read out the date. '1911. November.'

'Ah, I think if you keep looking we've got some Halloween artefacts from that year too,' said Tammy. 'Dated not too long before that letter. 1911 definitely rings a bell with me. I'm sure there's something between Elsie and her friend Pearl.'

'That's cool,' said Ryan. He liked Halloween. 'You'll have to let me see the letter.' He grinned at Tammy, read a bit more of the 1911 letter to himself, then spoke. 'So *here*, they're talking about getting together before the wedding. She wants him to come to London, she's got a dress fitting and bizarrely wants him there.' Ryan looked at Tammy. 'Damn sure I wouldn't want to get involved in dress fittings with my sister. Talk about a bridezilla. But Elsie's very kindly sketched her frock out as well to help. Look.' He showed Tammy the back of the letter and she nodded.

'Lovely sketch. But that *is* curious.' Tammy raised her eyebrows. 'Not sure *my* brother would be that interested in my wedding dress.'

'I can't actually imagine you in a dress, anyway, Tammy. But I don't suppose we'll ever find out why Elsie wanted her brother there. I heard Sybill say Elsie had been "capricious" once. Maybe that's just the way she was. Or maybe her brother could offer her good styling advice.' He looked at the box and its many layers of jumbled secrets, yet to be discovered.

Maybe the answer lay in there somewhere.

Or maybe he was the one being capricious and there was no secret there whatsoever, and no logical answer to his question.

Ah, well. He wasn't that bothered really.

It was just kind of . . . *interesting*. That was all.

But part of him held back from becoming too invested in Tammy's archives. Working in these musty attics, despite how absorbing the contents were, was a "for-now" job, and he was still pinning his hopes on Glasgow and the chance to handle Rennie Mackintosh artefacts instead of Pencradoc ones.

CHAPTER FOUR

1911

June had run into July, and then August, and fortunately — *fortunately* — Laurie had been spared the purgatory of seeing that Viola woman again. Although within those weeks, he'd had the joy of meeting his niece, Marigold, for the first time when she'd been brought to Pencradoc. Indeed, that was where he was heading today. Brunswick Square, in Bloomsbury, London, to see Elsie, Louis and Marigold.

Although Laurie was glad he hadn't seen Viola since the incident in Bodmin, he had a lot of time for Pearl and Ernie — especially knowing how close Pearl and Elsie were. Holly Andrews, wife of the successful novelist Noel Andrews, made up the triumvirate of friends. 'Thick as thieves,' Isolde said with a sniff now and again, when she was having a particularly jealous moment.

Once, when Elsie had been within earshot of Isolde's remarks, Elsie had cackled evilly and responded, 'Darling sister. The Unholy Trinity. Or the three witches from *Macbeth*. Pick one of those references, sweet Isolde, pick one.'

25

Laurie grinned to himself remembering that one. Elsie didn't help herself — she was constantly dressed in black and had a habit of throwing herself around dramatically and couldn't help but hold all the attention in every room. He sometimes wondered how two sisters had turned out so differently. Then he had to remind himself that they were only half-sisters; Elsie's real father, Ellory, the previous Duke of Trecarrow — the one before Uncle Jago had inherited the title — had died before Elsie was born. The rest of them: himself, Isolde, Medora, Clem, Enyon and Arthur shared the same parents, Zennor and Ruan Teague. Ruan was an incredibly talented artist and sometimes Laurie wondered how Elsie had those talents as well — but he was well aware of the rumours surrounding the family and Lady Elsie Pencradoc's true parentage, so he never dwelled on it too much.

His other sisters were quite handy with a watercolour palette themselves. Isolde's paintings were always more controlled and prettier than Medora's. Medora, modelling herself on her adored eldest sister, Elsie, was a lot looser and freer in her artwork. Elsie — and Ruan — agreed that at some point Medora would come into her own style, but she needed to do some growing up first. Medora, though, was already twenty, so Laurie, at the grand old age of twenty-three, wondered when that would actually happen.

But, here he was. In front of the tall, Georgian building in Bloomsbury Elsie had called home for the last few years. The garden square laid out neatly opposite was verdant, but Laurie knew that in a few weeks those trees would start changing colour and dropping leaves and autumn would be here.

He could see two figures in the square, a tall, fair-haired man and a small girl. The child was haring around the square, red ribbons flying free, her dark curls streaming out behind her as she yelled and whooped loudly.

Louis and Marigold. Of course. Laurie smiled again when he saw them and diverted to the square to greet them.

'May I join in?' he shouted as he approached the gate and Marigold spun around to see who had arrived.

'Unca Laurie!' She started running towards him instead, her arms outstretched and flailing like the sails of a windmill. Laurie caught her as she hurled herself into his arms and he started to swing her around. 'Faster!' she cried. 'Faster, Unca Laurie!' Obligingly, he spun her around a few more times until she was shrieking with laughter.

Then he placed her gently on the ground where she promptly fell over and declared the sky was moving too fast.

Louis came over and held his hand out to greet Laurie.

'Oh, I'm not spinning you around,' said Laurie with a laugh. 'Good to see you though.'

'I'm entirely disappointed,' replied Louis. 'Was it a good journey?'

'Not too bad, rather hot.'

'Yes, those trains leave something to be desired. But regardless, it's good to see you. We've been for a walk and then someone decided they had energy to burn off and swore there were pirates in the park, so we had to come and look for them.'

'Pirates,' muttered Marigold, but she made no effort to move and lay at the men's feet.

'Is Elsie around? She can't be at the Slade today, can she?'

'No. And much as she loves going there, she's enjoying her summer break. She's got a friend visiting at the moment, so that was another reason I took Marigold out for a breath of fresh air. Let them chatter in peace.'

Laurie nodded. He knew Elsie's good friend, Fabian Austen, often called round to see the little family. Ruan Teague, Laurie's father, had somewhat taken Fabian under his wing as a protégé and Fabian was in the midst of painting a series of portraits for the Teagues. He was meant to start with Zennor, but she had stepped aside until last, understanding how excited her daughters would be to have their portraits done first. After all, she was married to a world-famous portrait artist and Ruan had done dozens of pictures of Zennor throughout their lives together.

Isolde bore it stoically, her portrait in its final stages portraying a rather aloof yet incredibly beautiful young lady. Medora was twittering in excitement and had been wasting daydreams over how Fabian might fall for her, the way Teague had fallen for Zennor the first time he'd painted her. Elsie had to take Medora to one side and quietly advise her that it was highly unlikely, if not impossible, that Fabian would fall for Medora — or *any* woman he painted, for that matter. It had taken a little while for that to sink in, but Medora had eventually realised that she was never going to change Fabian's nature, and she determined to enjoy the experience regardless and turned her daydreams into someone else falling for her portrait instead.

That, the family could live with. And Fabian, God bless him, remained blissfully unaware of Medora's original fantasy.

If not Fabian, Elsie's visitor might be Lily Valentine, a family friend who had been closest to Elsie out of all of them. It would be nice to see Lily, Laurie thought, with her quiet Irish accent and her incredible tales of the stage when she'd been an actress so many years ago, before she'd married Edwin and had her children. Lily sometimes had Marigold stay at her house as well, so she was very special to all the family really. She had, he understood, been a great support to Elsie when she'd been pregnant with Marigold and had been absolutely invaluable to his sister over the little girl's first three years as well.

'I hope Elsie doesn't mind me intruding, then,' Laurie said to Louis. 'She is expecting me, I suppose?'

'Of course she is. The door is, I believe, unlocked, awaiting our return as well. Marigold, are you ready to go inside and see Mama again?'

'No, Papa. I think there may be a pirate *there*.' The child sat up and pointed to a copse. Then she scrambled to her feet and ran off towards it.

Laurie laughed. 'Have fun, Papa.' He waved at Louis as he jogged away after his small daughter. Marigold was delightful, but it was clear she had inherited more than her mother's dark hair and heart-shaped face. She'd inherited her exuberance and zest for life too, and my word, was that child energetic. Laurie had had to peel her off the Pencradoc Grand Staircase more than once as she'd scrambled up and decided she'd slide down it "just *so*."

He swore the child was like a limpet, clinging on so tightly to that banister with her knees and hands . . .

He walked across the road, pondering the layout in Elsie's house, wondering if Marigold tried to slide down their banister as well. Elsie's stairs were much more winding than Pencradoc's and he could see the attraction, he really could.

They'd all slid down those Pencradoc stairs at some stage, even serious Isolde. It was like a rite of passage, presided over, always, by Elsie. 'It's awfully easy!' she'd yell from the bottom. Laurie was inevitably the one at the top who had to push the children down. Elsie would catch them at the other end.

Mostly.

Laurie sometimes wondered who had pushed him or caught him the first time he'd done it? Maybe one of his Wheal Mount cousins, daughters of Uncle Jago and Aunt Alys, as Elsie held them in thrall too. The families had been one big mass of children growing up between the two properties, with Jago taking on the title of Duke of Trecarrow from his deceased brother.

Whatever, he held happy memories of growing up at Pencradoc and did a lot of work with his Uncle Jago to help out on the estate. One of his favourite areas was the garden room, where he'd sit with a notebook and pen and write his poems and stories, serenaded by the fountain in the centre of it, warmed by the heaters in there, whatever the weather outside . . .

But here he was in London, at Elsie's front door. Louis had told him it was open and a gentle push confirmed that.

'Elsie!' He stepped inside the black-and-white-tiled hallway, coloured light pouring in from the big stained-glass windows. 'Are you around? It's me.'

'In here!' came his sister's cheerful voice from a room on the right. As he might have expected, she was in her favourite room, a room full of soft furniture, warm fires in winter, and scattered with art equipment, cameras, sketches, books and photographs — whatever, basically, she was working on at the moment. And knowing Elsie it could be one, two or several more projects. 'Hold on, I'll pop out and get you!'

The door burst open and Elsie came running out, barefoot, dressed in flowing black as usual. Her dress was, even he could see, a dress out of time. Rather than the tall, slim silhouettes the streets were filled with, Elsie's dress would not have looked out of place thirty years ago at a society ball. It was off the shoulder, full-skirted and covered in lace. It suited her, though.

'Laurie! Oh, it's *so* good to see you.' She threw her arms around him.

'Vile sibling.' He smiled as he said it. It was part of their oddly affectionate shorthand. 'You look particularly pale and vampiric today.'

'Liar,' she said. 'I am always this colour. You, on the other hand, should be pale and vampiric, but you actually look hot, bothered and even more vile than usual. But come on — come and meet Viola.'

Laurie hesitated. Viola? No. It couldn't be. Could it? Oh, God, he hoped not. It wasn't that common a name, in his experience. But no — absolutely not . . .

Elsie took his hand, pushed open the door and stood back, gently urging him forward. His heart pounding, dreading what he might find within that delightful, airy room, he stepped inside.

Then . . .

'Oh, jeepers! Not *you*!' said *that* Viola, staring at Laurie, her face changing from open and welcoming to hostile and defensive in a heartbeat.

'Good God. Spare me *this*!' Laurie drew to a swift halt. '*Not* you!'

The pair of them glared at one another for what seemed like a lifetime.

'I say — anything I need to know?' asked Elsie, half amused. 'Anything at all?'

* * *

Viola was horrified. There was no other word for it. Utterly horrified.

She waited for Laurie to speak, but, as far as she could tell, he was just going to stand there and glare at her as if she was Medusa and had turned him to stone.

She guessed it was up to her to speak, then. 'Mr Teague and I have already met,' she said rather stiffly. Elsie looked from one to the other, amusement definitely written all over her face.

'May I ask — how?' Elsie asked.

Laurie lifted his hand and pointed to Viola, then ran it through his hair. He shook his head. 'In Cornwall.' He glowered at Viola. 'We were outside the same shop in Bodmin. She walked into me and dropped her parcels. I tried to help and she was, quite frankly, awful.'

'Disagree!' said Viola. 'Laurie was not looking where he was going. He quite definitely walked into me and not only did I drop the parcels, I also ended up sitting in a damned puddle of mud. And he wasn't helpful at all. He was the single most unhelpful person I've ever had the misfortune to meet. I swear he broke one of the gifts I had—'

'And *I* disagree with that.' Laurie fired back. 'The package that was apparently *broken*, was actually a jigsaw. Ernie told me.'

31

Viola shot a look at Elsie, feeling her cheeks heat up. That was the truth, but still . . . 'All right, maybe it *wasn't* broken, but it *could* have been broken . . .'

It sounded rather pathetic out loud and she had the grace to lower her eyes, then flick them back up. Laurie just looked confused, then angry, then she saw his mouth open to speak again.

'But it was *not* broken,' he repeated, very slowly, as if he was speaking to a rather stupid child.

'No. But it *could* have been. And — *and*!' She remembered something and pointed her finger at him. 'The marbles were *definitely* broken.'

'They were *not* broken. The packaging unravelled. They fell on the ground. I tried to help you pick them up!'

'I say!' Elsie finally chipped in and physically placed herself between Viola and Laurie. 'Is this *any* way to behave when there could be a small child quite possibly walking into this room at *any moment*?'

Viola bit back a retort and angrily took a sip of tea. Elsie was correct, of course. Sure, she had issues with that dreadful man, but it wasn't right to be stashing it up with him in Elsie's parlour. It was just too bad that he'd walked right in here when she was visiting . . .

'Beg pardon.' Laurie spoke stiffly. 'I just — hoped — it was Fabian or Lily here. When Edwin said a friend. I mean . . .' He indicated Viola. Viola knew exactly what he meant.

'I am *too* Elsie's friend. Does not mean I have to be *your* friend . . .'

'Enough!' Elsie was actually laughing now. She threw herself back into her seat and put her bare feet smartly on the table in front of her, crossed neatly at the ankles. Viola thought Elsie might take hold of her teacup again, but instead she scrabbled around and picked up a sketchbook and a stick of charcoal. The charcoal started moving swiftly over the paper, which was, Viola now knew, not exactly a nervous habit of Elsie's — it was more that her mind and her creativity never seemed to rest, and it was simply as much of a habit for Elsie to sketch her friends as they sat in front of her, as it was for anyone else to rub their nose.

'So, I take it you two *have* met before?' Elsie smiled at Laurie. 'Please. Sit down, vilest sibling.'

Laurie hesitated, then went to the furthest chair from Viola. Viola, despite not wanting to be anywhere near him, was quietly indignant that he had made that choice. She took another sip of tea, trying to focus on something that wasn't that pale young man sitting stiffly in the chair. She was sure a muscle was twitching in his jaw as he tried not to say anything else. He had the hump all right — but even so . . .

How *ignorant*!

'Tell me,' continued Elsie, a mischievous look in her eyes. 'How do you *really* know each other?'

'Don't pretend you don't know,' said Laurie. 'It's true that she walked into me—' Viola yelped indignantly — 'and I'm rather certain that Pearl and Ernie *already told you* that story.'

'Mmm. Perhaps.' Elsie clearly wasn't giving anything else away. 'But whatever the story is, it's jolly good that you bumped into each other here today. There's nothing nicer than having a lovely chat over a cup of tea and meeting new people. Or maybe not-so-new people. Is there?'

Viola saw Laurie narrow his eyes and shake his head in his sister's direction. She was inclined to agree with the man, but wouldn't give him the satisfaction. However, she couldn't actually bring herself to respond to Elsie and lie and agree with her, so she had yet another sip of the tea.

Tea was an acquired taste to her American sensibilities. She much preferred coffee, but when in Rome, and all that . . .

Elsie didn't seem to care that neither of her guests had agreed with her and blithely chattered on about this and that. Viola found her mind drifting a little and thought about what, in her mind, would be nicer than tea with Laurie Teague. Lots of things, really. She looked at him, not really seeing him, and thought that dancing somewhere like Paris would be much more preferable. She'd commented to Sam when they had been there how she quite wanted to dance at the Moulin Rouge. He'd laughed at her then and said for one thing she was too short, and for another, did she know the reputations of the girls that had danced there in the past?

Viola did, but she didn't pay it much attention. It just seemed like it would be quite fun, she'd told Sam.

A noise at the door dragged her attention back to the present. For a brief moment she focussed back on Laurie, and he was staring at her with much the same expression as she felt was displayed on her face. She raised her chin and looked away from him. *Not interested in you*, was what she wanted to portray, and she hoped he understood.

At the door stood a tiny Marigold-shaped whirlwind, along with her father. 'Aunt Viola!' the little girl shouted and threw herself at Viola, scrambling onto her lap. Viola just managed to put the cup and saucer down on a small table next to her before Marigold demanded her attention. 'I thought you'd gone *home*!' She took Viola's chin in her hands and placed a large kiss on Viola's lips.

'No, sweetie, I'm still here,' said Viola, her arms automatically going around the little girl to make sure she didn't slip off Viola's sateen frock and slide onto the floor.

'Yes, and so is Unca Laurie. We saw him out *there*. We saw him first.' Marigold pointed at the window that faced onto the square. 'We saw him first.' Then she shuffled and wriggled around so Viola had to let go of her, then, deliberately it seemed, used Viola's long, shiny skirt as a slide. Marigold ended up sitting on the ground. Then she laughed, scrambled to her feet and raced over to Laurie, where she clambered all over him and kissed him too. 'I think I may very much like a buttered crumpet,' she told him.

Laurie ruffled her hair and moved her around so she sat on his lap, holding her quite naturally and comfortably. Marigold proceeded to push his nose and his cheeks with her chubby fingers and he pulled faces at her and made noises like a duck, and

Marigold shrieked with laughter. Viola wondered how such an uncouth and annoying man knew how to amuse such a little girl, and then remembered that he had several brothers and sisters and cousins, so he'd probably grown up with small people everywhere. Viola was the youngest of three and hadn't done that. The only experience she had, really, was Pearl's brood, and even in the short time she'd been at Pearl and Ernie's, she had somehow acquired a reputation of being Fun Aunt Viola.

She loved it, she really did, but was nowhere near wanting to settle down and do that sort of thing herself.

Louis followed Marigold in and dropped a kiss on Elsie's hair. Elsie raised her hand and touched his cheek, without even looking away from her daughter and her brother. It was like she knew exactly where his cheek would be, like it was a well-played-out, entirely natural thing to do.

Which, of course, it probably was, even though she left a smudge of charcoal on his face. He didn't seem to mind.

'Oh, Viola?' Elsie suddenly asked. 'Did you write back to that boy who was so desperately in love with you?'

'Ugh.' Viola pulled a face, the uncomfortable memories surfacing. 'I did. I let him down gently. Or I guess I hope I did. I don't want to hear from him again.'

'Viola met a boy in Paris,' Elsie said to Louis. 'She had one dance with him, at the Printania Music Gardens, and he fell in love with her. So romantic.'

'It took me weeks to shake him off!' said Viola, one eye on Marigold, hoping that she didn't say anything out of turn in front of the tot. 'His name was Émile. Said he was a poet or a musician — or an artist.' She shrugged. 'Could have been any or all of those occupations. He kept changing it when I looked unimpressed with the latest one he came up with.'

'If you were that unimpressed with him,' said Laurie, in a muffled voice. 'Why did you give him your address?'

'Excuse me?' Viola frowned. 'That's none of your business.'

'Just asking.' Laurie shrugged and removed Marigold's fingers from his mouth.

But she couldn't help it — she found she needed to justify herself. 'My brother, Sam, got to know him as well and gave him the address we're at over here. Not that it's any of your business. Sam liked him. Said he seemed as if he adored me and would promise me the world.' She pulled a face again. Viola was not the sort of woman to put up with any soft soap. Émile had been awfully sweet, really, but she knew she'd soon become bored of him following her around with his puppy-dog eyes. Friendship was as much as she was willing to offer him and if he wasn't happy with that, well . . . it was better to cut their losses right now.

'Poor fool,' muttered Laurie.

'Adoration is overrated,' said Elsie cheerfully. 'I mean I know Louis adores me and I adore him, but . . .'

Louis laughed and ruffled her hair. 'But we know when to stop adoring one another and when to answer one another back,' he said.

'Correct.' Elsie nodded enthusiastically. Then she cast her eyes over the assembled company. '*Very* correct,' she repeated quietly, and a small, secret smile played around her lips. Viola wasn't entirely sure she liked where Elsie's thought process was going — because Viola's suspicions were written all over Elsie's pretty face . . .

There was only one thing she could say.

'Ugh.'

Elsie was not going to play matchmaker between her, Viola Arthur, and that awful man, Laurie Teague — Elsie's very definitely "vile sibling".

'Well.' Viola stood up and brushed some stray blades of grass — and more dried mud, it seemed, transferred from Marigold's feet — from her skirt. 'I must be going. Goodbye for now, Marigold. It was wunnerful to see you.'

Marigold giggled and blew her a kiss. 'Wunnerful,' she parroted.

Then Elsie stood up, and Louis was, of course, already on his feet, but Laurie, with Marigold clutched firmly on his lap, remained seated. He did make an awkward move to *begin* to stand up — more out of innate manners than a particular desire to stand and acknowledge Viola, she knew — but she turned smartly on her heel and began to walk off towards the door before he could fully struggle to his feet.

Ugh. If she never saw that man again, it would be too soon.

CHAPTER FIVE

Present

The next day, Tegan woke up in the unfamiliar bed to a sunny late-September morning. She stretched out, then rolled over so she was facing the window. She hadn't closed the curtains last night — she just loved sleeping with them open. There was something nice about looking out there, whatever time it was, and seeing a velvety dark night full of twinkling stars, or a deep rose-coloured sunset, or a golden sunrise — just like the one out there today.

She took a moment to appreciate the sunlight, then slid out of bed and padded over to the kitchen counter. She never bothered with breakfast and a strong black coffee was all she needed to set her up for the day — her first day in her new job!

And wow, what a great commute it was. She got showered and dressed, pulled her hair back into a smooth, high ponytail, dressed in what she felt was an appropriate outfit — black cigarette pants, white cut-off top, wedge-heeled sandals — and left the apartment. Then she headed along the corridor towards the Grand Staircase.

'Not using the servants' staircase today,' she said to nobody in particular. 'It's my first day and I'm making an entrance. Maybe tomorrow I'll do the other stairs.' She knew, of course, that she would *not* be using the other stairs at all, *no siree*. Wait, what? She smiled. She wasn't in the habit of using Americanisms — she'd obviously spent too long in Sicily with the group of lemon pickers who'd come from all areas of the world. There'd been a particularly nice couple from California, Meg and Jo. They'd laughed about their names the first night they'd all been there, sitting outside the accommodation block around a fire pit, drinking Aperol spritz and bottles of *birra*. *Little Women* was one of Tegan's favourite books. She'd studied it for a degree in Literature, before she'd decided after the first year that the course hadn't been for her and she'd rather travel.

'We just need to befriend a Beth and an Amy,' Meg had said with a laugh. 'And we'll have all the main characters.'

'Oh, I hated Amy!' Tegan said. 'She stole Laurie from Jo!' The Jo she was with joked she'd probably be more interested in a "Laura", and they all found that hysterical. But Tegan stood by her conviction, even though Jo March was much better suited to Professor Bhaer than Theodore "Laurie" Laurence. 'And even though *everybody* thinks it was best for Laurie!'

Today, at Pencradoc, Tegan smiled at the memories, recalling, as well, Angelo — a dreamy, dark-eyed musician who had been part of their group. All she'd originally wanted was a holiday romance, something to enjoy while she was in Italy, and Angelo had ticked all the boxes. But to her surprise, she had felt herself falling under a sort of Sicilian spell and finding it all becoming a little more serious. They'd begun to talk about her staying there, of her moving in with the charming, dark-haired, olive-skinned man and making a life in Italy.

And then one day, over her breakfast coffee of all things, she had, unaccountably, started to overthink things. Was she ready for that sort of commitment? Was she ready to settle down to days and evenings with the same person for, quite possibly, the rest of her life? She knew it happened, that instant connection with people — that feeling that you had found the other half of yourself. And while Angelo and Sicily had been a nice fit for now, that's how it had suddenly felt that morning — nice "for now". It had almost seemed as if there was something missing; the other half of her whole.

But what it was, she wasn't quite sure about. And certainly when Angelo had come in from the garden, smelling of fresh cigarette smoke and a lingering hint of weed and campfires from the previous evening and he'd kissed the back of her neck, she'd metaphorically shaken herself and told herself not to be so stupid.

Luckily, she hadn't expressed those doubts to anyone else, but when the chance had come up to work at Pencradoc, for reasons best known to her psyche, she had offered to take up the position.

It would, she'd told herself, take her away from this summery dream she was living in Sicily, plonk her back in the UK and force her to take stock of things in her own way.

Cornwall was, of course, a beautiful area to take stock in — especially the area where Pencradoc was. Bodmin Moor was wild, untamed and freeing. The Hurlers neolithic standing stones were there, along with abandoned pumping-engine houses and miles and miles of walks, pools and incredible geology.

And maybe Angelo and Sicily, the scent of suntan lotion and citrus fruit, and the sticky, sweaty feel of temperatures only experienced in the Med, might then end up seeming like prospects she wanted to be part of. If it was meant to be, it would be. They had, after all, been in touch quite frequently over the last few days, so that was good, right?

'I miss you,' Angelo had told her, just last night via FaceTime. Although his smiling face filled the screen, she could hear chatter around him, the clinking of glasses and faint music.

'Are you somewhere fun?' she asked, settling back onto the bed.

'Nowhere is fun without you!' Angelo laughed. 'I am drowning my sorrows. Is that what you call it?'

'I guess.' She smiled at him and her heart skipped a beat as his handsome face mirrored her expression. 'I went for a pizza earlier. There's a really nice restaurant in the village. Family-run Italian place. Checked tablecloths and everything.'

'Ahh! You miss real Italian food that much, yes?'

'I do! It wasn't the same, though.'

'But there was good red wine, yes?'

'There was indeed.'

'Then it was authentic.'

'As good as,' she said.

'It would have been better had we been together. Here. In Sicily,' he said, and she did feel as if she wanted to agree . . .

But she wasn't in Sicily, she was here, in Cornwall, ready to try something different, and, although she didn't want to admit it, she knew deep down she was here to decide what she really wanted.

Thoughtfully, she walked down the Grand Staircase, then made herself concentrate more on the moment and look around her. This was, actually, the first time she'd been down these stairs, but she remembered that she had to watch out for that snaggy bit of carpet or whatever it was, five stairs from the bottom . . .

'Woah!' She stopped, foot hovering over the offending stair. The carpet looked to be perfectly fine. But even so, she stepped cautiously onto it and stood for a moment, trying to sort her thoughts out.

Then a cheerful greeting rang out in the hallway, and she heard someone call her name delightedly.

'Tegan!'

Her attention shifted from the stair and she looked in the direction of the voice. 'Merryn! God — look at *you*!'

Tegan was genuinely shocked. At Christmas, Merryn had been — well — Merryn. Merryn-size, Merryn-shape, just *Merryn*. Now, her older sister looked as if she had a watermelon stuffed down her front. She was *enormously* pregnant and Tegan was surprised that she was actually standing upright.

How had the weight of that baby not made her faceplant the floor?

'Good to see you too, Tegan.' Merryn's voice was wryly amused. 'Come on. Give me a hug.'

'Not sure I can actually get my arms around you,' said Tegan. The odd feeling about the stair was forgotten as she bounded down the remaining steps to greet her sister, arms outstretched.

'You have to at least *try*!' said Merryn with a laugh, catching her sister as Tegan threw herself at her gently yet enthusiastically.

'I can just about manage it!' She hugged Merryn and kissed her on the cheek. 'Oh, wow, it's good to see you in person.'

'Isn't it great?' Merryn grinned. 'And you're here! At Pencradoc. Amazing. Can't *wait* for the place to start working its magic on you.'

'There are no bloody ghosts here, sis, don't know what you keep going on about,' said Tegan. 'I'm here to do a job — a doddle of a job, may I say, and only for a year.'

'Hmm.' Merryn was non-committal, then she laughed. 'A doddle of a job? Okay. Don't let Coren hear you say that, mind. And ghosts or no ghosts, I'm jolly pleased to see *you* too. Come on. Let's go and see the boss. I swear that man sleeps in that study; he's always in it.'

Merryn linked arms with Tegan and they headed to the office. 'Did you see Little Elsie last night?' Merryn asked, patting the marble girl on the head as they passed her. 'I would love to know what she was thinking when she posed for that.'

'Do you think it was done while she sat there? Posing?'

'Not at all. I think it was done from a drawing or a painting. But yes. It would be interesting to know what she was thinking. I bet she would have been full of it. Her little cousins and brothers and sisters wouldn't have heard the end of it.'

'And is that her mum? The lady in that beautiful portrait on the staircase? I know you've mentioned her to me, but I can't remember her name.'

'No.' Merryn shook her head. 'That's Duchess Rose. Sorry, Rose, Duchess of Trecarrow, if we want to give Rose

42

her formal title.' She paused, looking up at the portrait and studying it, as if she was seeing something far, far away. 'Rose died and Elsie's mum, Zennor, married the duke, the guy Rose had been married to first.'

Tegan couldn't help but notice the small, bitter twist to Merryn's mouth as she remarked upon the man. 'You're not impressed with the duke?' she asked.

'No, he wasn't a very nice person. From what we know, anyway.'

The sisters continued walking.

'Did the ghosts tell you that?' Tegan was amused.

'They didn't have to. We all knew it,' replied Merryn — cryptically, Tegan thought. But she didn't let the thought linger. They were now at Coren's office and the sisters disconnected their arms, and Merryn knocked on the door. 'It's just us!' she called, and walked in without waiting for an answer.

Coren looked up from his desk and a hint of a smile lifted the edges of his lips. 'Good morning,' he said. 'Thanks for coming up, Merryn. I know it's a long way.'

'It's worth it to see Tegan, if nothing else,' Merryn said. 'I think an hour away is the closest we've been for a long, long time.'

'Well, sit down and we can do this handover — then you can head back. I don't want to keep you too long. You shouldn't even be here.'

'I'm going to be here long enough to go to the Tower Tearoom. And help Tegan for the rest of the day if she needs me to.'

'I'm not totally hopeless, Merryn,' said Tegan. 'You've already been emailing me lists and lists and idiot guides and all sorts of stuff!' And by the look of her, she needed to be much, much closer to home in case that child decided to make an appearance. Much as she loved her sister, she didn't want her to hang around too long with *that* situation so imminent!

'Not idiot guides. *How-to* guides,' said Merryn defensively.

'*And* you mentioned what you fancied as the next exhibition,' said Tegan.

43

'Yes. I did.'

'First World War?' Tegan raised her eyebrows.

'Yes. It'll be perfect to work between Wheal Mount and Pencradoc. I told Sybill—'

'Honey, I've been thinking, and actually I'm *not* doing the War.' Tegan folded her arms. 'There's got to be something more uplifting to do. This is a temporary job for me. It's your permanent job, so you can do what you like. But for me, I'll do something else. There's got to be something Christmassy or festive we can think about.'

Merryn was just staring at her, apparently speechless. 'But the war . . .'

'No.'

'It's the natural progression for the one we did last time. We did Elsie's midsummer ball . . .'

'So we do Elsie's midwinter something. And why is it a natural progression?'

'Because it's the next chronological thing.'

'No. Chronological is overrated.'

'Coren . . .' Merryn turned to Coren pathetically. Coren was sitting back in his chair, his own arms folded, and very clearly trying not to laugh. 'Oh, Coren!' Merryn was cross now. It was her turn to fold her arms. They rested on top of her very large bump and she looked ridiculously indignant.

'I'm not getting involved,' said Coren. 'And let's just take a moment to reassess. You are officially on maternity leave. Your sister has the job at your recommendation. You really need her to make the decisions and allow her to do what she thinks is right. The war exhibition can wait. And actually, I like the idea of something Christmassy.'

Merryn looked even more indignant, but then she muttered something under her breath.

'What was that, Merryn?' asked Tegan, leaning forward. If it was what she thought she'd heard, that was rather interesting.

Merryn sighed theatrically, then lifted her head and glowered at Tegan. 'A wedding. A midwinter wedding. Elsie got married in the middle of winter. And *that* is all I'm giving you. Your project. Your research. Does that help at all?'

Tegan grinned. 'Perfect. A midwinter wedding. Coren, does that sound good to you? Are you happy for me to work on that?'

Coren nodded. 'That sounds great. I'll mention it to Sybill and we can chat when they come up tomorrow. I'll see if her archivist can lay his hands on anything to help you. Good call, Tegan. And thanks, Merryn.' He nodded at Tegan and winked at Merryn. 'Nothing like being thrown in at the deep end, Tegan, eh?'

'Coren! I think I sometimes preferred you when you were miserable and *weren't* in a relationship with Sybill,' muttered Merryn.

But Tegan knew her sister, and, looking at Merryn, Tegan knew that Merryn knew that she was well and truly beaten on this one.

* * *

'Here we are.' Sybill pulled on the handbrake and looked at Pencradoc, smiling as she apparently took in the grey stone frontage and eager, it seemed, to be getting on with the job in hand.

Sybill looked really happy to be here and Ryan guessed it was mostly because she got to see her partner, Coren, every time she came up under the pretext of "work".

It was his first time at Pencradoc, though. He'd definitely been sequestered a little at Wheal Mount, and, despite his longing to be back in Glasgow, he did feel a strong attachment to his current place of work. But Sybill had thought it a good idea for him to come up to the edge of Bodmin Moor and visit the place, seeing as he'd soon be working closely with the team — even if, he thought, it turned out to be temporary, if he got that other job.

'So what's the plan for today? Remind me,' he asked.

'We're meeting Merryn's replacement first. And then we can talk about the winter wedding exhibition, which will, of course, be a joint project. That's it. Nice and simple. Coren said last night that Merryn's World War One project was definitely off the cards — for now at least.'

'Yeah. A World War One project sounds a bit daunting, if I'm honest.'

As he looked at Pencradoc towering in front of them, he did think it had a sense of familiarity about it in some ways. Perhaps it was just because they had leaflets and postcards relating to Pencradoc at Wheal Mount. He supposed that Pencradoc would have some sort of merchandise about Wheal Mount too, as the two properties had belonged to the same family members over a century ago. And obviously Tammy and Sybill talked about it quite a lot as the two properties worked closely together, both being arts centres and all that.

But he did think the place looked comfortable and happy, as if he could just walk in there, throw himself into a chair and start leafing through a book or something, perfectly at home.

'Do you like it?' Sybill asked. 'You seem a bit dazed by it.'

'Yeah. No. It's good. I've just never been before and it's weird seeing it in real life, I guess.' He reached around and grabbed a document case from the back seat. A document case! When had he become the sort of man who transported a document case?

Sybill had told him it looked professional and it was the best way to present the information they'd found for the wedding. She'd given it to him this morning and told him to fill it before they left.

While Sybill had waited, he'd quickly stuffed it with copies of letters and photographs relating to the 1911 wedding of Lady Elsie Pencradoc and Louis Ashby. He'd found the documents, thanks to Tammy's excellent system and his recent, timely discoveries in those old boxes, but, to be fair, there wasn't a great deal to actually present today. However, he thought there would be more if he had the time to rummage.

There was, at least, a copy of a wedding photo of the bride and groom Sybill had provided — she said the original was at Pencradoc — the letter Elsie had sent to her brother Laurie to ask him to come to London and see her wedding dress, and a letter to her sisters asking if they would be her bridesmaids along with their cousins and a friend — or rather, telling them that was the case.

'You'll get used to Pencradoc.' Sybill undid her seatbelt and opened the door. 'You might find yourself working between the two properties a bit, especially with having their archives at our place. Honestly, it's not scary at all once you're in there.'

'I don't think it looks particularly scary at all,' said Ryan.

'Really?' Sybill paused, the door half open, and looked at him curiously. 'That's a good sign. Come on then.'

'Whatever.' He grinned and got out of the car. Ryan followed Sybill up the steps. 'I'm glad we're not doing the War,' he said. 'There's so much in those archives about that. It's a lot of information to pull together. I—' Ryan halted as he set foot inside the big hallway. 'Wow.' He looked around. The place seemed familiar — weirdly so. He could have sworn he'd been in a place like this before. That staircase . . . His gaze was drawn to a step about five up from the bottom.

An image shot into his mind of someone falling . . . someone lying at the bottom of the stairs . . . No. No, it must have been a film he'd seen. He honestly had never been here before.

'You okay?' asked Sybill curiously.

'Yeah. No. Sorry. Just — wasn't what I was expecting in here. That's all. This way?' He pointed towards the back of the hall.

'Yes, that's right. You *sure* you're okay? You've gone a bit pale. Seen a ghost or something?'

Pale was Ryan's default colour. And he didn't believe in ghosts. So . . . . 'Nope. I'm good, thanks.'

Sybill just laughed and headed towards where the study — no, the office — was. 'One thing you need to know about

Pencradoc, Ryan — this place gets a hold of you, you know, and it's not always easy to let it go.'

'Sure, sure.' But his mind was elsewhere — had anyone actually called Coren's room the "study", or had he thought that one up as well?

As if she was reading his mind, Sybill said, 'This is Coren's office. It used to be Louis' study — Elsie's husband.'

Okay. He, Ryan, didn't think that anyone had mentioned study or office before now, so he clamped his lips shut and tried to stop his brain whirring so hard that it was genuinely making more things up. He must be more nervous about this trip to Pencradoc than he had thought.

They were met just before the door by Coren, and Ryan spotted the wedding photograph hanging up on the wall as he greeted them. That was good. It was a link of sorts — something familiar. Ryan vaguely knew Coren of course — how could he not, the amount of times the man had been to Wheal Mount. But still, it was different seeing him on his home turf as it were.

'I saw the car pull up,' said Coren. He welcomed Sybill with a kiss — fair enough. They were having a child together after all. Yet they still didn't live together. Tammy had commented that she thought it was a bit late in the day to take it slowly, but that was Sybill and Coren all over.

'Liar,' said Sybill. 'You couldn't see us from the office, so you must have been lurking in the morning room or something.'

'Or something,' he said and smiled. 'Good morning, Ryan, good to see you. Come on — come and meet Tegan.'

Ryan hesitated. Tegan? That name rang a bell as well. No. It couldn't be. Could it? Oh, God, he hoped not. It wasn't that common a name, in his experience. But no — absolutely not . . .

Then Coren opened the door and stood back. Sybill entered first. 'Hey, Tegan, good to meet you!' she said cheerfully.

'Hello. You must be Sybill. Nice to meet you too,' said a voice that was all too familiar to Ryan. And not in a good way.

His heart pounding, Ryan followed Sybill in.

Then . . .

'Oh, God! Not *you*!' said Tegan, staring at Ryan.

Ryan shook his head. 'Good God. Spare me *this*! *Not* you!'

The pair of them glared at one another for what seemed like a lifetime.

'Umm — anything we need to know?' asked Sybill. 'Anything at all?'

CHAPTER SIX

1911

'El, I am entirely disappointed in you,' said Laurie, once Viola had — thank God — left the room, and it was just the four of them. Marigold was quite settled on his lap, a warm, soft weight, not unlike Biscuit the dog back at Pencradoc.

Biscuit was Elsie's dog. She'd had him since she was around eight years old, which now made him the grand old age of sixteen, but he showed no signs of shuffling off his mortal coil any time soon. Since Elsie had left for London, he showed no particular loyalty to any of the Teagues, but seemed to love everyone equally.

Biscuit would quite happily seek affection from whomso-ever was close by, although Medora was, Laurie knew, of the opinion that she was the most favoured soul in the house now. The truth was, that if Elsie walked back in the door, Biscuit would launch himself at her as if he was a puppy again, and had even good-naturedly accepted Marigold and her well-meaning, babyish tweaks and pulls to his ears on her visits.

Laurie felt somehow disloyal likening his toddler niece to the family's ancient dog, but the weight was the same in his lap and he felt himself patting Marigold's back even as she snuggled in today. Her breathing grew shallow and her weight seemed to increase and he knew the child was asleep — which also meant he was trapped here a little longer so, again *thank God*, he was pleased the hideous Viola Arthur had flounced out.

'Well, please excuse me,' said Louis cheerfully, and tip-toed out, saying something about having work to do for his father's estate and how he was dreadfully sorry but it simply couldn't wait. Privately, Laurie thought Louis was heading into his study to lock his door and have forty winks after playing pirates so furiously with his daughter. There was a nanny or a nursemaid or something, he knew, but it was clearly her day off. Or maybe her week off — who knew? But Marigold was certainly making the most of having her father around. It was good for them both.

'Why ever are you disappointed in me?' Elsie's eyes were wide and far too innocent. 'I was entertaining a friend — you turned up. Is it *my fault*,' she asked, spreading her arms wide and dramatically, 'that there is clearly a frisson between you two, and you have yet to notice it yourselves?'

'There is no frisson. Viola is an awful person — she's loud and outspoken and jumps to conclusions. I swear she thought I'd made her fall over on purpose.'

'Darling, it's fate. That's what it is.' Elsie shrugged, unconcerned. 'Now, on to other things.' She rummaged around on one of the tables, moving a paintbrush or two, sorting out some mail, discarding the sketch she'd been working on, and finally finding the letter she was after. 'Look.' She handed it to Laurie. 'It's from Pearl. We've decided we're having a Halloween party for the little ones. Delightful, yes?' She swooped down and gently scooped Marigold off Laurie's knee, cuddling her close and kissing her hair the way Louis had kissed hers earlier.

Laurie unfolded the letter properly and read it. Some words jumped out at him that made him cringe inwardly: *I'm desperately hoping Viola will still be here for Halloween. Yes, I agree, let's show the little ones how we do Halloween properly. I am happy to host it here, but I know how keen you are for that little poppet to spend time at Pencradoc — and to hell with all that snobbery. American Aunt Pearl and Aunt Viola will make sure Marigold is as merry as a grig when she sees our jack o' lanterns!*

'Well, I am sure that Pearl is the only one who is desperate for Viola to be here,' he said. 'And please can you translate it for me?'

Elsie rolled her eyes heavenwards. 'You *know* what it means. Don't be awkward.'

But Laurie was feeling in an awkward sort of mood. He obviously wanted to be part of the Halloween celebrations — he loved a good ghost story as much as the next person and there was always an eerie magic about the night at Pencradoc. However, he also knew that Aunt Pearl would not do anything by halves.

'And will Holly and Noel be involved as well?' he asked, resigned to the fact that the "little ones" would also include the "littlest one", as in Holly and Noel's newborn, Joe.

'Of course. It will be *wunnerful*, Laurie. I promise.' She grinned, deliberately using one of the words her friend was famous for saying.

'There will be small people overrunning the place,' he said grumpily. He wasn't really grumpy, to be honest. He was just irritated that Viola might appear again. He hoped she'd have had enough of England's autumnal weather by then, and disappear back to New York. Or turn tail and head to Paris, and go back to that poor sop who apparently adored her.

Vile.

Oh. Actually . . .

'El, do you think we can call her Vile-ola?'

'Laurie! No! Of *course* you can't! And please — *not* in front of Marigold!' She pulled the little girl closer into her black lacy bodice and cupped her hand around the ear that

52

was exposed, just in case the sleeping child heard anything. 'You're more of a child than she is at times! Dreadful boy.'

Oh, well. She might be correct. "You can't win 'em all", as he was sure Viola would say.

It was just — *wunnerful* — that they might be thrown together again at Halloween . . .

Not.

'Oh — something over there for you on the table,' said Elsie, nodding to where she'd left her most recent sketch. 'Top one.'

Laurie got up and went over. He picked up the top paper, and, to his horror, saw a charcoal sketch of Viola. It was definitely her — the attitude, the turn of her head, everything.

'Elsie! What the h . . .' He cast a glance at Marigold. 'Heck is this?'

'It's a gift from me to you. No! No need to thank me. Fresh off the page.' She held her hand up and closed her eyes. 'You must promise me you'll take it home with you and not to destroy it. Not yet, anyway. Please keep it for a while. Then, after a few months, perhaps when — or if — she goes back to America, you can decide what to do with it.' She opened her eyes and glared at him. 'Best Sibling Promise.'

A "Best Sibling Promise" was something they'd done as children, when they'd been up to mischief together. It was an unbreakable bond, always had been, always would be.

'Elsie Pencradoc. You are *not* the best sibling, you are the *worst* sibling.' Laurie was furious. But Elsie's gaze remained fixed on him. His mouth worked for a moment, then he rolled his eyes heavenwards and whipped the picture off the desk. 'You have me over a barrel. I will *do* as you *ask,* but I am *not* happy about it.'

'Nobody said you had to be happy about it,' she said easily. 'Not one person.'

Laurie just shook his head.

Yes. His sister was utterly, *utterly* vile.

But once again, she had the upper hand and he wasn't very happy about it at all.

* * *

Viola hadn't intended on being in England any longer than she had to be. *No siree.* The intention had been that she would be heading back to America with Sam — sometime in September, they'd said, sitting in their rented house in Bloomsbury, planning what they'd do.

Elsie had found them the property, when they'd decided to extend their stay a little. Sam had, of course, travelled to London first just after that crazy midsummer ball, and fallen in love with the place. Viola was sure the truth was that he'd fallen in love with a girl he'd met at the theatre, then another girl he'd met at a museum, and another girl he'd met in Hyde Park . . . the list went on.

But a few days after the awful re-introduction to Laurie Teague, she and Sam got an invitation to a ball. It was the end of the Season, as they so charmingly called it over here, and there was some celebratory ball going on in Mayfair.

At first, Viola was reluctant to go. As far as she was concerned, the Season was nothing more than a meat market. That was, she knew, how Pearl had ended up meeting and marrying Ernie on such a brief courtship. She, Viola, had been much younger, of course, when Pearl had come over here to fulfil her parents' dreams. Viola, was twenty now and felt grateful that she hadn't been herded down the same track as her elder sister.

The truth was, that once Pearl had gained her status in England by becoming a "Lady", her parents were quite happy that their wealth had put their family on the map in Cornwall's High Society — so they currently weren't pressuring Sam to marry, and Viola was in no imminent danger of becoming a Dollar Princess herself. She'd grown up in Washington Square North and everyone at home knew how well their neighbour, Flora Davis, had done, marrying Terence John Temple Hamilton-Temple-Blackwood. 'Second Marquess of Dufferin and Ava,' Mrs Arthur always said breathlessly.

To Viola's mind, Pearl had done her bit to raise the profile of the Arthur family by marrying Sir Ernest Elton, so there was no need for Viola to try to compete with the beautiful Flora — or even Pearl — right now.

It would happen, it definitely would — there would be an expectation *somewhere* along the line — but, for now, the two youngest Arthur siblings were footloose and fancy free, as the saying went. It helped that they had no financial concerns, and maybe, Viola thought, perhaps it was a good thing to be over here with Sam, away from the machinations of her mother . . .

Whatever. Right now, there was a ball to attend and she did like a good party. Pearl's fabulous midsummer costume ball had been delightful, despite all the craziness and the drama, and Viola hoped that this one would be the same.

And here they were this evening — at the Mayfair Ball!

'I doubt they'll appreciate us dancing the way we did at Pearl's,' her brother said as they pulled up in a carriage in front of the vast townhouse the ball was taking place at. The house was owned by some distant member of the nobility — Viola wasn't even sure they would know her if they fell over her, but they obviously knew of Pearl and Ernie, and as the Society grapevine went, they'd also know she and Sam were here for a little while.

'Mmm. It was fun, though, at Pearl's.' Viola smiled as she recalled ragtime dancing the bunny hug and the turkey trot and the grizzly bear . . .

'It was. Well, here we go. See who I can fall in love with tonight.' Sam knew exactly what he himself was like, and it was a laughing Viola who alighted the carriage before him and went up the steps to the house.

Almost the first person she saw when she went into the ballroom — a ballroom! A proper-sized *ballroom* in a townhouse, though! — was Elsie.

Tonight, Elsie was dressed in black again, but in a far more fashionable ball gown. The frock had a dove-grey underskirt, which was covered in intricately patterned black lace, and half the bodice was covered in rich black velvet, which then wrapped around her waist and trailed into a sash that hung prettily down the front.

Although Viola's frock was mint green with a pink sash, she felt dowdy next to her friend, and even more so when Elsie swooped down on her, with arms wide and welcoming, and a huge smile lighting up her face. Elsie's hair was tonight piled up on the top of her head with strings of pearls wound through it. She looked utterly breathtaking. Viola patted her own fair hair, set off with a pink ribbon to match her sash, and didn't feel much more confident.

That was entirely unusual for Viola — she usually felt composed and self-assured in *any* company — but Elsie outshone every woman in that room.

'Viola! And Sam! How delightful!' said Elsie. 'Come. Louis is over here.' She linked one arm through Viola's and one through Sam's, and marched them through the crowds. Viola felt all eyes turn to look at them and raised her chin a little higher. They would not intimidate her, not at all, even though she keenly felt how *short* she was tonight! That was the only thing she wished she could change about herself, really. But beyond that . . . Elsie wasn't exactly tall, but she was still taller than Viola and she felt, for a moment, like a tot being dragged in from the yard for supper.

'Here we are. Louis, look who I found.' Elsie smiled and released the pair of them, and then Louis took her hand and kissed it politely.

'Jolly good to see you here. Glad you could make it.'

'Oh, we had nothing else planned,' replied Sam, shaking his hand, his eyes already searching out a belle of the ball he could approach just as soon as. 'And it is dreadfully good to see you. Now — you must excuse me. I think I have already spotted someone I know.' He bowed politely, smiled again and headed off in the direction of a pert little brunette who was making big eyes at him.

Ugh.

'Don't worry,' said Elsie, holding Viola's hand. 'You shan't be left alone. Stay with us. I'm just looking for the third member of our party, but he's escaped my notice at the moment. Oh, look. Yes. There he is. Jolly good.' She squeezed Viola's hand and Viola suddenly realised quite how vice-like Elsie's grip was on her.

She couldn't have moved away even if she had tried — well, without a big, showy struggle — but dear God did she wish she had struggled when the realisation struck as to who the third person was, and clearly why Elsie had secured her in such a fashion.

Good Lord, no.

Laurie Teague was weaving his way through the crowds, smiling and waving as he spotted Louis and Elsie, but his face dropped into a *dreadful* scowl as soon as he saw Viola!

Viola forgot herself for a moment. 'Elsie! No! I'm sure we don't want to spend any time together. That's quite all right.' She shook her arm fruitlessly. Yes. That grip was *definitely* vice-like.

'Oh, no. Not at all!' Elsie would not be dissuaded. 'Laurie would, I'm *sure*, prefer to spend some time with you, rather than be paraded like a prize piglet for the ladies here tonight.'

'Prize *piglet*?' Viola was stunned. What was the "prize" with Laurie Teague?

'Yes. They all know *me*, of course,' said Elsie, but without a trace of entitlement. It was simply a fact. 'They know my father was the Duke of Trecarrow, and all about Pencradoc and Wheal Mount and everything. In fact, the reason I'm even here tonight is because our dearest hostess wishes me to recommend her godson to the Royal Academy.' Elsie pulled

57

a face. 'Not sure if she knows I have no influence over that whatsoever. Quite. Anyway. Laurie — the son of the famous artist Ruan Teague — is, of course, Ruan Teague's heir. And as such, is a good catch.' She raised her eyebrows, watching her brother gradually come back to life from his stance of frozen horror. 'So inevitably, once our delightful hostess realised Laurie was in the vicinity, she of course invited him too. In the hopes that a young lady here will indeed reel him in.' She left loose of Viola's arm and mimed a fishing rod.

'I do not envy the young lady who does succeed in reeling him in,' Viola somehow managed to say. Silently, she added, *But it won't be me!* 'But seriously, Elsie, I can just find my brother and help him manage his moral compass tonight, and all will be well.'

She made to leave, but she was too slow and all of a sudden *he* was in front of her.

It annoyed her that he was so *tall*. Even in her heels, all ready for dancing, she really felt unbearably *short* tonight. And the fact that, for a brief moment, she had seen him smile and knew that expression would never light on her. It gave her a feeling she was unaccustomed to, deep in the pit of her stomach: jealousy. Pure and simple jealousy.

The feeling made her start. Why would she be jealous that Laurie Teague would smile at other girls in a way he wouldn't ever smile at her? Surely, she shouldn't care one jot. But she didn't have a chance to ponder it further as he was only inches away from her now.

'El,' Laurie said, not looking at Viola. 'And Louis. I thought I saw you hiding over here.' He raised the glasses of champagne he was holding, two in one hand, one in the other. 'Just went to get some refreshments.'

'We found Viola and Sam when you were . . . refreshing,' said Louis with a smile, taking one of the glasses.

'Not for me, thank you,' said Elsie, looking at the sparkling liquid. 'I want to keep my wits about me tonight, thank you. I shall just have some — normal — wine.'

Louis looked at Viola wryly. 'I'm not speaking out of turn, because she would be the first to say it — but Elsie and champagne don't go well together.'

'Oh, I'm sure Viola can recall Pearl's last ball,' said Elsie comfortably. 'Champagne definitely didn't suit me then — but look at the outcome.' She touched Louis' cheek. 'I'm rather glad I was so outspoken.'

'I am also rather glad,' said Louis, taking hold of her hand and kissing it.

Viola did indeed remember Elsie's declaration. It had been an education. But she was too polite to agree, so she simply smiled.

'Laurie, perhaps Viola would like that spare glass of champagne?' said Elsie. 'And also, you two haven't greeted one another yet.'

Laurie fixed his gaze on Viola, his eyes like burning embers, emanating something she couldn't quite decipher.

He bowed, rather stiffly. 'Good evening, Miss Arthur.'

She bobbed a tiny curtsey and inclined her head just a smidgen. 'Good evening, Mr Teague.'

He offered her the champagne glass and she hesitated, then took it with another quick nod of thanks.

She was spared any further horror by the reappearance of Sam.

'Laurie!' he said expansively. 'Good to see you! I was just talking to that delightful young lady over there,' he indicated the pretty brunette, 'but then her beau reappeared and I was sadly sidelined. Viola, would *you* care to dance?'

'Oh — yes. Please. That would be *wunnerful.*' Viola was so relieved to be able to escape Laurie's immediate vicinity, she would have agreed to almost anything at that moment.

'Even though it's quite old-fashioned compared to our ragtime routines?' Sam smiled.

'Even so,' she replied.

'A little Parisian waltz, then? Just to mix things up here?' Sam and Viola had made up their own version of the waltz in

Paris and, rightly or wrongly, enjoyed the look of confusion on peoples' faces when they started dancing.

Viola agreed and allowed her brother to whisk her away, far away, from Laurie Teague.

Well — as far as she could get, anyway, in a full-sized ballroom in a house in Mayfair.

CHAPTER SEVEN

Present

Tegan was horrified. There was no other word for it. Utterly horrified.

'Ryan and I know one another,' she said rather stiffly. Coren and Sybill were standing looking at each of them, confusion written all over their faces.

'May I ask — how?' asked Sybill carefully.

Ryan pointed to Tegan, then ran his hand through his hair. He shook his head. 'From Glasgow.' He glowered at Tegan. 'We were at the same gallery. She was awful.'

It had been six years ago, Tegan realised — but the memories haunted her to this day.

'Disagree!' She could recall it all in vivid Technicolor. 'Ryan was there on a summer job. And he wasn't very good at it. He was the single most unhelpful person I've ever had the misfortune to work with.'

'Hey! Just wait a moment! You were the one that made things difficult up there! You never carried anything through that you said you'd do. I just got fed up of starting stuff you kept changing your mind over!'

'You have to flex when you need it! Change things up, make things *better*—'

'Get one thing out of the way before you mix it all up again—'

'Woah!' Coren flapped his hands at the pair of them and Tegan clamped her lips together and folded her arms.

Strike Three! seemed to be flashing in neon lights behind Coren's head. Bloody hell. Would she ever learn to shut *up*?

Although — hold on. She stood a little straighter. Hadn't she defended herself from Ryan's accusations?

Oh, no.

You hollered at him first, a little voice said in her head. At least she hoped it was in her head — the voice was American, and quite loud, and if it wasn't in her head, she'd swear an invisible American woman was standing right beside her ear telling her she'd been rather stupid.

Just for once, could she be less impulsive? And work on that filter other people claimed to have?

Not a great first impression. Tegan felt herself flush hotly, to the very roots of her hair. Sybill was staring at the pair of them, at her and that dreadful Ryan, and that old adage came back to her: *you never get a second chance to give a first impression*, or whatever it was.

'Okay.' Coren spoke calmly. 'I guess Glasgow was a long time ago, yes?'

'Yes,' Tegan said. 'Six years ago. But I remember it *very* well.'

'Yes. It was a while ago.' Ryan's arms were also folded and he was glaring at her. He apparently remembered it well too.

'Then — do we think we can kind of — move past Glasgow? And work together? Because if not . . .' Coren shrugged as he let that sentence hang there ominously.

Ryan scowled at Tegan, and Tegan scowled at him. But deep down, she knew this was an amazing opportunity and if she walked out now, she'd not only be letting Merryn down, but she'd be letting Coren down, and letting Sybill down.

Letting Pencradoc down. And, most of all, letting herself down.

And also giving *him* the satisfaction that she'd scuttled away like a coward.

She took a deep breath. 'Yes. I can move past it,' she said. 'It was a long time ago, like you say.' Part of her wanted to scream, *but regardless, I can't* stand *this person!* Wisely, she clamped her lips shut and said nothing.

'Ryan?' Sybill spoke to the Enemy.

'What? Me? Yes — of course.'

Tegan chanced a glance at him. His mouth was set in the same way hers was and she could tell he was fighting a comment down as well. But he said nothing else.

There was a beat.

'Good,' Coren said simply. 'Okay. Let's reacquaint ourselves after so long, and see what we can do to move things forwards, yes? Sit down. Please.' He indicated some chairs around a small circular table and Tegan made sure she sat as far away from Ryan as possible. Which, yes, happened to be dead opposite him.

But she couldn't do much about that. She'd just have to bear with it and be professional. But, dear God, *why* did it have to be Ryan Jackson she was supposed to be working with?

* * *

Ryan took his seat opposite Tegan and the tension was palpable across the table between them. Honestly, she had been the worst person to team up with at the gallery. She planned gallery events, and he, being a temporary member of summer staff, and of an age with her, had been paired up with her.

She was pretty, for certain, but back then, she was definitely not his type. Ryan hadn't found smart, sassy blondes who flicked their shiny ponytails over their shoulders about a million times a day attractive at all. When she walked, her ponytail bounced and swung from side to side, something that annoyed him intensely. Ryan felt more of an affinity with the goth girls and the emo girls who dyed their hair black or crimson, and glowered out of dark eyes hidden under long fringes. Tegan had always played bouncy pop music in the office, and once or twice he'd come in and found her dancing around the room singing along with the tunes. He, on the other hand, loved the old eighties goth music from bands like the Cure, the Mission and the Damned.

Yes, even now, he still loved wearing black, and still loved his goth music; but he was less moody and miserable, and had softened somewhat towards blonde girls. He had even dated a few.

But Tegan, he felt, was still not a person who he would want to spend a lot of time with; not based on their previous relationship, anyway.

For some reason, they just hadn't clicked at all.

With the distance of years, he just couldn't put his finger on it — perhaps it was because at the time they were polar opposites? She was outgoing and cheerful, and he was mired in his own company, still trying to find his way, still unsure of what he wanted to do.

But, also, sometimes, she'd just been nasty. *Pointlessly* nasty, to his mind.

He remembered how one day she'd come bursting into the office when he'd managed to put his own playlist on the computer, as he'd thought she was away for a few hours. "Butterfly on a Wheel", his current favourite Mission track, had been playing. He'd been enjoying wallowing in some post-break-up tunes — one of the emo girls he'd met from the Glasgow School of Art had dumped him for someone studying geology, no less — and Tegan's infernal peppiness that day had irritated him beyond measure.

'I can't bear that noise!' she'd said.

'I can't bear *your* noise either!' he replied, and thus ensued a good ten minutes of argument when they were meant to be finalising an exhibition-catalogue layout together; how she didn't believe in wallowing, and the only good thing to do after a break-up was to move on, go out with your friends and play upbeat music. He disagreed. He felt a break-up deserved a good couple of days in mourning and a damn good wallow and the most angst-ridden playlist you could find . . .

Also, he didn't really *have* any friends to go out with, but he wasn't going to admit that to her.

They sniped at each other all day after that and the catalogue went to print with several errors in it, which made neither of them very popular with the gallery owner.

They were both taken into the owner's office individually. Ryan listened silently and made sure his face remained impassive and expressionless. Tegan came out with red eyes and locked herself in the loos for fifteen minutes afterwards. Then she was vile to him all afternoon and refused even to look at him.

Thinking about that time, Ryan shuddered. Actually — what a stupid argument to have, now he thought about it. It didn't excuse her appalling taste in music, but they'd both been at fault. She'd powered off onto some other project after that, apparently managing to brush the gallery owner's comments off, her butterfly mind probably already moving on to the next big thing. He'd read and re-read the typo-ridden catalogue and churned it over and over in his mind, berating himself for the mistakes he should have spotted, and becoming gloomier and gloomier over it all.

"Butterfly on a wheel" indeed.

Today, Ryan took a deep breath and studied the woman Tegan had become, sitting across from him now. Her hair was lighter, but still irritatingly bouncy. Her face was tanned and her cheekbones were more pronounced, but that might have been the result of clever make-up or because she had her lips compressed tightly. Her clothes were still casual but somehow professional. And her eyes were narrowed, as she appeared to be studying him just as much as he was studying her.

He wasn't going to risk a smile.

it would be a bit embarrassing if she didn't smile back, so he remained stony faced and stared right back at her.

One of them would have to give in eventually.

Wouldn't they?

CHAPTER EIGHT

1911

Laurie watched Viola and Sam disappear into the whirling couples on the dance floor. Soon, they stood out, because they were dancing completely different steps to the other waltzers — standing on one foot, with the other being dragged into position or simply suspended in the air for a beat or two. The faster the music, the more they hesitated.

It was odd, yet strangely entrancing.

Laurie did enjoy dancing in his own, quiet way. But he followed the crowd and preferred not to stand out, so he wouldn't even dream of making a dance up as this pair seemed to do.

But he simply could not stop looking at them — well, looking at Viola, which appalled him. She held her head elegantly, occasionally looking up at her brother and laughing. Her face was rounder and her cheeks fuller than Pearl's as she smiled up at him — the fact that she was a few years younger than her sister was also evident by her lack of "London polish", as Laurie privately called it.

A strange thought entered his mind at that point — he didn't want her to be subsumed into this world of Society the way Pearl had been. And his next thought was: why should he even *care* that much about Viola's subsummation? It was her choice, her life — but she reminded him of Elsie in some ways. Pearl was extremely happy with Ernie and the life she'd married into, but Viola just seemed different, somehow. Whereas Elsie used her art to express her free spirit, it was clear to him tonight that Viola did the same with dance.

Elsie had told Laurie about the turkey trot, the bunny hug and the grizzly bear dance, which Sam and Viola had performed at Pearl's. And indeed, on one of Elsie's visits to Pencradoc with Marigold, she had shown Marigold the steps and they'd all had fun taking the little girl on as their partner and dancing with her. Laurie had been quite possibly the most out of step of the lot of them, and had only redeemed himself in Marigold's eyes by performing a perfect galop dance with Medora, as the little girl had laughed and clapped along in time with the music.

So to see Viola so free and uninhibited on the dance floor tonight was startling.

He realised the music was coming to an end and turned away. No need for her to see he was watching her out there — no need at all. But even as he turned away, his mind's eye was filled with images of Viola Arthur laughing and dancing and smiling, and a very small part of him wished she was doing that with him, and not her brother.

* * *

Viola laughed as the dance ended and she curtsied at Sam. He bowed theatrically back at her and they were just about to check what the next dance was to see if they could adapt that one to their own ends as well, when Viola became aware of a young man approaching her.

'I say,' whispered Sam in a made-up English accent. 'I think you have an admirer.'

Viola's stomach turned over. The last thing she wanted was for anyone to think she was husband-hunting. But she was too slow to say anything and cursed herself, because instead of asking Sam to stay with her, or turning around and heading purposefully back to Elsie and Louis, she looked across at Laurie, and in that split second two things happened — the young man who was approaching her tapped her on the shoulder and bowed, and she saw that Laurie had already turned and walked away.

She felt ridiculously cross and also terribly disappointed. But she couldn't dwell on why she felt like that; she could only switch on a fake smile and turn her attention to the young man.

'I couldn't help but notice your dancing,' he said. 'May I ask where you learned that? Oh—' he turned his attention to Sam — 'and also, my *deepest* apologies to your partner in advance for my intention to steal you away from him.'

'She's my sister,' said Sam. 'You're very welcome to steal her. *Adieu*, sister, *adieu.*'

He saluted Viola and walked away, heading back to Elsie and Louis — and Laurie.

Dammit!

Oh, well. She had to ride this one out herself.

'He's correct,' said Viola with a forced laugh. 'That's my brother, all right.'

'Splendid. Then you won't mind spending some time with me.' The man smiled. His top lip was rather shiny and damp, fleshy-looking in a not particularly pleasant way, especially when he licked it. *Ugh.* 'I'm Richard Bedford. One of the Sussex Bedfords?' He said it as if she should know who the hell he was, or who his family were. He didn't wait for an answer, but took her arm and manoeuvred her around the edge of the dance floor towards the refreshments. 'I can't help but notice you're American.'

'Yes. I am.'

'And . . .' He looked at her curiously. 'Are you going to avail me of your name?'

'Viola—' she started to say, but wasn't able to finish the sentence before he was off again.

'Lady Pearl Elton is American. Married into the Bodmin Eltons. I believe she has done wonders for Elton Lacy. Well, her fortune has.' He laughed, as if that was the most amusing thing in the world and Viola was treated to moist breath that smelled of alcohol washing over her face. She felt her stomach turn a little. 'Lady Elton is one of the New York Arthurs — not sure if you're *familiar* with them?' He didn't wait for answer but blithely continued. 'I hear her father works on Wall Street, so they're not short of a bob or two.' *Jeepers! How did he know that?* 'It really was the talk of Society when the Eltons married.' Viola and Sam had not been at the wedding — Viola had been deemed "too young" to travel halfway across the world, and Sam had been travelling, so she was completely unaware of any of this. 'Why,' Richard continued, smirking, 'a couple of us put bets on how much she'd brought as a dowry!'

Viola went hot and cold all over. She wasn't going to tell Pearl *that* one, although Pearl probably knew herself what the gossips were saying. How awful. How utterly awful!

'The rumour is . . .' *Does this man* ever *stop talking?* 'That Lady Elsie Pencradoc attended the wedding — but it seems that woman is allergic to the state of matrimony herself.'

'We—'

'I mean, their situation is highly unusual,' he said before Viola could say she'd come with Elsie. 'Living as they do, and all that.'

'Living as what?' Viola was confused. Did he mean the fact that Elsie and Louis lived in London, away from Pencradoc itself? It didn't seem that unusual . . .

'Living together outside of wedlock, of course!' Richard leaned in, all *faux* shock, and laughed loudly, right in her face; Viola could smell even more alcohol on his breath. 'And truth be told, I'm *damn* surprised they've upheld their station in Society for so long, but I suppose she may have used certain charms to stay where she is. She's here tonight, of course, brazen as anything.'

'Pardon?' Viola was thoroughly confused now, only half-listening and thoroughly hung up on his earlier comment about wedlock. Elsie and Louis not being married? The thought hadn't even entered her mind.

'Shocking, isn't it? I mean, the apple doesn't fall far from the tree in that family. Rumour also has it that half her siblings are—'

But whatever he was going to say about Elsie's siblings was never to be uttered at that point.

Because Laurie suddenly appeared out of the shadows, looking for all the world like an avenging vampire, and planted himself in front of Viola's companion.

'Is this gentleman bothering you?' Laurie asked. His voice was chilling. 'Because he's bothering me.'

'Excuse me?' Richard took a moment to focus on Laurie. 'I'm having a conversation. You . . .'

Laurie took one more step and the flickering candlelight from the table, from the wall sconces and from the chandeliers seemed to pool around him, illuminating him.

His mouth was compressed in a tight, angry line, his brows were drawn together, a scowl darkened his face. And he looked glorious!

Viola blinked — she could do nothing but stare at him. Jeepers, her knees were practically jelly and that had *nothing* to do with her dancing . . .

'No. I shall not "excuse you",' Laurie said coldly. 'You have insulted my sister, you have insulted me, you have insulted my family. You are an arrogant bigot and this young lady is so far above you in both manners and decorum that she should no longer be subjected to your drivel.' He paused and looked Richard up and down in disgust. 'You are actually an embarrassment to Society yourself. Do you know that?'

'I—'

'*Do* you?' Laurie's voice thundered, not letting Richard follow through. 'No. I bet you do not.' He shook his head. Then, in one smooth movement, he took Viola's hand and drew her close to him.

Her legs really were going to collapse beneath her; she had to hang on to Laurie's hand awfully tightly and found herself taking a couple of steps closer to him, so it felt like she and him were definitely on the side of the angels together. Well, the fallen angels, she amended, chancing a quick glance at the tall, dark, angry man next to her.

My word. Her arm was tingling all the way from her fingertips to her shoulder, and it was all because *he* was holding her hand . . . like that. Like he really cared about her and cared about removing her from such an obnoxious presence as Richard Bedford.

Her rational side told her it was probably because Laurie was so angry at what he'd overheard about Elsie and his family, but for that brief moment, she'd felt a total connection to the man beside her and it made her feel faint.

My word.

'I'm now going to walk away from you,' Laurie told Richard. 'And I'm taking this young lady with me. I feel it's safest to put a considerable distance between you and me. Good evening, *Sir.*' The last word dripped with sarcasm and Viola was rather impressed, despite the situation.

'Now wait just one moment!' Richard began to bluster, suddenly finding his voice. 'Violet may not want to go with you. She would much rather stay with me, I'm sure. Violet?' He held his hand out and wiggled his fingers, beckoning her to him. Viola found that gesture rather sickening to be honest. And actually . . .

'Who's *Violet*?' she asked. 'My name is Viola. Viola Arthur. One of the New York Arthurs. And don't worry, I'll be sure to send your regards to my sister.'

She dropped a brief curtsey and turned to Laurie, not waiting to see Richard's reaction. She curtsied to Laurie as well. He bowed to her and the pair of them walked out of the ballroom, her heart thumping so *very* loudly. They continued until they came to the balcony. Then Laurie threw the door open and strode out onto the balcony . . .

Where he very quickly let go of her hand, took three steps backwards and folded his hands behind his back.

CHAPTER NINE

Tegan knew he was looking at her, so she stared him out. He had changed a bit since those days in Glasgow; his long, dark, horrible hair was shorter now — well, more styled at least. He had a side-parting sort of thing, and his hair flopped over his forehead, and he didn't look like he'd shaved for a couple of days. His brown eyes stared unblinkingly back at her.

Taking him at face value — if she didn't know him as she did — he looked like an earnest, intelligent and deep type of young man. The piercings in his ear hinted at a more edgy personality, well hidden, and on another man, that floppy bit of hair might even be classed as "endearing".

However, this was Ryan Jackson and he had crap taste in music, still apparently wore all-black clothing and preferred wallowing introspection to living real life.

Ugh.

If this was karma having a laugh on her behalf, karma was still a bitch, but no longer *her* bitch. Tegan thought of Angelo, and his dark hair and dark eyes, of Angelo sitting, cross-legged, plucking at his guitar while the sparks from the campfire danced to the melody.

Oh, how she missed that feeling — that feeling of relaxation and completely giving herself over to the warmth of Sicily and the dark, sultry skies.

Babes, said the latest text on her phone. *I miss you so badly. I cannot sleep, I cannot play my guitar, I want you back in my bed.*

Why on *earth* had she left Angelo and come *here*? Back, unwittingly, into the world of bloody Ryan Jackson?

But she had to tear her gaze away from Ryan, and her thoughts away from Angelo, as Sybill was talking.

'So,' said Sybill. 'I take it you two know each other? And, no, we don't want the history. What we want, Coren and I, is to make sure we all work together professionally and Pencradoc and Wheal Mount can continue supporting one another as they always have done.'

Ryan and Tegan murmured consent, even though Ryan turned red — it must have killed him to agree to that. That seemed to satisfy Sybill, who smiled at them brightly. 'Good. Okay, I'm not sure how much Merryn has told you, but these are the sorts of things we do between the two arts centres . . .'

Sybill talked for a little while about the joint exhibitions the places had run in the past. Even though the exhibitions were not joint in the true sense of the word, each property would usually try to have at least one gallery supporting the other.

Tegan found herself extremely interested in Sybill's words. Coren didn't say much, but appeared to hang on every word Sybill uttered, which didn't surprise Tegan. Merryn had said Sybill was definitely more people-focussed than Coren and gradually Tegan relaxed into the conversation enough to not be totally reliving the Ghosts of Galleries Past with Gothy Ryan over there.

'Coren told me that the next joint exhibition would be changing,' Sybill said eventually. 'Can you explain why you decided that?' She looked at Tegan.

Tegan nodded, trying to remind herself that this *wasn't* an interview, that she *had* the job, and despite Gothy Ryan, she needed to look and sound professional. 'Yes. It was felt that the War was just too expansive a topic and we needed to concentrate on something more seasonal and uplifting for people. It seemed too much going from a wonderful midsummer ball to conflict.'

'Ryan, what do you think?' asked Coren.

Ryan looked at Coren and nodded. 'Yes. I completely agree. Something more seasonal would be great — I mean, not only have we got evidence of a midwinter wedding for Lady Elsie, but Tammy said we've got some references to Halloween in the archives, and I've already seen a letter about it. Maybe we could look at that properly another time. Or as a lead up to the wedding.' He looked a little startled at what he had said. 'But yeah. It's fantastic that Merryn decided to focus on the wedding instead.'

'Actually,' said Tegan. 'That was my idea. The wedding, I mean.'

There was a silence at the table and everyone stared at her.

Strike Four!

Potentially?

Dear God, she hoped not.

'Well.' Ryan's face contorted through a few different expressions as the silence in the room grew uncomfortable. Eventually, he caught Sybill's eye, then dropped his gaze and raised it again. He fixed his eyes on Tegan and she blinked, suddenly aware of how piercing that gaze was.

Hell, yeah, it's like he knows your soul and he's staring . . . Right. Into. It! came that American voice again and Tegan felt a little sick. She took a deep breath and refused to lower her own eyes.

'It's . . . a good idea,' he said, then dropped his gaze again.

It must have killed him to say that.

Inwardly, Tegan wanted to run around and do a celebratory lap of the room. Instead, she nodded — she hoped — graciously, and muttered, 'Thank you.'

'Excellent!' said Sybill. 'We're all on board. Ryan — can I ask how much information you have relating to Halloween in the archives? I'm not sure it's a traditional thing for the family to be celebrating.'

'Oh — yes. The only thing I've seen so far is a letter, really. Between Elsie and is it Petra? Patricia? Someone — a "P" name.'

'Pearl?' said Sybill.

'Yes! That's the one.' Ryan nodded. He still looked a bit confused, though. Great. He was still useless and couldn't carry a plan through then, spoke before he thought and all that jazz.

Like other guys we know.

Tegan wanted to tell her conscience or whatever it was to shut the hell up — and to stop talking to her in a New York accent.

'Pearl and Ernie, yes, that makes sense,' Coren was saying. 'Pearl was American and I suspect she brought some traditions over with her.' He looked at Sybill, then at Ryan. 'We're already arranging a pumpkin trail here for the kids, so if you've got a letter, we could display it somewhere to complement the trail.'

'Let me have a look for the letter,' said Ryan. 'Just to be sure. And I'll check for photos or pictures in the archives. And run it by you all.'

'It does link really well into the wedding,' said Tegan suddenly. Hang on — where the heck had that come from? But she knew it — she absolutely knew it. There was some sort of link between the events, just nudging at her consciousness. 'It leads up to it well,' she said again, almost disbelieving what was coming out of her mouth. How? How did Halloween and Christmas weddings go together at *all*?

'Really?' Sybill was curious. 'In what way?'

'Let me pull the information together.' Tegan felt her cheeks heat up. 'I'm — I'm sure Merryn mentioned it.'

'Great.' Sybill smiled around the table. 'Now, Coren and I need to have a discussion about some other things.'

Tegan knew it was more than likely to be private matters that concerned nobody but Sybill and Coren — like antenatal appointments, or how they were going to co-parent this child if they lived an hour away from each other — and she didn't really want to intrude on that. 'Great.' She picked up her notebook and smiled blankly around at everyone. 'Well, I have research to do. Wedding traditions of 1911 and all that. Exciting stuff!' She couldn't wait to escape from this room and from Ryan. She wasn't actually sure where she wanted to work though . . . her office across the hallway just seemed too close to this whole situation for comfort, and anyway—

'Why don't you take Ryan for a tour around Pencradoc?' said Sybill breezily. 'He's never been before — it'll be good for him to see what it's like.'

'Oh, no, it's fine,' said Ryan quickly.

'I don't think so,' said Tegan at the same time.

'Yeah, it's fine,' they both said together.

Sybill looked at Coren and raised her eyebrows in amusement. 'Maybe another time, then,' she said.

Tegan nodded quickly and hurried out of the room clutching her book. She absolutely desperately needed to be away from the house and from Ryan. It was all a bit much, bumping into him today! She wondered if the Tower Tearoom might be a good choice.

But what if *he* decided to go there too?

It was simply too difficult!

Whatever, she needed to go and she needed to go *now*.

* * *

Ryan watched Tegan run out of the office. Thank goodness for that. The last thing he wanted to do was have some enforced time in Tegan Burton's company.

'I'll have a look around like you say,' he said to Sybill. 'Text me when you're ready to leave.'

'Will do.' Sybill smiled at him and he nodded farewell to Coren, and slipped outside.

Once he was in the hallway, he exhaled slowly. That was close. He thought he'd acted professionally, anyway. But he had no idea why he'd felt the need to throw Halloween in there.

Tammy had directed him to the letter after their conversation about it, and he had definitely seen it. Elsie had been corresponding with her friend — he now knew it was Pearl, thanks to Sybill — and had said that they were all looking forward to getting together for Halloween and the little ones would be excited about it. He needed to look at it properly.

It would be back at Wheal Mount, filed under . . . well, he didn't quite know what it would be filed under. H for Halloween was unlikely. Maybe he'd filed it under the year it had been written? And then a sub-folder of that called . . . Correspondence.

Tammy should never have let him loose in those archives.

He shook his head. Unimaginative. Someone would have to redo them all again and finetune it all. With any luck, he'd be in Glasgow looking at Rennie Mackintosh's correspondence to his wife or his friends before the you-know-what hit the fan . . .

By now, he was out the front door of Pencradoc, clutching his document case and looking around him as he stood on the top step . . .

Clutching the document case.

Shit.

That was full of stuff he should have shown to Coren — but Tegan's presence had thrown him and he'd totally forgotten to open it.

In his defence, nobody had reminded him though . . .

He hovered uncertainly for a moment, wondering whether to go back in and interrupt them, but then the view from the top of the steps caught his attention again.

It really was fantastic. The warmth of the day washed over him, the sun shining desultorily, the clouds casting slow-moving shadows across the gently undulating greenery

78

of Bodmin Moor, the moorland melting into blues and purples in the far distance. The edge of the moor was just over there, straight across the formal gardens, and it was exactly the sort of place a person could ride a horse across as fast as they could. He peered into the distance and sure enough saw a small figure doing just that. He smiled and closed his eyes briefly, imagining it, putting himself in the place of the rider, feeling the power of the horse galloping across the moor . . . not something he'd do in his day-to-day life, but he could imagine someone of that era, of Lady Elsie Pencradoc's era, loving it. Her brother, perhaps — Laurie, wasn't it? — the one who had fought in the War. When he'd done that, ridden his horse like he'd had no cares in the world, had he realised what was coming?

Ryan opened his eyes and shuddered, a cold chill suddenly creeping across his shoulders despite the warmth of the September day. Unable to resist finding out Laurie's fate after Tammy had mentioned him, he'd discovered from some military records that Laurie had come back from the War all in one piece, which was good — apart from the bullet wound in his leg, which had seen him invalided out and given a job at the War Office.

But at least the guy had survived.

He wasn't going to think about it any more, though, because they'd decided *not* to do the War, and were going to do a wedding instead.

Well — Tegan had. He preferred the topic, but really, really hated it that she had been the one to suggest it! Never mind.

Ryan looked back across the gardens towards the moor and blinked. Hang on — he couldn't actually *see* the moor clearly enough to identify lone riders galloping across it, or see shadows from the clouds drifting over the vast expanse — the trees looked much denser in that direction, almost as if they had grown in the few seconds he'd imagined Laurie riding his horse.

Was that who he'd been imagining then? It made sense, he supposed. He knew Elsie had written to her brother about the wedding, he'd been thinking about the wedding and about Laurie — so, yes. That made perfect sense.

He abandoned the idea of taking the documents back into the office and began to walk down the steps, still a little curious about the image he'd seen, but not worried. He'd head this way — towards the gothic rose garden that he knew the beautiful Rose, Duchess of Trecarrow, had created before her early death. It was just along here — if he followed the signs towards the Tower Tearoom, he feared he'd be walking straight into Tegan's territory, because what if she was the sort of person who would grab a table in a full café — probably for four people — and set up their laptop and strew their paperwork around themselves. Perhaps she'd have no more than a bottle of water she'd actually brought in herself — along with a snack in a teeny tiny Tupperware box — and eventually get a small, black coffee, just to prove a point when it started getting busier . . .

He reflected briefly that he had absolutely no basis for that supposition, and she hadn't flounced *out* of their meeting with a laptop, but she could possibly go and *get* a laptop, because there wasn't much research she could do quickly about Edwardian weddings without an internet connection, and he didn't think she'd want to take the time to look through the library at Pencradoc . . .

It was hard to find things on the shelves anyway — the little ones moved books around all the time — and all of his notebooks had to be well hidden or they'd go through them and read out his poetry and laugh about it, and then he'd lose his temper and the girls would look at him in horror and say, 'Why *did you get cross with us? It's* good *for us to read—'*

What on earth?

Ryan's heart was pounding crazily and he honestly wondered why he'd just plucked that thought out of nowhere. Sybill was right — this place got a hold of you and it was clear that a little knowledge was dangerous, because your imagination apparently made up the rest.

He'd spent too long in those archives reading Elsie's letters. That was the problem.

Ryan followed the pathway around to the gothic rose garden and went through the archway of Old English roses that formed a sort of secret tunnel into the garden. There were still big, blowsy flowers on the branches, along with one or two buds that promised to bloom before the frosts came. He sniffed appreciatively and thought that in the height of summer, this place would be magical. Even now, it was like a suntrap.

As he rounded the corner, he saw someone's legs stretched out and crossed at the ankles as they, too, made the most of the weather. They were wearing smartly heeled, black shoes, and a long, pale pink skirt that was apparently hitched up to their knees and trailing on the ground. In fact, the hem was muddy and so were the shoes — which was odd as there was no mud on the ground.

But as he headed towards them and the path took a gentle sweep to the right, he pulled up short suddenly as the sitter came into view.

It was Tegan Burton — only she was wearing wedge-heeled sandals and black trousers, and there wasn't a trace of a muddy pale-pink skirt anywhere. And far from being on a laptop, with paperwork spread out all over a cafe table, she was scrolling through her mobile, and writing notes down as she did so.

CHAPTER TEN

1911

Laurie looked at the girl in front of him, the moonlight and the lights from the ballroom catching on her hair and reflecting in her eyes. There were tiny crystals or something similar dotted across her bodice and skirt. He hadn't really noticed them before, but they shone like the stars right now. He felt that he was in some surreal otherworld with a sprite or a nymph or something fanciful that Medora would definitely have known the name of . . .

But that wasn't the issue right now, and he chased that thought out of his head and took a deep breath. This was Viola Arthur, for God's sake. His nemesis! Why was he likening her to an ethereal sprite?

But even that wasn't the issue, and to be honest he wondered if he was getting a little tired of fighting whatever his complicated feelings were about this girl.

No. The issue right here, right now, was that man he'd been so very close to punching, and what he'd been saying about his family.

'Laurie. What happened in there?' Viola asked quietly, breaking the strange, eerie silence wrapped around them. 'What on earth did he *mean* by all of that?'

It was, Laurie thought, perhaps the first time Viola hadn't screeched at him like a banshee. And for a few moments in there, they had felt . . . close.

'You were magnificent. That's what happened.' He gave a half-smile. 'I've got to hand it to you — that parting shot was an absolute corker.'

'He'd been very rude about my sister.'

'Not only your sister. My sister as well.'

Viola said nothing. It was an invitation to expand on the comments Richard had made, and Laurie debated whether he should take it or not. The silence seemed to stretch for eons, until Viola eventually broke it.

'You don't have to explain things if you don't want to,' she said. 'It doesn't matter.'

'You're right. It doesn't.'

'Good.' She nodded and picked up her skirt. 'I'll go back in and find Sam. Perhaps if I stick by him all night, jossers like that won't be able to talk to me. The problem is, Sam can be a josser himself and likes nothing better than flirting with young ladies. Perhaps I'm best-off finding Elsie . . .'

'Perhaps.' Laurie paused, then took a step towards her. There was a strand of hair falling over her face and he couldn't help himself — he gently moved it out of the way, then dropped his hand back down to his side. 'All I'll say to you is this world is full of Richards and the more you get involved with my family, the more you'll be drawn into gossip like that.'

She looked up at him and touched the lock of hair he'd moved. 'Gossip like that doesn't bother me. Unless, of course, you're trying to warn me off? Telling me to stop choosing my friends the way I do?' There was a challenge in her eyes and to his eternal shame, he found he couldn't answer her or reassure her or tell her that was ridiculous and he wanted her to be friends with his family — he wanted her, in that moment, in that moonlight, to be *more* than friends, perhaps.

But he was, for one of the first times in his life, lost for words.

Viola waited a moment more, then nodded. 'I see,' she said coldly. 'Please. Excuse me, then. But, you know — *thank you* for coming to my rescue and all that. For one moment, I thought we might be able to be friends ourselves. I can see, though, that you clearly don't think that's possible. And I guess I have to respect that. Good evening, Mr Teague.'

She turned and walked purposefully back into the ball-room, swallowed up by the colourful gowns and dark suits.

'Viola!' He suddenly found his voice and hurried to the door. He wasn't sure what he was going to say to her, but he had a feeling that whatever tentative connection they'd built in those few moments had fallen down like a sandcastle at the seaside. He saw her, walking briskly towards Elsie and Louis. A brief conversation ensued, then her brother appeared. There was more conversation and then Sam and Viola danced one more waltz, then left the party.

And in all that time, Laurie stood on the balcony, leaning against the doorframe, hands in his pocket, and never taking his eyes from Viola.

He remained there for a while after she left, staring at the way out of the ballroom, almost willing her to walk back in.

But she didn't.

And even though he was, to all intents and purposes, alone with his thoughts, he still couldn't make sense of any of them.

* * *

A couple of weeks after that dreadful ball — because it *had* turned dreadful, when she'd stormed out of that conversation and flounced back into the ballroom — Sam threw a curveball at her.

84

'I wouldn't mind staying in London a bit longer,' he said to her one evening over dinner. 'I think there is still so much to see and do here.'

'That may be,' she replied. 'But don't you *want* to go home?'

'Hey, the young gentlemen from years ago — they did the Grand Tour, did they not? Across Europe?'

'They did.'

'Then we can do a tour here.' Sam smiled at her. 'Or I can. I know you must miss home more than I do. If you really don't want to stay, you know, you don't have to. We can get you back to New York. Just let me know and we'll book passage for you.'

There was nothing stopping her either staying or going. And she knew that if she *did* want to go home, she *would* go home, and she wouldn't be reliant on her brother to book passage for her.

But Viola didn't think she really wanted to. And she wasn't sure why, although a tiny part of her had a huge suspicion . . .

But *ugh*!

'I don't know.' Viola pulled a face. 'I kind of *want* to go home — but there's still a lot *I* want to see here too. Also, I want to see more of Pearl. And the babies.'

'Pearl has said she'll be happy to come see us over there. Says it'll be good for the children to know their American heritage as well.'

'Mmm. But, you know, there are people here *I* want to get to know more as well . . .'

'Like?'

'Like Elsie.'

'And?'

'Holly.'

'And?'

'Other *people* as well. I don't *know* all their names yet. I quite possibly haven't met them all yet.'

85

'I see.' Sam grinned. 'Shall I ask Émile to pop across the Channel and see you as well? Seems like he wanted to get to know *you* more.'

In a very unladylike fashion, Viola threw a piece of bread at her brother. 'No, thank you — you did enough. Poor man. I had to tell him I was only interested in friendship. I just can't stand being . . .' She searched for the word and the conversation she'd had at Elsie's came back into her mind. 'Adored.' She screwed her face up. She knew how bad that sounded.

'I can think of someone who doesn't adore you,' said Sam teasingly. 'Laurie Teague.'

'Don't mention that man!' Viola practically growled at her brother. 'I've told you how rude he is.' She had given him the potted history of what had happened at the ball. Ugh.

'I like him.' Sam sat back in his seat and tossed the piece of bread up in the air, then caught it in his mouth and ate it.

Everybody seemed to like Laurie! She reminded herself how annoying he was most of the time.

Every time she thought of the man, she found her pulse racing and her temper building. He annoyed her. He just rubbed her up the wrong way. No matter what he did, whatever situation they'd ever find themselves in, it seemed that he would always be destined to wind her up like a bobbin.

'Some of the people I've met, though, I wouldn't want to meet again,' said Viola thoughtfully. She meant, of course, the hideous Richard.

'Ah, yes. You do know what he was insinuating, don't you, though?' Sam raised his eyebrows. 'Richard of Sussex or whoever he was.'

'No, not at all. He was being disparaging about Elsie living away from Pencradoc, I think. That was about it.'

'Oh, you are an innocent.' Sam smiled at her. 'Elsie and Louis aren't married — *that's* the scandal!'

Viola stared at him. She'd got that impression at the midsummer ball when it had all become quite chaotic — but hadn't thought about it much afterwards. She presumed that they had perhaps married quietly in the aftermath, because that's what people did, wasn't it? Especially people in Elsie's position . . .

'Well.' She didn't know what else to say for a moment. It *was* actually quite shocking, but really — who else did it matter to? 'I suppose that's highly unusual, *but* . . .' She verbalised her thoughts. 'Of what interest is that to a room full of people at a ball?'

'I suppose it depends on how very small these peoples' lives are,' replied Sam with a shrug. 'Apparently Elsie's mother lived in sin with Ruan Teague for a while as well. Had a few children before they got married. Laurie was one of them. That was the other thing your friend Richard was implying. And obviously why Laurie lost his temper with him.'

'Richard was *not* my friend. And anyway, none of that changes my opinion of Elsie at all!' said Viola, still indignant. 'I like her. I like Louis. I like . . .' She stopped abruptly.

'You like Laurie?' Sam's eyebrow raised.

'I didn't say that.' But Viola shrank down in her seat, nevertheless, and felt her cheeks heat up. 'I like Marigold.'

'Sure you do.' Sam grinned. 'But you like Laurie too. I'd bet my bottom dollar on that one. Oh — this came for you today as well.' He rummaged in his pocket and tossed an envelope over to her.

Viola didn't recognise the confident, beautiful handwriting on the envelope — she looked at it, half dreading that it might be another ball invitation, yet half hoping it would be, because *he* might be there as well . . .

Never mind betting her brother's bottom dollar, Viola would bet her substantial trust fund on the fact that Laurie Teague, with his dark eyes and his scowling expression, would be at the party, wherever it was.

As she opened the letter, Viola tried not to think how Laurie changed when he was in the company of his small niece, or his younger siblings, or how utterly nice and charming he could be to anyone who basically wasn't her.

How nice he had almost been on that balcony, how he had moved her hair away, so tenderly — and how she had hoped his hand would linger on her cheek for just a moment . . .

Ugh! *No!*

But she wouldn't dwell on it. No siree. The last person she wanted to be nice to her, she told herself crossly, was Laurie Teague.

Because then that would mean she would have to try to be nice to him, or she would look so, so bad . . .

And also — she would start to doubt herself and her opinions, and doubting herself was not something Viola Arthur would *ever* consider doing.

As she read the letter, however, she felt her lips tilt upwards into a smile.

It was an invitation to a Halloween party.

At Pencradoc.

Pearl apparently wanted to show the "little ones" in all the families what a proper ol' festival Halloween could be and Elsie had agreed to host it.

Yes. Laurie would definitely be there, then.

And despite herself and her conflicted emotions about that man, she felt that she might, actually, allow herself to look forward to it.

So, no. She would not be going home just now. No siree.

CHAPTER ELEVEN

Present

Tegan was aware of someone standing in her peripheral vision — a tall, masculine shadow, with what looked like a white shirt on, dark trousers and a dark waistcoat.

At least, it looked like that from the corner of her eye. When she turned to look at the person, she realised that, yes, it was a man — a tall, dark man at that — but rather than wearing a white shirt and a waistcoat, the person was wearing a black T-shirt. And that person was Ryan Jackson.

Dammit. Why had he come here? Why hadn't he just gone to the Tower Tearoom like he was *supposed* to?

'Can I help?' she asked, and even to herself she sounded clipped and unfriendly. 'But you'll have to wait a second. I'm just texting my boyfriend. Angelo. He lives in Sicily. He's a musician.'

Ryan's lip curled up at the corner and he looked at her strangely. Clearly, he wasn't bothered about Angelo and why should he be? She *had* been messaging him a few minutes ago — well, responding to a text that asked how she was, and which had included a photo of a Sicilian sunrise. But did she really need to share all that with Ryan?

No.

'Okay.' Ryan continued to look at her strangely. 'I'll leave you to it. Although I did somehow think that you were working, and perhaps you'd have gone to the tearoom to do that. To work, I mean.'

Ouch. Now it looked as if she'd been messing around with Angelo instead of doing what she was meant to be doing. It galled her that Ryan thought that, but that was pretty much the case to be fair.

'Why would I do that?' she asked defensively. 'Go and work in the tearoom, I mean. It's coming up to lunchtime anyway, and you might have been there. Also,' she shrugged. 'It wouldn't be fair if I commandeered a table, but to be honest Sorcha would pretty soon move me on if I tried *that*.'

Ryan nodded. 'Good for Sorcha.'

He hovered for a moment, before turning around to leave.

Something in Tegan relented. She sighed, then called after him. 'Ryan! Do you want to know what I'm *really* looking at?'

'Not particularly.' But he turned back around and took a few steps towards her. 'But you did say you were messaging your boyfriend in Sydney.'

'Sicily.'

'Whatever. Let me guess.' He sighed. 'Rubbish music? Your next job? Social media influencers who you think are super-cool, but who would *literally* do my head in?'

'Not smart, not funny.' She glared at him. '*No* music is worse than your crap and I'm sticking this one out for a year, despite you being part of it.'

'Despite your boyfriend being in Sydney.'

'Sicily.'

'Sicily. Is he coming over, then? Actually, don't tell me, I don't care.' He waved his hand around to illustrate. 'But you being here for a year is pretty unfortunate for me. Don't suppose you fancy reconsidering your post, do you? It would make me very happy. Unless, of course, I get the job in Glasgow I've applied for and then I'll be away from you. Which would *also* make me very happy. But, having said that, you're not chasing me out of *this* job with your attitude. I might have to stick it out for the long haul.'

'Whoopee-do,' muttered Tegan. 'Then you really oughta be interested in what I have in front of me here.'

'A pink phone?'

'Smart ass. No. The research I'm doing. If we really have to work together and you won't leave immediately — no? — okay, just checking again — then we should talk weddings.'

She realised what she'd said and knew the colour had drained from her face. It sounded a bit — intimate — that. Like they were getting married.

Ugh.

'Elsie's wedding, of course,' she said for clarity.

'Of *course*.' Ryan was emphatic — she couldn't be sure if he was being sarcastic or not, so chose to ignore him.

'So it's only recently come to light that she married Louis in December 1911. I've managed to dig a bit more, and I can confirm that Lady Elsie Alexandra Teague Pencradoc and Mr Louis William Ashby got married on Friday the twenty-second of December 1911, at St George's Church, Bloomsbury. The winter solstice, no less.'

'Perfect!' Ryan took a step closer, his guard apparently dropped, and he even managed to look fairly excited. 'That links really well to the theme.'

'My theme.' Tegan couldn't help but claim it. The winter wedding thing had been her idea after all — but the solstice thing . . . yes. As Ryan said (and she reluctantly agreed), perfect.

'So, my next idea—' she pretended not to notice that he had folded his arms — 'is that we go all out with a winter wonderland theme. Kind of like Narnia. Through the wardrobe door into Elsie's wedding. We have replicas of her dress, her bouquet, all that sort of stuff—'

'No.' Ryan shook his head.

'What?' Tegan was momentarily shocked. He'd disagreed with her? 'You disagreed with me?'

'Yes.'

There was a beat and they stared at each other.

It almost choked her to say it, but, 'Why?'

'Narnia.'

'What's wrong with Narnia?'

'It's the wrong era.'

'How do you know that?'

'Because the kids in the story get evacuated in the Second World War. Way after Elsie's wedding.'

'Oh.' There was no comeback for that. He was, annoyingly, correct. 'Ah.' Tegan began drumming her fingertips on the notepad. Narnia had been perfect. She had even sketched the flow of the Pencradoc rooms and where she would put the wardrobe door and what the corridor of trees would look like and where she'd have the lamppost . . .

'You could do *The Snow Queen*,' said Ryan. 'Fairy tale. Same sort of idea. Spectacular entrance into her world, corridor of trees, Snow Queen's sleigh. Could Elsie's wedding dress be the Snow Queen's gown, with her sitting in the sleigh?'

'Oh! No, because we really want to show off her dress. But she — well, she could be standing on a giant mirror, which could represent the frozen lake the Queen's throne sits on. And the splinters of ice . . .' The story came flooding into Tegan's mind, which was odd, as she couldn't remember ever reading the fairytale. All her ideas about the Snow Queen came from Narnia. But she *must* have read it, to know what she said next. 'The splinters of ice had to spell out "eternity" before the little girl in the story could rescue the little boy.'

'Gerda and Kai.'

'*That's* it. So we have something representing those splinters of ice saying the word "eternity" and that links into the wedding theme. Awesome!' Tegan would have high-fived anyone else. But she wasn't going to touch Ryan, no way. And anyway, he still had his arms folded.

'The corridor of trees,' he said suddenly. 'I think that could be a room. The ballroom's fairly long — I'd think.' He was quiet for a moment. Tegan nodded. It was, and Merryn had told her it was the permanent home to an exhibition of informal Pencradoc family pictures and sketches from the stores that probably didn't warrant full exhibits themselves, but were little windows into the domestic world of the Teagues. 'Yes. So you can have it in the ballroom and have the smaller room at the front — is that the morning room or something? — leading into the main exhibition—'

'Yes! That smaller room as you go in, on the right of the staircase — it's the drawing room — could be a pop-up gallery with photos, letters, that kind of jazz.'

'It actually sounds great. And not too much work.' Ryan smiled.

'Definitely manageable.' Tegan nodded.

There was a silence and it would have been the natural point for them to close down the conversation. But oddly, Ryan didn't make a move to leave the gothic rose garden.

Instead, he said, 'I've got some papers in my bag here.' He patted the document case, slung diagonally across his body. He almost looked embarrassed. 'I never thought I'd end up the kind of a guy with a man-bag.'

'It's not a good look on you,' said Tegan.

'Much as I hate to agree with you, I agree.' Ryan pulled a face. 'But I do have stuff you might be interested in. But you haven't asked, sooooo . . .'

'Oh, God. Don't make me physically *ask* you.' Tegan folded her arms. 'I refuse to play that game.'

'Fair enough. See you via email soon. Hopefully not in person.' He turned around and began to walk out of the garden, but curiosity got the better of her.

'All right then,' she said, cross with herself. 'Please may I see what you've got in your delightful man-bag?' She closed her eyes. Asking Ryan anything was anathema to her sensibilities.

He paused, back still turned to her, then he responded. 'All right. Seeing as you asked so nicely, I shall share the contents of my man-bag with you.'

Tegan rolled her eyes heavenwards in an extremely dramatic fashion to indicate her extreme exasperation with this annoying man, but sadly, the gesture was wasted on Ryan as he was still turned away from her.

* * *

It was just as well Tegan couldn't see Ryan's face. He was, some would say, smirking by this point. It felt good to have the upper hand, even for a moment.

And boy, was he going to savour it.

He turned, very, very slowly, to face her, then nodded, equally slowly. 'I'll see what I can find.'

He could tell she was biting her lip, trying desperately not to snipe back at him in case he came back with some smart retort. And then, let's face it, they'd get absolutely nowhere — even though they had apparently agreed on the content of the exhibition without any bloodshed.

'May I?' He indicated the seat next to her on the bench. He didn't really want to sit there, so very close to her, but it seemed the most appropriate option. To sit on the ground would a) put her in a higher physical position than himself, and b) be rather stupid when there was a perfectly serviceable bench right there.

Tegan nodded shortly. Ryan hid a smile and walked over. He perched on the edge of the bench — okay, he might be sitting on a perfectly serviceable bench, but there was no need to sit right next to her — and opened the flap on his bag.

'I just grabbed a couple of things,' he said. 'I'm sure there's more waiting to be found—'

'So you only did half a job then. Useful.'

'Spirited,' muttered Ryan. 'And worth ignoring. Here we go.' He pulled the treasures he'd located out of the dreadful bag and dumped the offending receptacle on the ground. 'I've got a letter from Elsie to her brother, dated from the November, asking him to go down to London to see her dress . . .'

'Well, I guess it is part of the run-up to the event. But does it give any more information beyond that?'

'Hmm. You're determined to be a teensy-tiny bit negative, aren't you, Tegan? But for your information, yes, it does give us more than you think. She says something about hoping he'll call a truce with Viola for her sake, and then there's this . . .' Ryan enjoyed his next move — he *flourished* the letter at his blonde nemesis. There was no other word for it. 'Elsie actually drew her dress. She sketched it out on the back of the page. See?'

'Oh! My word.' Tegan leaned forward to take a better look. Her ponytail fell across him and tickled his hand as he held the letter out and she peered down at it. He moved backwards slightly. He wasn't sure if the sensation was making him itch or sending weird little sensory prickles across his skin.

Regardless, he held the letter out at a distance and allowed Tegan to study it.

'This is actually — quite cool.' Tegan nodded. 'I've seen a photograph of her in her wedding dress, but only, like, the top half. You've probably seen it today as well. It's outside Coren's office.' She demonstrated by waving her arms around her own top half. 'And there was a bouquet. A huge bouquet.'

'This photo?' Another flourish. Ryan was starting to enjoy this. 'Yes. I already saw it, thank you.'

'No need for that attitude.' She sniffed. 'But yes. That's the one. Well. A copy. We've got the *original* one here. I noticed that it's been made into one of the new postcards they sell. I saw them yesterday when I was having a wander around the estate.'

'Yes, I'm *aware* this is a copy, thank you. Sybill got it for me — well, for the archives — it's a bit bigger than postcard size.'

'It's got so much detail in. Far better than the postcard. Thanks.'

Ryan blinked in surprise. Was she actually *thanking* him? Wow. 'Yes,' he said. 'And when you look at the sketch she sent Laurie—'

'Woah — *Laurie*?' Tegan looked shocked. 'Her brother was called *Laurie*?'

'Yes.' Ryan looked at her oddly. 'What's strange about that? I would have thought you would have known that.'

Tegan had the grace to blush and shrug very slightly. 'I mean, I knew Elsie had loads of brothers and sisters, but I didn't know their names. I haven't, like, *learned* them yet.'

'So you only did half a job then. Useful.'

'Spirited.' But he chanced a glance at her and she almost — *almost* — smiled. 'And I've only just *started* the job.'

'Whatever. Look. Here's another letter. It's from Elsie to her sisters — *Isolde* and *Medora*.' He emphasised their names, very slowly. There was no need for Tegan to know he'd only recently learnt the Teague family's names properly himself. 'She's telling them she expects them to be bridesmaids along with their cousins and Viola.'

Tegan took the letter and read it. 'So, if her sisters were Isolde and Medora,' she said thoughtfully. 'Who was Viola? The other girl she asked to be bridesmaid?'

CHAPTER TWELVE

1911

The autumn was generally Laurie's favourite season. It was not the hot, sticky time that summer could be, and not cold and wet like winter in Cornwall often was.

Spring was all right though. Spring was acceptable. But he still preferred autumn.

Only in autumn could he see the glorious colours spreading out before him — the reds and golds of the leaves turning, those odd, bright-blue days where the orange trees would pop against the cloudless sky. His sisters would dismiss it as simple colour theory — 'Blue,' Isolde would say with a sniff, 'is the complementary colour to orange. How do you not *know* that, Laurie Teague?'

'Because I don't really paint pictures,' he'd say. No, Laurie was much more at home with words. It was, he supposed, his guilty pleasure. He'd begin novels and poems and the like, but never get around to finishing them. Part of the enjoyment was *starting* new things. He liked playing with how the words sounded, writing them out, reading them in his head . . . that sort of thing. But he never wanted to try to publish anything or had any great ambition to be known as a writer.

He was Laurie Teague, he liked words and was rarely stuck for them. Unless, of course, he was in the company of Miss Viola Arthur. Even her name in his head made him shudder and forget what sensible thing he was stringing together in the form of a sentence.

Laurie used to have a habit of stuffing his notebooks and scraps of paper on the library shelves, but then his younger siblings had discovered his notes and tried to read them, and that was not for him. Especially when Medora had decided she wanted to act out one of his ghost stories as a monologue one Christmas Eve in her traditional guise as the family storyteller.

'And then the duchess *wailed* as she saw the roses in her garden *shrivel* and turn *black*, one by one, as she drifted past them on that moonlit night . . . she would not *rest*, her *spirit* would not *rest* and the *Tower* became the only safe haven she knew . . .'

Honestly, the story had sounded better when Laurie had written it, aged ten. It had been on those shelves for the best part of a decade when fourteen-year-old Medora had found it.

It was, he thought, hiding a smile, amusing now in a way that only the distance of years could make it amusing.

He had particularly liked autumn and the darker nights, though, when it came to creating those sort of stories — sitting by candlelight in his room, preferably with a full moon streaming through his window, scratching these things out with a traditional pen and ink, and wondering what exactly would terrify his younger siblings the most.

Now, as an adult, he preferred getting out into the fresh air and doing what he was doing right now — riding his horse as fast as he could over Bodmin Moor. He dug his heels into Jester's flanks, sensing that the horse too wanted to go faster. Obligingly, Jester took off at full pelt and Laurie leaned forward over his neck, clinging onto the reins, exhilarated by the sense of freedom and speed.

This was better than being hunched over a piece of paper, scribbling words down! This was far better.

Because by doing this, on this glorious autumn day, when, yes, the sky was blue and the trees were stark against it, he had no time to think about Viola Arthur. Because she — or a version of her, anyway — had crept, unknowingly, into his bedroom and he'd spent several evenings with that pen and ink, and that candlelight, and these thoughts in his head about words. And he'd written words down that made the outcome of that hideous ball quite, quite different.

In his version, she hadn't walked away from him and disappeared back into the crowd. He hadn't stood like a total incompetent and let her go. He had called her back, or he'd reached out and taken her hand, or she'd looked back over her shoulder and hesitated just long enough for him to take those few steps towards her. And the common denominator in all those versions and in all the words he was writing, was that there was a kiss somewhere. And, yes, had it all happened as he had written it, the ending of the evening would have been *very* different . . .

Laurie dug his heels into the horse's flanks again and grasped the reins more firmly as Jester lowered his head and bolted across the moor.

This was better, though, he told himself again. This was *much* better than words. He needed to concentrate on staying on his horse, which left absolutely no time for thoughts of words, or thoughts of Viola, or any thoughts at all beyond not falling off the beast and breaking his neck.

Because it would be Halloween soon, and he really wanted to be at Pencradoc in person and *not* as the resident ghost.

* * *

So there they were, heading up to Pencradoc on the night of 31 October 1911 — Halloween.

'The night where the veil is thinnest between the living and the dead.' Sam intoned the words as he peered out of the carriage window. '*What* has Pearl been up to? Are those things even available in England?'

'Outta the way!' Viola practically clambered over her brother to see what he was commenting on. She gasped — for instead of the dark, chilly, Cornish October night, there was an eerie orange glow coming through the window. The moon wasn't full — it would be another week or so before that happened — but what light there was, was practically dulled by flickering jack o' lanterns, lining the carriage drive.

The pumpkins had all been carved with grinning faces, and candles lit inside them, and Viola could only marvel at the work Pearl must have done to bring them to life like this — and even to her acquiring the things in the first place.

'I wonder if she grew them on the estate?' Viola whispered in awe. 'She might have had a proper pumpkin patch created, knowing Pearl.'

'Wouldn't surprise me,' replied Sam. 'Those children are going to be mesmerised.'

'*I'm* pretty mesmerised!'

'Is that what you call it?' Sam glanced at her, amused. 'You look more like a vampire.'

'Oh, funny.' Viola was indeed dressed as one, in a confection of red and black, with her hair standing out around her head and a considerable layer of face powder caked on to give her a ghastly pale complexion. Sam had gone as the male version and accepted the face powder under sufferance, but not the messy hair. He was a man of standards, her brother. 'Oh, here we are. Right at the door.'

They had travelled from Elton Lacy with the carriage swathed in black velvet, and even the horses had black plumes on their heads. It made Viola deliciously shivery. She'd always enjoyed the celebration in New York

— apple-ducking and storytelling and all the wonderful traditions — and it made it even more exciting that she was attending this party today.

She refused to acknowledge the fact that she might be even more excited at the prospect of Laurie being there.

They alighted the carriage and the door opened as if on its own.

'Good evening,' boomed a voice from beneath a white sheet. 'Welcome to Pencradoc! Mwah ha ha!'

Viola fought a smile back as a small hand emerged and lifted the sheet so the person beneath could get a better view. A boy peered at them. 'I say — are you the Arthurs?' he said in a normal voice.

'We are,' replied Viola.

'Yes, indeed we are. Viola and Sam,' said Sam.

'Jolly pleased to meet you! My name is Arthur as well! Arthur Teague.' The boy bowed, his sheet trailing on the floor as he did so. Then he stood up, remembering his role and put on his very deep Halloween voice again. 'Please go into the *paaaaaarlour*. But beware of the witches! Oh.' He turned and pointed at a very old dog wandering around with a little white sheet attached to his collar, like a very small opera-cloak. It had some sort of hood that kept flopping over the dog's ears until he stopped and shook his head vehemently and moved the thing. 'That's Biscuit. He'll try to eat anything within his reach, so you have been *waaaaaarned*. Mwah ha ha.'

'Wunnerful.' Viola laughed. 'And is the parlour this way?'

'Yes.' Arthur Teague nodded beneath his sheet. 'We normally call it the morning room, but I think *paaaaaarlour* sounds more scary, don't you? Oh, and watch out for the cobweb. Medora made it and I've already broken it.'

Privately Viola thought changing the name to "Mourning" Room by adding a "u" would have been fine and dandy. But she nodded back at Arthur, realised he might

101

not be seeing her too clearly through the unevenly cut eye-holes, and agreed verbally that "*paaaaaarlour*" sounded ideal.

Then she and Sam wandered towards the room he'd indicated and saw a huge, white, crochet spiderweb hanging over the door with a long, trailing piece of wool, which was slowly unravelling. Sam lifted the edge of the web and Viola ducked under and entered what was seemingly a witches' coven.

Everything had been draped with dark fabric and a huge bucket was in the middle of the floor full of apples bobbing around in water. Goblets and red punch in a decanter labelled *Dragon's Blood* were on a serving table pushed against the wall — obviously for the adults — and what Viola assumed was a children's version, labelled *Bat's Blood*, was next to it, with a collection of smaller glasses. Biscuits shaped like bats and witches' hats lay on plates, and everywhere she looked, there seemed to be a small person dressed as a creature of the night or a wolf or a bat or a black cat shrieking and running around. One small black cat, her tiny black ears half-hidden in her mass of dark curls, clutched a biscuit in each hand. A black taffeta skirt and a long velvet tail completed the outfit, and Viola laughed to realise it was, of course, Marigold.

'Aunt Viola!' Marigold charged over to her. 'Hello! I'm a *cat*!'

'I can see that,' said Viola. She managed a quick hug before the cat wriggled out of her grasp and started prancing around. 'Mama is the witch I belong to. Look!' She pointed a sticky finger towards the back of the room where three witches were indeed sitting together — Pearl, Elsie and Holly, all dressed in black. Holly was dandling her baby on her costumed knee. Elsie's frock was the most embellished, obviously, embroidered with moons and stars. She was also wearing a pointed hat. A silver rope hung loosely around her waist and the lace sleeves were long and full. She looked stunning.

'Off you go, then,' said Sam with a laugh. 'I'm going to investigate the Dragon's Blood, and talk to Ernie and Louis and Noel. Oh, delightful. Fabian is here as well. Just spotted him.'

Sam headed over to the men — there was another younger man with them as well, Elsie's brother Clem, who it seemed had come back from university for the party. He looked awkward, as if he'd much rather be apple-ducking with Arthur — who had abandoned door duty and joined the party now they were all there — and another young boy dressed as a warlock. The warlock was Elsie's other brother, Enyon. Two other boys she didn't recognise were also with the apple-ducking group, but she suspected from the copper hints in their hair that they were related to the same family. Someone had also hung apples from pieces of string on the ceiling, the idea being that people could try to bite those as well.

And sure enough, as Sam approached the men, Clem peeled away and joined his brothers. Viola looked around. There was one man missing. Noticeable by his absence in fact: Laurie.

Her heart sank into her boots. Perhaps he wasn't coming after all. Arthur had left his post at the door. Even Biscuit was lying on the floor by a group of six girls — two dark and four fair-haired. Elsie's sisters and cousins likely.

It just didn't look as if he was coming.

Dammit.

She hovered for a moment or two, checking and double-checking the guests. And, no, no siree, no sign of Laurie at all.

Well, she couldn't just *hover* there, *could* she?

So she pasted a smile on her face and headed over to her sister and her friends. She couldn't let them know how she felt.

To be fair, even *she* didn't really know!

But the first thing that she said when she approached was, 'Is everyone here who's coming now?'

Elsie, who was half lying and half sitting in a large comfy chair, looking even paler than usual, perked up at that. 'Good evening, Viola. *Delightful* to see you. Mama and Teague are in London, and at the theatre with Aunt Alys, Uncle Jago, Lily and Edwin, so they won't be here. And Laurie . . .' She looked around vaguely. 'No Laurie. Not here. Oh *dear*.' She slumped back in the chair, a plate of biscuits and a goblet of Dragon's Blood, both seemingly untouched, close to her. 'He and Evie must be delayed. Oh, well. It's only four thirty. Train must be late. Those boys over there — Lily and Edwin's sons, Albert and Edward. Very sweet.'

'Oh dear, indeed,' said Viola wryly, hung up on the fact Laurie was definitely not there. She couldn't stop herself. And also . . . she wanted to shout, "*Who's Evie?*" But fortunately she didn't, and fortunately Elsie seemed as if her mind was elsewhere, or as if she was recovering from rather too much champagne, so she didn't pick up on the original comment. *Thankfully!*

And actually, would it be worse if Laurie came with another woman or simply didn't come at all? Now *there* was a dilemma.

Elsie seemed to make a great effort, leaned over and patted Viola's hand. 'But *we* are here. Jolly good. And a *stunning* costume, darling. Stunning. Make sure you have your photograph taken. Look — we've got it all set up over there.' She nodded to a corner of the room draped with black velvet, looking for all the world like a photographer's studio. 'Isolde and Medora painted most of the background, I added the spooks and demons and some finishing touches, and I've designated Clem as the photographer. Letting him use my camera and tripod, though.' She frowned. '*Think* I made the right decision. *Think* I trust him. But we really need to record this party and all the costumes. We've all had our turns. You simply *must* do it.'

'Your costume is stunning too.' Viola looked at the three friends and couldn't help but smile, even if Laurie was apt to arrive with a lover at any time soon. 'In fact, you all look wunnerful.'

'Don't we just.' Pearl stood up and kissed her sister. 'I am just certain that we look *absolutely* Macbeth in our photograph. And the little ones are having a *wunnerful* time already!'

Pearl's twins, although a little older than Marigold, were running in her wake, totally in thrall to the girl, and Pearl's other two smaller children were staggering around and falling down in that way small children do when they are unsteady on their feet but desperately want to play with the others.

'Just wait until that apple-bobbing starts.' Holly handed over her tiny baby, Joe, to Elsie, and also got to her feet. She kissed Viola too. 'It will be chaos. Marigold suggested she could hold Joe over the bucket to help him, but *we* suggested it wouldn't be appropriate, seeing as he has no *teeth*. So she's taking his turn instead.'

'That seems sensible.' Viola took a seat nearby. 'I have to ask, *are* you the three witches from Macbeth — or did you just not consult before you came out?'

Pearl laughed. 'Number one, sweetie — we have a reputation to uphold, so we may as well uphold it. Although . . .' She frowned and leaned in closer. 'Elsie isn't her usual self,' she murmured in a low voice. 'Don't know if she's feeling rather punk or just has a case of the blue devils.'

Viola studied Elsie and she definitely didn't look herself — perhaps she *was* feeling ill or a bit miserable. She knew fizz could do that to a person. The dark circles beneath her eyes and her pale cheeks could suggest that.

'I'm sure if she felt too bad, she wouldn't have had the party,' Viola whispered back to Pearl. 'But look — the boys are doing very well with those apples!'

CHAPTER THIRTEEN

Present

Who indeed was Viola? It was intriguing. And also a little embarrassing, because Ryan had had to tell her, Tegan, that *her* people from Pencradoc were called Laurie, Isolde and Medora. Tegan really felt she should have known that. But — ah! She did know there had been girls at Wheal Mount too.

It was worth a try and would show off a little bit of knowledge. 'Might it have been one of the Wheal Mount girls? Elsie's cousins?'

There was a flicker of a smile at the edge of Ryan's lips and she knew immediately that she was wrong and he was going to impart a bit more knowledge to her . . . *dammit*!

'The Wheal Mount girls were Clara, Mabel, Lucy and Nancy. No — Viola was Elsie's friend Pearl's sister. That "P" lady I couldn't think of before. Pearl.'

'American Pearl?' Tegan was surprised — and a little disappointed in herself — she'd remembered that nugget of information, but didn't know the names of Elsie's siblings. Again, a quick mooch around the gift shop yesterday had offered up a postcard of Elton Lacy, one of the big stately homes in the area. She had picked it up, immediately drawn to it and curious to know more. It was tucked in her notebook today, as a sort of bookmark, and Tegan was suddenly awfully conscious it was there. It seemed like it would be an awesome place to visit . . .

It sure is! came that weird New York voice in her ear again.

Tegan pushed the odd feeling aside. Viola. Of course. Of *course*. Of course she was Pearl's sister. She was the one who loved to dance and perform and travel . . .

She cleared her throat and lowered her eyes to her notebook. She was surprised to see her hands shaking a little. She really hoped Ryan hadn't noticed that. But regardless . . . 'I picked this up yesterday,' she said. She slid the postcard out of her notebook and handed it, almost reluctantly, to him.

As he hesitated, then took the card, a vision came into her mind of a fair-haired girl sitting somewhere that looked like the inside of a church. The girl had clearly started the day with a complicated updo, but by now it was coming loose, her hair still threaded through with red and green ribbon. A dark-haired man turned and looked at her, and Tegan had the feeling that he was desperate to say something earth-shattering to her.

But then the image faded and was replaced with a picture of the two people in the middle of a snowy landscape, a horse behind them, and the man in nothing more than his shirt sleeves, riding breeches and long boots.

Tegan blinked the image away, her heart pounding. She'd always had a bit of an imagination, so it wasn't surprising that the vibrant Viola had burst into her consciousness.

What *was* surprising was that the young man she had seen looked exactly like Ryan.

'Where's this? Oh — the Lacy,' the modern-day Ryan said, jerking her back to the present.

'Yes. I found it in our gift shop.'

'I went on a visit last year,' he said. 'It's way bigger than our two properties put together. I hear they had some fantastic parties there. Midsummer balls and things.'

'Like — um — wedding celebrations as well?' asked Tegan. 'Perhaps like Elsie's?'

'No idea.' Ryan passed the postcard back to her. 'But if you recall, Elsie got married in London, so I guess any celebration she had was based at her home down there.'

'Ah.' Again, she flushed. 'So should we *not* do the solstice wedding thing? I don't want any Elsie purists complaining.' For the first time, she began to doubt herself and her idea. Maybe Merryn had been right about the World War I thing . . .

Ryan looked at her oddly. 'I can't see any reason why we shouldn't do it. As long as we specify that the wedding was in London, because she lived in Brunswick Square.'

'How did you know that was her address?' asked Tegan, hoping, wildly, that he had had a weird moment as well.

'It's on her letters,' Ryan replied smoothly.

'Ah.'

There was silence for a moment.

Then Ryan spoke again. 'Want to see what else I have in here? I think there's something else just at the bottom . . .'

Tegan shrugged. *Why not?* He took her silence for consent and suddenly grinned. It changed his whole face from a moody emo/goth person to a handsome, cheerful . . . man. One she felt she could actually — like.

No. She couldn't think of him like that. The image she had just imagined had thrown her and it was Horrible Ryan here. No matter what he looked like, they would never be friends. Colleagues would be more than enough. She had to basically be polite until this exhibition was over.

She made herself wonder, in fact, whether Angelo would like to come and visit soon — maybe he'd enjoy it. Perhaps he'd like to see where she was living. Meet her family. Stay at Pencradoc for a little while . . .

Force thoughts of a smiling Ryan out of her head, because goodness, Ryan in a shirt and boots and *that* smile . . .

It was wrong. So very wrong.

She was in love with Angelo and shouldn't be imagining Ryan like that at all.

Ugh.

However, Ryan didn't seem to notice her discombobulation. Instead, he looked down and sorted through some documents, then his forehead creased.

'Okay — apparently I put this in too. I can't remember doing it — maybe it was stuck to another letter. They must have been filed together after all . . . not sure where though . . . hmmm.' He looked up at her, looking a little confused. 'Oh well. It's appropriate, anyway. It's the Halloween letter.' He read it quickly. 'It definitely fits the scene. I can confirm it's between Elsie and Pearl. And oh — your friend Viola is mentioned in it too. Look.'

He handed it over to her and she accepted it, half reluctantly. No more weird images? That was good. That was very good.

A couple of lines jumped out at her: *I'm desperately hoping Viola will still be here for Halloween. Yes, I agree, let's show the little ones how we do Halloween properly. I am happy to host it here, but I know how keen you are for that little poppet to spend time at Pencradoc — and to hell with all that snobbery. American Aunt Pearl and Aunt Viola will make sure Marigold is as merry as a grig when she sees our jack o' lanterns!*

'I still have no idea what those weird words mean,' said Ryan. 'But I kind of get the gist.'

Tegan pulled a face. 'As "merry as a grig". It means lively, full of fun, sort of thing. They're implying that Marigold is going to have a jolly good evening.'

'Well done.' Ryan smiled at her, quite genuinely, and it made her blink. *That* was unexpected. 'How did you know that?'

'Oh, my friends Meg and Jo,' said Tegan. 'They're American. I learned a lot from them.'

And she had — but what she *wasn't* going to tell Ryan, was that Edwardian slang that sounded rather American was never one of the things they'd talked about in Sicily.

She didn't know how she knew that at all — she just . . . did.

***

Ryan was actually impressed at how professional Tegan sounded — and a little stunned at the fact she seemed willing to discuss things with him, but he mentally high-fived himself at the fact he'd managed to correct her a couple of times.

Here, in their new jobs, they were both on an equal footing. In Glasgow, she had been the permanent employee and he'd been, as she had said, just summer staff. She flounced around as if she knew everything and on occasion it was apparent that her enthusiasm and confidence outweighed her knowledge.

'Tegan,' he suddenly found himself asking. 'Why did you leave the gallery in Glasgow?'

'Why?' She shrugged. 'Well, it's none of your business really, but I got bored. I wanted a change. And . . .' she glanced at him. 'That manager really, *really* pissed me off.' She held his gaze and there was almost a smile on her lips. 'Do *you* think that catalogue was an appalling reflection of the gallery and the staff in it?'

'What? That one we argued over?'

'The very one.'

'Well. Yes. I suppose one *could* say that. But did it really matter?' There was a beat. 'It was a rubbish exhibition anyway and we sold how many tickets?'

'Twelve.'

'Twelve.' Ryan nodded. 'I was pleased to get of the place that night — he really went to town on me.' Suddenly he grinned, remembering how he'd glowered at the man silently until he ran out of steam and stopped shouting. Then he remembered again how Tegan had looked when she came out of the office and felt, for the first time, perhaps, a little guilty. 'You genuinely looked upset though. Sorry. I maybe should have checked on you when you disappeared into the bathroom.'

'You think I would have let you in there with me?' Tegan scowled and shook her head vehemently. 'It was all your fault for playing that crap music. And also, I wasn't sad-crying, I was angry-crying and there's a difference.'

'Fair enough. But my music was great.'

'Was not.'

'Was.'

'You were a weird gothy type and you liked weird music. Do you still like that music?'

'I do.'

'So are you still a weird gothy type?' There was a certain twitch at the corner of her lips that may or may not have been amusement.

'It was a phase. An art student phase.'

'Really?' She raised her eyebrows ironically.

'Yes.' He followed her gaze as it swept across his black outfit. 'I *am* allowed to *like* black clothing, you know. There's nothing weird about that!'

'Hmmm. Anyway, it's all ancient history and it was all fine, because I went out that night and drowned my sorrows. Stupid manager.'

'Ah. Yeah. You did. So did I . . .'

'Did you? I wouldn't know.' Tegan turned away and busied herself with her notebook. The conversation about that night was, Ryan realised, at an end.

But his mind flew back to that night, and even if Tegan didn't want to remember it, or, less likely given her current demeanour, *couldn't* remember it, he did.

He remembered sitting at the bar, on his own as usual, and a movement catching his eye at the door.

Tegan had swept in, looking defiant and confident and swishing that damn ponytail around, as if she was looking for someone.

Whoever it was she was looking for, clearly wasn't there though, as she sat down alone at a table. Within minutes, an inebriated guy had stumbled up to her and was talking to her, swaying as he did so, indicating the bar and waving a credit card around.

Tegan gave him a confident, dismissive smile and shook her head. Ryan watched as the man seemed to become more animated and implied that he would *definitely* like to buy Tegan a drink, and here was the card to prove it — right up in her face.

Tegan shook her head again, more firmly, and shifted position so she was turned away from the drunk. The drunk, however, staggered around the table so he was facing her again.

'What the hell?' Ryan heard himself say. Regardless of what argument he and Tegan had had that day, watching the behaviour of that guy towards her was unacceptable. He dithered for a moment — Tegan was, as he knew, eminently capable of defending herself; but this guy was going too far for comfort.

By now he was up in her face, as well as his damn credit card, and Tegan was no longer looking confident, but a bit scared.

Which was unusual for her.

So — no more.

Ryan couldn't sit and watch that.

'I think that guy needs to be thrown out,' he said to the barman. 'He's causing a bit of a nuisance.'

'Who? Phil? He's harmless.' The barman grinned over in his direction. 'One of our regulars. He'll give up in a second.'

'*What?*' Ryan was appalled. 'He's bothering that girl!'

'He's fine.'

Ryan stared at the barman in horror. God, was he going to have to do something himself? Okay — he *would*. He had to.

Without giving himself time to think, he got up and started to head towards Tegan. He wasn't sure what he'd do when he got there; maybe tell her that her taxi was here; maybe sit down and pretend he was the guy she'd been waiting for all this time . . .

However, he was within a few steps of Tegan, when there was a commotion at the door. Three girls practically fell through it into the bar.

'*There* she is!' hollered one of the girls, and ran unsteadily across to Tegan.

'Tasha!' cried Tegan and stood up. Neatly, she circumvented the drunk who was swaying, apparently confused now as to why his prey had disappeared, and ran over to Tasha. 'Great to see you! Come on — let's go somewhere else. I'm bored of this place already.'

She'd linked arms with the girl and they'd turned and hurried out of the bar, the other two girls running after them.

She'd passed Ryan with inches to spare, but apparently didn't see him, as she didn't acknowledge him at all.

Ryan stood there in the middle of the bar, staring after her as she left. He felt like a bit of a fool. He was only intending to do something to help her — but she clearly didn't need his help after all.

And that made him feel rather stupid, and also made him wonder if he'd misinterpreted the whole thing and Tegan had the situation under control the whole time.

He guessed he would never know.

Regardless, he left the bar and knew he would never go back — not if the barman was happy to let people like Phil wander around unhindered.

Tegan turned up at work the next day, seeming absolutely fine, full of her usual confidence, and it made him doubt his perception of the evening all over again.

Ryan often wondered if she'd seen him coming towards her, but he never knew. And it didn't seem the time or the place to bring it back up today.

Instead, today, in the gothic rose garden, he said: 'You were right to leave. That manager — he was an utter dick.'

Tegan suddenly smiled. 'He was *utterly* a dick.' Then she looked up at him. 'At least our managers here aren't dicks.'

'No.' Ryan looked at his hated man-bag. 'Even though mine makes me carry this thing around.'

'But it has some really cool stuff inside it,' replied Tegan. And that, he couldn't deny.

CHAPTER FOURTEEN

1911

As the Halloween party picked up pace in Cornwall, Laurie was elsewhere — in a carriage, to be precise, travelling from the railway station. With him, was a very dusty, very excited girl. That girl was fourteen-year-old Evie Griffiths, red-headed daughter of Lily and Edwin Griffiths.

'That's the first time I've travelled on a train by myself!' she was telling Laurie happily. 'When Mama and Papa waved me off, I *swear* I was going to cry — I mean, all the way to Cornwall on a train!'

The arrangement had been that Laurie would collect Evie at the other end. She'd had a piano examination earlier that day at Trinity College, in London, and hadn't wanted to miss it — she and her older brother, the quiet, shy Albert, had a friendly rivalry going on. Albert was one grade ahead of Evie and if she'd missed this — well, he would be *two* grades ahead of her and that would never do . . .

The boys had travelled up yesterday after lessons had finished, and stayed at Pencradoc. They got on very well with Laurie's younger brothers and the evening had been an uproar of yelling boys and rough-and-tumble games. Elsie, normally in the middle of it all, had stayed out of it for once, helping Pearl as she prepared the house for the party.

Laurie's aunt and uncle had also dropped his cousins off earlier today, and then Alys, Jago and Laurie's parents had travelled in the *opposite* direction to Evie, to meet Edwin and Lily in London, and to stay with them for the evening in their beautiful house in Primrose Hill. It was all pretty complicated — the point Laurie was focussing on right now was that he was escorting Evie to Pencradoc to join them all for the party. The train had been half an hour late, she had explained, as there'd been a delay while they'd shooed a cow off the line, but once the cow had decided to wander back to its field, the train had started up again and Evie had eventually made it.

Laurie allowed her to chatter happily all the way back and to discuss the best way for her to wear her costume. It was an old stage costume of her mother's — Lily had kept one or two of her favourites from her life before Edwin — and this one was a gypsy fortune teller.

'Will everyone be dressed like they were in Alva Vanderbilt's ball?' Evie asked, her mind dancing to something else entirely. It was the first time she'd been to anything like a costume party and she was practically bouncing.

'Not really,' Laurie said carefully. 'This is more for the children. I don't think there'll be any cat headdresses tonight beyond the traditional witch's cat outfits.' He referred to a hideous costume someone had worn at the Vanderbilt ball in 1883, which included a stuffed cat as a headdress. Evie loved reading Lily's magazines, and there had been an article about the Vanderbilt ball, along with a selection of astonishing photographs a little while ago, and they had clearly made an impression on her.

'Oh.' She was disappointed for a second, but soon perked up again. 'Whatever. It will be splendid anyway!'

'Medora is going as Mary Shelley. Or Lady Byron. Or someone like that,' Laurie said. 'She *always* does that.' He knew his sister adored the black Regency-style dress she had inherited from Elsie and dragged out whenever possible. 'Isolde is going as Mina from *Dracula* — she's dug through the dressing-up box and come up with something corseted and uncomfortable-looking.' Privately, he thought it would suit Isolde to sit primly. Situated between Elsie and Medora in age, Isolde often seemed as if she was trying to prove that she was the sensible one of the family, which was a shame because Laurie knew that she could be one of the funniest, kindest girls he knew — she just didn't show it very often. He definitely felt there was an element of jealousy there, but who was he to try to mediate between his sisters. He had given that up a *very* long time ago.

'What are you going as, Laurie?' asked Evie.

'Me? Byron, I suspect. Or maybe I could be Shelley — after the vampire got 'em in Switzerland, though. Going for the half-decomposed cadaver look. No choice. Outfit ancient. Medora swooned when I suggested it.' Laurie had also rummaged through the dressing-up box and come up with a collection of clothes he'd thought might be appropriate. He knew Fabian had a fondness for Regency dandies as well — indeed, there was a wonderful photograph of Elsie and Fabian from the summer when they'd been to Pearl's ball, where it all blew up about Marigold — but Laurie's clothes were quite tattered compared to the outfit Fabian had worn so well. And there was that famous story about the Villa Diodati, where Mary Shelley had written *Frankenstein*, and Byron had written a story about a vampire, and Laurie believed in artistic licence, so . . .

Also, Laurie did enjoy writing his poetry, even though he had to keep hiding it from the rest of the family, so why couldn't he be a Romantic poet tonight?

The thought made him smile.

Evie laughed. 'A vampire didn't get them,' she said.

'I know.' Laurie smiled back. 'But we can *pretend* it did. It's scarier that way.'

'Oh, definitely! Yes, it is!'

They continued to debate how scary that sort of story could be, all the way to Pencradoc, and, when they eventually reached the place, Evie gasped with delight at all the jack o' lanterns on the driveway . . . .

'If it's as scary as this outside,' she exclaimed in delight, 'it will be marvellous inside!'

'I'm sure it will be.' Laurie helped her out and took her Gladstone bag out of the carriage as well. It was only an overnight stay, so she hadn't brought a great deal, but he knew her precious outfit was folded up in there.

The light was spilling out along the side of the house as they approached and as Laurie pushed the door open and stepped into the hallway, they heard the party in full swing. Children were shrieking, adults were laughing and Evie looked delighted.

'Come on.' Laurie grinned at her. She reminded him a lot of Medora with her *joie de vivre* and her exuberance over everything. 'I'll take you up to your room and you can get ready. Would you like someone to come and help?'

'Oh, no!' She shook her head. 'I'll be awfully quick. Then is it all right if I just — go in?'

She almost looked worried that he'd say no.

'Of course you can,' he said. 'You can surprise them. I'll be down as soon as I'm ready — but you know everyone, I think.' Mentally, he counted out who he thought would be there — truth be told, he hadn't taken much notice when his siblings were discussing it. After that appalling ball in Mayfair, he had tried to put thoughts of socialising out of his head.

And maybe thoughts of a certain blonde American girl, to whom he felt he'd acted appallingly as well. Still. He'd managed to avoid her thus far and she was probably living it up in London with her brother anyway. No need to keep revisiting the dreadful evening.

Tonight, he knew without a doubt it would be Holly, Noel and the baby; Pearl, Ernie and the children; Evie's brothers; his cousins; Elsie, Louis and Marigold, and the rest of his brothers and sisters. Oh. And Fabian, of course.

Yes, Evie would be fine walking into that lot.

He dropped her off at her door and she ran inside, already trying to get the straps off her bag, then he went along to his own bedroom.

The outfit was laid out on his bed. It wouldn't take too long to get washed and changed, then he'd head down to the party as well.

At least this time, nobody would be critical of his sister's marital status, and not for the first time he thanked whatever powers that be for his genuine friends and his family.

* * *

The apple-ducking — or apple-*bobbing*, as Viola was told it was called over here — was being taken very seriously by the boys. Unfortunately, at one point, Arthur had to be fished out of the bucket as he'd overbalanced trying to grab one of the floating fruits between his teeth, then a howl to rival a werewolf followed as one of his previously wobbly teeth embedded itself in the apple he'd won.

Arthur continued to roar in horror as blood dripped into the bucket and some of the smaller children cried as it stained the water red and simultaneously spread all over Arthur's chin, dripping onto his no-longer-white ghost outfit.

'Oh, Arthur!' Elsie came to life, jumped to her feet and went over to him. 'Are you all right, darling? That's been ready to come out for a while, hasn't it?'

'Yeth.' Arthur was trying to speak and staunch the blood at the same time.

'Jolly good timing for Halloween,' said Elsie. 'Good prank.'

'Not a prank,' said Arthur grumpily. 'With it wath . . .'

'Why is Arthur bleeding?' asked Marigold. She ran up to her young uncle and patted his cheek, getting blood all over herself in the process.

'Goodness me,' said Elsie's friend Fabian, obviously trying not to laugh. He swooped on Marigold and gently removed her hand from Arthur's face, dunked her hand in the water, then shook the liquid off it. Then he picked the bucket up and hurried out of the room to dispose of it, shouting over his shoulder as he went. 'Don't worry, I'll wash the apples! No harm done! You can use the ones hanging up to play with in the meantime!'

Enyon pulled a face. 'Ugh, Fabian, I'm *not* doing that! The girls have been at those — trying to see who'll get married first!'

'Have not!' said Medora, while simultaneously flushing bright red. She was wearing a black lace dress with a high waist that wouldn't have looked out of place in Regency times. In addition, she was wearing long, black gloves and a black tiara.

'Have too!' said Enyon. 'I saw you all there squawking about it! And I heard you practising that poem and it sounded *stupid*! Who has a raven called Quoth anyway?'

'The words are "Quoth the raven",' said Isolde icily, siding with her sister. 'And if you studied your schoolbooks you would *know* that means the raven quoted the phrase "nevermore". Stupid boy.'

'I say,' said Holly suddenly as Pearl, Viola and Holly watched the drama unfold. 'Do you do that thing in America with the apple peel?'

'What, where you pare the skin off in one long ribbon and drop it on the floor?' Viola asked, tearing her attention away from the centre of the room.

'That's the one!'

'Why, yes, we do. Although Pearl didn't get an "E" when she did it, so we never thought she'd marry an Ernie.'

'An "E" is quite a hard one to get,' said Pearl defensively, but she sounded amused anyway.

'It's not hard at all,' said Holly. 'If it was a lower case "e".'

'Ah. No. You're right.' Pearl nodded. 'Well, it must be a silly game anyway, as it wasn't correct like Viola says.'

'Viola, you should do it,' said Holly. 'You're the only one we need to matchmake, and we need a clue.'

Viola laughed. 'Fair dos. All right. I'll get an apple.' Confident as ever, she stood up and headed over to the hanging apples. 'Boys. Anyone got a penknife?' she called, and Sam obliged, handing her one.

'There you go, sis,' he said, grinning. 'Let's see how you're gonna use it, then!'

'Oh, I know how to use one of these, dear brother.' She was just about to use it to cut the string, when Nancy, Elsie's youngest cousin, stopped her. 'No, Viola. You need to do it properly. If you grab it with your *teeth*, you're getting married.' She gnashed her little white teeth together to push home the point.

Viola blinked. 'Very well. But if I can't grab it, you have to let me cut it.'

'Of course — because we need to see the initial anyway, don't we?' the girl said, grinning. 'Go on. Try the game first, though.'

Viola laughed and shook her head. She ducked down and aimed at the apple, not expecting to get a bite at all now she was in company — her luck was like that! She had played this dozens of times at home, even with the dangerous addition of lit candles stuck to the tops of the apples, and she knew the best way for her to attack the fruit was to put her arms behind her back and go from beneath. She rarely missed if she attacked it logically.

Sometimes, it helped being short.

To everyone else's surprise, it seemed, she managed to win the apple, and the girls all clapped and cheered.

'Viola is the next to get married!' cried Nancy.

'I wonder who to?' said her sister Lucy, and they all started chattering excitedly about a fictional prince who would meet her and fall in love with her at first sight, and sweep her off her feet, and simply adore her.

'I don't *want* to be adored,' she said, curtseying her thanks to them, then opening the blade on the penknife. 'I know someone who *would* do that, and, no, thank you, I don't want that at all!' She fervently hoped that she wouldn't get an "e" with her peel, even as she carefully pared the apple from top to bottom — Émile was not even to be entertained in that respect!

Finally, after a few cautious minutes, she had it — one long piece of peel, dangling from the knife. Everybody was around her now, watching eagerly as she tossed it over her shoulder — even Arthur was watching. He seemed to have forgotten about the tooth, he probably had his eye on her brother's penknife more than the peel, but still . . .

Viola heard a gentle, slithery sort of noise as she tossed the peel over her shoulder and it landed on the floor. There was a beat, then a confused voice — Medora, Viola suspected — said, 'But it's just landed in a *line*. That's not an initial!'

Viola turned to look — and the girl was correct. There the peel lay, defiantly in a straight line. 'Jeepers,' she said. 'What sort of apples do you *grow* over here? We've always had something that at least *looked* like a letter in America.'

Everyone stared at it for a moment;, then Marigold, who was just learning her letters from her papa, knelt down and peered at it. She reached out a chubby finger and pointed at it.

'Luh,' she said. 'It's a little *luh*. Look. "Luh" for lollipop. Light. Lily.' Here she smiled, naming one of her very favourite people in the entire world. 'And luh for Unca Laurie.' She looked up at Viola proudly. 'Luh,' she said again. 'Unca Laurie.'

'What? *No!*' Viola was shocked. It was only the innocent words of a tot learning her letters and proud of what she knew, but, even so, she felt herself flush and she knew her face would have displayed all of her feelings, for everyone to see. 'No. Not Unca Laurie. Viola *won't* be marrying Unca Laurie.'

'But it's Halloween!' the little girl said, all wide-eyed and innocent. 'It is magical on Halloween.'

'It is,' said Pearl, stifling a laugh. 'Listen to Marigold. She's a very wise witch's cat.'

Viola could see the little girl nodding proudly. 'No,' Viola said again, weakly.

'One way to find out!' said Medora. 'The mirror and candle game.'

'Oh, *yes*.' One of the blonde girls clapped her hands — Viola thought it was Mabel. 'Clara, please could you go and find a mirror? I think there's one in the study. Isolde's been using it to check her hair when Fabian's been here painting her portrait.' There was an indignant squawk from Isolde, but everyone ignored her and the tallest blonde girl added, 'We need a candle as well — but that might not be very safe, actually. Because we don't want the little ones copying and she has to walk up the staircase backwards . . .'

'Wait. *What?*' Viola felt completely cornered. 'Walk up the staircase *backwards?*'

'Yes. Traditionally, you'd hold a candle and look in the mirror at the same time, but I think we can just do it with a low lamp in the hallway this evening,' said Medora. 'Come on. Oh, this is *so* exciting.' She reached out and took Viola's hand and practically ran out into the hallway, dragging Viola with her.

Fabian passed them in the hallway with a bucket of clean water full of freshly washed apples, and swung it out of their way. 'Easy, girls!' he said, laughing.

'Fabian, could you keep the little ones busy in there?' asked Medora. 'And the boys. With the apples? We just need the *girls* out here!'

Fabian shook his head and pressed himself into the wall as seven young women hurtled past him. 'As you command,' he said, waiting until they'd gone past before resuming his travels.

Viola looked helplessly over her shoulder at the morning-room door, hoping that one of the three adult witches in there would weave a spell and rescue her. But it was to no avail. The three witches themselves were at the door, eager to join in, and Viola had never felt more in the spotlight — and not in a *good* way. If she was dancing or something that would be a *good* spotlight experience. But this — this was *not* a good spotlight experience.

'Here's the mirror,' said Clara, handing it over. 'And now the lamplight.' She lowered the lights in the hallway and blew out a few candles that were dotted around atmospherically. The hallway was plunged into an eerie gloom, but, despite herself, Viola began to feel a little excited. She didn't believe in the folklore, but she could have some fun here. She could make up a man — who was *nothing* like Laurie — and spin them all a tale. It was a night for stories after all . . .

'All right,' Viola said. 'I'll do it. But you must all be *quiet*.'

There were rustles of skirts and sudden, nervous giggles, but, eventually, the girls settled down and Viola stood on the first step, facing them, her natural confidence bubbling to the surface.

'"Shade of a shadow in the glass,"' she said in a low, resonant voice, looking around the assembled faces. '"O set the crystal surface free! Pass — as the fairer visions pass — Nor ever more return, to be . . ."' She walked slowly up the steps, backwards, as instructed. There was a delicious sigh from Medora and Mabel as the words of Mary Elizabeth Coleridge's Gothic poem, *The Other Side of the Mirror*, echoed around the darkened hallway. '"The ghost of a distracted hour . . ."' More steps backwards, as she held the mirror aloft and stared into it . . . '"That heard me whisper—" *Jeepers!* What the *hell*?'

Because, looming up in the background of the mirror, was a pale, dark-haired man, dressed in tattered Regency clothing. Then it all seemed to happen at once — she screamed, the girls screamed, she tried to move and her foot caught in the long skirt of her gown.

She clutched in vain for the handrail and lost her balance on the stairs . . . but before she actually tripped, tumbled and fell to certain doom, the man in the mirror reached out a bone-white hand and grabbed the back of her dress, hauling her backwards so she was suspended, half lying, half sitting on the stairs, rather than rolling inelegantly down them.

There was another scream from the top of the stairs and almost simultaneously, a voice which sounded not unlike Laurie Teague's. 'What the hell are *you* doing *that* for? It's bloody dangerous!'

CHAPTER FIFTEEN

Present

The conversation Tegan and Ryan had just had about the after-work drinks on that awful day had made Tegan a little uncomfortable.

Of *course* she remembered the night in the bar — that horrible drunk man trying it on with her was just the icing on a very shitty day.

And of *course* she had seen Ryan in the bar. How could anyone have missed him, all dressed in black, hunched up glowering at the world like a very grumpy storm cloud? She knew that he was coming over to her, and to be honest he looked totally scary.

She was actually a little terrified that she would run over to him and try to hide behind him, and then he'd think she wasn't as confident or as feisty as she liked people to think. When her friends had walked in, that had proved the perfect excuse to exit the scene stage right and get out of there.

And of course she'd been too embarrassed to say anything to him the next day. Or the next. Or the day after that. And then it didn't seem appropriate to say anything at all, because he left and it seemed like a good time to draw a line under it all and forget it had ever happened.

She was pleased she'd left the gallery though — despite the boss being annoying, she knew it was time to move on. She loved new experiences and had learned to channel that philosophy into work and had loved most of her jobs, to be fair.

And then, during one of these great experiences, she had met Angelo. There was no doubt she'd been attracted to him when she'd first met him, as he had been to her. And suddenly, she was happy and felt content. Sicily was amazing, Angelo was amazing and it was *good*.

Well, she *almost* felt content, at any rate...

There was, though, just something missing in her amazing life, and she couldn't put her finger in it.

Before she could second-guess herself, she picked up her phone and texted him again.

Hey, just thinking — why don't you come over for a visit? I miss you already and would love to see you! How about Christmas? Could you come for Christmas? Xxx

She looked at the phone, half expecting an immediate YES! to come back, but of course it didn't. People weren't surgically attached to their phones. Stupid to think otherwise.

Ryan's voice, however, jolted her right back to that September day in Cornwall. 'Okay, I'll be off then,' he said, standing up and bringing her back to the present. She turned the phone over quickly, hiding the screen, hoping that Ryan hadn't seen the message. It wouldn't do to be texting her boyfriend in the middle of a business meeting.

Even though he'd caught her at it earlier, she acknowledged . . . but it was senseless to give him even more ammunition, wasn't it?

But she feared it was too late, as he was *definitely* looking at the pink phone and his voice was suddenly businesslike and professional. 'Sybill will be wanting to head back down to Wheal Mount soon and I think we've got enough here between us to keep us going.'

'I agree.' Embarrassed, she stood up as well. It made her feel she was more on an even footing with him. Then she sat down again. He would be heading back to the house and she didn't really want to walk with him. She'd got as close to Ryan as she wanted to, today. 'I guess this is where we say we'll be in touch with each other and we email or something when we have more information.'

'I guess.' Ryan hitched his bag more securely over his shoulder. 'Do you need copies of any of these documents?'

'I think we'll need them for the exhibitions, yes. Do you think we convinced them about the Halloween thing?'

Ryan almost smiled. 'Not sure. There's a link somewhere to the events. I just can't put my finger on it.'

'Me neither.'

'I'm going to have a look at that ballroom when I go back to the house,' Ryan said. 'See if it's suitable for frosted wonderlands and suchlike.'

'Enjoy,' she said. 'I'll . . . be in touch.'

'Yes. Me too.' He hovered a moment longer, as if he wanted to say something else.

Then, it was as if that New York voice was impressing upon her the urgency of saying something to him, of saying that *thing*.

You might as well tell him, the voice said. *I guess you ain't too proud to thank him? Or are you?* There was a hint of amusement there and Tegan could swear she was nudged, not so gently, from behind.

She spun around, just in time to see the bottom of a pink dress disappearing behind a rose bush.

Ugh!

But . . . 'Ryan!' she suddenly said as he walked off. 'Just to say . . .'

He turned and looked at her curiously. 'Just to say what?'

'Umm. Thank you. For that night in the bar with the drunk guy.' She paused. 'I — um — saw you — coming over to me. But, well, I was too embarrassed, I guess, to say anything before now.' Ugh — how to show someone your vulnerable side! But it was too late, and she found she had to continue. 'I'm usually pretty good at looking after myself, and he just wouldn't go away. If my friends hadn't come in, well, I don't know what I would have done. Maybe I would have acknowledged you. Pretended you were my boyfriend or something.' She tried to make a joke of it. 'And that would have been horrific for us both!'

'You're welcome,' said Ryan after a moment, his cheeks and ears turning pink. 'Not sure what I would have done had I actually reached your table, to be frank. I was kind of winging it. Wouldn't have wanted people to think I was your boyfriend, that's for sure — you were so not my type. You were too . . . cheerful.' He smiled. He was joking as well, so that was a relief.

Tegan relaxed a little. It actually felt good to be acknowledging that evening now. 'I just didn't want to seem like I was helpless,' she said, 'but, like I say. Thank you. It's, um, long overdue.'

'No problem. I'm — um — glad I could help.' Ryan flushed bright red, cleared his throat and nodded smartly. He turned away properly, striding out across the grounds in the direction of Pencradoc.

Tegan watched him go, then dashed behind the rose bush to see who was wearing that pink skirt.

But there was nothing and nobody there.

* * *

Ryan kept heading towards the house, not sure what to think. Certainly, he'd been a bit thrown after catching sight of that text message she'd just tapped out — in his head, he was lost in Glasgow, six years ago, still thinking of Tegan as the girl who enjoyed time with her friends, and didn't take life too seriously. To see her asking her boyfriend a fairly normal question had disconcerted him.

Maybe it was the fact that he'd never envisaged her in anything long term and serious and it was a bit of a culture shock to find out that she had potentially now done that — when he hadn't had a relationship that had lasted longer than six months, let's be honest.

Also, he kind of hadn't expected any thanks about saving her from Drunk Guy after so long, and the fact she *had* actually noticed him that night was news to him. He knew though, that if he could go back to that moment, he would have done the same again and, had her friends not come in, he would have just kept walking towards her and did whatever he had to do.

He had left the gallery a few days after that night and had never expected to see Tegan again. They'd certainly not hugged or anything on his last day. He'd logged out of the computer, the manager had done some sort of banal speech wishing him well and Tegan had kept working away on her own computer, not looking at him.

Now, he wondered if she had genuinely been struggling to show him her softer, more vulnerable side, and the speech she had just made seemed to suggest that. Perhaps that had stopped her from even taking the slightest interest in his farewells. Cringing, he remembered that he'd picked up his coat and glanced at her, feeling like he maybe *should* say goodbye; say *something* to her, anyway. But she just kept tapping away and not looking at him, so he turned and just walked out of the office; and they went their separate ways, never to meet up again.

Or so he thought at the time.

What on earth were you thinking of? he asked himself crossly. *Was it so important to maintain that prickly, angry, loner persona, that you couldn't even say a polite goodbye to a co-worker?*

Quite. Absolutely not *the smartest move, old fellow*, said a voice nearby.

Ryan stopped in his tracks and stared around him.

He must be imagining it.

Or the legendary ghosts were deciding to throw their opinions in.

Just in case, he hurried up. The grounds felt weird and he felt kind of alone, as if there was a silence that had dropped all around him and the world had become too still for his liking.

Nope. There was the house, and if he hurried he'd get there before his imagination played any more tricks on him.

He took the outside steps two at a time, his long legs making easy work of it, and was soon in the hallway looking at the Grand Staircase.

But even in there, in Pencradoc itself, there was an odd feeling, He blinked and looked around. There was Little Elsie, her marble figure cheerily greeting everyone who visited, but on the wall was a painting of a man. A man with fair hair and grey eyes, where Rose, the duchess, should be.

He stared at the picture, wondering how they had managed to take Rose down and hang this man up — *Ellory, that was it, Elsie's father* — in the short time he'd been in the garden with Tegan. At Wheal Mount, it took a whole team of people to do things like that and it wasn't a five-minute task.

His eyes travelled up the staircase and he felt as if it would be the most natural thing in the world to walk up those stairs and check something was . . . yes. Was where he'd left it.

Because he couldn't let anyone see what was written there and he couldn't take the chance of Medora getting her hands on it . . .

He hurried up the stairs, still energised from his race across the moors earlier, and strode along the corridor to his bedroom. He could hear Enyon and Arthur arguing about something in Enyon's room, a game or a story, or one of the many things they agreed or disagreed on at regular intervals.

He pushed the door open to his room and went over to the desk by the window. He opened the drawer and riffled through the papers. Yes, there it was. Under that picture of her Elsie had given him a while ago. He scanned it again and half smiled. Words on a page. He was better off just burning the damned thing — in fact he thought he might. It was probably the safest option. It wasn't going to change the outcome of anything.

He carried it over to the fireplace, fully intending to crumple it and toss it among the ashes, but a commotion in the hallway stopped him in his tracks.

'Let's ask Laurie for his opinion!' Enyon was shouting. 'I'm sure he'll agree with me!'

'I think he will not!' said Arthur. 'I think he will agree with me!'

Laurie looked around quickly and stuffed the papers into a hole in the chimney breast. He'd deal with them later — he couldn't take the chance that the boys' sharp eyes would see the papers unfolding tauntingly in the fireplace. It had happened before and they'd teased him mercilessly about a poem he'd been trying to write . . .

Just as he withdrew his hand, his door burst open and the boys tumbled in.

'Laurie! Laurie! Can we just ask . . .'

Ryan caught his breath and woke up from some sort of daydream he'd been experiencing. Good grief! What the hell was he doing in this room? The last thing he remembered was standing in the hallway and thinking there was something up here he needed to retrieve . . .

He looked around him and half recognised the room. It certainly wasn't the ballroom he'd intended to visit when he'd returned after his chat with Tegan — it was definitely a bedroom. But, in his memories, there was a desk by the window, a four-poster bed against the wall and a large wardrobe there, and the dressing room was right through that door *there* — which was shortly, it seemed, to become an ensuite. Because he was actually in a room that was, seemingly, getting turned into a guest room. He knew that

Pencradoc Arts Centre ran artists' retreats and he could only assume this was one of the soon-to-be-released new phase of retreat rooms.

He turned and looked at the fireplace. That was, as yet, untouched by renovation. But looking at the tools next to it, it was next on the list to be refurbished. Sympathetically, he was sure — but there was a bucket and a bag of ready-mix concrete there, and he knew that any loose bricks or holes in the chimney breast would be well and truly sealed up very soon . . .

It was almost as if someone was urging him to look, to check the place he thought he'd seen in that weird daydream.

He wondered if there was, by some incredible chance, something there . . .

'Okay. I might be crazy, but I'm going to look,' he muttered. One of his favourite Mission tracks was knocking at the back of his mind, the one where they sang about other days and times and places.

If it was good enough for the Mission, it was good enough for him.

He took a deep breath and, his heart thumping, leaned into the fireplace. He closed his eyes and reached in, feeling around as if he knew exactly where his fingertips needed to search.

He opened his eyes in surprise as he found the opening and he reached deep inside. Whatever was there would have been pretty safe from over a century of leaping flames, especially if it was pushed right to the back.

A thought came into his head. *I didn't care if it went up in flames. In fact, I wanted it to! Sorry it hasn't, really.*

Ryan tried to ignore the voice and pushed his fingertips further into the rectangular gap. Sure enough, they touched the corner of a piece of paper, and he closed his fingers around it, gently easing it out of its hiding place.

As he brought the piece of paper into the daylight, he saw that it was actually two or three sheets, folded up.

Carefully, he unfolded them, hoping at the same time that nobody would burst into the room when *he* was here.

As he cast his eyes over the neat, cursive writing, he could hardly believe what he was reading. It was an account of a ball in Mayfair, but it had several different endings and was written as a piece of fiction.

But all the endings had one thing in common: the author made sure that, each time, he kissed the heroine and declared how much he loved her.

The heroine's name was Viola.

The author's name, however, was unknown.

CHAPTER SIXTEEN

1911

Laurie was hanging on to Viola by a handful of frilly material, his other hand on the handrail. He wasn't sure how he could get out of this one. Let go of Viola and she would fall down the stairs, let go of the handrail and they would *both* overbalance and fall down the stairs.

'Evie — could you help, please?' He shouted for her over his shoulder. Oddly, he felt Viola stiffen under his hand, but he couldn't wonder why right at this moment.

'I'm fine. I don't *need* any help!' Viola muttered. She began to wriggle, trying to get herself into a better position . . .

But then . . . a ripping sound, a gasp, and the sound of a body bouncing down the stairs and landing in a heap on the floor. Laurie was left grasping a piece of cloth as he watched in horror as the crumpled form of Viola Arthur lay motionless at the bottom of the Grand Staircase.

'Viola!' he yelled and raced down the stairs towards her, jumping the last two or three.

'Oh, *God*!' Elsie was running towards them from the door of the morning room, quickly pursued by Pearl and Holly.

'Viola!' Pearl's face was white as she threw herself down next to her sister and touched her shoulder.

Medora howled. 'Oh, nooooo! She's like the duchess. She's dead! Dead on Halloween, at the bottom of our staircase! She'll haunt Pencradoc forever! But she won't haunt the rose garden, she'll haunt *here*!'

'Don't be so *stupid*.' Isolde pushed her overly-dramatic younger sister out of the way and knelt down beside Viola, on the opposite side to Pearl. She leaned down and checked her breathing, checked her pulse. 'Rose died on the Tower staircase and *not* at Halloween, and Viola isn't *dead*,' she continued. Then, in a softer voice, 'Viola. Vi — can you hear me?'

Laurie, by this time, was there as well, kneeling beside her.

'Shall I get Sam?' asked Clara.

'No — no. Keep the rest of the boys out of this for now,' said Holly, looking concerned. 'We don't need everyone crowding around her. They're in the smoking room now anyway — they'll not even know this has happened.'

The girls took the hint and moved back a couple of steps. Laurie touched Viola's cheek. It was cold, but he could see her chest moving up and down, so he knew, thank God, that Isolde was right and Viola was breathing. There was also blood on her face from a nasty scrape where she must have caught her chin and forehead on the way down.

'We need to move her if we can,' he said shortly, frowning as he said it, because oddly he couldn't let anyone see how upset he was. She was an annoying American girl he'd crossed swords with on a couple of occasions under less-than-ideal circumstances, but the idea of her not being there anymore was awful. It was hard seeing her so helpless — it wasn't what he was used to. 'We need to get her somewhere more comfortable than the floor.'

Suddenly, there was a little moan from Viola and he leaned over, moving her hair from her face, gently lifting the strands that were stuck to the blood from the scrapes. Her eyes flickered open and for a moment fixed on his. He hadn't realised how green they were before and they looked almost otherworldly right now, with the candlelight from the hallway flickering in them.

'What happened? Why are you so *close*?' Viola asked.

'You slipped on the stairs,' said Laurie, as his heart hardened a little more, as was usual when he was near Viola. He sat back on his heels. If she didn't want him *close*, he wouldn't *get* close. *Well. It was good to see* some *things hadn't changed*, he thought ironically.

'Can you move everything?' asked Pearl gently, ignoring the atmosphere that had started to fizz and bubble between Laurie and Viola.

Viola turned her attention to her sister and wiggled her fingers and toes. 'Yes. Everything seems to be working,' she said, and then tried to sit up, blinking like a baby owl. She rubbed the side of her face and looked a little shocked when her hand came away with blood.

'See, Medora. I *said* she was alive.' Isolde produced a lace handkerchief from somewhere and efficiently handed it to Viola. However, in a rare display of emotion, she leaned across, put her arms around Viola and hugged her. 'Medora was worried you'd die on Halloween and haunt Pencradoc for ever.'

'Why was I . . . ? Oh. *Oh!*' Viola had clearly remembered something about her exploits. 'The mirror. I was walking backwards up the stairs, wasn't I?'

'Why on earth would anyone *do* that?' Now the danger was past, Laurie could not see the logic in that at all.

'Did the mirror break?' asked Viola, apparently looking around for it and ignoring the question. She did flush a dark pink, though, as if the answer was not going to be looked upon favourably by him. 'That's seven years bad luck and I sure don't need that!' A touch of her usual sparkiness was back, Laurie noticed.

'It's to see who you would marry, isn't it?' Evie came downstairs fully and smiled at Viola. 'Don't worry, the mirror looks fine. I'm Evelyn Griffiths.' She held her hand out to Viola. 'But I always get called Evie. I'm sorry if we startled you.'

'Evie. Right.' Viola looked stunned. '*You're* Evie.' It was almost as if she was fitting a puzzle together in her head.

'I am. That was a beautiful poem you were saying. My mother was an actress and I can imagine her saying it too, on stage. My brothers are already here, but Laurie collected me from the station because I had a piano examination.' Viola's eyes flicked up to Evie's bright-red hair and another piece of the puzzle seemed to click into place. Viola's cheeks reddened again. 'So my parents put me on the train in London,' Evie continued blithely, 'and Laurie met me at the station here so I wouldn't have to travel alone.'

'Oh.' Viola blinked. 'Yes. Quite. Um — nice to meet you, then, Evie.'

Evie kept hold of the hand Viola offered in return and gently helped her to her feet. 'Do you feel a little swimmy?' asked Evie. 'Or are you all right? I think you bumped your head a little. Laurie was going to carry you to a sofa or something — quite romantic.' Evie smiled as Viola looked horrified. 'Perhaps he might have fled on a horse to get the doctor to you after that. He saved you, you know. You would have plummeted to your death had he not been so quick to react. He was a true hero. You — *bounced* — rather than — *plummeted*. So that's very good, actually.'

Laurie was aghast. He'd forgotten how much Evie was influenced by those awful novels Elsie said she enjoyed. Also, she had Lily Valentine as a mother, so obviously she had a dramatic bent . . .

'I'm quite all right, thank you.' Viola's answer was stiff. 'If I need a doctor, I'm sure I can make my way to one, without relying on Laurie.'

Laurie felt himself flush. Because of course that was exactly what he would have done had the situation demanded. It wouldn't have been the action of a romantic hero. It would have been the rational response to a medical situation.

However, as Laurie plucked self-consciously at the lace cuffs on his billowing, tattered, Byron-or-Shelley-esque shirt, he knew in his heart that his soul was more poetic than practical, and he would never have heard the end of it from his sisters. Ugh. He still had hold of that lace from her frock as well!

Evie persisted. 'But wouldn't Laurie have looked *quite* the part of the romantic hero?'

'I don't *want* Laurie to play the part of a romantic hero!' Viola growled the words, but her cheeks flushed bright red. 'Even though he *looks* like one—' She bit her lip, clearly stopping herself saying any more.

'I wouldn't do it anyway. Not for you. But it might be worth *getting* a doctor,' he said stiffly. 'I believe you were out cold for a minute or two. Or maybe, because you were actually *silent* for once, and not arguing with me, I only *thought* you were out cold . . .'

'Just one thing.' Elsie's voice interjected. She sounded amused. 'We probably *will* get a doctor out, just to check you over, darling. But tell me, when you were walking up those stairs, declaiming your delightful poem — what did you see in the mirror? Or should I say, *who* did you see in the mirror?'

'Nobody,' said Viola, her face turning bright red again. 'I saw nothing and nobody. I simply caught my foot on my frock and fell.'

Elsie turned to Holly and raised her eyebrows. '*Quite*,' she said, and folded her arms triumphantly across her stomach. 'Actually, on that note, vile sibling, I invite you to have your photograph taken for posterity.' Elsie bowed at Laurie and swept out an arc with her arm, indicating that he should go into that hellish room Elsie had commandeered and have his hideous photograph taken at that awful makeshift studio she'd been daubing things on earlier.

Ugh.

'I don't think—'

Elsie held her fingers up to his lips. 'Hush, hush, hush,' she said in that irritating way she had. 'Marigold is too small to remember much about this, so the photographs are for her. *Please* tell me you won't let your niece down, Laurie.'

'Blackmailer,' he said.

But, actually, it was a bloody good excuse to leave that carnage behind on the staircase. He just had one thing to do first. 'Here, take your bloody lace. It's no good to me.' He thrust his hand out and Viola's eyes widened, before she snatched the scrap of fabric from him.

He did not wait for a response.

And thus it was, he stalked into the drawing room and walked towards the hideous studio.

Anything to get away from *her*.

And this time he didn't mean Elsie.

* * *

There had been no ill effects from her tumble on the staircase at the Halloween party. A doctor had been called, but it had been one of the staff who'd gone to fetch him, and not Laurie dashing through the moonlit night on horseback, with his costume on.

It would have been *dreadfully* romantic in some ways and Viola briefly allowed herself to daydream about it in her weaker moments. Then she shook herself out of it, because why would she will herself to be so damned incapacitated that Laurie — or anyone for that matter — would have to go get a doctor by galloping across Bodmin Moor at night?

And on Halloween night, at that. The tales the guests at the party had told, of will-o'-the-wisps, and the "pobel vean" — or the little people — and old Jan Tregeagle at Dozmary Pool, meant that anyone out riding wildly that night would be risking their own life, never mind anyone else's.

Which was also utterly romantic that someone would do that for you, but not something she would allow herself to dwell on . . .

It was bad enough that she'd seen Laurie in that mirror — that was what had startled her. What with Marigold talking about "luh for Unca Laurie" and his face looming up on the mirror, it was not a surprise then that she'd caught her foot in her gown. However, the bunch of lace that had been torn off the frock and eventually handed unceremoniously back to her was proof that he had actually tried to save her, and not just stood back and watched her roll down those damned stairs.

She had, of course, considered expressing how cross she'd been that he had ruined her dress; but on balance had thought that might be a step too far, even for her.

But the main thing she thought about, when she thought about that evening, was waking up at the bottom of the stairs and having his face right above her, and those dark eyes and that furrowed brow showing exactly how much he had been worried. It was an expression he had been quick to hide, but she'd seen it, sure enough.

And in her confused state, she'd wondered what it would be like to wake up each morning with those dark eyes looking at you and the expression in them being one of love and — no, not adoration, of *course* not that — but something deeper. Something that told you, that above all, above everything else, you were soulmates and wherever you went in life — and beyond, perhaps — you would always, always come back to one another . . .

And then, a week or so after the Halloween party, she got the message from Elsie, which threw everything else into disarray.

The bruises on the side of her face had begun to fade, the scrapes had healed up and she was no longer stiff and achy where she'd bumped herself on the stairs, so she was feeling much more chipper than she had done for the first couple of days.

And Evie! Evie was just a *child*, for goodness' sake. What on earth had predisposed her, Viola, to dislike the girl before she'd even *met* her?

It was, of course, because she'd thought Laurie was her beau. Nothing could be further from the truth — and Evie had actually turned out to be lovely.

Viola had had a *divine* letter from Evie, hoping she was well and recommending some "delightful romantic novels, should she want to read and recuperate". Holly had smiled when Viola had shared that, and said Noel's younger sister, Marion, was similarly entranced by "delightful romantic novels" and they would probably get on well.

But the last thing Viola had wanted to do for *too long* was rest and recuperate. She had too much to do! Most definitely, she'd had some lovely messages and gifts from the guests at the party, and had stayed, at Pearl's insistence, with her at Elton Lacy for a few days, so, Pearl had said, 'That you can be thoroughly spoiled because Sam just will not do that.'

And it had been nice, and Pearl had been right of course. Sam had found it amusing that she'd careered down the stairs because of a shock she'd received in an "amusing little mirror game" — once he'd realised she was fine, he wasn't *that* heartless — so she'd enjoyed being waited on for a day or so at the Lacy and then, when she'd felt less fragile, had enjoyed spending time with her sister, out and about in the town and visiting Holly and baby Joe.

Elsie, Louis and Marigold had already returned to London, taking Evie and her brothers with them, but Medora and Isolde had met Pearl and Viola for tea and buns in Bodmin. They'd brought a big bottle of fizz from Elsie, a bunch of autumn flowers from the grounds of Pencradoc and Laurie's "best wishes", but Laurie himself hadn't come.

Viola hadn't known whether to be pleased about that or not, but she'd chosen to smile, because there would be none of that awkward "thank you for rescuing me" piffle.

Obviously she'd been grateful, but it had just seemed difficult to face him just then . . .

At one point, though, she'd looked up and out of the tearoom window, and had seen someone she'd been convinced was Laurie stalking along the street. The man had had his coat collar pulled up and his hat pulled down, and, really, his face hadn't been visible, but Laurie had a certain gait when he walked — he strode, slightly hunched over, as if he was thinking deeply about something, and he walked *fast*. And this fellow had been doing exactly that.

Pearl had called her attention back to the conversation and the next time she'd looked, the man had disappeared.

But here she was, now back in London, and there was a card with her name on it on the mantelpiece when she walked into the house.

'Obviously, I left it for you,' said Sam, when he saw her picking it up curiously. 'None of the exciting invitations are ever for me.'

She flashed a look at him, ready to dispute that fact, when she spotted the twinkle in his eyes.

'Sure,' she said mildly. 'And you've never been invited to an exciting party back home in New York, have you.' It was a flat sort of statement, rather than a question. They both knew the answer. The Arnolds, the Astors, the Vanderbilts, the Kings — the list went on. Half the people on the *Social Register* had invited Sam Arthur to their parties. He had probably kissed the other half of the people on that register at those very same parties.

'Well, this one is definitely addressed to me, so I am opening it right now,' she said, and slit the envelope open.

Inside the envelope was an invitation. And not just any invitation . . .

'It's from Elsie!' Viola said. 'It's a *wedding* invitation! For her and Louis!' She looked at Sam. 'You were right. They really *are not* married!'

'Yet,' said Sam, with a shrug. 'I wonder what's brought that on? A marriage! Good Lord.' He had the audacity to shudder.

Viola kept reading. 'It's for December twenty-second,' she said. 'So it's pretty quick.'

'Really.' Sam raised his eyebrows. 'Shotgun, anyone?'

'Sam!' Viola was cross. 'A quick wedding does *not* mean she's pregnant, for God's sake!'

'Doesn't mean she's not pregnant, either.' There was no denying the logic, so Viola chose to ignore him. Her mind flitted to the last time she'd seen Elsie, at the Halloween party.

Ah.

Well, yes. She *had* been damned pale and listless . . .

Oh, whatever. It was Elsie's life and Viola loved a good wedding, so . . .

'I shall send my acceptance,' she said, hunting for a pen.

'So you're going to be here in December, are you?'

Viola's hand hovered over the desk, where she knew a fountain pen lurked in the drawer. 'Guess so,' she said, without looking at her brother.

'All right,' he said. 'Am I invited too?'

'You are.'

'Fine. Accept for me too, please.'

'Will do. Oh. Hold on one moment . . .' Viola pulled an extra piece of paper out of the envelope. She read it, then let out a delighted whoop. 'Hey!' she said. 'I'm gonna be bridesmaid as well!'

'You definitely need to stay then.' Sam grinned at her.

'Yup. Apparently she's already got a design in mind for her dress and she'll invite me over to see it when she's had it made up.'

'Exciting times,' said Sam.

'Very exciting.'

'And definitely shotgun.'

'Shut up, Sam.'

144

CHAPTER SEVENTEEN

Present

Tegan tried to put the discussion in the rose garden out of her mind. She didn't see why she needed to dwell on something so unpleasant when she had something so perfectly wonderful to plan in the shape of a "Winter Wonderland Wedding" exhibition.

She stayed away from Pencradoc for a good couple of hours after she'd had that conversation with Ryan to ensure he and Sybill had left. When she eventually got back to the office, Coren didn't query her absence but she made a point of telling him exactly what she — well, she and Ryan — had planned.

'*The Snow Queen* idea. I like it.' He nodded. 'I'm not sure how you're going to get that dress replicated though. Am I right in thinking that all we have is a sketch on a letter?'

'Yes. But I can ask someone. Wheal Mount has had costume exhibitions in the past too. And I know when you did the Lily Valentine event, you got a dress for Merryn's friend Cordelia from Sybill. My sister told me about it. I found some photos online. So I guess I just need to speak to someone.'

'You're best speaking to Sybill. Or Ryan.' He pulled a face. 'For a start, we're having a bit of difficulty keeping Merryn away from the place as it is, and no way do I want anyone delivering babies on this premises if she decides to spend even more time here. And, as I recall, the Lily Valentine dress was kind of wrecked in some incident at the Mill House. Not sure that Sybill will want to give us anything more from her stores, but she might know the details of a seamstress who can help.'

'I'll check with her.'

'Or Ryan.'

Coren's voice was mild, but Tegan dropped her head anyway so he couldn't see her expression. 'Yes. Quite. Right. I'll get on with this then. Planning and everything.' She swallowed and managed to choke out, 'Planning with . . . Ryan.'

'Good luck. I've got every faith you can sort it all out.'

She looked up quickly, wondering whether that comment had a double meaning or not. Coren's face gave nothing away. In fact, he was looking back down at his desk again, shuffling some paper importantly. She took that as a dismissal. 'Sure,' she said.

She checked her phone again subtly. Still nothing from Angelo.

'Oh — Ryan left some things for you over on the photocopier,' Coren added, just as she turned to leave his office. 'I suspect they're useful for you. He said he'd managed to have a tour of the house as well after your meeting.'

'That's good.'

'Found his own way around, apparently.'

Tegan's cheeks burned. Yeah, perhaps she should have taken him for that tour. She had no more right to Pencradoc than he had and he needed to know where things were as well. 'I'll take him next time. Once I know more about the place myself.'

Coren looked up and half smiled. 'Believe me. If Pencradoc wants you to know about it, you will.' Then he looked back at the papers on his desk and Tegan finally managed to grab Ryan's papers and hurry out of the room.

Ugh.

Embarrassing!

She took herself off to the main office and laid the papers out in front of her. Sure enough, they were the documents they'd looked at in the garden. She flipped the letter over with the sketch of the dress on the back and pulled over the photograph of Elsie and Louis, laying them next to one another. But really, all she had was the top half of Elsie covered by a ginormous winter bouquet and a rough sketch that looked all together . . . *thinner* than the flounces behind that bouquet.

She stared out of the window. *Think, Tegan, think.* Her gaze then settled on a copy of *Darling!* magazine someone had left next to the kettle. On the front was some non-A-lister's wedding photo. Tegan curled her lip slightly. No matter what Ryan might have implied, she actually had no time for shallow social media influencers, and this person on the front was definitely one of those.

However . . . she sat up straighter in her chair. Elsie was a *kind* of celebrity in her day, was she not? Would it, perhaps, be plausible, that the Edwardian version of the paparazzi would have lurked near the church to grab some photos? Actually, there had to be some official photos somewhere. The photograph of the couple looked professional and she knew that Elsie's friend Pearl was one of the "Dollar Princesses" who had travelled over from America and married into the British nobility.

Surely, *that* was newsworthy — especially if Pearl was a guest there, and Pearl's sister, Viola, was a bridesmaid?

Her heart pounding, she pulled up a search engine on the computer. Some swift detective work brought up some wonderful American magazines of the era: *The Delineator* magazine, *The Ladies' Home Journal* . . . and, a gem which she thought was worth investigating further — *Portrayal* magazine.

Whereas, the internet informed her, some of the magazines focussed on fashion, sewing patterns, articles and the like, *Portrayal* was rather like a Society magazine that ladies in America were fond of, as it told them tales of what their friends over the pond were up to.

Some further digging revealed that some of the issues of the magazine were online — the originals were held at the British Library and had been digitised as part of the American Collection.

'Bingo!' Tegan said, clicking into the pages. A little longer and she had located what she wanted . . .

Miss Viola Arthur, of Washington Square North, New York, presided as maid of honor at a Society Wedding on 22 December 1911, the text coyly reported, probably knowing that their audience would be more interested in the American contingent than the English one. *The wedding, at St George's, Bloomsbury, London, also boasted attendance from her sister, Lady Pearl Arthur Elton, wife of Sir Ernest Elton, of Elton Lacy, in Cornwall, England. The happy couple, Lady Elsie Alexandra Teague Pencradoc and Mr Louis William Ashby also hail from Cornwall and have now made their home in Bloomsbury, London.*

A couple of clicks more and Tegan had scrolled down to a small collection of photographs.

'Oh my God!' She stared at the screen. In front of her was a group photograph of so many people that she wondered how the photographer had got them all to stand still for so long. In the centre was, of course, Elsie and Louis. This time she had a full-length shot of Elsie's gown, which helped a lot in her quest for a copy of the dress. In front of them were a little girl and, strangely, a dog. Ranged to either side, was a collection of young women and young men. Rarely had she ever seen such a depiction of sheer beauty in those faces — whoever they were they all had bloody good genes.

The girl who seemed to be maid of honour, by virtue of the fact she was standing closest to the bridal party, had dark hair and a striking, if fairly haughty, expression. Something about that didn't sit quite right with Tegan, though. If this was Viola, she was nothing like she'd imagined.

That's because I wasn't maid of honour!

The computer flickered and the lights in the office blinked on and off. Tegan shot out of her seat and stood up.

'What the hell?'

I wasn't maid of honour! The press liked to make things up so us New Yorkers sounded more important.

The lights flashed again and then went off completely. Her hands shaking, Tegan managed to right-click on the page and bookmark the link before the computer switched itself off completely.

I mean, I look nothing like the maid of honour! It's clearly not me!

Out of the shadows in the room, the figure of a young woman appeared, quite small, fair-haired, wearing a long dress and clutching a smaller bouquet, walking slowly towards Tegan.

The thing was, though, it seemed that she was silently laughing. Almost, it seemed, at the ridiculousness of the report.

This is me. This is who you're looking for . . .

Tegan thought she was going to faint. The room started swimming and going in and out of her vision, then to compound matters, another figure materialised close by the woman — a man, this time. Tall, dark and, even though his back was towards Tegan, she knew he'd be handsome.

Did I tell you how beautiful you looked that day? Tegan heard the man ask. He held his hand out to the girl.

No, she said simply. *You didn't . . .*

Then Tegan's phone rang and the lights came back on, and, thank *God,* the spell was broken.

Good God . . .

She sat down, shaking. She'd missed the call and for one bizarre moment she thought that it was going to be a voice from beyond the grave speaking to her. When she managed to fumble the phone towards her and saw an unknown number and a voicemail icon blinking, she was almost afraid to listen to it.

Nervously, she clicked the button and had to use both hands to hold it up to her ear. Part of her wanted to run out of the office, but another part of her was frozen to the spot. While she listened to the call connecting, she stared at the area the girl had appeared from. Nothing was there, and, of course, with the lights back on, it didn't look sinister at all.

'Tegan. Hi. Um. It's Ryan. Can you call me back? There's something I need to tell you.' There was a beat. 'Something — weird. Yeah. Thanks. Talk soon.'

It was almost as if he couldn't find the words to describe what he needed to tell her, judging by the pauses and breaks in the message.

There was only one thing to do. She needed to speak to a human and really didn't think Coren was the best choice right now. She looked at the call log and her finger hovered over Angelo's number. But then she moved her finger up, pressed the unknown number and called Ryan back.

* * *

Ryan had found Tegan's number in the notes Sybill had given him. He hesitated several times before finally calling her. It was work — sort of. Despite how weird it all sounded. And despite that it seemed like he'd lost his mind — or at least himself — for a few minutes as he'd walked through Pencradoc, his feet seeming to know exactly where to go.

His first thought had been to speak to Sybill. She was, to be fair, probably the best-placed person to talk to. Her knowledge of the two families at Pencradoc and Wheal Mount seemed, at times, encyclopaedic. She was bound to know, or at least have a good guess at, the provenance of the note — who, for example, in the Teague or Pencradoc families used to enjoy writing, and who, possibly more importantly, was involved with Viola.

Sybill was, he thought, unlikely to believe his story of where he'd found the notes and would probably know that it was a lie when he trotted out his cover story of how he'd discovered them. There were, of course, tons of hitherto undiscovered boxes and trunks and cases in the attics — part of his job was, he knew, to go through them all and log everything. But even though he was prepared to tell Sybill he'd discovered the papers there, he knew he had one of those faces where he couldn't lie without it showing.

He actually wondered how he'd managed to keep his Glasgow job application secret from Sybill these last few days.

But, if he called Tegan, a) he wasn't looking *right at her* when he said he'd discovered the papers in a trunk, and, b) she possibly already knew something of this Viola. Especially if she knew she'd been a bridesmaid at Elsie and Louis' wedding.

He talked himself in and out of calling her several times before he finally took a deep breath and dialled her number.

Typically, though, there was no answer. He wondered if it was because she knew it was him calling and was deliberately ignoring the call — then logic took over and he reminded himself that they had never exchanged numbers and there was no reason why she'd ignore him when his name didn't actually come up on the call log. Especially as Tegan did not seem the sort of person who would have already programmed the Wheal Mount contacts into her phone.

She rang back a few moments after he'd left a message and at first he wasn't sure it was her. She sounded completely different on the phone. Guarded and edgy and insecure. And pretty nervous, actually.

'Ryan? Sorry, I missed your call — someone — someone was in the office, And, um, we had a — a — power cut — or something. And my computer went off. And, yeah. Sorry . . .'

'No problem.' His voice, he knew, was equally odd. He put it down to his own nerves and awkwardness and not being sure he'd one hundred per cent made the correct choice by calling her. But he had made the decision and had to carry it through. 'There's — there's another document that's turned up. About Viola. Well. I think it's about her. It's, like, a story.' He frowned at the papers. They were carefully placed on the edge of his desk. He didn't really want them too close. 'I — I was just wondering if you knew anything that could help me fit the pieces together.'

'Viola. Right. Of course . . .' There was a beat. 'Okay. What pieces do we need to fit together?'

'Might she have been at a ball in Mayfair? Around about August 1911?'

'I don't know — possibly. She was a bridesmaid at Elsie's wedding and the letter asking her to be bridesmaid is from November, isn't it.' There was some rustling. 'Yes. November. The letter asking her to go and see the dress is December and we know she was around for the Halloween party.'

'But we've got nothing to say she was in England before October?'

'No. Not really.'

'And guest lists or invitations to balls? Do you think they would have existed somewhere?'

'They might have done. But if it was a ball at Mayfair, then I don't think any of the families we deal with had houses there.'

'Ah.' He didn't really know what to say.

'I could ask Merryn?' Tegan said. 'She'll maybe know a bit more about the family? Like — who Viola partnered with at Elsie's wedding.' There was a moment of silence. 'I say that, because something turned up here as well.'

'Anything exciting?'

152

'Yeah. I think so. I found an article in an American magazine about the wedding. It names Viola as maid of honour.'

'Seriously?' That was pretty exciting, even to him.

'Yes. But she wasn't maid of honour. Just a bridesmaid,' Tegan added hurriedly.

'Typical press. Lie about everything,' he said wryly.

'I guess so. But, anyway, this article. It has photos. The computer crashed. But I can go back onto the site. I think.' That nervous tone had returned. 'If we don't have another power cut.'

'Do you — do you want to send me the link? And I can have a look as well.'

'I think that might be a good idea,' she replied. 'In case . . . anything dodgy . . . happens here again.'

'Okay, I'll give you my email,' said Ryan.

'Thanks. I'll send that on shortly. As far as I can remember, there were a couple of photos and they had full-length shots of Elsie so we could use those to help with the dress design.'

'We can. I'll have a look at our stuff as well to see if anything else comes up for Viola and that Mayfair ball. Tammy or Bryony might already have found something and filed it. I think there are some mirrors in storage. I might search them out and we can use them in the Snow Queen display. Reflecting back on stuff, kind of thing. I don't know — that sounds a bit hipster and arty, doesn't it?'

'No, it actually sounds great.' The relief in her voice was evident and again that seemed pretty weird. The Tegan he remembered from Glasgow could be irritating, but you had to give her points for her confidence.

'Right. I'll get on with it. We've got each other's numbers now. Not sure if that's a good thing or a bad thing, though, right?' It was an attempt at humour and he was pleased to hear a nervous chuckle from the other end of the phone.

'Right now, I think that's a good thing. Um — thanks for calling. I actually needed to speak to a real, living person this afternoon.'

And Angelo wasn't available? he wanted to ask, then thought better of it.

Then Ryan was going to make a joke about the Pencradoc ghosts, but remembering his wanderings earlier that day, he decided not to go there, even in jest.

'No problem. I'll let you go and we can pick this up another time.'

'Yes. Talk soon, bye for now.' said Tegan.

'Goodbye,' he replied, and they rang off.

The phone call hadn't been as difficult as he'd anticipated, in the end. But, it had been a long day, strange things had happened and he was ready to call it quits.

But perhaps he'd just wait for that email to come through first.

CHAPTER EIGHTEEN

1911

One day at Pencradoc, as everyone was sitting at the dining table after breakfast, the butler brought in a whole raft of letters, one of which was to be shared by Zennor and Teague, one of which was to be shared between Isolde and Medora, one for Laurie on his own. And one to be shared between Clem, Enyon and Arthur.

'Lady Elsie's handwriting, sir,' the butler said in a low voice to Teague — but as Laurie was sitting beside his father, he looked up to see what was happening. His parents passed a look between one another and he was fairly sure he saw a fleeting smile on his mother's face.

'Shall we open them all at the same time?' she asked.

'Might be good to do that,' said his father. 'Take one and pass it along, son,' he said to Laurie, as he held on to their own particular letter.

'Of course.' Laurie found his letter and passed the remaining two to Isolde. She and Medora looked at one another, then passed the final letter to the boys at the end.

'Poor Clem will miss out,' said Enyon, greedily looking at the letter. 'Ah, well. We can't wait until he's home. We'll just have to open it and pass the news on.'

'On the count of three, then,' said their father, and there was a sound of ripping envelopes.

A moment of silence was soon replaced by the sound of delighted screaming, as Isolde and Medora read the news. Enyon and Arthur were more restrained and looked at each other with frowns on their faces. Laurie read the news and raised his eyebrows. The smile on his mother's face grew and his father looked flustered.

'What's so exciting about a stupid wedding?' asked Arthur, turning the frown towards his sisters. 'Will there be cake?'

'Bound to be cake,' said Enyon with a nod. 'Worth going for cake.'

'We're going to be bridesmaids!' cried Medora.

'I'm maid of honour,' said Isolde, barely keeping the pride out of her voice. 'As I'm the next eldest girl.'

'*We're* meant to be groomsmen,' said Arthur. 'Whatever they do.'

'Laurie?' His mother looked at him. 'What about you?'

'Yes. I'm to be a groomsman too,' he said. 'Apparently Drew, Louis' brother, is to be his best man. But my role is to escort Marigold and . . .' He almost choked on the name. 'Viola down the aisle. Good God.'

'Why does *Viola* get to escort Marigold?' asked Medora.

'Because *you're* in charge of Biscuit,' said Isolde. 'Look — it says so right there.' Biscuit, hearing his name, apparently sat up from his prone position beneath the table and nudged Medora, who, Laurie saw, dropped a crust of buttered toast right next to his nose.

Their father pretended not to notice. 'Well, *I* am to give her away,' he said. There was a little note of pride in his voice as he said it.

156

'And I am to simply, and I quote, "look beautiful with Aunt Alys and Lily in the front row",' said their mother. 'What glorious news to start the day with!'

'Lily's children are to be in attendance too,' said Enyon. 'And so are our cousins.' He looked at Arthur. 'This means there will be a *lot* of cake, for the bridal party alone.'

Arthur and Enyon looked satisfied at that, and then, their interest piqued then dispersed, moved on to squabble over the last piece of toast on the table.

Nobody seemed to wonder at the fact that it was November, and the wedding was set for 22 December, less than six weeks away. Except Laurie, who, having seen the state of Elsie at the Halloween party, and, worse than that, the state of her in the morning after the party — where she'd looked as dreadful as she normally did after too much champagne, but without drinking the stuff, or eating much at all — had wondered then if she was coming down with something.

It seemed that whatever she'd come down with would possibly not be cured until next summer, perhaps.

He hid a smile and went back to his coffee. Typical Elsie. But he couldn't understand why she'd mentioned he'd be escorting Viola. And worse than that, why she'd mentioned she would "be in touch" about her gown.

Her wedding dress was the last thing on his mind and he really didn't know why she had mentioned it to him, rather than one of the girls. Perhaps it was because he was in London more than they were and she just wanted a second opinion.

But second opinions didn't really matter that much to Elsie. She usually did what she wanted to anyway. "Curiouser and curiouser", as Alice in Wonderland would say. Which reminded him — next time he went up to visit, he would take Marigold a copy of that book. It was never too soon to start appreciating literature, even the nonsense poems in the book. Because if Marigold turned out not to be an artist like her mother, she could always be a poet like her uncle — hopefully she'd not have to hide her poems from a whole raft of siblings like he did.

* * *

November crept into December and the weather began to turn more wintery. There was even some snowfall, which delighted Viola. She was desperately hoping that the Thames would freeze and she could skate on it, or attend one of the famous frost fairs, but, as her brother pointed out, the last frost fair had been held almost a century earlier in 1814, so it was highly unlikely they would have one in 1911, just because she happened to be in London.

But she had Elsie's wedding to look forward to! And Christmas gifts to buy and cards to write and deliver, and the excitement of going to Pearl's for Christmas. With all of those children, it sure would be magical. She was especially looking forward to helping decorate the Christmas tree on the twenty-fourth and had already started adding holly, mistletoe, yew and laurel to their own house in Bloomsbury. Sam pretended to be horrified every time he discovered a new piece of decoration, but she knew he was as excited as she was about the season.

And it made it even more exciting that today, her hands cosily hidden inside a warm hand muff, she was trudging through the snow to Elsie's house to see this mysterious wedding gown. She didn't really know why Elsie had requested her presence. Surely one of her sisters would have been the natural choice, but perhaps because she was there, in London, and they were in Cornwall, it was just a second opinion she was after.

Still, what woman would *not* want to look at a wedding dress, and she understood the seamstress would be there today and Elsie had drawn out the design herself. How utterly exciting! She'd already met one of the seamstresses from Lucile Ltd, the highly regarded fashion house Elsie had chosen to make the gowns. Viola was, after all, getting a beautiful gown of her own to wear for the day — an adult version of Marigold's little red dress, only in green satin, to go with the Christmas theme. She shivered delightedly and smiled to herself.

It was as she was contemplating the dresses, how excited Marigold had been to show off her little gown, and, especially, what Elsie's might be like, that she rounded the corner to Brunswick Square and slipped on a patch of ice. Her hands were still trapped within her hand muff, but before she overbalanced and landed on her bottom, a hand grabbed her elbow and steadied her. Woodsmoke and tobacco and leather . . . Oh, God. That scent. She knew who it was already.

'Can't you ever keep your balance? If it's not puddles you're falling into, it's staircases you're falling down.'

She recognised the gruff voice, which compounded the identification of course, and stiffened. 'Laurie,' she said. 'How fortunate you were there.' But, even though she tried to make her voice ironic, bizarrely, she liked the feel of his hand on her elbow. He released her rather quickly and she didn't know how she felt about that. She looked up at him, saw the snowflakes that were settling in his dark hair and the touch of pink on the tip of his nose and on his cheekbones. 'Are you going to Elsie's as well?' she asked, in a not-so-ironic voice.

He must have noticed the change in register as something akin to a smile lifted the corners of his lips before it fled again. 'Yes. I am.' He pulled a face. 'Something about looking at a dress.'

'Snap.'

'I'm not very au fait with women's fashion,' he said. 'But I assume it's because I'm here and the girls are in Cornwall.'

'I wondered the same. Why she asked me, I mean.'

'Who knows with El?' Laurie shrugged. Viola noted that it was possibly the longest, most rational conversation

159

they'd had. 'It's not so icy here,' he said as they approached Elsie's front door. 'You should be able to keep your footing from here on, I hope.'

'I should imagine so. Um, thank you for — Halloween — by the way. For not letting me kill myself on the staircase.' Inwardly she cringed. How would he take that? Would he be all superior and arrogant and I-told-you-so?

'Would have been too much mess for the family to clean up.'

She darted a look at him. He didn't seem arrogant. In fact, maybe there was a little amusement there. A joke, perhaps? 'Agreed,' she said.

And that was it — she'd thanked him. Maybe time had dulled the embarrassment, the way it had healed the bruises on her face. Or maybe she was just ready to give up fighting with the man. Temporarily, at least. They were, apparently, escorting Marigold down the aisle at St George's, Bloomsbury, in two weeks or so. They should really try to get along with one another — or at least not scream at one another — even if the truce just lasted the length of the ceremony.

'Please,' said Laurie, indicating the door. 'You can knock. Announce our presence. I'll be pleased to get into the warmth.'

Viola extracted her hand from the hand muff and rapped the door knocker. Within moments, it was opened by a young maid who smiled at them. 'Lady Elsie said she was expecting you,' she said. Obviously, she recognised both Laurie and Viola. 'Please come this way.' It was odd, though, to hear Elsie referred to as "Lady Elsie", when Viola knew her just as Elsie, her sister's friend.

The maid led them into Elsie's familiar reception room, but there was no sign of their hostess. 'I think she's upstairs,' said the maid. 'I'll go and check.' She went off, closing the door behind her, and Viola and Laurie were left standing together in Elsie's drawing room, standing far too close together for Viola's liking. It felt odd, and somehow forbidden, yet weirdly exciting to be trapped with Laurie in a room accompanied only by the ticking of a clock.

'Well now,' Viola said.

'Quite,' Laurie said.

They said nothing else and the silence grew and thickened between them, Viola not exactly sure what should be happening. She felt quite tongue-tied, but also as if she wanted to start talking to Laurie and have a conversation, a conversation that would address the elephant in the room. A conversation that would go something like: "What exactly are we doing? Why can't either of us properly back down and actually, you know, be friends and be able to have proper conversations with one another?"

Viola looked around the room, as if it was suddenly the most important and interesting room she'd ever experienced. She noticed, from the corner of her eye, that Laurie was doing the same thing, his hands crossed behind his back, rocking forwards and backwards on the balls of his feet. He looked as awkward as she felt, but, when she studied him, the realisation took her breath away like a punch to her stomach. He was just a man, for goodness' sake. A man no worse than any other man she'd ever encountered. A man who was, it had to be said, a lot more handsome than many men she'd encountered. A man who might be gruff and quiet and not sugarcoat his words, a man who spoke to her in the way she spoke to him — which wasn't always polite, she acknowledged shamefully — but did she really have any respect for a man who *did* sugarcoat everything? She shuddered, remembering the rather slimy, greasy personage of Richard Bedford and his gossipy discussions about Pearl and Elsie, said in such a nice, polite voice . . .

'This is ridiculous,' Viola said suddenly. 'Laurie, we need to—'

But then the door flung open and the maid was there again. 'Lady Elsie says if you wouldn't mind coming upstairs, she would be delighted to receive you there. Could I take your coats?'

'No, thank you,' said Viola quickly, hoping that Laurie would forget she had actually tried to start a conversation. 'I'm fine.' And as she was nearest the door, she was first out of the room, leaving Laurie to follow behind. A thing she was pleased about, because then he might not see how red her cheeks were.

And it was nothing to do with the heat in the house.

CHAPTER NINETEEN

Present

Tegan decided not to stay in the office on her own any longer that day. She emailed Ryan the website link, then re-saved all the photos from the site, and then she was out of there.

Fortunately, time was getting on so she didn't feel bad giving herself a reasonably early finish.

She went for a walk around the village, all the way to the church where Rose was buried, and stopped at a pub called the White Lady for dinner. She treated herself to a large glass of wine — she felt she deserved it after having shadowy figures loom up at her in the middle of the office. It was, however, a mistake to read the potted history of Pencradoc on the back of the pub menu.

"Pencradoc House and village are said to be haunted by the spirit of Rose, Duchess of Trecarrow, an unhappy woman who died under mysterious circumstances in 1884 . . ."

'Bollocks to that,' muttered Tegan, quickly putting the menu down and picking up her phone instead. She scrolled through her social media, answered a couple of emails and did a little online stalking of her friends and family to see

163

what they were up to. Meg and Jo were back in America, Merryn was posting pictures of food, and Ryan was . . .

Well, Ryan wasn't on her friends list. And, annoyingly, he had his accounts hiked up on the privacy settings.

'Bollocks to *that* as well,' said Tegan under her breath. She hovered over the "Add Friend" icon, and then, before she could overthink it, she clicked it.

She looked at her phone, almost willing the confirmation to her request to come back in — but it didn't. Which was a little annoying, but also a bit of a relief, as she knew she would have then wasted ages scrolling through his posts and photos to piece together what had gone on in his life since they'd last met.

Perhaps she had misjudged him all those years ago, had never given him a chance. After all, she knew as well as anyone that you could put a front on and hide your real self from everyone, even from your closest friends and family. Heaven forbid anyone ever thought she was anything but confident and bubbly and knew exactly what she wanted out of life.

Oh, well.

She moved on to Angelo's profile. He had posted a picture of the sunset, his sandals tossed to one side, a pair of flip-flops upended near them, a guitar lying in the sand and two sets of footprints leading up from the ocean. A huge heart drawn in the sand encompassed the guitar and the footwear. She smiled at it, remembering the day it had been taken, and scrolled back through the older photos — selfies of her and Angelo on the very same beach, her raising a cocktail to him over a plate of pasta, a picture of him posing in his sunglasses in front of Mount Etna. Further back, she knew, were pictures of him with other girls, friends of his, draped around him at beach barbeques or standing in silhouette against the sunrise, arms raised greeting the new day in skimpy shorts and a bikini top.

Even the odd photo of him kissing a stunning brunette was laughed over as two friends enjoying a party and too much red wine.

So she stopped scrolling before it got to that point in his feed and sighed.

Overcome with some sort of nostalgia for her life in Sicily — and a sudden longing for Angelo's soft, melodious voice — she called him.

He answered straight away.

'Tegan!' His warm voice had a smile in it, even though he seemed a little distracted. 'My love. How are you?'

'Hey, Angelo.' She smiled into the phone. 'It's so good to hear you. How's things?'

'Good, good,' he said. 'Busy, though. So very busy!'

'I can imagine.' Tegan settled back in her seat. 'Are you at a gig, then?' There were clinking glasses and sounds of laughter in the background, as if he was using the phone in a busy bar or restaurant.

'Gig!' He laughed. He always laughed when she said "gig" because, he claimed, the word sounded so peculiar to him. 'Yes, yes. A gig.'

'Did you get my message before?' she asked.

'Your message?' He sounded confused. 'What message?'

'The one about coming over here. To visit. Maybe for Christmas? Like I mentioned?'

'About me coming to you?' He still sounded baffled. 'I — I do not recall that. I think I did not get that. My phone has been, how you say, flaky?'

'Oh. Okay. Yeah — I was just asking basically if you might like to come here and see me? I'm not going to get a holiday soon, so I can't come back for a while and wondered if . . .'

'Ah!' The penny must have dropped. The smile was back in his voice. 'I would *love* to visit.'

'Awesome.'

'But . . .' He sighed. 'I cannot.'

'Wait. What? You can't come?'

'No. I have too many commitments. I am *so* sorry.' He sounded genuinely gutted. 'I have a lot of — gigs — on.

And I cannot afford to lose out on them. The money is good and I want to save up. I would like, you see, to come to you in the New Year.'

'The New Year? But what about Christmas?' It was her turn to be confused.

'Flights will be expensive then. I will work, you see, on these gigs, to get money for New Year. For January. I will come then.'

'January seems a long time away,' she said.

'It is. But you know, *next* Christmas, we will be together in Sicily again.'

It should have sounded comforting. It should have sounded blissful — Christmas in Sicily with Angelo. But it just — didn't.

Not really.

Tegan liked Christmas at home, with her family.

'Okay. Not to worry. We'll sort something out nearer the time,' she told him. What she would "sort", she had no idea. But it wasn't a discussion she wanted to have in a pub a couple of thousands of miles apart. 'Anyway, you're busy, so I'll let you go. Go and gig and make some money. Oh — I love the photo on Instagram. The beach one you posted.' She smiled. 'With your guitar and the footsteps.'

'The beach one . . . ? Oh! Yes. Yes. That one. From ages ago!'

'Yes. Ages ago.' She laughed. 'Happy memories.'

'Indeed. Happy memories. Goodbye then, talk soon! Oh! I must go — they are calling me onto stage . . .'

There was a rustle and a click, some muffled Italian words and then, just like that he was gone.

She stared at her phone for a moment. Then, for want of anyone else to chat to — and to not overthink the rushed goodbye and the no mention of the "love you" phrase — she decided to call her sister instead.

'Merryn!' she said in delight when Merryn answered. 'How *are* you?'

'Bloody fucking hell, Tegan, I think I'm in labour,' Merryn said.

Oh, God. Bad call, Tegan, bad call!

'Oh. Okay. You'd best — go then.' Tegan held the phone at arm's length, looking at it in horror, as if her sister would step through it, contractions and all.

'No! Please distract me until Kit comes back. He's on his way from work now. Argh!'

'Shit, Merryn! What on earth can I say to . . . oh! Oh, yes. I know.' Even as she closed her eyes and prepared to ask the question, Tegan knew that it was, on some level, a poor show. But you didn't get anywhere in life without grabbing the bull by the horns sometimes. *Carpe diem* and all that. 'What do you know about a girl called Viola?'

'What? *Viola*? Oh my God, oh my God . . . hang on . . .' There were a few deep breaths from the other end of the phone and Tegan screwed up her face, making a mental note not to get pregnant any time soon. 'Viola. Right. She was Pearl's sister . . . ow, ow, ow. Sketch of her in ballroom. By Elsie. *Owwwww!* She married . . . Hell, this *hurts*!'

Tegan yelped. 'You need to go!'

'Yeah, yeah. In a minute. She . . . *Kit!* Thank *fuck* . . . Can we go now? Straight *away*?'

'Okay, Merryn — Merryn, can you hear me? Go. Go now and I'll talk later.'

Merryn rarely swore so it was a bit of a shocker to hear her on the phone in that state.

'Yes. Yes. Talk later . . .' There was a clatter as Merryn apparently dropped the phone. Then it disconnected and Tegan was left looking at her mobile in horror.

She wished her sister well, she really did, but there was no way on this earth that she was wandering around Pencradoc that evening looking for random portraits. Viola or no Viola.

For one thing, she'd had enough of the creepiness of being alone in a room there today, and, for another, she had an awfully sick feeling that, once she found the portrait, the girl would look exactly like the woman who had appeared out of the shadows with a bouquet earlier on in her office.

* * *

Ryan was feeling similarly discombobulated at Wheal Mount. He needed to set some time aside to search for some things in his archives for the Snow Queen exhibit, but had made a point of reading the email Tegan had sent about the American Society magazine.

He ended up totally going down a rabbit hole with it, scrolling through the whole magazine, as well as the article he was *supposed* to read. He downloaded the pages and photos that Tegan had located. Of course, they weren't fantastic quality, being over a century old, but there was enough information to show what Elsie's dress would have looked like. As Tegan had said, there was a full-length picture of the bridal party, flanked by so many young men and women it made Ryan wonder at the cost of the ceremony and the clothes and everything that went with it. He was very much of the opinion that, if he ever got married, it would be a pretty quiet do. Nothing on this scale. In fact, did he even have that many brothers and/or good friends to have as ushers? He shook his head. No. The answer was no.

He closed the computer down for the evening, having decided to carry on after a good night's sleep. And maybe he needed to have a word with Sybill as well.

He managed to catch her a few days later — she'd had a couple of days off — and he was quite relieved to see her.

'Sybill, can I have a quick word?' he asked, knocking on her office door.

'Sure!' She smiled at him. 'Are you over the shock of Tegan at Pencradoc now?'

'Not sure about that, to be honest.' He half smiled. 'But I think we'll work around our differences — I don't think we're going to spoil the relationship between the two arts centres just yet. Actually, that was kind of what I wanted to talk to you about.' It wasn't — not at all. But he felt a bit stupid asking her what he really wanted to find out.

'Oh? Come in, take a seat.' She gestured to a chair. Ryan sat down almost reluctantly. It did feel as if he had gone to see the headteacher at school.

'I was just wondering,' he said, 'if you were happy for me to dig around for Halloween things in the archive, as well as the Christmas thing? It wouldn't be much, you know? Just displaying the letter from Pearl and other bits and bobs in the ballroom at Pencradoc.'

'That sounds great. But,' she looked at him and smiled, 'you don't need to run that by me — we'd agreed you could do it. Just remember the focus is on the Christmas wedding — so something that can be easily dismantled is ideal.'

'It would definitely be temporary,' Ryan added hurriedly. He felt his cheeks flush.

'I'm sure. Now. What did you *really* want to ask me?' She leaned on her elbows and put her chin in her hands. 'No references required for jobs elsewhere? No "actually, if I'm honest, Sybill, I *can't* work with Tegan, so I *have* to leave Wheal Mount" conversations.'

'Ah.' He looked down at his own hands. The woman was *definitely* a witch, but he wouldn't give her the satisfaction of knowing about that application — not at all . . .

He pushed the thought out of his head. Perhaps he should just come semi-clean about the stories he'd found. 'I wouldn't mind knowing, actually, if any of the family were writers?'

'Oh?'

'Yes. For — for — World Book Day. In March.'

'Hmm. Really, Ryan?'

'No. Not really.' He sighed. 'Okay. I found some papers that looked as if someone had been writing a story about Viola. Elsie's bridesmaid, you remember?' He hoped she wouldn't ask him where he'd found it and luckily the gods were with him as she didn't query that at all.

'Interesting. Well, we know a family friend, Noel — Holly's husband — was an author, but he was successful for his children's books. I doubt he would have written anything about Viola, unless it was a skit or something they were having fun over.'

'It doesn't seem as if it was a skit. From what I understand, the papers were originally well hidden. So unless he fancied Viola and was creating some sort of fantasy world . . .'

'Absolutely not.' Sybill was vehement. 'That wouldn't have happened. I think I can probably shed some light on it for you. Were the papers found at Pencradoc by any chance?'

'Yes.' He didn't volunteer any further information and she didn't ask for it.

'So, we know Viola actually married into the Teague family just before World War One. Can you guess the link? Who she might have married?' Sybill was smiling now.

Ryan thought for a moment. 'Before the War. I suspect, possibly, Elsie's brother — the one that went off to fight?'

'Exactly right. Laurie Teague. He was the only one of the children who didn't paint, he apparently preferred to write. When he was invalided out of the frontline, so the family stories go, he worked for the War Office and put all those skills to use with his reports and things. Does that help?'

'It does. Thanks. I knew he'd gone to work for the War Office, so that makes sense.' Ryan was thoughtful. He probably needed to pass that extra information on to Tegan. But perhaps she knew about the story anyway. Which reminded him. 'Tegan found a magazine online with some American social stuff in it. We think we've got the style of Elsie's wedding dress now.'

'That's fantastic! Well done. See, we knew you two could do it.'

'I don't suppose you know anyone who can make the dress up for us, do you? I'm happy looking for things upstairs — mirrors, lamps, lanterns — that kind of thing to reflect the dress, but we need a dress to reflect, I guess.'

'You guess correctly. Yes. Here you go — try Ianthe Shelley.' Sybill rummaged in her desk and brought out a business card. 'The girl is a marvel. Based in Covent Garden.' She looked at Ryan impishly. 'You and Tegan could take a business trip there.'

'Or perhaps not,' said Ryan firmly. Things were better with Tegan, he thought, but not business-trip good.

'Or perhaps yes,' said Sybill, quite smugly. 'Anyway, I've got shedloads to do, so if you can send me that link and the photos, that would be amazing.'

'Yes. No problem. I'll get searching upstairs for stuff too.'

'Excellent. Let me know how you get on.'

'Will do.'

'And if you need me to book tickets for London.'

'Won't do.'

'Sure.' Sybill grinned. 'Sure, Ryan. *Sure.*'

Ryan thought it best at that point to exit stage left — so he did.

CHAPTER TWENTY

1911

Laurie stood for a second in Elsie's reception room, wondering what exactly was "ridiculous". He had hoped, secretly, that Elsie might have delayed herself a little longer and that he and Viola might have been able to clear the air a little. He was rather tired and quite bored of this feud. And it didn't seem that Viola would be out of his life quickly — for God's sake, they had to walk a three-year-old up the aisle soon, one on each side of Marigold, he presumed. It would not be good if they could only stare straight ahead at the altar with fury on their countenances, or look anywhere but at each other.

Also, he wasn't sure anymore whether he actually disliked her as much as he had initially thought. It had grown old and become a habit. Today would have been ideal to corner the woman and get a few things straight.

Ah, well. Instead, he found himself climbing Elsie's winding townhouse staircase and walking through a door into her huge salon. It wasn't a room he'd been inside often. He'd witnessed, for example, Marigold sliding around the polished floorboards in her stockinged feet one day, but largely he was used to staying downstairs.

At one end of the room, Elsie had yet another easel and a lot of painting equipment — sensible, really, as the big windows let in a wonderful amount of light and looked over the garden; at the other, Elsie was standing holding her arms out to them dressed in, what he assumed, was her wedding gown. A small, nervous woman stood nearby, a tape measure around her neck and a table beside her that was covered in fabric, pins, bobbins of thread . . . everything a person would need to concoct such a gown.

'What do you think?' Elsie asked delightedly. 'I have the best seamstress in the world. She can disguise a multitude of sins with this dress — I just adore it. I shall be forever grateful to Lucile Ltd. And I shall make a particular point of telling Lady Duff-Gordon how much I recommend her designs and her staff.'

'Ohhhhh!' breathed Viola. 'Elsie! That's top-hole! It's wunnerful.' Viola addressed the last comment to the seamstress who blushed prettily and smiled.

'It's been a pleasure,' the lady said. 'My favourite job of the year.'

The dress was fairly modest, high-necked with those big puffy sleeves that were all the rage now, and absolutely covered in white lace — tons and tons of the stuff. The waist was quite high, with a thick, white satin ribbon tied around it, making a huge, fat bow at the back, trailing ribbons down to the hem. The hem was just above Elsie's ankle and she wiggled her toes as she saw Laurie's gaze travel downwards.

'I was thinking my hair up and something Christmassy for my headdress and bouquet,' she said. 'And look! I can do this after the ceremony!' Deftly, she untied the sash and the dress transformed into a loose, sheath-sort-of dress. 'So I can breathe,' she informed them cheerfully.

'So you can hide what you haven't told any of us yet,' Laurie said, leaning over and whispering in her ear. 'Hence the rush.'

173

Elsie just laughed, although she did colour slightly. 'Oh, Laurie. You amuse me. Quite. Anyway. Do you like it? As I say, my designer has been the *soul* of discretion and *most* accommodating.'

As accommodating as your dress needs to be, thought Laurie wryly.

His sister turned slowly, giving them the benefit of the lace confection. The dress was also studded, Laurie could see now, with tiny crystals that caught the wintery light and would catch the candlelight in the church even more. 'I think I'm going to get another layer of tulle on it as well, just to give it a bit more structure,' she said thoughtfully, plucking at the end of the ribbon strung now between her hands. 'Make it . . . *puff* . . . out a bit.' She indicated the skirt. 'In fact, maybe that puffy layer can be separate? So I can get rid of *that* as well as the sash afterwards.'

'Oh, like an overskirt?' said Viola. Laurie shot a look at her and saw that she was entranced. Her eyes were wide and excited, her hands clasped in front of her chin in an attitude more suited to Medora than Viola.

'*Exactly* like an overskirt.' Elsie nodded as if all that was decided, thank you very much, and smiled at them. 'I'm going to wriggle out of this now.' She nodded to a screen with another garment thrown over the top, and headed behind it. The seamstress followed her, and, after a few moments, Elsie re-emerged with a sort of wrapper dress on, belted around her middle, looking like her normal self and not some sort of fairytale princess. It had been a shock for Laurie to see her in white, to be honest — but the wrapper dress was black, as per usual for Elsie's wardrobe.

'Thank you *so* much,' she told the seamstress, who was now swamped with armfuls of fabric but wore a huge smile on her face. 'I'll ring for someone to come and help you tidy up, then ask them to take you down for a cup of tea and a biscuit as a thank you before the hansom cab comes for you.'

'Very good, Lady Elsie,' replied the seamstress and bustled off to her table.

Elsie turned to Laurie and Viola. 'Marigold is at Lily and Edwin's with Nanny, and Louis is working, so it's just us three. Could I tempt you into a hot cup of tea yourselves?'

'Thank you, that would be *wunnerful*,' said Viola.

'I'm in no real hurry,' said Laurie, and gestured for the women to go ahead of him. What he really wanted to say, though, was, 'Elsie, why on *earth* did you bring us here together?' Because he had the feeling that that excuse for the viewing of the dress was simply a ruse.

* * *

Once they were settled back in Elsie's reception room, with Elsie sitting back in her chair, bare feet on the table as usual, Viola was desperate to ask why indeed Elsie had felt it fitting to bring both herself and Laurie to her house today, to see a dress which clearly wasn't even finished.

But before she could ask, Laurie asked the question for her. But in a very subtle way, which she had to give him credit for.

'El,' he said. 'A question, if I may.'

'Oh, of course!' replied Elsie.

'I think I speak for Viola as well, when I ask — why *us*?'

'Why you what?' Elsie was overly innocent.

'Why did you ask us to come and see your dress — for all of five minutes. We've trekked halfway across London in the snow, and, actually, I don't really know why I did, or why you asked us?' Laurie blinked, looking confused and — Viola hated to admit it — terribly attractive.

To divert her attention, Viola chanced a glance out of the window. The snow was falling more thickly now. She was glad of the hot drink her hands were wrapped around.

'Well, the viewing of my dress only took a few minutes, granted, but you did spend a few more minutes downstairs here, did you not? On your own?'

'Elsie!' Laurie sounded horrified. 'I knew it — you planned that delay, didn't you. Vile sibling!'

'Perhaps. Really, I just need to make sure you two are happy in each other's company before you escort my daughter down the aisle at my wedding. I've said it before and I'll say it again. There is a definite frisson when you two are together and—'

'And nothing, Elsie!' He clattered his cup down onto the tray and stood up. 'Viola and I are perfectly capable of deciding when we speak to one another, and, even, if we speak to one another. We don't need you creating drama and talking about "frissons".' He cast a glance at Viola. 'If we want to walk down that damned aisle in a frosty silence, then . . . So. Be. It.'

'Laurie!' Elsie actually looked a little startled — a look Viola had never seen on her before. It made her look rather young and rather vulnerable. 'I'm only trying to . . .'

'To make sure we don't spoil your wedding. I know. Well, here it is, El. We won't. But we don't need you to manipulate us, thank you very much. We are both adults, and, well, we don't even like each other that much. You can blame being emotional, or whatever it is you want to blame, or the fact you're in an interesting condition — you know, the condition we don't *know about yet* — but please don't treat us like idiots. I'll see you soon, no doubt. Goodbye for now — and I want no more invitations to see your dress or to be thrown together with Miss Arthur at any point before the wedding. Understood?'

He gave a short bow and stomped out of the room, slamming the door behind him.

'Well now.' Elsie stared after him. She pulled herself together, placed her cup and saucer neatly on the tray next to Laurie's abandoned one, and looked at Viola. 'If *that* doesn't prove there's a frisson there — I honestly don't know what will!'

Viola wasn't quite sure what to say next, so she took another sip of her tea. 'I'm not sure about a frisson,' she

176

said eventually. 'But I do know we are both stubborn creatures and nothing and nobody will make us do anything we don't want to do. But you have my word as well — I promise we won't spoil the wedding. And, for what it's worth, I adored coming to see your wedding dress and I can't wait to wear my bridesmaid one!'

'The final fitting for that is a few days before the wedding, isn't it?' said Elsie. 'In case you've ballooned or shrunk terribly since we took the measurements, I assume.'

'I won't be doing either of those things!'

'I might be ballooning.' Elsie looked down and patted her stomach. 'I'm eating *far* too much right now. We will see. Regardless, do you know why I chose so many of you as bridesmaids?' She grinned at Viola, the cross words of her brother apparently forgotten or passed over.

'Because you have a large number of sisters and cousins and friends' daughters?' Viola knew that Isolde, Medora, the four cousins from Wheal Mount and Lily's daughter Evie were part of Elsie's day. They'd all exchanged delighted letters comparing their dresses and had met up for one gloriously exciting day in London, at Lily's beautiful home, for the seamstresses to work their magic. They were to be dressed in reds, greens and golds, the men escorting them in matching cravats. And Biscuit, of course, had his own cravat — gold, to match Medora's outfit.

Elsie nodded. 'That is part of it. But also, because so many people think I am a witch, I need to confuse the evil spirits who may come to the wedding. Traditionally, you'd all wear veils so they kidnapped one of you instead of me.' She shot a smile at Viola. 'But your faces are far too pretty for that and I am *not* having you all in white, although some people think that is the done thing to do!' She paused while she wrinkled her nose in disgust at the thought of the "done thing". 'So, yes. Quite.' Then she slumped in her chair a little. 'But Laurie . . .' She shook her head. The conversation was not forgotten, then. 'Quite.' She was silent and stared at her cup.

Viola leaned over, put her cup on the tray and patted Elsie's hand. 'I'm sure we will behave ourselves on the day,' she said, crossing her fingers out of sight of Elsie. 'Trust us.'

Elsie studied her for a moment. 'I wish I could,' she said. 'But not in the way you say, for behaving yourselves on the day, I mean. I *know* you'll do that. I just wish I could trust you to see what *we* all see.' She smiled at Viola, then shrugged. 'Ah, well.' She patted her stomach again and this time let her hand lie on the folds of her loose wrapper dress. To Viola's shock, she saw a little rounding of Elsie's stomach. Laurie's suppositions were possibly true, then! 'Put that down to the ramblings of an overly emotional woman and ignore me. Crazy Elsie, the eccentric one of the family. I may as well be a fantasist. People think I am anyway.'

'Normal is overrated,' said Viola with a smile. 'I'm leaving now — you get some rest before Louis and Marigold come back. Guess you might need some after all that excitement over your gown!'

'Guess I won't be *able* to rest,' said Elsie with a smile. 'You know me, can't sit still for a minute. No, I'll go up to the salon and throw paint around. It's the only remedy for me.' She stood up and held her hand out to Viola, who took it and allowed herself to be helped to her feet. 'I will see you *very soon*, Viola.'

'On the morning of the twenty-second, if not before,' replied Viola. 'How utterly exciting.'

'I'll see you before that — at the rehearsal! Oh, I can't wait!' Elsie clapped her hands.

The two women walked to the door and, Elsie being Elsie, opened it for Viola, without summoning a maid or a butler or anyone in between. Elsie peeped out of the door and shivered at the sight of the thickly falling snow, which now blanketed the square and had turned the trees and bushes in the park into weirdly rounded humps and bumps. 'Yes. Definitely the salon. Get a good fire going in there and I'll be happy for the rest of the day.'

'Enjoy, darling.' Viola stepped outside and took a deep breath. She *did* love the snow. Being from New York it was nothing new to her, but she was very happy to be experiencing snow here in London as well.

Wunnerful!

Although . . .

She tilted her head up, closed her eyes and stuck her tongue out, catching a small herd of snowflakes as they drifted down over the heavy sky.

Then she opened her eyes, stood on the step and stared around her at the winter wonderland. Beautiful though this was, and despite how exciting Elsie's upcoming wedding was — and of course how welcome the chance would be to wear her absolutely beautiful bridesmaid's gown . . . there was one thing that she really wished for this Christmas — one secret wish that she dared not utter to a soul.

No. She shook herself, tucked her hands firmly into her hand muff and stepped off onto the pavement. She wasn't even going to allow herself to think about that.

When she was small, Pearl had encouraged her to make a wish on the first snowfall of the season. It had to be her heart's desire, Pearl would tell her seriously. Two little girls, peering out of a New York townhouse and wishing for pretty dolls, or sweet treats or a new dress for the next party they'd go to.

The wishes had always worked, funnily enough.

But this time, no. She wouldn't allow herself to go there, even though last night she'd seen the most perfect winter star in the sky and been so very tempted to wish right there and then as well.

And was it her heart's desire? Maybe.

And might it come true? Again, maybe.

But she wasn't going to verbalise that wish for *anyone*. No siree!

CHAPTER TWENTY-ONE

Present

Tegan plucked up courage a few days after her conversation with Merryn to go into the ballroom and locate the picture of Viola.

First of all, she had to go and congratulate her sister on the birth of her daughter, Rosie Loveday Penhaligon. That had happened on 30 September, and, once the excitement had died down a little and their parents had been and visited, she felt she could focus a little more on her job. She also realised with a start that if she and Ryan were to do something for Halloween, to tie in with the pumpkin trail, that they really needed to get a wiggle on.

They'd exchanged a few emails; he'd passed on the details of a seamstress in Covent Garden and Tegan had sent her the photos and sketches they'd collected. Ianthe Shelley — what a fantastic name — had promised she could work her magic and recreate the dress. And even though Tegan was secretly disappointed that Elsie's dress had either not survived the years or been lost to the family — Elsie's children had, she knew, scattered around the globe — she immediately trusted Ianthe to do her very best with what she had.

And as well as that, she knew that Ryan was looking for artefacts in the archives to help with the Snow Queen exhibition, and, in the meantime, she'd ordered some huge glass floor tiles to make a frozen lake and some frond-y stuff to decorate it all with.

She thought back to when she and Ryan had started discussing the event and that he had suggested a sleigh, but, realistically, she thought that might be pushing both the budget and the fact that a huge thing like that would need to be brought inside that old house. Nope. Not a good idea.

The only thing that hovered over her was the location of Viola's picture. Something was stopping her from searching for it — probably the same feelings that she had harboured when she'd thought that the girl in the sketch might be the same one who had approached her in the office that time. The thought still made her shudder and she had avoided wandering around Pencradoc after hours in case the couple — because now she was convinced they were a couple — appeared again.

But today — today, she felt as if she needed to go and hunt for it. Something was just pushing her to do it. She found it difficult to concentrate on much else. There was something knocking in the back of her mind anyway which was unsettling her. She couldn't quite put her finger on it, but she knew if she kept busy, her subconscious mind might just figure it out.

She made it to six thirty, well after closing time at the arts centre, and well after she should have left herself — but she didn't relish the thought of a long Friday evening stretching out in front of her, alone with her thoughts in her room at Pencradoc House. She hadn't even had Coren to distract her with his gentle demands this afternoon. He had been off to meet someone about the wedding packages they wanted to offer and then he was coming back to spend the weekend with Sybill.

But, now, she really had no more excuses to stay at her desk, stuck there like a limpet.

Go find it! She imagined the New York voice was speaking in her ear. Or, at least, she thought, as she sipped a cup of strong, black coffee while staring into space (well, staring at the corner that apparition had appeared from), she was imagining it.

Ugh.

'Right. I'm going,' she said out loud. She stood up and glared at the corner of the room. God knew how she was actually working in that room. She texted Coren, just to say she was finally finishing up for the day and would be heading to the ballroom for one final task, in case he checked in on her, then, still looking at her phone, she realised she couldn't resist texting Merryn.

How haunted is the ballroom at Pencradoc? she typed out. She suspected Merryn would take a while to respond, probably being knee-deep in bottles and nappies and things. But, to her surprise, Merryn typed back almost immediately.

Haven't seen anything there myself! came the response. *Not to say there isn't anything there, though.*

Ugh.

Why ugh?

I have to go there and look for Viola.

Haven't you done that yet?

Why aren't you with your child? Tegan pulled a face — guilt-tripping her sister maybe wasn't the smartest thing to do, but the texts were implying there may actually be a ghost there.

She's sleeping — *SLEEPING, THANK GOD* . . .

Tegan grinned. *Okay. Give her cuddles from me and I'll report back.*

Will do. And you make sure you do! xxx

xxx

Tegan took a deep breath and walked out of the office. It was one step after another, that's all it was. She went along the corridor, along the hallway, through the drawing room. There wasn't a soul around — a living soul, anyway. Her heart pounding, she kept walking, keeping her eyes fixed straight ahead.

The house was — she could feel it — taking on a different personality. It was almost waking up around her, all these silent rooms, filled with modern-day things, but she could swear that as she walked through, everything was changing behind her, ironically taking on new shapes of the old things that used to be there.

Oh, shit. Maybe this hadn't been a good idea at all.

She didn't feel like it was polite anymore to challenge the house on the existence of its ghosts . . .

All she wanted to do was keep going forwards — she was, literally, too scared to go backwards and retrace her steps. She was terrified at what she might see, but she was also terrified of what she was leaving behind.

Forcing herself to keep going, she walked through the door into the ballroom, trying to imagine it decorated for the Snow Queen event, leading into the morning room behind. None of the pictures on the walls would be removed, but instead she would have frosty trees and blue-and-silver stuff going on — maybe some classical Christmas music or carols from a church choir singing . . .

Yes, that was nice. That was a nice thing for her to imagine — not to imagine the ghostly figures she felt were filling the room around her. Laughing children, couples dancing and residents from centuries ago walking purposefully through the room . . .

She whimpered. 'Oh God. Please be pretty close Viola's picture, please be pretty close . . .'

She stopped suddenly and looked to her left. Later, she would kid herself that she had caught sight of the sketch out of her peripheral vision, but, in reality, she knew that something or someone had made her stop in that exact spot and look at the wall.

The picture she found herself staring at was relatively small — no bigger than A4 sized, but beautifully framed in a simple gold rectangle. It was, as Merryn had said, a charcoal sketch that looked as if it had been swiftly transferred onto the paper, hugely informal, with the sitter looking off to the right and laughing.

That's right, she thought. *Marigold was there, asking so prettily for a buttered crumpet. I wasn't sure what Elsie was sketching, until I saw it here, so long afterwards . . .*

'Woah. Stop it!' said Tegan, batting the thoughts back from whence they came. Or were they thoughts? Were they actual memories? She felt, for an odd moment, as if she was actually there, in a cluttered, friendly drawing room in London, surrounded by someone else's possessions, and definitely in someone else's life.

But still she found herself staring at the picture as if she knew the girl in it so very, very well, unable to tear herself away from it, lost somewhere between two worlds. It really didn't help that the longer she looked at it, the more it seemed that she was looking into a mirror; that the girl in the sketch was her. Tegan, in another time and another place.

It was also clear, comparing this sketch to the photograph of the wedding that Viola was the small, fair-haired girl she had suspected she was. And, Tegan realised with a shudder, the person who had appeared to her in the office with that bouquet of flowers held in front of her.

In fact, she could smell it now — that odd, green scent of Christmas foliage. Holly and ivy and mistletoe, fresh from the woods. It was wrapping itself around her and she genuinely thought she would either throw up or pass out.

What the hell was going on?

'Oh, God,' she muttered again. Realistically, she knew that ghosts couldn't harm her, but also, she seemed rooted to the spot. She was also conscious that, outside, the sky was seemingly growing darker with the promise of heavy rain and everything just seemed ominous. Like a classic haunted-house movie. And here she was, in a haunted ballroom, looking at a picture she seemed to remember being created.

184

Then the door flung open with a bang and she heard footsteps at the other end of the room hurrying towards her, and she screamed.

* * *

Ryan had already found a few items in the archives at Wheal Mount. He knew that they needed to get the Halloween things ready and then, once that was done, he would see what he could find for Christmas. There were bound to be Christmas cards, or invitations, or, hopefully, photographs.

He just needed to go through Tammy and Bryony's system logically. Logic didn't come easily to Ryan — he was much more of a creative thinker. So, yes, the job he had found himself in was challenging at times, but extremely interesting. Nothing, though, had been as weird to come by as the story he had found in that chimney breast. He didn't want to dwell on it too much and even now was starting to think of it as some kind of dream.

But to his delight, he had found a load of spooky things in a large hatbox. Bryony's logic had, indeed, extended to "H/P" for "Halloween/Pencradoc" and he sent a silent thank you to her for being as absolutely descriptive as he would have been in that case. The box contained a pair of dress-up black velvet cat ears attached to some ribbon, a long, black velvet tail and a stiff little black skirt. Also, there had been a pointed hat, rather battered now, and a silver rope, still loosely knotted. A random, ornately decorated hand mirror and, oddly, a white sheet that looked too small for a person, but had ties attached to it too.

The mystery was solved when, at the bottom of that box, he found a photo album with a collection of pictures in. Entranced, he sat down on another trunk and carefully flicked through it. *Halloween party, 1911*, it proclaimed on the first page.

'Yes!' He almost punched the air. The year and the event matched with the invite they had. And, to make it even better, the book was full of photos of the party. The first picture was of a little girl dressed as a cat, making a claw shape with her hands. In another photograph she was sitting on the floor, her arms around the neck of a dog, which was dressed in the small white sheet.

Three women, dressed as witches, posed theatrically around a giant cooking pot that was supposed to be, he guessed, a cauldron — one of the women wore the pointed hat and what looked like the silver rope belt. Other people took their turns in the photos and he smiled at the younger boys who he could tell were thoroughly enjoying themselves.

The background to all the photographs was a depiction of Pencradoc House itself, made to look scary and forbidding, placed in what was supposed to be a haunted forest judging by the ghosts and ghouls peering out from behind trees. There were even figures at the windows of the house itself. Ryan suspected it had taken a good deal of time and skill to do that, and wondered which of the family had been involved.

The girls. Always the girls . . . came a voice so close to him that he jerked his head around to see who had crept up into the attics with him, dropping the album in his fluster. There was nobody there, but he couldn't shake the feeling that someone was watching him and enjoying reminiscing over the photographs as he turned the pages.

Ryan shivered and picked up the album. It had landed face down and as he picked it up, he saw that it had opened at a page he hadn't seen yet. On one side of the book was a photograph of a petite, fair-haired woman dressed as a vampiress apparently. She again was doing the claw-thing with her hands and baring her teeth. Her hair was messy and back-combed or something as it stood out around her head like a dandelion-clock, with some curls hanging down over her shoulder. She was, however, he could tell, desperately trying not to laugh.

Ryan stared at the picture for what seemed like an age. It was almost as if he had seen her first hand — almost as if he knew exactly what that girl's laughter sounded like, even

186

what perfume she had been wearing that night. Something like violets and lilies.

He blinked and pulled his thoughts away from it, forcing himself to look at the opposite page. He went hot and cold as he looked. A young, dark-haired man glowered out at the lens, almost as if he was reluctant to stand there and have his picture taken. He was tall, slim and slightly hunched over as if someone had told him to pose like a tortured Romantic poet. One hand was on the back of a chair and the other was on his hip, his legs crossed at the ankles as he stood there. His clothes were a raggedy version of Byron or Keats or Shelley, but the most astonishing thing was his expression. Ryan knew that expression well. It was exactly the same as the one he himself used when he was grumpy and cross and just wanted to be left alone.

Bloody awful night, that . . . she looked top-hole, though, don't you think?

The voice interrupted his thoughts again and Ryan closed the book rapidly. Something slid out of it and he picked it up. It was another photograph, but this time of the same young man in an army uniform. His hair was shorter and parted at the side, and he looked even more like Ryan in this one, although, bizarrely, the scowl had gone and he was almost smiling.

Ryan's stomach turned over as he flipped the photo and read the words on the back.

Laurie, 1914, it read.

And at that point, Ryan tossed everything back in the hatbox, picked it up and left the attic just as fast as he could.

Had it been up to him, he would have left the damned hatbox up there, but he knew that box of treasures was what he needed to take to Pencradoc and, if he left it there, he would have to pluck up a lot of courage to go back and retrieve it.

Better to just — do it.

But even as he reached the safety of his office, he still couldn't shake the feeling that someone had accompanied him all the way downstairs.

CHAPTER TWENTY-TWO

1911

God, it was cold out there. Laurie was grumpy. Why the hell had he decided to storm out of Elsie's house like that? And not even to sensibly stomp outside, hail a hansom cab and get back to his own accommodation where he could pour a brandy and huddle by the fireside.

The family had a house in London, which didn't really belong to any one of them individually. The Pencradocs had bought it many, many years ago, a tall, thin townhouse near Kensington Palace Gardens. It made sense for the family to still have a *pied-à-terre* up there, especially when Jago was travelling to town for business, and, latterly, when Laurie — as the eldest boy — was working with his uncle on estate business and needed to be there as well.

In years gone by, the young ladies of the family would have been expected to stay at the house while they took part in the Season and the ridiculous — in Laurie's eyes — Queen Charlotte's Ball, where twittering debutantes would be presented to the Queen, who held court next to a giant birthday cake.

Nowadays, it was a place for the family to stay if they were in London. Much to the secret chagrin of the Wheal Mount girls and Laurie's sisters, the Pencradoc family was no longer devoted to the Season. If any of them happened to be there, all well and good — they could enjoy a party or two. But the families would not be making a special effort to find the girls husbands during the Season.

But Laurie had not done the sensible thing and headed back to the cosy house near Kensington Palace Gardens. No. He had walked around the streets near Brunswick Square, huddled in doorways and stomped around the garden square itself — all in the vain hope that Viola would leave Elsie's and he could apprehend her for a quick word.

That's all he wanted — a quick word, out of earshot of his sister.

He was just cursing his own stupidity, promising himself that he would give up in five more minutes, when he saw the door to Elsie's house open and Viola step outside. She tilted her head up, closed her eyes and stuck her tongue out. It looked like she was catching snowflakes as they drifted down over the heavy sky. Then, opening her eyes and smiling, she looked along the road and stepped out onto the pavement.

Thank the Lord!

Laurie hurried along the snow-covered street — he could barely feel his fingers and toes right now, despite his thick boots and warm gloves, but he caught up with Viola and reached out, touching her shoulder.

'Hey!' she cried, swivelling around, anger in her face. 'What the . . . Oh! Laurie. It's you.' The anger disappeared from her face and was replaced with a startled expression instead. 'Sorry, I . . .' She gestured wildly with her hand muff but as her hands were still tucked inside it, it all looked a bit odd. 'A girl from back home, Dorothy Arnold — she disappeared last year from New York. She was taken from the street, maybe, and I thought you were . . .'

'Going to grab you from behind and spirit you away?' he asked. 'Oh, hell. I'm sorry. I didn't think. I should have called your name and got your attention that way.' Would he ever do anything right? Or was he fated to always make huge mistakes any time he was near this girl?

'More or less.'

'I'm sorry — I honestly didn't mean to scare you. That's dreadful about that girl — Dorothy, you say? Doesn't anyone know what happened to her?' The thought of one of his sisters vanishing like that was horrendous.

'No.' Viola shook her head. 'There are lots of stories, but nobody knows the truth.'

Viola looked upset and Laurie could have kicked himself again for not thinking before he approached her.

'Again. I'm so sorry. I didn't mean to scare you.'

'Oh, I'm not scared now I know it's you,' she said. She nodded, pulling herself together. 'Well. Good day, Mr Teague. Unless there's a particular reason why you tried to get my attention beyond just for the hell of it.'

Laurie pushed his hands into his pocket and tried his best to look contrite. It didn't come easily to look contrite around Viola. A scowl felt much more natural. 'There *was* a reason I waited for you—'

'You *waited* for me? In *this*?' She looked up at the cold grey sky, thick with falling flakes. 'Why ever did you do that? Couldn't you have just come back into your sister's house?'

'So many questions.' He fought against a smile. 'Look, can we walk for a little? I really think I'm going to freeze to the spot if I stay here any longer.'

'Sure.' Viola looked surprised. 'I'm heading this way.' Again, she gestured with her hand muff.

'Thank you. Shall we?' He gestured for her to begin walking and fell into step beside her. 'Now, to answer your questions. Yes, I waited for you — as I told you. I'm not in the habit of lying to make myself look more gallant. I did indeed wait for you.' He raised his eyes heavenwards. 'In this.' He thought he saw a smile twitch at the corner of her mouth. That was a good sign.

'I don't want or *expect* any gallant or grand gestures,' she said hurriedly. 'Let's just get that straight between us right now! Never!'

'All right. I believe you. Which is just as well, because all that is something I could never really be or do, and have *never* been or done. Much to my chagrin. But also, and here I switch your questions and answers around a little, I didn't want to go back into my sister's house today because I've had enough of her machinations and it always feels good to storm out on El, because you very rarely get the last word in otherwise. Trust me. I've known her all my life.' The smile appeared to grow, although Viola kept her head studiously down, seemingly watching where she was going for patches of ice. 'And the reason why I waited, Viola, is because I wanted to apologise to you.'

'Apologise to me?' Now he had her full attention and she looked at him, confused. 'Why ever do you need to apologise to me?'

'Two more questions!' He took his hand out of his pocket and held up his thumb and his forefinger. 'One,' he said, folding his thumb back in. 'Yes. I do need to apologise. And two.' He folded his finger in. 'I didn't really mean what I said about us not liking each other. Obviously. I can't speak for you liking me, but I wanted you to know that I don't — *dislike* you.' There. He'd said it. 'I actually do quite — *like* you. In a weird way.' It was his turn to put his head down and frown at the snow underfoot. 'I mean, you and I haven't exactly had the best of introductions to one another. First of all, I knock you into a puddle.'

'Oof. Yes. But then I guess I was a little mean to you as well. The jigsaw puzzle was not broken. I just wanted to make you feel tiled for being such a clodpole.'

'Pardon?' It was Laurie's turn to smile. 'In English, please?'

'Sure. Sorry.' She laughed — she actually laughed. 'I guess I *am* trying to talk to an English person. I wanted to make you feel guilty for being such an idiot.'

'You sure did that, honey.' Laurie's American accent was so bad it verged on comical — even he knew that — but she laughed again. 'Then next, we meet at my sister's. Where we argued again.'

'Very true.'

'And then more arguments at that wretched ball . . .'

'I'm not sure we actually argued at the wretched ball. We just — didn't say *enough* to each other. You did rescue me from that fellow who was so entirely obnoxious that I could not have stood another minute in his company. That was a nice thing to do.'

'He was utterly vile. Can't stand the man. And after that, Halloween. Less said about that the better.'

'Yes.' Viola wasn't going to elaborate on that one either. They stood in an uneasy silence for a moment. 'Then here. Today. I nearly slip on the ice and you appear again.'

'And El tries to be the most indiscreet matchmaker I have ever encountered.' Laurie shuddered, then indicated that they should keep moving. It was bloody cold out there. 'I can only apologise for her.'

'I know. It's not your fault. It's fine — you had every right to shout and stomp like that. I might have done the same if it was Sam doing that.'

'But I am right in thinking that we can tolerate each other well enough to not spoil the wedding, am I?'

Viola smiled. 'Oh, I should think we can do that well enough, Laurie.' Then her attention was caught by something further up the street. 'Oh, *look!*'

Laurie looked, and, towards Russell Square, there was music and laughter, and something altogether festive going on.

'Shall we go and see what it is?' she asked. 'You know — to try to have a better time together than we usually do. So we know how to play nice with one another on the twenty-second?'

Laurie looked at the beautiful, perfectly oval face staring up at him, her eyes dancing and a smile most definitely on her lips now. He felt his heart and stomach do an awfully strange *kerchung* sort of swooping movement and he blinked.

'Yes,' he heard himself saying. 'That would be wonderful.'

* * *

Viola laughed. She put on an English voice as bad as his attempt at an American one. 'That would indeed be wunnerful — wunner — wun . . .' She reverted to her normal voice. 'No. I can't say it. Why *is* that?'

'You obviously need to spend a little longer in England,' Laurie told her. 'Anyway — shall we?' He nodded up ahead to the Christmas fair or market, or whatever it was. He didn't offer his arm, or ask to take her hand, or any of those terribly gallant things young men usually did, and Viola didn't know whether to be relieved or put out at that. *Be relieved*, her sensible side told her. *You are aiming for a truce, nothing more.*

It would have felt awfully awkward to walk up to that square on his arm as if they were — together. But she did notice a little movement where Laurie pushed his hands further into his pockets and if she was a romantic at heart — which she was *not* — then she might have taken it as a sign of gentlemanly restraint and been a little hurt that he hadn't offered his arm.

But she wasn't interested in him romantically and she truly didn't care if he took her arm or not, so she straightened her shoulders, tilted her chin up and walked as smartly as she could towards Russell Square . . . making sure, though, that she didn't actually walk *too* smartly, in case he thought she was trying to walk away from him and that she did not want his company.

'Doesn't it look beautiful with the snow everywhere?' she asked. 'We have some dreadful snow in New York, but this is nice snow. Not too much of it and just thick enough to make it look really Christmassy.'

'In a few hours it will have turned to slush,' said Laurie. 'So you really have got the best of the day here.'

'I am inclined to agree. And I wonder what we have in the square — oh! Can you hear that?'

As they got closer, they could hear the festive noise and cheer resolve itself into the familiar words of Christmas carols — a group of people were singing beneath a tree that had been hastily decorated in holly and ivy — as evidenced by the bucket containing that festive greenery, which was being carefully looked after by a very stern lady in a red coat. Children were running around in the snow, building snowmen and playing games. A toboggan or two was being dragged around the grass, and a mulled-wine stall and a roast-chestnut stand were cosily situated in an area radiating warmth from the fires the stallholders had lit. People were standing listening to the carols, enjoying the wine and chestnuts, and smiling at the children scattered around them.

'Oh, how utterly *perfect*!' said Viola, entranced. 'I didn't know this was happening today. Would someone have said?' She looked up at Laurie.

He shook his head, but there was a smile on his face. 'Not necessarily. The choir might have decided to come out because of the weather and once the chestnut and mulled-wine sellers found out, they would have come along too. And — well — children gravitate to places like this in weather like this, so it's just a perfect scene, really.'

'It is. It's . . . magical. I've never had a roast chestnut before. They smell divine.'

'They're an acquired taste. And take some skill to eat. Wait here — I'll show you what I mean.'

He headed towards the chestnut seller, and, after a quick conversation and some money changing hands, Laurie was presented with a bag of the hot, delicious-smelling festive treats. 'These are better than that thing for warming your hands,' he said, returning to Viola and nodding at her hand muff. 'I promise.'

Viola extracted her hands, and, laughing, took the bag of chestnuts from Laurie. 'You're right!' she said, holding the knobbly parcel carefully. 'It's almost a shame to eat them.'

'Trust me,' he said, pulling a face. 'You may prefer to keep them as handwarmers. One moment. You need something else.'

He slipped away again and Viola saw him go to the mulled-wine stall. He came back with bought two small cups. 'To take the taste away. Cheers. However, I shall hold them as you'll need both hands to eat those things.'

'Deevie,' she said. And it was divine, actually, to be standing in Russell Square, listening to Christmas carols with the delicious scent of roast chestnuts tickling her nose, and the aroma of mulled wine tempting her into a warming drink. She opened the bag of chestnuts carefully and sniffed again. The shiny, brown nuts were looking awfully tempting and she took one out and looked at it for a moment. Then she looked at Laurie.

'I find it easier to break it open,' he said. 'If you can use your nails, that works well.'

'All right. I'll try that.' She pierced the shell with her thumbnail and exposed a strange, pale centre with a texture she couldn't quite describe. Not what she was expecting at all. She eased a piece of the nut out and popped it in her mouth. In there, it was an even stranger texture, and, although she valiantly chewed and swallowed it, she found it all coated the inside of her mouth quite unpleasantly.

'Ugh,' was all she could say.

Laurie laughed. 'Here. Take a sip of this. It should help.' She took the mulled wine gratefully and sipped it, the spices filling her nose and mouth in a much more pleasant way.

'I ain't gonna give up on these devils,' she said, handing the wine back to Laurie. 'They ain't gonna beat me.'

'I salute you, then,' he said, doing exactly that and bowing for good measure. Luckily, he managed not to spill any of that precious wine and by the time Viola had chewed her way through five of the devils, and he had taken the last one from her out of pity and pulled a face while he ate the thing, it seemed like the mulled wine really was, as he'd said, the best thing in the world to accompany the roast chestnuts.

'Jeepers, what a disappointment,' Viola said. 'I was so looking forward to those. All traditional and everything.'

'My family would be the first to tell you that "traditional" doesn't always mean good. But, you've tried them, and . . .' He looked around and held his arms out, encompassing the glorious scene before him. 'What could be better and more Christmassy than this?'

'Not much.'

They stood in silence for a moment, neither of them seemingly knowing where to look or what to say. Some form of unsaid words hung between them, as clearly as the choir was singing the notes of "In the Bleak Midwinter".

Laurie fixed his gaze on her and scowled, and seemed about to speak, and her heart began to pound quite treacherously in her chest.

Perhaps this was a good time for her to reiterate that Christmas wish she'd been toying with, the very first time she'd seen that winter star in the sky . . .

But then—

'Unca Laurie! Viola!' The pair of them swung around to see Marigold gamely trudging towards them, waving at them, her own little hand muff hanging at an angle across her body. 'It's fun here! Look at the snow!' The little girl stormed ahead, in front of an efficient-looking woman who Viola assumed was "Nanny", and stooped to pick up a pile of snow. She squashed it in her hands in a childish attempt at a snowball and threw it, then clapped her hands and laughed delightedly.

196

'Marigold Ashby,' said Laurie, crouching down so she could run at him. She almost knocked him over as he closed his arms around her, then he stood up and swung her around before placing her back on the ground. 'Good afternoon.' That little scene did something even more strange to Viola's stomach. He looked so happy and natural in the child's company. Yes, he was clearly well used to small people.

She shivered. It wasn't just that, though, that made her shiver. She had the oddest feeling that they were being watched and she couldn't work out why. But someone, somewhere, was watching the events here unfold and something was happening somewhere that she couldn't see, despite the fact she quickly glanced around the scene to check.

Jeepers!

'Good afternoon.' Marigold curtsied prettily, bringing Viola back to the present, and Laurie bowed back.

'I'm sorry, sir,' said the nanny, hurrying up to them. 'She saw you and ran, and I couldn't catch her quickly enough.'

'It's not a problem.' He smiled at the nanny. 'I thought you were at Mr and Mrs Griffith's home with her?'

'We were, but we saw this on our way back and of course we had to stop the carriage and get out, and come and investigate.'

'I'm not surprised. Well, I suspect Lady Elsie will be pleased to have you back in the warm before too long.' Then he turned his attention to his niece. 'Hot milk for you, Miss Ashby. And perhaps a buttered crumpet when you get in?'

'Buttered crumpets are my *favourite*,' said Marigold. Then she leaned confidentially into her uncle, who bent down to hear her. 'I had a buttered crumpet at Lily's,' she whispered — although Marigold's whisper was not exactly a whisper and quite loud enough for Viola to hear. 'But I may have *another* one when I get home. And. *Hot chocolate!*' She clasped her little hands over her mouth and made her eyes wide. Laurie copied her gesture and Viola bit her lip to hide her smile.

'I shan't tell your mama you had one at Lily's,' Laurie said. He bowed again. 'And I wish you well in your quest for extra buttered crumpets, young lady.'

Marigold spluttered a laugh and reached up for her nanny's hand. Then she yawned. 'Yes. I think I am ready to go home now. I am quite cold.'

'All right. Be a good girl and we will see you soon.' He bent down and hugged her, then Marigold looked up at Viola and smiled. Viola couldn't help but bend down and take the tot in her own arms and hug her as well.

They waved at Marigold and Nanny as the pair headed off, and then, finally, they were alone again. Well, as alone as they could be in the middle of a carol concert in Russell Square.

'I'm afraid,' Viola said, 'that I must echo young Miss Ashby and advise you, sir, that I am also ready to go home now. And also quite cold.'

'Fair enough. Could I get you a cab or something? Or we could share — if you wished. I'll need one myself as I don't think I can stand being out here in the snow much longer — although, I have to say, it was worth it.' Laurie studied her and Viola felt her cheeks redden and heat up. Did he mean it was worth waiting for her outside of Elsie's or that it was worth walking through the snow to find this magical little scene? Or even, worth it to exchange a few words with his niece.

She cleared her throat. 'It's fine and dandy. Really. I'm just up there.' She pointed to her street, which wasn't very far at all — you could see it, straight up from the square. But it was, she knew, out of his way. 'I'll just walk, no need to escort me. You go ahead and get your cab. You must be frozen.'

Laurie seemed to think for a moment, then nodded. 'Very well. I'm — um — I'm glad we managed to clear the air a little. So we can behave on the twenty-second.'

'Yes. I agree. Oh — and Laurie?'

'Yes?'

'You waiting in the snow — I agree. It was definitely worth it.'

Then she put her head down, turned in the direction of her street and hurried away through the still-falling snow. Her cheeks were now molten — she could feel them burning — and he could take that comment about it being "worth it" in whichever way he chose.

She knew which way she had meant it.

CHAPTER TWENTY-THREE

Present

'What on earth are you screaming for? It's only me!' Ryan
was standing at the end of the ballroom. 'I'm not going
to hurt you!' Tegan stared at him — Ryan was the person
who had invaded the ballroom, startling her in the process.

She found her voice. 'Just don't — creep *up* on people
like that!' Her heart still thumped like mad. '*And we are
closed*!'

'How did I creep up on you?' His voice matched hers
for snappiness. 'I'm way up here. You're way down there.
Coren told Sybill you were still here, so I came to find you!'
Ryan was glaring at her and Tegan felt the truce they'd sort
of agreed on wobbling. She took a deep breath. She was
getting tired of this, tired of the shouting and the grouch-
ing. And there were, actually, worse things to be dealing
with than Ryan. Things like the Pencradoc ghosts.

The only thing was, his entrance had forced her to
turn away from the charcoal sketch of Viola, and she could
see that the ballroom was exactly as it always was. Light,
bright and elegant, lined with beautiful watercolours and

little oil paintings produced by the Teague family at the height of their occupancy here.

'Okay. I'm sorry. You did startle me, though.'

'Okay.' He walked towards her, carrying what looked like a hatbox. 'I guess I'm sorry too — for startling you. I came up with Sybill in the van after work so I could drop this stuff off for the Halloween trail. She was heading here anyway for the weekend and I kind of suggested I drive us so I could get this done.' He raised the hatbox slightly as if to show her. 'Coren's apparently taking her back home Sunday evening. Like I said, he thought you might be in here so I headed along to see you.'

'It's fine. And thank you. I was in here looking for this.' She gestured to the sketch. 'Truth be told, I'm kind of pleased you're human company.' She could have bitten her tongue off as soon as she'd said it. How stupid did that make her sound — especially when she saw Ryan's expression change from his habitual scowl to one of surprise and disbelief.

'You expecting non-human company?' he asked.

Oh, sod it. She had to tell someone and he was as good as anyone, she supposed, and, actually, she was still quite relieved it was him and not a see-through person instead.

'Think I had it.' She closed her eyes briefly in embarrassment. She opened her eyes again and looked straight at him. 'Non-human company, that is. Downstairs. And in here.' She shivered. 'Just — voices, And the sense that someone's with me. You know?' She looked across at the sketch. 'I came to look for that and it's creeped me out. It's Viola. Elsie's bridesmaid.' She stared at it for a moment longer. 'It's creeped me out, because she kind of looks like me, I guess. Same hair, same smile. It's just a bit weird.'

Ryan came closer to her and looked at it. 'Ah,' he said after a moment, in an odd little flat voice. 'So it is. She does look a lot like you. Um. Do you want to see what I have here? I have another photo of her. But it might creep you out more. In fact, I was pretty creeped out myself when I saw a couple of the pictures I found.'

'Oh, God. Okay then.' Tegan was slightly scared of what she'd see and she didn't know if the ballroom was the best place to look. But the whole house could potentially be swarming with ghosts, so there was probably no "good" place to go to. 'Come on then. Let me see what you found.'

'I found a load of Halloween artefacts, bits of costumes and the like.' He put the box down and opened it. 'See? Cat ears and things. Witchy gear. And, believe it or not, a dog's ghost costume. I can prove that's what it is, because I have evidence. And the evidence is in this photo album.' He took a black, ornately embossed book out of the box and Tegan saw he had it bookmarked with a card or something at one of the pages. 'It's family photos, from a party. The 1911 one we had the invite for. I can maybe guess at some of the characters involved, but it'll take more of an expert than me to name them all.'

'Wow.' Tegan leaned over as Ryan turned the pages carefully. 'I recognise these people. They were in the wedding photo.'

'Perfect,' he said. 'But the most interesting page I thought — for us, anyway—' Tegan noticed he didn't look at her when he said that, and his voice was oddly guarded — 'is this one.' He slipped the bookmark out and presented the open album to Tegan.

On one side of the page was a girl dressed as a vampiress and on the other was a young man who looked angry and annoyed at something, but enormously sexy in billowing white shirt sleeves and a waistcoat, both of which were artfully distressed, or perhaps just tatty. Tegan didn't know which it was.

Again, she had that weird feeling that she could remember the photograph being taken . . .

'Stand still, Viola. You have to hold the pose for a few seconds so we can get it right. You can smile if you want, but you don't have to.'

'Can I just look kind of spooky and scary?'

'If you want to.'

'Wunnerful. I'll do that then . . .'

Then, later on, she was aware of a banging pain in the side of her head and the most excruciating embarrassment she had ever felt in her entire life.

From above her, she heard Elsie say to him, 'Actually, on that note, vile sibling, I invite you to have your photograph taken for posterity.'

'I don't think—'

'Hush, hush, hush. Marigold is too small to remember much about this, so the photographs are for her. Please tell me you won't let your niece down, Laurie.'

'Blackmailer . . .'

The present day swooped back in on Tegan, along with one, resounding word in her heart, in her mind, on her lips. 'Laurie!'

'Yes. Elsie's brother.' Ryan's voice brought her fully back to her own world. 'This is him in 1914.' He handed her the card he'd been using as a bookmark. She took it, her hands shaking. It was a photograph of a young man, who looked very much like Ryan, practically smiling as he posed in his army uniform.

'Laurie . . .' she whispered, holding on to the photo just as tightly as she could, as if she was frightened to let it get away from her again.

'He married Viola. And that, I suspect, was her at the party.'

'She looks just like the bridesmaid in the wedding photo. And the sketch here. And . . .' She stopped short at mentioning her otherworldly visitor with a bouquet. Instead she laughed, even though, strangely, she wanted to cry as well. 'Laurie was my literary crush, you know. From *Little Women*. I've always loved him.'

'Really? I've never read it.'

'I doubt it's the sort of book you'd have been interested in. But it's my favourite one. Remember when we first met up again and I was a bit shocked that Elsie's brother was called Laurie? I obviously wasn't going to tell you then, but I used to have dreams about me marrying Laurie instead of Amy marrying him . . . God. Under the circumstances, and given my apparent likeness to Viola, that's *incredibly* creepy.' Tegan stared at the photo again.

Then, with a touch of her usual sass where Ryan was concerned, and perhaps as a little bit of her defence mechanism kicked in, she said, 'And *this* Laurie looks a bit like you. If I'm creeped out about Viola, it's only fair you should be too.'

Ryan went paler than usual. 'Well, thanks a lot, Tegan. I don't need you to creep me out. I did spot the likeness. Remember, I said it was weird when I came in here?'

'And it's got even weirder,' she said quietly. Then she shivered. 'And colder.' She looked around and saw a mist starting to form behind Ryan, coming slowly down the ballroom towards them.

Nope. No. That wasn't happening.

'Come on,' she said suddenly, grabbing his hand. 'We need to get out of here. Leave the hatbox.'

'I am not leaving *anything*,' he said, shaking his hand free. 'Because who the hell is going to come back in here and get it?' He ducked down and picked up the box and tossed the book into it. He might have seen the horror in her eyes and that she was looking over his shoulder; their eyes connected for a second, then he looked behind him. The mist was getting stronger and closer and starting to form shapes — legs, perhaps, coming out of it, arms, maybe.

Shit.

No.

They couldn't hurt you, but who was mad enough to stay and risk it?

Not them.

She yelled at Ryan. 'Let's go!'

'Right with you.' And somehow, they were holding hands and running through the ballroom as if all the demons of Hell were after them, and not, God forbid, a pre-war version of themselves emerging out of the shadows to say "hello".

* * *

Ryan couldn't believe what he'd seen. It definitely looked as if something was coming along the ballroom, gliding towards them.

He felt a little sick and a lot scared. Not that he wanted to admit it to Tegan, although it had probably been crazily obvious when he'd grabbed her hand and they'd pelted out of the room.

Or had she grabbed his hand? He wasn't sure — all he knew was that, somehow, they were still holding hands and were in the hallway, at the bottom of the Grand Staircase, both breathing heavily.

'Oh my God. This *place*!' said Tegan. 'You saw it, didn't you? Saw — them?'

Ryan nodded. 'Yeah. I think so . . .' He was still trying to process it. 'How do you *work* here?'

'I don't know. They were in my office as well—' She stopped herself short, then shook her head. 'No. Never mind. Forget I said anything.'

They simultaneously seemed to realise they were still holding hands, released each other and both took a step backwards.

'I can't actually *do* that. Forget it, I mean. If it makes you feel any better, that story I found? It was here as well.' He closed his eyes briefly, rubbed his hand across his face and then re-opened this eyes. 'Up in one of the rooms they're refurbishing.'

'What were you doing creeping around up there?' asked Tegan, looking shocked. As well she might.

'I don't know. That's the thing.' He was mortified now. 'I just — found myself in there. Poking around inside a chimney breast.'

There was silence. 'Wow. That almost trumps my story.'

'Almost,' he said miserably. He raked his hand through his hair. 'Now I'm wondering if it was Laurie's room and he took me there.'

'Laurie.' She shook her head. 'If Viola keeps popping in to see me, it makes sense that he came to see you. But he's *my* crush. I'm actually jealous.'

Ryan blinked and looked at her in astonishment. He realised, though, that she had actually been joking. He felt himself relax a little. 'You're welcome to him.'

Tegan sat down on the bottom step. Cautiously, he sat next to her, the hatbox between them. 'So, what else is in there?' she asked after a moment. 'And more to the point are we safe to look?'

'Like I said. Some old costumes that would look good in the display. Next to blown-up pictures of the photos they relate to. And a random old hand mirror.'

'A hand mirror. I think they used to play games at Halloween with mirrors, you know. I did it myself when I was a kid.'

'You know more about it than me then.'

'Hmm. Can I see it, at all?'

It was an odd sort of request. They'd just been chased by ghosts and she wanted to look at a mirror.

And not actually leave Pencradoc and whatever might be floating around in that ballroom? What if it followed them?

But Tegan didn't seem open to the fact this was an option, and Ryan didn't dare question the wisdom of that request. He understood perfectly that sometimes distraction was the best thing to do. And he would just have to pray the ghosts would remain where they'd left them . . .

'Sure.' He tried not to think about that odd mist, and opened the hatbox, the photo album looking innocuous now, then handed her the mirror.

'Thanks.' She took it and held it up in front of her. The lights had been dimmed in the hallway for closing time and it was quite dark by now outside, being the beginning of October, but from somewhere up the stairs it seemed, a shaft of light glinted off the glass surface and reflected back on her face. For a moment, Tegan looked unlike herself and Ryan felt a shiver of unease.

'Tegan?' he asked. 'You okay?'

'I'm fine.' She lowered the mirror and looked at him. 'I can see I'm getting a spot on my chin, but beyond that . . .' She shrugged. 'They used to walk up the stairs backwards with these things, you know. Supposed to show you the person you're going to marry. And there was candlelight. Usually.'

'Gotta love a bit of folklore,' he said wryly. 'If you don't mind contravening health-and-safety guidelines.'

'It would have been fun, though.' She stood up and again he got that flash of someone else's face overlaying hers. 'Look. Just like this.'

And before he could stop her, she held the mirror up in front of her face again and began to walk carefully backwards up the stairs, her gaze fixed on the mirror.

'Tegan, I don't think—'

But she held up her other hand as if to silence him and continued to walk. Her eyes definitely didn't look like Tegan's eyes and Ryan started to panic a little.

'Tegan, that's dangerous. Look, if you fall, it's your own fault. I'm not picking you up off the floor . . .'

Then a couple of things happened at once.

Obviously, because she was being ridiculously stubborn and carrying out a stupid manoeuvre, she stumbled, but at the same time she stumbled, she yelled out in surprise, 'You! What are you doing *behind* me?'

And then, seemingly, she missed her footing while trying to recover from the stumble and ended up in a tangled, tripping heap that slithered down the stairs.

Ryan flew up the steps two at a time and managed to catch her before she actually fell properly and ended up on the floor. Her weight and momentum had them both stumbling down the last few stairs, but finally he managed to set her on her feet again at the bottom.

He had never been this close to her before, even if they'd held hands briefly a few minutes ago. That was completely different to holding her around her waist, somehow pulling her a little closer as she looked up at him, her lips slightly parted, her eyes asking so many questions. He felt her hands settle on his shoulders, almost pulling him down to meet her.

He was, he suddenly realised, way too close for comfort. But even so, he found himself tilting his head down towards her, looking in her eyes, wondering exactly what it would be like to kiss her, wondering exactly why he'd left it so long . . .

Then he blinked and dragged himself back to reality. He took his hands away from her waist, forced himself to paste a scowl on his face and said, 'I *told* you so. You could have broken your neck.'

Tegan seemed to come back to life at the same time. Quickly, she moved her hands from his shoulders and shifted her footing so she was planted more squarely on the floor.

'What *I* don't understand, then,' she said, with another touch of that sparkiness, 'is if it was so dangerous and unadvisable, how or why you snuck up behind me and got yourself right there at the top of the stairs! And then *looked in my mirror*! You must have known it would startle me!'

'Exactly!' said Ryan. 'I *know* it would have been dangerous, *if* I had done a trick like that. But I promise you. I didn't. I've been right here, all the time. Ready to catch you if you bloody fell down the stairs!'

They stared at one another for what seemed like an age as they both processed the information.

Tegan was the first to break the spell. 'I have to get out of here,' she said, almost in a whisper. 'Right now. I've had enough.' *Finally! Thank the Lord, they could leave Pencradoc!* 'I'm going to see if the pub has a room for the night. I literally cannot be here tonight. It's just — too much.'

The words were out before Ryan was fully aware that he'd said them. And given his current thinking about escaping from the place, he could have bitten his own tongue off by suggesting it. 'If you want to get some clothes, I'll come up and wait for you outside your room,' he heard himself say. 'I think we could both do with a drink tonight. I'll stay in the village too.'

'Where? In the pub?' Tegan looked surprised.

Ryan shook his head. 'No. In my van. It's a campervan. Great for transporting things here, there and everywhere. And great for unscheduled stopovers. Like this one.' There was a beat and he tried to swallow down any lingering animosity there was between them. 'In all good conscience, I can't let you cope with this on your own tonight. I'd rather spend some time with you and make sure you're okay.' He cringed. He had just given Tegan Burton an opening to throw his offer back in his face.

But, to his surprise, that didn't happen.

'Thank you.' The words sounded strained. 'I would — appreciate that. Would you — would you come with me now? Up the servants' staircase.' A smile struggled to appear on her lips, then died. 'I'm not going up these things any more tonight.' She nodded over her shoulder, indicating the Grand Staircase.

Ryan nodded back. 'That's fine. Lead the way. And this — hatbox. Where can I leave it?'

'I'll lock it in a cupboard in the office. Do you think we can take the photo album, though? I think I'd like to look at the photos in a neutral place.'

'That sounds great. Surely they can't get us in the pub?'

'I bloody hope not,' she replied. 'Come on. And — thanks.'

'No problem.' He gestured for Tegan to take them through the maze of corridors he knew Pencradoc consisted of and tried to batter down the thought that, actually, if he was left to his own devices, he could probably lead Tegan there himself.

It was, very much, as if he was starting to recognise that he, Ryan, knew this place like the back of his hand.

CHAPTER TWENTY-FOUR

1911

The day of Elsie and Louis' wedding — the twenty-second of December, the winter solstice — finally dawned. It was one of those beautiful winter days where the snow blanketed the ground, but the sky was blue, and everyone woke up in a cheerful mood.

Laurie and his entire family — including the Wheal Mount contingent — were in the Pencradoc London house and although it was a reasonably large property, they were practically falling over one another to get ready, or to take their turn with the seamstress, or to have their hair done, or to grumble about the arrangements for walking down the aisle.

Elsie had given them all very specific instructions. Zennor had a list with everyone's names on and she was going to take it with her, but Laurie had committed it all to memory anyway. Words were his thing and it wasn't hard for him to retain the information.

He recited it in his mind once more.

Isolde would precede the bridal party, along with Louis' brother, Drew. As maid of honour and best man, it was only correct.

They would be followed by him, Laurie, with Viola and Marigold.

Then would come Medora and Biscuit. Oh, yes — Biscuit had travelled to London as well and was as excited as a puppy, exploring the house and garden and getting under everyone's feet, his long tail wagging constantly. Medora and Biscuit would be accompanied by Fabian. And Biscuit was also the ring-bearer.

Coming after Medora, Fabian and Biscuit, were Clem and Evie.

They would be followed by Clara, and Lily's eldest son, Albert. Then it would be Enyon and Lucy, Arthur and Nancy, and Mabel and Edward — Lily's youngest son.

The bridal attendants, Laurie feared, would fill the aisle before the bridal party actually entered the place.

However.

The day before, on the twenty-first, they'd all arrived at the church for a wedding rehearsal, and Laurie preferred not to think of the jumble of excited girls and dour boys trying to find their places and step over dogs and toddlers — both of whom had also been over-excited — and argue over who had the best view and when could they expect to eat the wedding cake, please.

Louis had just looked worried — he'd admitted later that he could just imagine chaos descending over the place — and Elsie had beamed at everyone, wrapped up in a loosely fitted black walking coat she'd refused to take off.

Laurie had to wonder why. Everyone had guessed the reason for the speedy wedding, and, to be honest, nobody cared. And surely, the situation couldn't be *that* obvious yet, but he had to allow his sister her foibles, the cross words between them a couple of weeks ago long forgotten.

More importantly, he had seen Viola there, for the first time since their snowy afternoon in Russell Square. They had nodded politely at one another and walked down the aisle as instructed, and not a bad word or argument had happened between them.

211

It was a Christmas miracle.

He wondered whether that time they'd spent together had shifted something in the atmosphere between them and he had been pleased he'd waited in the snow for her — he really had been. But he wasn't sure whether she knew the reason for that pleasure or not.

All he knew, was that he felt a whole lot better in her company now and he was actually looking forward to the wedding and sharing the aisle with her.

Which made him feel a little odd and wonder whether, in some ways, it was something they were destined to do again at some point . . .

But no. He shuddered. It was the magic of Christmas and the idea he'd built up of her after that last meeting in Russell Square.

He found that he certainly did not dislike her at all now.

He found that, perhaps, he might even like her.

A lot.

Perhaps even love her.

Just a little.

Then he shook his head to clear it of such ridiculous thoughts and headed downstairs to the predicted chaos, as the bridesmaids and canine contingent got ready to clamber into a carriage and be delivered wholesale to Brunswick Square to meet the other bridesmaids — including Viola — and carry out their duties, and the male attendants waited, sullenly or otherwise, for the carriage that would take them to St George's Church, Bloomsbury, to meet everyone there.

* * *

The wedding had been — perfect. Absolutely perfect.

'It's — wunnerful!' Viola had muttered to Laurie, of all people, as they sat beside one another, Marigold between them, in the church.

212

There had been, of course, a slight change of plan. Marigold had, like her mother, been particularly single-minded that morning, and, instead of walking nicely between Viola and Laurie as they held her hands, she had decided she wanted to walk in front of them and scatter greenery in gay abandon in the aisle.

Somebody had made the mistake of saying that if it was a summer wedding, wouldn't a scattering of rose petals have been delightful, and, in the absence of rose petals, Marigold had been determined to find an alternative.

This had resulted in all the bridesmaids raiding the Christmas decorations and the garden for things Marigold could put in a basket — therefore, she had acquired the more traditional items of holly and ivy, as well as some cyclamen flowers, some Christmas roses and a fine green shrub from the garden with little white trumpet flowers that was apparently called Christmas Box.

Nobody claimed responsibility for the mention of rose petals.

Unsurprisingly.

But anyway — here they were. Elsie and Louis had just exchanged vows, and Elsie was, quite possibly, the most stunning bride Viola had ever seen. She absolutely glowed with happiness, a wreath of holly, ivy and mistletoe in her hair, and also in her bouquet. She clutched the bouquet very firmly in front of her, the gorgeous white dress even more divine since the extra layers of tulle and lace had been added. The sash, however, was no longer white — Elsie had chosen a red sash to complement Marigold's dress and it looked utterly perfect. Viola had helped her tie it and adjust it just so before the ceremony. She'd hidden a smile when Elsie had asked her to "loosen it just a little bit, sweetums", and Elsie had laid her hand briefly on her stomach as if she'd been *definitely* trying to hide whatever was going on around that area.

The bridesmaids had ribbons of red, gold and green woven through their elaborate hairstyles, but already Viola could feel her style dropping out and the ribbons unravelling. She didn't care, though. Nobody would be looking at her and if her hair only stayed up as long as it took for the photographs to be taken, that was long enough.

Well, she *thought* that nobody would be looking at her — but the odd time she had felt Laurie's eyes on her and once she had turned and caught his expression, and it had made her surreptitiously smile.

She hadn't forgotten her secret Christmas wish. She wondered if, perhaps, it might *not* be too much to wish for after all.

But yes, the wedding was "wunnerful".

She looked around and saw Pearl and Holly clutching each other and crying what she assumed were happy tears while their husbands sat either side of them looking embarrassed, and the children lining the pews beside them. Sam was there too. He caught her eye and grinned, rolling his eyes heavenwards and nodding towards Pearl. She grinned back and looked around a little more.

There were Zennor and Ruan Teague, Laurie's parents. Ruan Teague had escorted his stepdaughter down the aisle to give her away, looking just as proud as any biological father would. And there were Louis' parents and his sister-in-law, Felicity. And a couple who she assumed were Laurie's aunt and uncle, Alys and Jago, the Duke and Duchess of Trecarrow, looking happy to be there as well. The likeness between Alys and the fair-haired Wheal Mount bridesmaids was astonishing, apart from the fact they all had their father's serious, dark eyes.

There was a movement next to her and she realised it was Marigold, trying to clamber up onto her knee.

'Isn't Mama *bee-you-tee-fool*,' the little girl whispered. 'And Papa is bee-you-tee-fool too.'

'They are both very bee-you-tee-fool, honey. And so are you.' Viola scooped the child onto her knee and caught Laurie's eye again. This time, she found that she couldn't look away. His eyes were fixed on hers, the way she knew hers were fixed on his. The packed church seemed to melt away and it seemed as if it was just the two of them in the world.

'Yes,' he whispered. 'You're wunnerful.'

But as Marigold had coughed at that point, Viola couldn't swear that was exactly what Laurie Teague had said.

CHAPTER TWENTY-FIVE

Present

Tegan didn't take long to sweep what possessions she
needed into an overnight bag. She was used to travelling
light and packing smartly, but she had to admit that she
was awfully glad Ryan was actually lurking in the corridor
like a dour sort of bodyguard, waiting for her. It must, after
all, be a bit scary for him as well. He was probably expecting something to jump out on him as much as she was.

After dropping the hatbox in at the office, they'd gone
up the servants' staircase as planned and that didn't feel as
bad, or as eerie, perhaps, as the Grand Staircase did that
night. It was like the ballroom thing — the atmosphere was
fluid and shifting, and Tegan didn't really know how to
deal with it. She had scoffed at her sister's stories about the
ghosts of Pencradoc but now she was here, in the middle
of it all, it was no scoffing matter.

Ryan had, she noticed, studiously ignored the other
wing as they'd headed up to her room — not even looking along the corridor curiously or commenting on the
refurbishments.

It was no surprise. Finding yourself randomly in a room, with your hand stuck up a grotty old chimney breast was on a par with things coming out of the shadows at you in your place of work — definitely.

'Okay, I've got everything I need,' Tegan said, coming out of her room. Ryan was peering out of the window at the end of the corridor, almost as if he didn't want to see what was coming at him from the other direction. She could have, she supposed, asked him inside to wait, but that would have been a bit awkward. There wasn't enough privacy in there for a guy you worked with to not see you grabbing your smalls out of a chest of drawers. As an afterthought, she'd tossed her battered old copy of *Little Women* into her bag. It was her go-to book and tonight she felt she would really need to "go to" it.

'Great.' Ryan turned around, and, for a moment, with the uplighting from outside the building illuminating his silhouette through the window, he looked more like the chap in the scowling photos than he looked like himself. He adjusted the way he was carrying the photo album, fiddled with his cuff and walked towards her, and her heart began to pound. It was a gesture she'd seen before, and not on Ryan.

'Let's just — go,' she said and turned away, hurrying along the corridor. Ryan's footsteps followed her — at least, she hoped it was his footsteps, but wasn't going to look behind her to find out.

She headed to the servants' staircase and straight down it. 'I'll text Coren when I get to the pub, tell him what I'm doing tonight.' She was babbling just to hear noise in that eerie old place. God, it was a big house when you were practically on your own in it. She didn't know how Coren lived there all the time. Surely, he must just stay in his apartment and not go out of his front door at night! 'I'll just say I'm staying over at a friend's this weekend. I'm not sure of the protocol, when you're kind of in staff accommodation . . .'

'No, me neither.' Ryan caught up with her, his strides longer than hers. 'Wheal Mount just doesn't feel like this at all.'

'Does Wheal Mount have — guests?' She didn't want to say the word "ghosts", just in case Laurie or Viola appreciated the attention and jumped out at them at *that* point.

'Not that I've heard,' Ryan said. 'But who can say?'

They had reached the front door now and Tegan pulled it open, stepping out into the chilly evening air. Only then, did she feel she could breathe properly.

Ryan had his van parked in the staff bays and he drove them the short distance to the White Lady in the basic but apparently cosy vehicle, and, luckily, the pub had a vacancy. By the time Tegan had checked in and dropped her stuff off in the room, Ryan had managed to grab a table in the corner and there was a large glass of red wine in front of her seat, and a pint of real ale in front of Ryan.

'Just guessed at what you might like.' Ryan shrugged. 'I think you had a bottle of red at some event in Glasgow. I don't know — it was a while ago . . .'

'Red wine is fine. Thanks. Next round's on me.' No way was Tegan letting Ryan buy her drinks all night, like they were on a date or something. This was strictly two colleagues who'd had ridiculous experiences at the same place and were bonding over the horror of it all.

'That works for me,' said Ryan, and seemed to visibly relax a little. Maybe he'd been thinking the same thing. 'Maybe after we've had our second, we can have a look at the book.' He half smiled. 'We might be a bit more relaxed by then.'

'I actually feel wound up as tight as a bobbin.'

Ryan grinned. 'That's an old-fashioned phrase!'

'Oh, God!' Tegan took a slug of her wine. 'I seriously hope I'm not morphing into our Edwardian Dollar Princess!'

'If you are,' said Ryan, matching her with a slug of his ale, 'start worrying if I quote romantic poetry at you and then try to rewrite history.'

* * *

Ryan had never thought, in a million years, that he'd be finding himself sitting in a country pub with Tegan Burton on a Friday night, not sniping at her nor having her snap at him. It was a relief, actually. This job would be so much more difficult if they maintained that awful attitude towards one another.

And it seemed that they had bonded, willingly or not, over some people who had lived over a century ago.

Which reminded him. 'Did you keep a copy of the magazine link in your emails? We could try to match the people in the photos to the characters in the album.'

'I did better than that,' she said with a grin. 'I downloaded the photos after I sent them to that Ianthe person. I'll pull them up in a second. But I'll get the next round in anyway and then we can settle down.'

'Good idea.'

He watched her head to the bar, and was impressed at how Tegan managed to weave her way between the people propping up the bar and emerge not too long after with two glasses. The people parted like the Red Sea for her — she just had that sort of confidence. *That* was the Tegan he remembered from Glasgow.

'Here we go.' She put the drinks on the table and sat down, scraping her chair a little as she moved it closer to him.

He pulled the photo album towards them and opened it up as she clicked through her phone to find the wedding pictures.

They spent a pleasant half hour or so comparing the photos. Elsie was easy — she was the witch in the middle of the Macbeth shot and looked just as radiant in her wedding photograph.

'I'm not sure who those other two girls are,' said Tegan. 'I'm guessing at Holly and Pearl. She was besties with them.'

'They aren't on the wedding group,' said Ryan. 'But that little girl is — and so is the dog.'

They both smiled at the little cat and the cheerful-looking mongrel.

'I'm not sure who they are,' said Tegan. 'I don't know enough about the family history yet.' She blushed. 'Which is shit to admit when you're in charge of the history side of the arts centre.'

'You're new to the post,' said Ryan, surprised on some level that he was sticking up for Tegan . . . and she was admitting to not being very good at something.

'Yeah. But I bet you know more about your family at Wheal Mount than I do about mine at Pencradoc.'

'They're the same family, really.' Ryan grinned. He pointed at the four blonde girls in the wedding photos — the four who were not Viola, because God knew they were both pretty familiar with what she looked like now. 'Those are my girls. Clara, Mabel, Lucy and Nancy.' He pointed at them from tallest to smallest.

They flicked through the album until they found the pages with the girls on to compare them.

'That one must be Louis' brother,' said Tegan, pointing at the apparent best man. 'He looks like Louis.'

'He's not in the photo album,' said Ryan. 'But that guy is.' He indicated a dark-haired man who wasn't Laurie. Again, he knew enough to know who Laurie was.

'Those must be Elsie's brothers and sisters, then,' said Tegan, looking at the sea of genetically blessed people. 'Again, God, I don't know their names.'

'And I don't know who this lot are.' Ryan studied two boys and a girl who didn't look like anyone else in the wedding photo, but were at the party. 'God, we're useless.' He laughed. 'How are we still employed?'

'I have no idea!' Tegan laughed with him.

And it was while they were both obviously having a good time, that Ryan heard a delighted, yet half-curious voice speak. 'Well, isn't this nice! Good to see you both networking.'

Shit.

'Sybill. Hello. And, um, hello, Coren.'

Sure enough, it was their employers, walking into the White Lady hand in hand.

'Are we okay to sit here?' asked Sybill pleasantly. 'Place is a bit busy tonight.'

Tongue-tied, Ryan nodded and out of the corner of his eye he saw Tegan subtly move her seat away from him a fraction to make it look a little less cosy.

'What can I get you all to drink?' asked Coren, equally pleasantly. Ryan had the feeling that he was trying to stifle a laugh.

Tegan and Ryan muttered their requests and sat in silence as Sybill fussed around and sat down. 'Coren got your message,' she said to Tegan. 'Said you were staying at a friend's tonight. And then we saw Ryan's van in the car park here, and wondered what he was doing there. And here you are. Together. How lovely.'

'We're working, actually,' said Tegan stiffly. 'As you know, Ryan brought the Halloween things over and we decided to come here and look at them.'

'What's wrong with working in the office?' asked Sybill. 'Although, I must say, it's nice in here.'

'It's got a totally different atmosphere,' muttered Ryan dryly.

Sybill studied him for a moment. 'I suppose it has. Yes. Oh — thanks Coren.' She smiled up as Coren came over with a tray of drinks, then took his own seat. 'Tegan and Ryan tell me they're working tonight.'

'That's good,' said Coren and smiled at them. 'What are you doing?'

'Looking at this photo album,' said Tegan, clearly giving up. 'Trying to spot the people in the wedding photos. But we, um, don't know enough of the people in the family to know them all. We don't know these three people, or this guy. Or the names of Elsie's family. Or the dog or the little girl.'

'We know practically nothing,' added Ryan miserably.

'Don't worry about it. It's a big family,' said Sybill. 'Took us a while to work our people out, didn't it?' She looked at Coren and something unspoken passed between them, which was gone in an instant.

'Yes. It took way too long. Can we have a look? Maybe we can help.'

'Sure.' Tegan pushed the album and her phone over to them. 'The article it relates to is linked there too if you want to read that first. We know the Wheal Mount girls, the bride and groom, the best man, but we don't know his name. We know Viola and Laurie—' there was a pause, which, unless you were aware of the situation, you wouldn't know exactly how weighted it was — 'and that's about it. Oh, the maid of honour — I think that's Elsie's sister. Dunno which one though.'

'Thank you!' Sybill and Coren bent over the phone, read the article, clicked back onto the photo and flicked through the album pages, punctuated by agreeable noises and nods.

'Okay, so this might help,' said Sybill, eventually. She pointed at the wedding photos. 'Marigold and Biscuit — Elsie and Louis' daughter, and Elsie's dog. Huge scandal, not surprised the magazine didn't expand on the relationship. Why tarnish Miss Viola Arthur from New York with an English scandal? Fabian, Elsie's best friend — went to Paris and fell in love with a wonderful man by all accounts. Edward, Albert and Evie — Lily Valentine's children. Isolde, she's the maid of honour. That's Medora, Clem, Enyon and Arthur. Elsie's other brothers and sisters. And Drew, Louis' brother. How does all that sound?'

Ryan was stunned and looked at Sybill. 'That sounds great, but how on earth did you know all of that?'

Sybill half smiled. 'When you've been involved with the Pencradoc family as long as we have, you learn a few things along the way. Is there anyone else you need us to identify?'

'These two from the witches' picture,' said Tegan.

'Easy. Holly and Pearl. And those chaps at the end of the album are Noel, Ernie and Sam. Holly and Pearl's husbands, and Viola's brother.'

'Wow. Thank you,' Tegan replied. 'It all — makes sense — now.'

'Splendid. Happy to help.' Sybill sat back in her chair. 'So — where does your friend live?' she asked Tegan. 'Is she local? Or is *he* local?'

'Quite local,' Tegan replied vaguely. 'I mean nothing is set in concrete yet. I'm waiting for her to confirm it's all okay.' She retrieved her phone and waved it around, as if she was indeed waiting for a call. Ryan bit his lip and dipped his head, frightened he would start laughing quite inappropriately.

'I see. And Ryan — are you staying in the car park tonight?' asked Sybill. 'I mean, with your van being here and all that? And . . .' She nodded towards his empty glasses. Gosh, there were three in front of him now . . . 'You're obviously not driving.'

'No. Not driving tonight,' he said. 'Heading home in the morning.'

Coren chipped in. 'You could always stay at Pencradoc. We've got the Retreat rooms free. There aren't any sessions booked in this weekend.'

'No, thanks,' Ryan said hurriedly. 'The van is fine. Absolutely *fine*.'

'Hmm.' Sybill studied him and he felt his neck growing uncomfortably warm beneath his t-shirt. 'Has anyone told you, actually, that you look a bit like Laurie Teague, Ryan? The likeness is quite astonishing when you see those photos. I didn't realise before.'

'Not something we've — I've — noticed,' he said, glancing at Tegan as she dropped her head and looked extremely interested in whatever was on her phone at that precise moment in time.

'Okay. Well, maybe it is best if you don't stay at Pencradoc tonight,' said Sybill. 'Either of you. I know it can sometimes be intense if you're living the job.'

'Exactly,' said Ryan.

'Very true,' added Tegan.

Ryan was just about to breathe a sigh of relief that he didn't have to explain himself away any more tonight, when Sybill threw her curveball in. 'Oh, I've been in touch with Ianthe Shelley and on Monday I'm going to book your tickets to London — the pair of you — to go and see how Elsie's wedding dress is getting on. I'll book them for after the Halloween event, so you can go up closer to Christmas. You can check out where Elsie used to live if you want. There's not much of it left now, but it might give you more of a sense of her as well, along with the church she got married in and all the rest.'

'Should be nice near Christmas,' said Coren. 'Get you in the festive mood for our work. I might ask you to try to nab some ideas from the Hyde Park Winter Wonderland.' He grinned, then looked at Sybill. 'Think our budget'll stretch to any of that?'

'Absolutely not!' said Sybill, smiling back at him.

They began to talk about other things relating to Pencradoc and Wheal Mount, and joking with one another about various things.

But Ryan didn't hear half of it — all he was hung up on was the phrase: "On Monday I'm going to book your tickets to London — the pair of you."

And, when he cast a quick glance at Tegan to see if she had picked that up as well, he could tell by the look on her face, and the slightly slack jaw and the trepidation in her eyes that, yes, she had heard that too.

224

It looked as if they were going to be in each other's enforced company in London near Christmas.

But, strangely, the thought of that didn't bother him half so much as it would have done a few weeks ago. Tegan was actually turning into someone he thought he might like to spend a bit of time with. He glanced at her again and this time she caught his eye. Her expression changed and the trepidation left her face, and a smile took the place of that anxious look she'd had . . .

And he chanced a smile back at her and her smile grew wider, and he thought that she might not be as bothered as she would have been a few weeks earlier either.

And that felt pretty good.

CHAPTER TWENTY-SIX

1911

Unsurprisingly, Laurie thought, Elsie had decided not to host a traditional wedding reception. Instead, the wedding party went to Claridge's for afternoon tea and, to the boys' delight, lots and lots of cake.

First of all, though, they had to suffer the indignity of wedding photographs. Laurie felt he looked particularly stiff and unpleasant on them, his habitual scowl the expression of the day. Probably because he didn't have the opportunity to spend any more time alone with Viola. He kept glancing at her, though, all the while wishing it was just the two of them here.

The photographer seemed to be a perfectionist and even Elsie started to get annoyed — she was, after all, a keen photographer herself. 'Natural photographs are *so* much better,' Laurie heard her mutter to Louis at one point, all the while fixing a smile on her lovely face. If you saw the pictures afterwards, unless you knew Elsie extremely well, you'd not understand how irritated she was becoming.

'Excuse me, Miss Arthur, can you confirm you are maid of honour here today?' There was seemingly a reporter lurking nearby, his American accent thicker even than Viola's. 'The New York socials will be *delighted* to see this report. Say, Mr Photographer, I'd be interested in buying some of these shots. Just name your price.'

"Mr Photographer" initially bristled, but looked interested and afterwards they went off together — possibly to discuss prices.

Viola had not had the chance to respond to the reporter, though.

'I swear,' Laurie heard her say to Pearl, once they were taking their seats at Claridge's. 'If that report goes out and says I'm maid of honour, I'll come back and haunt the fellows who think that!'

Laurie, from his table too far away from her, could see the pent-up rage in her face and it softened his heart towards her again. She and he were very alike in some ways. That afternoon in Russell Square had definitely changed his opinion of her, and, despite his proclamations of not being very gallant and all the rest, he wanted to do something to make her see him in a different light. Because he was still afraid that she might not see him as Laurie, a flawed Byronic-hero type, who could be bad-tempered and speak without thinking, but deep down, actually, he wanted to tell her how he felt. How he realised he now felt and how, perhaps, he had felt since they'd first bumped into each other that day outside the toy store in Bodmin.

He fiddled with the cuffs of his rather fancy wedding shirt, while tuning in to a conversation Elsie was having with their mother.

'I think we'll come to Pencradoc on Christmas Eve,' she was saying. 'It will be Marigold's first Christmas there and we want it to be incredibly special for her.'

'Oh, that will be delightful!' their mother replied. 'She'll love it. Our first family Christmas with her. We'll be decorating the tree on Christmas Eve and we'll leave the star for her to put on top. It's always been the tradition that the youngest Pencradoc does it, although I think Arthur might be a little put out that it's not his job this year.'

Elsie laughed. 'Oh, we'll let Marigold have her time this year. After all . . .' She let her voice taper away and flushed. But Zennor placed her hand on Elsie's and said, 'It's all right, darling. We'll let her do it again next year because her little brother or sister won't be quite big enough, will they.'

'Indeed.' Elsie replied, flushing even pinker. 'Quite.'

Laurie dipped his head and hid a smile. And there it was. *Congratulations, Elsie and Louis, then.* He wasn't quite sure why Elsie hadn't revealed that news earlier, if he was frank. But then she had kept Marigold secret for three years — even from Louis. God knew how she'd done it but perhaps old habits died hard, even with Lady Elsie Pencradoc.

Then, as if she was changing the subject quite quickly, Elsie rushed in with her next question, which made Laurie jerk his head up and stare at her. 'Do you think we could ask Louis' parents, and Pearl and Holly and everyone as well? Just for part of the day, perhaps?' she asked hopefully.

'I don't see why not.' Zennor smiled at her daughter. 'I'm sure Louis' parents are just as anxious to spend Christmas with their granddaughter as we are, and it will be lovely to have them at Pencradoc. And I did hear that Viola and Sam were to spend Christmas with Pearl and Ernie. They said they might even come to midnight mass with us, so Viola and Sam experience a proper Cornish Christmas this year. We can't promise snow, of course. Not in Cornwall — but we can certainly be merry otherwise.'

Laurie sat up straighter. That was certainly good news. Obviously, the fact that Elsie, Louis and Marigold would be part of Christmas at Pencradoc, but also that Viola might be there as well. And, even more splendidly, that they would be there at midnight mass in the little church in Pencradoc village that the family had been attending for more years than anyone could count. The church had always, he knew, held an odd sort of fascination to Elsie — her father's first wife, along with her father, Ellory, the duke who had preceded Jago, were buried there.

Laurie cast a glance at Elsie, catching her profile alongside his own father's, and, possibly, for the first time, he saw how similar they were . . . He blinked. It was rather obvious, really, when you saw something like that. Perhaps there *was* something in those rumours after all, then . . .

When he was very young, he remembered asking his mother why Elsie had a title and he didn't, and was his father not as important as Elsie's? Zennor had smiled and replied that in her eyes all her children were equal and equally loved, and nobody was as important to her as Laurie's father and Laurie and his brothers and sisters.

The response had satisfied him at the time and he had thought no more of it. But now, as an adult, it made him wonder a little more than he possibly should as to the intricacies of Zennor's response . . .

He pushed the thought out of his mind. It really didn't matter. What mattered was the fact that Viola would be at Pencradoc church on Christmas Eve. And he would be there as well.

He looked across the room and saw her at a table with Pearl, Ernie, Holly, Noel and Sam. The children were with them and it was clearly a noisy, happy meal. Viola had, apparently, given up on her hairstyle and her long fair hair was now in a plait, hanging down her back, the red, green and gold ribbons wound through it.

Almost as if she could sense him watching her, she turned and looked at him. For another moment, they caught each other's eyes and he tentatively smiled. She smiled back — also tentatively, and then, after another moment, she turned back to her family and friends.

Laurie, though, was still smiling — he must look rather stupid, he thought, smiling at nothing. So he forced the expression off his face and replaced it with his more usual semi-scowl.

'You quite all right?' Fabian, who was sitting next to him, asked. 'Do you need more champagne? Or more cake?' He nodded at the younger boys who were manfully chewing their way through some enormous slices of fruit cake.

'What? No. Thank you.'

'Fair enough. Just let me know if you do need anything. I'm damn sure I'm having more champagne. It's dreadfully good.'

'Enjoy it! That's what it's there for.'

Fabian nodded his agreement and poured a glass, and Laurie twiddled with the annoying shirt cuff again — the sleeve was far too long and far too flouncy for his liking, and would *definitely* be more suited to a romantic hero such as Byron or Keats or Shelley. Then he paused for a moment and a plan began to formulate and then crystallise in his mind . . .

'Actually, old man, you could help me,' he said to Fabian.

'Fire away. Anything at all. Just ask.'

So Laurie did.

* * *

It was Christmas Eve! The most magical day of the year, as far as Viola was concerned. Obviously, when she was younger, she much preferred Christmas Day, with all the food and the gifts and the music and the company . . . But as an adult, and, more specifically, an aunt ensconced for a few days among four small nieces and nephews, she was far more aware of how special Christmas Eve actually was.

That was the day the tree went up — or rather the trees, plural — at Elton Lacy, because there was one in the hallway, one in the morning room, one in the dining room, one in the nursery . . . the whole day seemed a mess of greenery and candles and baubles, and then it was story time for the children as they imagined a world inhabited by dancing sugar-plums, miniature reindeer and a jolly old fellow called St Nicholas coming to call on them at midnight. That book had been rapidly pulled off the nursery bookshelf, to replace the story Viola had originally begun to tell them, as *The Snow Queen* had resulted in four pairs of eyes getting rounder and rounder, and then wails of horror at the fact the little boy was trapped with the evil queen and bad things were happening.

Viola was appalled. She had never been scared of the story like that, but then she'd certainly not been as sensitive a child as these four treasures seemed to be.

She must have been an awful, awful little girl!

After the story — the *nice* story — there were some slight tantrums by the twins as they found that their stockings were not hung up on the fireplace in *exactly* the same way, so that had to be rectified before they were chased good-naturedly off to bed by Sam, who then had to prance around the night nursery reciting, "'Now, Dasher! now, Dancer! now Prancer and Vixen! On, Comet! on Cupid! on Donner and Blitzen!'" as the children clapped along in time.

When they had finally been settled and had asked for the fifth time would Father Christmas land on the roof atop of their nursery, Viola was relieved to back out of the night nursery with her brother, and leave Pearl and Ernie in there to give final kisses before they all went to Pencradoc for midnight mass.

'Jeepers,' Viola said to Sam as he helped her on with her heavy winter coat. 'How do parents *deal* with small people?'

'Practice, I guess,' he said with a laugh. 'What are you betting that it's chaos at Pencradoc as well?'

'I shall bet the coal from my Christmas stocking.' She grinned. 'I think I'm probably on the naughty list, so I don't expect anything else in there. Anyway, it's just Marigold, so it'll be a little calmer I think — unless Enyon and Arthur have wound her as tight as a bobbin, of course.'

'They may have done. But hopefully it'll be the older people at midnight mass, so we may escape the worst of it.'

'Hopefully.' They made their way outside and were soon joined by Pearl and Ernie as they waited for the carriage that would take them to Pencradoc. When it finally came to the door, Viola gasped with delight as even the carriage and the horses had been decorated festively.

'Oh, Pearl! This is your doing. It has to be!' she said in delight, fingering the tiny sleigh bells and ivy wound around the door handles.

'It most certainly is.' Pearl smiled. 'I've heard that there could be snow tonight, so I thought what better way to travel than in a fine-and-dandy Christmas carriage.'

'My car,' muttered Ernie. 'It would get us there more quickly.'

'But *would* it really?' asked Pearl. 'And could four of us fit in it comfortably? Perhaps not, darling.'

Ernie, knowing the truth of her statement, said nothing and tucked his chin further into his overcoat. Viola hid a smile. She knew how proud Ernie was of his car, but she too could see the logic — and the magic — of travelling in that beautiful carriage on Christmas Eve.

Eagerly, she clambered in and made space for Pearl to sit next to her, while the men sat opposite. And with a lurch and a clip-clop of hooves — but perhaps not the "prancing and pawing of each little hoof" the children might have been waiting for — they were on their way to Pencradoc!

'Oh!' As they headed down the well-lit drive — because, again, *someone* had had the foresight to put lanterns on the driveway — Viola saw some small flakes of snow begin drifting into the lamplight. Not enough to cover the ground yet, perhaps, because the little flakes were melting onto the surface of the driveway, but, of course she was hopeful that it would settle tonight and complete the magic.

No. Actually, that would not complete the magic.

Something else would — her secret Christmas wish. It seemed foolish now she was an adult, yet . . .

Pearl leaned over to her and whispered. 'It's the first snowfall of the season — have you made your secret wish yet? Your heart's desire wish?'

'Honey, it snowed when I was in London,' Viola replied. 'So technically it's not the first snowfall of the season for me.' But still, she smiled out into the night.

'But it's the first snowfall of our season down here,' said Pearl. Her hand crept over the seat and she took Viola's and squeezed it. 'You gotta try.'

Viola lied. 'There's nothing I really want to wish for.'

'Sure there is,' replied her sister. 'I haven't known you all your life to not know when you're lying.'

Viola's smile widened as she remembered someone else saying something similar about their sister. 'Sure,' she said mildly.

But she had to try. She actually, really had to try.

Didn't she?

So she closed her eyes and she wished her wish.

CHAPTER TWENTY-SEVEN

Present

It felt like ancient history now, so close to Christmas, but Tegan couldn't stop mentally congratulating herself — and Ryan — on the Halloween event. It had gone extremely well. The pumpkin trail had been well-received by the families and the temporary exhibition of the Halloween-party artefacts had gone down equally well. Once the witch's hat, the silver rope, Biscuit's ghost outfit and the cat outfit had been checked over and tidied up a little by some experts, they'd formed the centrepiece in a case in the morning room.

Tegan had managed to get some of the photos blown up for display as well — the main ones being Elsie, Holly and Pearl doing their Macbeth thing, and of course Marigold and Biscuit were there in A3 size as well. In fact, the exhibition was accompanied by crazily spooky music, the occasional childish giggle and the odd bark from an unseen dog, which Tegan considered genius.

Tegan herself had been entranced at the detail on the reproductions. She hadn't intended to use the ones of Viola and Laurie, but, possibly against her better judgement, she'd put those digital files in for enlargement as well. She'd told herself it was international relations of a kind — an American friend of the family and the traditions associated with Halloween coming with her to Pencradoc. The letter from Pearl to Elsie had been included too.

At the last moment, she'd added Laurie's soldier photograph to the files as well, along with Fabian's. The addition of Laurie's soldier picture had given a poignant reminder to the viewer, she'd thought, that those had been the days before the War and things would change for that generation of young people in unthinkable ways. Fabian had been a famous war artist, so that had been the reason he'd gone in there too. It had also been a nod to Merryn's idea about the World War One exhibition that she, Tegan, had dismissed. She felt a bit guilty now that she'd refused to do it. Truth be told, it had seemed like too much work — but she acknowledged, her original reasons still stood. A wedding was so much nicer.

She wondered if part of the reason she'd been so against the idea in the first place, though, was because she'd known, on some level, that it would have involved her much more closely with Viola and Laurie, and that was something she hadn't been at all ready to do back in September.

'The Lost Generation,' Merryn had said when she'd brought little Rosie to Pencradoc, the baby dressed as a tiny, round pumpkin. 'Elsie knew Rupert Brooke as well — he was at the Slade when she was. He was one good-looking chap, but rather a tenuous link to Pencradoc, so maybe just as well you didn't add him.'

Tegan remained silent. She hadn't even considered Rupert Brooke. She knew who he was, of course — even *she* had a knowledge of famous war poets. But she'd had no idea of his link to Elsie.

'However, Rupert certainly wasn't at this party,' continued Merryn. 'But goodness me, I bet they had a blast that evening! And who's this? Viola? I recognise her from that sketch.' She pointed to the picture of Vampiress Viola. 'But she looks different in the photo — more like . . .' She paused for a moment, then looked at Tegan. 'More like you, actually.' Merryn grinned. 'How unsurprising. I'm supposed to look like Alys, Elsie's aunt. And you look like her friend. We were clearly meant to work here.'

'Hmm,' Tegan said, all the while thanking her lucky stars that Ryan wasn't there for Merryn to comment on how much he looked like Laurie.

Ugh.

But as Tegan now acknowledged, that event was ancient history and today she was in London with Ryan.

At the platform, waiting for him, she had anticipated her usual "ugh" reaction to happen when she thought of the day ahead with him, and it didn't come.

Surprising.

But, to be honest, she'd felt a lot happier over the last few weeks working with Ryan and exchanging emails, calls and visits. The "ugh"ness had definitely dispersed and she felt a lot happier because of it. And he'd definitely helped the Halloween exhibit work well. So there could, actually, be worse things to be doing on this chilly December morning than being in a Christmassy London with Ryan.

He had the address of Ianthe's studio on his phone and as they headed in the general direction of Covent Garden, Tegan could certainly feel her spirits lifting. Ryan was dressed from head to toe in black. His scarf was black and his gloves were black and he had a huge, long, black overcoat on, atop of big, clunky, metal-buckled boots — black, of course. He was, it seemed, still a goth at heart, even though he'd changed his hair, told her it had been an "art student phase" and they were six years down the line from Glasgow. It honestly made her smile at the irony — because she, on the other hand, was dressed in pastel-blue trousers, a long white coat that was made of bobbly white wool, a pale-blue-and-white pom-pom hat and navy-blue ankle boots. They must have made a bizarre sight walking down the street together, but, then, this was London, this was almost Covent Garden and this was almost Christmas. So, she supposed, they could literally be anyone heading to the capital to do some Christmas shopping and enjoy the Hyde Park Winter Wonderland.

'It's just along here,' Ryan said, pointing along a side street. 'Sybill said she was brilliant at what she did. I'm not sure I'm the best placed of the two of us to consider fashion and what's good or bad.' He gestured to his outfit. 'One colour and one colour only. That's largely my wardrobe. So I'm pretty glad she forced us both to come.'

'Yes. We were kind of cornered, though, weren't we?'

Ryan laughed, clearly thinking back to that night in the White Lady. 'We had no chance. Once Sybill saw us in there, I think she thought we'd be safe to send off on an outing together. She could maybe see we'd called a truce.'

'A truce. Of course.' Tegan smiled. 'I have to say, thanks again for the Halloween stuff. The exhibition got some great feedback.'

'And so it should. Everything's back at Wheal Mount now for next time.' He held up his forefinger. 'Correctly filed under H-P.'

'Halloween at Pencradoc.'

'Of course.' Neither one of them acknowledged, though, that the enlarged photos of Laurie and Viola were hidden in the Pencradoc attics with some other exhibition things from older events. It had seemed wrong, somehow, to remove them from the house.

Also, they both found the photos rather eerie to look at, almost as if they were staring into their own souls. Ryan didn't want them anywhere near where he'd be working, e.g. in the Wheal Mount archives. And Tegan didn't want them anywhere near where she could stumble upon them accidentally. Hence, they were well away from her office and she hoped they — and their associated ghosts — would haunt up there for a little while instead.

'This is it.' Ryan came to a halt outside a dark-blue door and she pressed the buzzer. A pleasant voice answered, the door clicked open and soon they were inside, climbing up some steps to the first floor of the building.

'Hi!' A young woman Tegan assumed was Ianthe Shelley greeted them with a smile. Her hair was in a messy bun and she was wearing a patchwork minidress, red socks and high-top trainers. 'Welcome to where the magic happens. I'm Ianthe, although you probably guessed. And, yes, that is my real name and, yes, I was named after Percy Bysshe Shelley's daughter. That's usually what people want to ask me. Tegan and Ryan, yes?' They both nodded. 'Cool. Over here.' She led them to the other side of the room, where what Tegan assumed was a tailor's dummy was covered with a white sheet. 'I've done my best with her,' she said. 'The pictures and sketches you sent were really helpful. It was good to have all those different angles. She's all ready for you. I've also spoken to my friend who's a florist and I can get you an evergreen headdress and bouquet made up to match Elsie's. It should last the length of your exhibition. Is that okay? I'll be sorting out delivery tomorrow. Unless you want to take her with you today?' Ianthe grinned, seeing their expressions. Tegan imagined hers must match Ryan's. 'No? Too high risk on the train? Don't blame you!'

'Um, we just want to see how it's getting on today. We've got some other things to — do — in London, soooo . . .' said Tegan quickly.

'It's fine. Just kidding. I'd never trust anything so precious to an average person. Not that you two are average, mind — just saying.' Ianthe took hold of the corner of the sheet. 'Are you ready?'

Tegan nodded and Ianthe whisked the sheet off the dummy.

'Oh, my word!' Tegan was mesmerised. 'It's — beautiful. Absolutely stunning. May I touch it?'

'Yes, of course. If your hands are clean?'

Tegan nodded that they were and she touched the delicate fabric. She could see the original sheath dress from the sketch, pulled in under the bust with some sort of overskirt that stuck out into those frothy layers. There was a sash tied under the bust and the length was just above where she guessed the wearer's ankles would be.

But there was just something . . . something that wasn't quite right with it. She couldn't put her finger on it, but she knew that something needed to change.

'Ryan . . .' She didn't need to say any more. He was as stunned by the dress as she was. 'What are you thinking?'

'The sash,' he said, after a moment. 'The sash should be red.'

* * *

Ryan didn't know where that comment had come from. But he knew, even as he marvelled at the dress, that the sash should, indeed, be red.

That was the way he remembered it.

'Am I right, Tegan?' he asked quietly. 'Is that the way you — interpreted it?'

'I did.' She nodded, looking just as confused as he knew he did.

'Red?' Ianthe stared at them. For one horrible moment, Ryan thought she was going to complain and shout at them, and refuse to release the frock . . . but, surprisingly, she nodded briskly. 'That's easily sorted. Give me a moment.'

She went over to a wall full of shelves containing all sorts of materials and fabrics. Ryan knew nothing about types of fabric — if it was shiny, it was likely satin. If it was fluffy, it was likely velvet. That was, basically, where his knowledge started and ended. But he could appreciate all the different colours laid out like a bag of tempting sweeties.

'This one, I think.' Ianthe pulled a ream off the shelf, cut a length off it and brought it back to the dummy. Expertly, she folded it into a long sash shape, removed the green one and tied the red one efficiently under the dummy's bust. 'There.' She gave it a couple of tweaks and it hung down the gown as if it had always been there.

'Perfect,' said Tegan.

Ryan nodded. 'Exactly right.'

'Cool. I'll hem it up and that'll be in the package as well.' Ianthe smiled. 'All happy with it?'

'It's . . . wonderful,' said Tegan. 'Truly it is.'

'Great. Can you hang around while I finish up the paperwork, invoices, all that boring stuff?' asked Ianthe. 'It's mainly a Pencradoc thing — for Tegan, I suppose. Is that okay with you, Ryan? Are you happy to stay with us?'

Tegan looked at Ryan — they did have other things to do, but, really, it was no problem. He didn't particularly want to do any of those other things on his own, either.

'I'm in no real hurry,' Ryan heard himself say. He gestured for the women to go ahead of him into Ianthe's office. He realised shortly afterwards though, that what he *really* wanted to say, was, "Sybill, why on *earth* did you make us come here together?"

Because he had the feeling that that excuse for the viewing of the dress was simply a ruse. To get them to spend some time together before Elsie's wedding.

No.

He corrected himself.

Before Elsie's wedding *exhibition*.

To distract himself, he picked up his phone and checked his emails. There was one from the Glasgow gallery and his stomach somersaulted. He clicked into it and read it.

Good afternoon, it said. *We are pleased to advise that you have been shortlisted for the role at the new gallery and we will be arranging an interview with you in the near future . . .*

CHAPTER TWENTY-EIGHT

1911

Over at Pencradoc, much the same Christmas Eve scenario was playing out with excited children. Marigold was, obviously, the focus of the entire day. She had turned up with her parents and Uncle Fabian, rosy-cheeked and be-mittened, scrambling out of the carriage and falling up the steps in her haste to get into Pencradoc.

A good, caring licking from Biscuit soon had her back on her feet, the holes in her stockings forgotten, along with her grazed knees, as the dog urged her into the house.

Laurie, leaning on the doorframe, arms folded, was smiling in his own quiet way at their antics. He'd already been out and about, doing some last-minute errands, but had made sure he'd returned in time for the newlyweds' arrival. He followed them in after he'd greeted his sister and her new husband (husband! Goodness gracious), and almost fell over Arthur, who was standing manfully in the hallway, legs planted far apart, a serious expression on his face. He had his hands behind his back, but, as Marigold ran up to him, he produced from its hidden place the family star for the top of the tree.

The tree had already been largely decorated — mainly by Isolde and Medora who felt that the boys could not do it *quite* as nicely as they could — but the top of the tree was naked, waiting for the youngest member of the family to finish the task.

'Marigold Louisa Ashby,' said Arthur importantly. 'It gives me great pleasure to hand the Pencradoc Christmas Star over to you.' He bowed and held the star out.

'Thank you!' Marigold's eyes were wide. She curtsied very prettily and took the star. 'But I do not think I can reach the tree. I may have to put it somewhere else.'

She looked at Biscuit thoughtfully and Elsie stepped in. 'Darling, your papa will lift you up. Biscuit does not want the star attached to him, I promise.'

'Because your mama did that when she was small as well,' said Laurie. 'And I was even smaller, but I can remember that Biscuit was not a very happy dog.'

'She only did it so that I couldn't put it on the tree,' said Clem. 'She was cross with me that day.'

'Hush, hush, hush,' said Elsie, flapping her hands around. 'Once Biscuit had calmed down, it was quite all right.'

Laurie could remember Biscuit racing around, trying to shake the annoying object off his head, knocking little Nancy over in the process. All the Wheal Mount girls had been there that Christmas and Nancy had been just small enough to get under everyone's feet and in everyone's way. He didn't know how Elsie had attached it to Biscuit, but the dog had caused even more chaos than was usual for a Pencradoc Christmas Eve.

So, on this particular Christmas Eve, Louis very gallantly lifted his small daughter up in the air and allowed her to place the star on top of the tree, and everyone clapped and cheered, and Marigold — her mother's daughter all over — curtsied again.

Stories, games, hot drinks and food ensued, after which Marigold was safely settled in bed — and Laurie was once again lurking in the hallway, peering out of the open door, with one eye on the clock . . .

Because a certain carriage was supposed to be coming to Pencradoc tonight and he really wanted to be there to welcome the occupants.

'Everything good, old fellow?' Fabian appeared with a glass of sherry in his hand and another glass for Laurie.

'It will be. I hope,' said Laurie, gratefully accepting the drink. 'Just a few things I need to get right first.'

Fabian grinned and clapped Laurie on the back. 'Have no fear. I'm here. And look — it's beginning to snow. Surely that's a good sign!' Fabian was spending Christmas with the family as he had a somewhat difficult relationship with his sister, the only family he had. Elsie had called the sister a "damned bigot" to Laurie and had absolutely no time for her. She was very unlike the Pencradoc clan, who accepted anyone for whatever they were.

Fabian was a good friend and Laurie knew that tonight was a night he'd be relying on his friend, and he crossed his fingers, hoping it would all work out.

'I say,' said Fabian, peering out of the door over Laurie's shoulder. 'That can't be them, can it?'

'Not unless they've walked,' said Laurie, watching the lamplit procession coming up the drive towards the house.

As the procession became closer, he saw that it was a group of carol singers. He smiled, remembering the choir he'd seen in London with Viola just a couple of weeks ago.

'Best let everyone know we've got company,' said Laurie and headed back into the house to rally the family. Soon they were all outside Pencradoc, on the top of the steps, listening to the carol singers.

So involved was Laurie in the visit — because of course the musical wassailers then had to be offered a hot spiced drink and it turned out that apparently that was *his* job — that he must have missed what he was waiting for, because once all the drinks had been handed out he felt warm breath on his neck, making a shiver run down his spine. And he turned around and there she was, at his shoulder, smiling.

'They took the carriage straight to the stable — we got off just around there.' She pointed around the corner. 'Didn't want to intrude on the festivities. So we snuck in.'

'Very good,' he said, before he could think or speak or come up with any rational conversation whatsoever. 'I mean — yes — sorry. Good to see you. You're not intruding, not at all. Would you like some warmed cider? Or mulled wine, perhaps?'

'No. Thank you. I think for now I just want to enjoy the music and then head into the warmth.' She shivered despite her warm-looking coat and the inevitable hand muff. 'It's utterly charming out there, what with the snow and everything. But it's still damned cold.'

Laurie couldn't help but smile. The family entertained the wassailers a little longer, then waved them off, and he was just about to offer to escort Viola into the drawing room, where he knew a huge fire blazed, and where soon they'd be lighting the Yule log, but, before he could speak, Isolde and Medora swooped on the girl and bore her away. Sam, he saw, had been adopted by Clem and they were talking earnestly at the bottom of the stairs, and Pearl and Ernie were with Elsie and Louis beneath the Christmas tree in the hallway. Then Louis and Ernie wandered away, into the drawing room.

'Yes,' El was saying. 'Marigold put the star on the tree tonight.' There was a wobble in her voice, though, and Laurie cast a glance over to her. Then El suddenly howled. 'Oh, Pearl! How could I have kept her away so lo-o-o-ong?' Then there was general weeping and a friendly patting of his sister on the arm and murmurs of "there, there", and he, Laurie, shook his head in despair. He knew that women could often become over-emotional when they were in a certain condition, and in this area, it seemed, his sister was very traditional indeed.

He turned his back on the girls and strode purposefully into the drawing room. He checked the clock. They had a few hours before they needed to head to the church. Plenty of time to enjoy supper (his brothers), tell ghost stories (his sisters — Medora already had her Lady Byron dress on) and, of course, light the Yule log.

Laurie privately wondered whether his parents had considered the future traits of their children when they'd named them after such literary characters. Apart from Elsie, of course. She had, apparently, just "looked like" an Elsie.

* * *

Viola didn't think she had ever enjoyed a Christmas Eve so much. They'd all sat down to a noisy, happy supper, and plenty of mulled wine for the adults. The younger people had had ginger beer, with sticks of cinnamon and orange slices floating in it.

Their supper had consisted of a Yule cake each (Arthur had eyed Elsie's up hungrily and she had passed it on to him), mince pies, plum pudding and something very odd and porridge-like, but curiously tasty and filled with almonds and currants, called "furmity". And afterwards, they had retired to the drawing room where she'd witnessed the tradition of the Yule log. Ruan Teague had lit the log, and, she'd been told, the idea was that it would burn until twelfth night.

'Traditionally,' Laurie told her now as they settled down before the fireplace and Enyon ran to switch off the lamps, 'we'd light this before supper, but none of us are particularly traditional at Pencradoc.' She was aware of just how close he was to her, how he'd kept looking at her throughout supper with that funny little scowl on his face — which now she knew did not dictate his temperament — and how he'd made sure he'd been right next to her as they'd walked into the drawing room. And then, of course, he'd sat next to her on the long sofa.

Once the lights were off and all the cheery, festive candles in the room had been blown out, Arthur, the youngest person present (and, apparently, still allowed to do this, even though Marigold had trumped him in the placing of the star on the Christmas tree this year), solemnly lit two long candles from the log.

'Just so Sam and Viola know,' he said, just before igniting the first one. 'You have to be quiet when I do this. You can make a wish, but you have to keep it secret. Then you can talk again when they're on the table over there.' He nodded across the room. 'Then we have to keep the lights off for the rest of the night. But it's all right. Medora is useless and her ghost stories aren't scary at all, so you'll not be scared. And we're not using one of Laurie's about the old duchess and her garden, so you don't have to listen to that either. Not that anyone knows much about Rose. She was Elsie's father's first wife and she is dead, so . . .'

'Arthur . . .' Laurie raised his eyebrows at the boy at the same time as Medora began to shriek a protest, but some harsh shushing from her siblings had quietened her.

Then Arthur did his job and lit the candles: *one, two*.

He carried them over to the table and put them in the candlesticks, and then stood back sombrely. After a moment of watching the flickering lights, he spoke once more. 'The candles are now lit. Your wishes must remain secret. Thank you.' Then he bowed to the candles and Viola was desperate to clap. So, actually, she did. Which, everyone agreed, certainly lightened the mood and made it more appropriate to a magical, snowy Christmas Eve.

'What did you wish for?' asked Pearl innocently.

'Oh, it's a secret,' she said with a smile. But she hoped that, after her wish in the snow and now this one, that her wish would indeed come true.

But there wasn't much time to ponder. After Medora's ghost stories, it would be time to leave for church.

CHAPTER TWENTY-NINE

Present

The paperwork was definitely the dull bit. Seeing the wedding dress had been the exciting part, but Tegan knew that along with the fun stuff there was the work stuff and at least she'd been trusted enough to do this.

She couldn't help but imagine the exhibition in all its glory, with that wonderful dress in the middle of the frozen lake and all the mirrors and things reflecting around the room. Should she, though, have it spinning around, like a musical box, or just somewhere people could walk around it . . . just somewhere it could be walked around, she decided, or it would end up more *Chitty Chitty Bang Bang* than *The Snow Queen* — too much like the bit where Truly Scrumptious did a ballet dance in front of the Baron and the Baroness. Then she remembered the Child Catcher was in that scene as well, and shuddered. It probably wasn't the best thing to put in a family-friendly display.

'Okay, so that's us done,' said Ianthe, bringing her attention back to the present. 'I'll get that sash tidied up and, like we said, I'll get it sent down to you tomorrow.'

'Fantastic. Thanks — we can get it set up in good time at Pencradoc.'

'Send me some photos,' said Ianthe with a smile. 'I like to see my girls *in situ*, if you like.'

'Most definitely.'

They shook hands and headed back into the studio where Ryan was lurking beside the dummy, staring at the dress again. He seemed a million miles away though, and he was certainly scowling.

'Ryan — that's us done,' said Tegan.

'Hmm?' he asked, without looking at her.

'I said, that's us done.'

'Oh! Great.' Ryan turned and quickly smiled at them both. Tegan got a little shockwave of something — she hesitated to call it "desire" — but, heck, when he wasn't scowling and smiled a genuine smile, he was pretty good-looking. 'Um. Thanks for your help, Ianthe.'

'Any time. Give my best to Sybill.'

'Will do,' he replied.

Then, after a final few words, Ianthe walked them to the door and they found themselves on the pavement again, the sharp scent of winter in her nostrils. Unsurprisingly, as, in the time they'd been indoors, the skies had turned grey and promised rain, sleet, snow or a combination of them all.

'What now?' asked Ryan, when the door had closed on them. He looked up at the sky and pulled a face. He was right to pull a face — a gentle drizzle had started. It then became heavier and the clouds seemed to lower and glower at them, taunting them to stay out of doors.

'Elsie's house?' Tegan suggested. 'Or Hyde Park?'

'I think I'd quite like to see where Elsie lived. And it's a bit closer than Hyde Park.' Ryan held up his phone. 'Thank goodness this is waterproof. I was doing some checking when you were with Ianthe. Um. Emails and stuff. And . . . well, directions. We're just under half an hour to Elsie's. Just a bit longer to Hyde Park. On foot, that is.'

'Elsie's, then. I think it would be a nice walk. I love this part of London,' said Tegan. 'I worked at a hotel here one summer. It's a bit vile in the rain, though.'

'We could maybe grab a coffee on the way? We're bound to pass somewhere. This is London, after all.'

'Sounds good.' She was a little surprised at how easily she'd agreed. 'Let's see how far we can get before we drown.'

'Challenge accepted.'

They started off along the path and, despite the rain, chatted remarkably easily about jobs they'd had, and things they'd experienced in them. She found herself telling Ryan about Angelo and how she was expecting him after New Year, but they just needed to confirm the details . . .

Oh.

Guiltily, she realised she hadn't thought about Angelo much over the last couple of days. She wondered if she'd deliberately parked those thoughts in the excitement and horror of the Ballroom Incident, as she'd privately named it. Which, actually, reminded her . . .

'You haven't accepted my friend request yet!'

'Oh, so we're friends now, are we?' Ryan looked down at her and grinned, the drizzly drops of rain sticking to his hair and his black overcoat.

She knew he was teasing and she shrugged nonchalantly. 'Maybe. Maybe that truce is working.'

'It's certainly easier not to fight all the time,' said Ryan. 'I mean, look at us—' he extracted his hand from his pocket and waved it around expansively, '— walking happily around London, not fighting, not sniping and actually communicating with words and things.'

Tegan hunched her shoulders up and wriggled her chin into her scarf. 'It's like we're adulting. It's *weird*.'

'Definitely weird.' Ryan laughed. 'Oh! Look. What's going on over there?'

Tegan followed his nod. They were approaching Russell Square, and, through the haze of mizzle that was rapidly turning London damp and grey, it looked as if there was some activity going on, some sort of Christmas fair, no less.

'Ah! Christmas stuff!' she said. 'Shall we go and have a look? It's not quite Hyde Park, but it looks pretty. We can cut through and then Brunswick Square is just to the left, if I remember correctly.'

They stepped through the gate into the square and Tegan drew up short. It was decorated exactly like a Victorian Christmas or something. Fake snow was piled up and people were milling around dressed in old-fashioned clothing.

A choir was singing and children were running around, weaving in and out of roast-chestnut sellers and mulled-wine carts, the earthy, spiced scent drifting tantalisingly around the stalls.

'Wow.' She stared at it. 'This is amazing!'

Ryan looked up and held his hand out. 'The rain's turned to snow. I'm not sure they'll need the fake stuff for much longer. It'll get covered in the proper stuff before long.'

Tegan stuck the toe of her boot into a snowdrift. 'It's good, though. I wonder where they got it from. It would be good for our wedding exhibition.' She realised immediately that she'd said "our", but decided not to correct herself. Ryan had helped out a lot, she knew that.

Ryan seemed to let it go too. 'It's very effective.' He bent down and picked up a handful of the stuff, experimentally crushing it into a snowball. Then he tossed the snowball towards the edge of the path, where it exploded in a cloud of very realistic snow. 'Bloody good snow indeed.'

They walked further into the square, stepping aside as people walked purposefully towards them, and the carollers sang about the bleak midwinter. Nobody seemed to pay them one iota of attention.

As they got further into the crowd, though, Tegan began to feel a little odd. She couldn't explain it, but it was as if she was invisible. Not really there, not really inhabiting that space. Almost as if she'd stumbled into a dream. If she looked away from someone or something, for example, then looked back, it was all slow motion and jerky, like the reels on a very old spool of film coming back into focus.

She stopped in the middle of the path, looking at a child in a red coat running towards them. The girl had dark curly hair flying loose and made no attempt to avoid her. She didn't even seem to see her.

What would happen, she thought, *if I just stayed here and didn't move . . . ?*

It was a risk she was willing to take and, for some reason, she was prepared to do so. And not because she wanted to hurt the child or see her fall over, or force the little girl to move instead of her, Tegan . . .

Instead, she felt Ryan's hand take hers and tug her out of the way.

'Careful,' he said. 'Nobody wants to end up sitting on their bums in the snow today.'

'Ryan,' she said, carefully. 'I don't think she saw me.'

'Kids are like that,' he said. 'Never take notice of anyone but themselves.' He was smiling as he said it. 'Look at her — she's got a purpose and she knows exactly where she's headed.'

They both turned and watched the girl. She'd slowed to a purposeful trudge.

'Unca Laurie! Viola!' she cried. Two people swung around, obviously hearing the child shout. She began to wave at them, her hand muff hanging at an angle across her body. 'It's fun here! Look at the snow!'

* * *

Ryan's hand was still in Tegan's and he felt her stiffen as much as he did when the child yelled out those names.

Watching the scene unfold, his heart pounding and his stomach churning as he tried to make sense of it all, he saw the little girl storm ahead of a woman dressed in a formal sort of uniform. The child stooped to pick up a pile of snow, just as he'd done. She also made it into a snowball, threw it, then clapped her hands and laughed.

'Marigold Ashby,' said the man she'd approached. He hunkered down and the child ran at him and almost knocked him over as he closed his arms around her. Then he stood up and swung her around before placing her back on the ground. 'Good afternoon.'

The woman with him, with "Unca Laurie", was standing slightly to the side. Small, with fair hair under a warm-looking hat, and her hands encased in a muff, she blinked and looked at the man as if she was seeing him for the very first time.

Then her gaze travelled around the square briefly, a slight look of confusion on her face, and Ryan got a good look at her as she scanned the park past him.

Viola.

It was her. It was definitely her. And Ryan knew that this wasn't the first time he'd seen her, or the first time he'd been in Viola's company — the real Viola, that was. Not the ethereal version that seemed to be hanging around him and Tegan in Cornwall.

In that moment, it was as if all the pieces of a giant jigsaw puzzle had fallen into place. He found himself hanging on to Tegan's hand as if he was scared to let it go. He could feel her fingers digging into his, too.

'They're not real,' he heard her whisper. 'This Christmas fair. It's not — real. Is it?'

Ryan shook his head slowly. 'No. I think it *was* real. For them. But it's not real for *us*.'

'Is it . . . Laurie and Viola?'

'I think so. And Marigold.'

'Then where the hell *are* we?' Tegan sounded scared.

Ryan swallowed back some panic. '1911,' he replied. 'Or thereabouts.'

'Fuck this for a game of soldiers.' Tegan began to pull him back the way they'd come. 'Not surprised the snow's so bloody real!'

Ryan wasn't going to disagree with any of those sentiments. With some difficulty, he tore his gaze away from the group of people whose lives they had somehow gate-crashed and hurried out of the gate they'd come in. All thoughts of his shortlisting and upcoming interview fled from his mind — all he was concerned about was getting out of Russell Square, circa 1911.

Once they were outside and walking really, really quickly away from the place, towards a warm coffee shop and the twenty-first century, he took the chance of looking behind him.

Russell Square was looking just like itself. Slightly grey and soggy, damp benches scattered around it, people walking dogs there, people carrying shopping bags through it . . . just the way it should look today in modern-day Bloomsbury.

Not a scrap of snow anywhere, just a huge Christmas tree in the middle of it, right next to the fountain, decorated with modern fairy lights.

'In here.' Tegan pulled him into a coffee shop — one of the popular chains which was, quite possibly, the best grounding experience he could have hoped for at that particular point in time.

'Good call.'

'I'll get them,' said Tegan. 'I want to do something — normal!'

Ryan didn't argue. He was still half in that life he'd just witnessed and didn't think he'd be able to formulate a sensible request to the smiling barista.

Within a few minutes, Tegan was back with two large coffees — some sort of festive spice version, piled high with whipped cream and marshmallows.

'Don't judge me,' she muttered. 'If I hadn't have given up smoking a few years back, I'd be bloody lighting up right now. This is my vice. Whipped cream and Christmas coffees.'

'Worse ones to have,' he replied. 'Do you want another marshmallow?'

Tegan nodded and he spooned the confection off his drink and plopped it on hers.

'The more sugar the better,' she said. 'I'm not wrong, am I? That really happened there.' She pointed her spoon in the general direction of Russell Square. 'We were at some Christmas fair in the past?'

'It's just weird we both saw it. Having said that, I'm kind of glad you were there. I'm not sure anyone else would believe me.'

Tegan shook her head. 'I can kind of understand it happening at Pencradoc. I mean, I've sort of accepted it now. Viola and Laurie were obviously an item and want us to know about it.'

'We know they were an item — they got married for God's sake!'

'Yes. But . . .' Tegan blushed. 'What if it wasn't all sunshine and roses. Right from the beginning, I mean. Didn't it say somewhere that Elsie wanted them to call a truce before her wedding?'

Ryan nodded slowly. 'Yes. In the letter she sent to Laurie about going to see the dress.'

'And that story you found — didn't he try to rewrite the story of the ball? So they actually enjoyed themselves? Like he'd regretted whatever had happened that night?'

'I guess he did. Tegan, you're quite good at this.'

'Shut up.' He knew she didn't mean it in a bad way, but the comments had relaxed them a bit. 'But if it *was* them we saw just now—'

'It definitely was,' he said drily. 'Looked a bit like us in a period drama, but whatever.' *Because, dear God, it* had *looked like them.* He felt a bit sick again and it wasn't the mountain of cream causing it.

'Okay. Whatever.' She waved her spoon around and showered the table with globs of melting whipped cream. 'If it *was* them, it looked to me as if they'd called that truce when they visited Russell Square. For whatever reason they were there.' Her cheeks were pink and she was tumbling over her words. 'I mean, just consider for a moment,' she said, 'that they were trying to tell us something. They chose to tell us when we were together, at the same time they were together. Kind of.'

'Only we were at the same place, like, over a century later.'

'Stop splitting hairs. You know what I mean.'

'Do I?' asked Ryan. But he thought he did and his heart began to pound. He was looking in her eyes, and, he realised, they were leaning across the table, very close to one another. 'Do you — want to explain what I think you mean.'

'Not really.'

'Are we supposed to be calling a truce?'

'I thought we'd done that.'

'So what do we do next?' Ryan couldn't understand the feelings she was stirring up in him. This was Tegan! His nemesis, the girl he'd disliked so intently at Glasgow that they could barely tolerate the other person breathing the same air.

'Do we — wait and see what happens?'

'That's one way to approach it.'

They stared at one another for a moment more. Then they both jumped as Tegan's phone rang.

'Shit.' She looked at her bag and pulled her phone out. 'Hello? Oh! Coren. Hi. Yeah, yeah. It's gone well. Thanks for checking in — Ianthe sorted the invoice when I was there. Yeah, the evergreens — I agreed that. Is that okay? I know you said I had authority to do whatever was best . . . fantastic . . . thanks . . . oh, brilliant . . .'

Ryan sat back in his seat. The moment, whatever that moment had been or whatever it had been leading up to, was lost.

Ah, well.

He looked at the half-drunk coffee in front of him. There was one lone marshmallow wallowing in the murky liquid, bobbing and turning to and fro. Thank God she'd got that call, actually, because he was sure his next comment was going to be something stupid, like, "do you want another marshmallow?" Good grief, he was useless. He knew in his heart what he wanted to do — and, yes, what those ghosts were actually trying to tell him. But he wanted to choose his moment. And a knee-jerk reaction to a weird, freaky, old-fashioned-Christmas-fair experience was, he considered, not the best time to blurt it all out — to blurt out what he really wanted to say.

What exactly are you waiting for? came a stern, frustrated voice. *What* is *it, man?*

Christmas, he told the voice silently. *I think I'm waiting for Christmas.*

Tegan ended the call and tapped around on her phone for a moment. Ryan wondered whether she was playing for time and transferred his attention to the marshmallow, which was slowly sinking into the coffee. It was better than staring at her, and he absolutely *knew* he was staring at her . . .

'Well now.' She looked up at him and held her phone up. 'Angelo messaged back.' Her face was pale, but her eyes sparked a little with anger or frustration — he couldn't really tell.

'What? Boyfriend Angelo?'

He'd almost forgotten she had a boyfriend.

'Yeah.' She shrugged. 'So — here it is. Remember I was saying we needed to confirm when he was coming over? I asked him *again* when he thought he could make it. Reckons he can't get over here in *January* either. First he says he can't make Christmas, then he says he'll come after New Year. Now he thinks February or March might be more affordable.'

'Ah.' Ryan didn't really know what to say. 'Might it be possible for you to go over there? I'm sure you'll get

256

some holiday entitlement after we've finished the midwinter exhibition.'

'Yeah.' She stared at her phone again, then laid it down, perfectly square in front of her. 'I could. I guess.'

Ryan didn't answer. If she wanted to go, nobody was going to stop her.

'But we could be busy after Christmas, couldn't we? I mean — me and you.' She held his gaze, with huge green eyes he could almost — almost — drown in, if he stared too long into them. 'Easter. Stuff like that to plan. We're sort of vital people. Like — a network.'

Ryan nodded, then opened his mouth. Then closed it again. Then scowled.

'What?' Tegan scowled back at him, then said in a quiet, clipped, snappy tone, 'Has this been too horrendous for you? Don't you think we'd be able to do it again?'

'No! No, I mean, it's been great. It's just . . .' His voice trailed off.

'Just what?'

'Just . . . I don't know if I'll be staying on, is all.' He forced himself to look at her. 'I applied for a job. At Glasgow. Working with Art Deco things and researching the Glasgow Boys in a new gallery that's opening. And we'll be including the Glasgow Girls of course. Don't want to leave them out.'

'What?' She looked genuinely horrified. 'You're going? You're leaving Cornwall?'

He nodded briefly. 'Yes. I think so. I mean — if I get it.'

'Have you been interviewed?' Her voice was almost a whisper.

'Not yet. But I've been shortlisted, so an interview is coming. I should know what's happening soon with it all, anyway. Whether I've got it and stuff. Like, before Christmas.'

'Oh,' was all she said. 'I see.' Then she dropped her gaze, picked up her phone again and scrolled idly. 'Oh.'

'Yeah.'

'Well, if you need any help for the interview, I'm happy to help. God knows I've had plenty of interviews myself over the years.' Then she looked up at him and smiled, and it seemed genuine. 'Not that I'm trying to get rid of you. But I know how much you loved it up there. I'm sure you know what you're doing and it's an amazing opportunity for you.'

'Yeah. It is,' he said. And smiled back at her. 'I might take you up on that offer.'

'Fab.'

'Great.'

Silence.

There wasn't really much else to say.

But, actually, he wasn't really sure of anything anymore.

Not after today.

CHAPTER THIRTY

1911

They walked to church in the village, as was traditional, but Laurie couldn't engineer walking there with Viola — Ruan Teague led the party holding a lantern and Laurie was bringing up the rear with a lantern as well.

Also, Viola was flanked by her brother and her sister, and, besides, he needed to speak to Fabian. So the two men walked together, their feet crunching in the snow, which had come down thicker and faster, and was now, most definitely, settling on the ground.

'Whereabouts will you be sitting?' asked Fabian, the tip of his cigarette glowing red in the darkness.

'I'm going at the back of the church,' Laurie said. 'I'll hang back and the rest of them can have the family pews. It will be utter chaos trying to get everyone settled, so nobody will realise I'm missing.' He grinned at his friend and Fabian laughed.

'You should try that expression more often,' Fabian told him. 'Then perhaps people might smile back at you. Some people in particular.'

'She's actually smiled at me a couple of times tonight,' replied Laurie. 'That's an improvement.'

'Let's see if she's still smiling after midnight mass,' said Fabian.

'Oh, dear Lord. I hope so.' Laurie wasn't quite sure what he would do if she wasn't.

* * *

They reached the church at Pencradoc village and filed into the old building to join the villagers. Viola was entranced by the candles and the soft music that welcomed them in, and the greenery that wreathed the pillars and the old plaques on the wall. One caught her eye: *Miss Adeline Spencer, Faithful Nurse and Companion.*

Viola wondered just who Miss Adeline Spencer had been the faithful nurse and companion to, and hoped the old lady was looking down on the church that evening and enjoying seeing the village come together to celebrate Christmas, as Viola was sure she had done for many years with her charges. *Actually* . . . Viola looked around for Laurie — it would be an excellent excuse to ask him who the lady was, but he was nowhere to be seen.

Oh. One moment. He was right at the back of the church, standing up and letting someone squeeze in past him, so he was right on the end of a pew. He and Elsie's friend Fabian exchanged a few words, then, deliberately, it seemed, he didn't look at the front of the church where his family and friends were, not even to wave at them. Instead, he studied the order of service, that scowl back on his face, and Fabian strolled down the aisle instead.

Viola frowned. She had no idea why on earth Laurie had chosen to stay all the way up there. She calculated that if they all shuffled along *this* pew, he could just as easily squeeze onto the end *here*.

'Do you mind if I sit here?' asked Fabian instead, who was the *actual* person approaching the pew. 'Laurie said he preferred to stay at the back, out of the way, and sent me down here. No idea why.'

'That makes two of us, then,' Viola muttered wryly. But she nodded, and some of the shine was taken off the evening. She had, herself, deliberately hung back to see if she could possibly, at all, sit next to Laurie. And clearly that had not worked in the slightest.

So much for her secret Christmas wishes.

But she didn't have too much time to dwell on that fact, because the music had changed from a gentle background music to a strong melody that was clearly intended to grab everyone's attention. And so the service began.

Viola spent the next half hour or so surrounded by, it seemed, every other member of Laurie's family, listening to Enyon and Arthur's lusty, out-of-tune singing as they tried to outdo one another, the sweet baritone of Clem and the beautiful voices of Elsie, Medora and Isolde, harmonising perfectly.

She had no idea what Laurie's singing voice sounded like . . . *because he was at the other end of the church!*

Ugh.

However, she tried to put it aside because the vicar was clearing his throat and preparing to launch into his sermon.

It was just as the short sermon was drawing to a close (it had been largely about Christmas and loving everyone as Mary and Joseph had loved Baby Jesus) and they were standing up to sing "It Came Upon a Midnight Clear" — which was, oddly, she realised as the organist began to play, a little different to the version she knew from home — when she felt a light touch on her hand.

She looked up at Fabian, who was smiling at her. 'Someone said to give you this,' he whispered, handing over a folded piece of paper. 'I can't tell you who. So ask me no questions and I'll tell you no lies.' Then he winked at her and went back to singing the carol, and she unfolded the note.

For the prompt attention of Miss Viola Arthur. Come to Rose's garden at midnight on Christmas Eve, it said. *Your carriage awaits.*

She read it and re-read it, and then realised there was something fundamentally wrong with it.

She had no clue how to get to Rose's garden. Or where the heck she was expected to get a carriage at almost midnight on Christmas Eve!

She spun around, her suspicions about the author of the note quite possibly confirmed when she saw that Laurie was missing from his space in the church.

'Fabian!' she whispered, not quite sure what to think or say. All she knew was that her heart was pounding in her chest and she wanted to run out of the church and find her way to Rose's garden just as quickly as she could. 'How do I get to this place? And how do I find the carriage?' She thrust the note at him and he smiled.

He leaned down and whispered. 'Don't worry — I know exactly where to find one. Apparently, the vicar always finishes his service a good half hour before midnight, so you've plenty of time.'

Viola realised the service was indeed coming to an end and the vicar was beaming around and blessing everyone and wishing them a Merry Christmas. She responded just as loudly as everyone else in the congregation and they began filing out.

As she left the church, the clock tower said it was eleven thirty. Thirty minutes. Thirty minutes to midnight, thirty minutes to Christmas Day.

And, in the time they had been in the church, even more snow had fallen.

'Come on,' Fabian said to Viola, taking her arm. 'I believe there may be a carriage just along here.'

They peeled away from the group, Zennor and Ruan Teague remonstrating with their youngest boys for throwing snowballs at one another, and slipped down a lane by the side of the church.

Sure enough, there was a carriage, the driver huddled in a big overcoat, his hat pulled down over his ears and a huge scarf wrapped around him. Snowflakes were settling on his hat and his collar, and, by the way he was sitting, Viola could tell he wasn't the happiest of people to be out there that night. His horse didn't look much happier, but at least that too had a huge blanket covering it.

'Poor man!' she said to Fabian, aghast. 'He's had to come out for me?'

'I suspect he just did what he was paid to do,' replied Fabian with a shrug. 'But yes — one can think of *better* things to do in the snow.' He opened the door for her and helped her up the step. 'However, this was all done with the very best of intentions, I can assure you. Merry Christmas, Viola!' he said, and shut the door. Then he rapped on the side of the coach and Viola felt the thing lurch as they pulled away — and headed towards this mysterious Rose's garden, wherever that may be.

CHAPTER THIRTY-ONE

Present

Unsurprisingly, after the experience in Russell Square, they hadn't felt much like continuing to Brunswick Square, or even turning around and heading to Hyde Park to enjoy the Winter Wonderland.

'There's a haunted mansion attraction,' Ryan had said.

They looked at one another for a moment.

'No way.'

'Nope. Absolutely not.'

They spoke together. Tegan was pleased they were in agreement, even if Ryan had thrown her a little with his Glasgow news and Angelo had upset her a little with his flowery, apologetic message. So they decided, instead, to head back to Cornwall on an earlier train, had a couple of hours in the pub, and again Ryan spent the evening in his van before going back down to Wheal Mount the day after.

Neither one of them mentioned Glasgow or Angelo.

Ryan hadn't parked up in the pub car park this time. He had made it as far as the grounds of Pencradoc, and, as Tegan closed her curtains that evening, she could see his shadow moving around inside the vehicle. She had leaned on the windowsill for a little while, peering down at him, before she decided that she felt a bit like a Peeping Tom and how would she like it if he, Ryan, spent some time staring up into her window? She wouldn't like it at all.

But the idea that he was so close, yet technically so far away, kept her awake and tossing and turning most of the night. Coren had again offered Ryan a room in the house itself, but he had politely refused. Tegan sort of understood that as well. After the odd things that had happened in London, it was somehow as if the air might be charged and Laurie and Viola would spring out on them again, if they were in the same place, just yards apart.

He'd gone by the time she got up and it was business as usual at Pencradoc. The only good thing was that Laurie and Viola had, it seemed, decided to stay in London for a bit. The atmosphere just felt different and a bit empty; Tegan could only hope they stayed away for a little while longer. At least until she got the exhibition up and running.

And that, indeed, was what occupied her mind and took up the bulk of her time over the next couple of weeks.

Elsie's dress arrived the next day, as promised, and one of the Christmas staff, Katy, gave her a hand setting it all up in the ballroom. Katy was lovely, just in her mid-to-late-twenties like Tegan, and part of her remit was to help out where she was needed, be it in the tearoom, the studios, the exhibition rooms or wherever Coren deemed it necessary. She was a dab hand at creative things, and, between them, she and Tegan had created a perfect Snow Queen room.

They'd used the ideas Tegan and Ryan had come up with so many weeks ago to base the exhibition on, and the morning room, which led onto the ballroom, had been filled with a tasteful blue, silver and white forest. From there you walked into the realm of the Snow Queen. Elsie's dress was displayed beautifully on the mirrored tiles and Katy had piled up holly and evergreens around it to disguise the hard edges. "Tilly", the tailor's dummy that had been in the Pencradoc family for generations, had been brought out of Coren's private quarters and the wedding dress was arranged on that. Mirrors and lanterns flickered around her and fairy lights were strung across the ceiling to make a crazy, sparkling crystal realm.

To make it even more special, the evergreen crown and bouquet perfectly matched Elsie's, as far as Tegan could tell from the wedding photograph. The final touch was the bright-red sash. Tegan felt a weird little tingle when she carefully tied it, again making sure it matched the style of the sash in the photographs. She could almost imagine herself there, at the wedding, adjusting the sash, then following Elsie down the aisle, next to Laurie . . . For some reason, just after she thought that, she untied the bright-red sash and slackened it a little, and *then* it was perfect.

However, Tegan was sad she hadn't managed to get a sleigh. She had, on the off chance, run that by Coren again, though, and he had just looked at her silently.

'All right,' she'd said, almost backing out of the room. 'I'll adapt.'

"Adapting" had been speaking to Cordelia and Matt, good friends of Kit and Merryn, and, as they both worked in a school — Cordelia teaching drama and Matt teaching art — they had managed to rustle up a cardboard cut-out, covered in glitter and tinsel and icicle lights. It was, sadly, just one side of a sleigh, but Matt had set his class to work on a background and behind the sleigh was a painted winter forest, with winding paths leading off between the snow-covered fir trees.

As Tegan admired it, she was reminded of the painted background in the old Halloween photographs. She wondered if the family had painted it, and was fairly certain they had done.

The wedding photographs had been put up on display in the morning room, along with anything else she and Ryan had come up with — from invitations, to letters, to a copy of Elsie's sketch of the dress. Ryan had found a couple of invoices in the archives. One of them was from Lucile Ltd, a high-end designer of the time, for an eye-watering price covering Elsie's dress and all the bridesmaids' dresses. The yardage of fabric quoted was enough to thoroughly shock Tegan. The most she'd ever sewn was a handkerchief at school and a felt roll to keep her make-up brushes in. It was supposed to hold pens and pencils, but teenage Tegan preferred lipstick and mascara to essay writing. The other invoice was from Claridge's where it seemed the wedding reception had been held.

The invoices had gone in the display too.

So, all in all, the place was looking incredible. As Tegan stood there in the early morning before it opened, though, she had the feeling that she needed to add something else to it — just something to sit among the shards of crystal that spelled out "eternity" and the twinkling lights that set off the wedding dress.

Flowers, she thought. That's what she needed.

She headed out into the gardens, not sure exactly what she would find, or what would be available at that time of year. Grubbing around, sending silent prayers up to avoid any lurking gardeners who might get cross with her, she collected a large bagful of different items, some of which she even recognised: cyclamens, Christmas roses and a green shrubby thing with little white trumpet flowers on it. She scattered them on the mirrored tiles and stood back, folding her arms.

There, she thought. *Just perfect.*

Proud of her handiwork, she whipped out her phone to take a photograph. It was, to be honest, massively Instagrammable anyway, and she fully intended to share it on her personal page and also the Pencradoc arts centre page.

While she was on her phone, she sent it to Angelo. He always appreciated beautiful things and she really wanted to show him what she'd been busy with as well.

Look! Isn't this fabulous? she typed. *It's been such fun.* She thought for a moment, then continued. *It's a shame you'll miss it, but I'll send some more photos soon.*

It was a few moments before the message came back.

Bellissima! I hope you do something similar at Easter. I will look forward to seeing it! I hope to be with you at Easter, my love.

'Easter?' she said out loud. Hang on. She stared at the screen for a moment, then started to type.

Easter? What happened to February?

I have many gigs. Valentine's Day and all that. They are baying for my blood! I cannot afford to miss the events — I am so sorry. I should have told you.

But Valentine's Day. You won't be here?

I am so sorry, my love.

She waited in case he expanded on that.

Fine.

Her lips pressed together in a thin line, she fired off: *Shall I come to Sicily for Valentine's then?*

He responded a little too quickly for her liking. *Ah, no. It isn't worth it. I will be working. I have so very little time. Next year. Next year, we will do something fun. Like go on the beach again!*

'The beach.' She looked at the phone, her heart thumping. There had been something niggling her since she'd seen that picture of his on Instagram — the one of the sandals and the guitar and the flip-flops. And now, with all the crystal clarity of the mirror that Elsie's gown was displayed upon, she knew what it was.

The flip-flops.

She hadn't worn flip-flops that day.

The toe bar on her flip-flops had broken and she'd worn white, strappy Roman sandals instead.

She felt the bile rise in her throat and carefully clicked through Angelo's Instagram.

The flip-flop picture was still there, but, as she scrolled back in time, *way* back in time, she saw *her* beach photo — staged exactly the same as the recent flip-flop one. Only in her photo, a pair of white strappy Roman sandals were discarded to the side of the heart drawn in the sand.

'*Really*?' A dozen emotions churned up inside her at the same time. '*Seriously*?'

Wow.

Before she could second-guess herself, she took a screen-shot of the flip-flop picture. She sent it to Angelo, with the comment, *Whose flip-flops are they?*

There was a brief pause, then he responded.

Yours. Of course.

I don't think so. These were my shoes. The day we went to the beach and took that photo. Then she attached the Roman sandal one.

Then they must have belonged to someone else on the beach that day. I was missing you and wanted to remember our days in the summer.

It was plausible, she supposed. But . . .

But they are in a heart.

I didn't realise they were in the shot.

She paused for a moment. She could take the comment at face value. Or she could take it further.

She did know there were other girls in his Instagram feed — but for the first time she wondered whether they were just friends of his. Or friends with benefits.

Or ex-girlfriends.

She went hot and cold all over, and it was nothing to do with whoever or whatever might have been lurking in Pencradoc that day.

She sat down, legs crossed, facing Elsie's gown, and looked at her phone. Then she looked up at the figure in front of her.

What would Elsie do? What, in fact, would Viola do?

She knew without a doubt that they would fight for a love they believed in and set themselves free from a situation that did not make them one hundred per cent happy.

Life was too short.

As Tegan studied the gown, she went over some of the things Angelo had said and done over the few months they'd been apart. He was putting off seeing her. Every time she'd called him, he'd had another excuse as to why he'd been too busy to talk. He had, she realised, stopped making the first move and didn't call or text her.

It was always her chasing him, grateful for whatever crumb he threw her way.

Unbidden, thoughts of Ryan — bloody Ryan — wormed their way into her mind. Yes, their relationship was work-based, but they were getting there on a personal level, weren't they? They had begun enjoying each other's company — socialising, calling and messaging each other with little bits of daily nonsense.

Fate had a funny way of working, didn't it? People came into your lives when you needed them. And if someone was meant to come back *into* your life, they would.

Tegan took a deep breath and her heart began to pound.

Okay, she typed to Angelo. *Not to worry. I'm pleased I saw it actually, as there's something I've been meaning to talk to you about.*

There were a few moments of silence on the phone. Then:

Cool. But can we talk later? I'm busy.

'I bet you bloody are!' muttered Tegan.

Then she typed: *What's her name?*

I do not know what you mean!

Yes. You do. Angelo — just tell me. It was fun while it lasted (because it had been, she reasoned). *But you can't tell me that you honestly thought we had a whole lifetime ahead of us?*

We will talk later. I have to go to my gig. I will call you.

Tegan shook her head. Of course he wouldn't call her. She bit her lip.

Angelo, please don't call me. I suspect there's nothing to say. Honestly. It's fine. I wish you well. I just don't see the point in fighting for this. You're an amazing musician, your life is in Sicily. Mine is here. Peace out. Xxx

It was a corny phrase, but one he used a lot.

The phone told her he was "typing" and she waited.

*If that's what you want. Peace out, Babes. It was good. I wish
you well too. If ever you are over here again, I will be happy to meet
you xxx*

And that was it. He, it seemed, didn't want to fight for
them either. Had it really been *that easy*?

If anything, that proved her point. But . . .

'Not gonna be a friend with benefits, mate,' she said to
the phone. But she couldn't help smiling, just a little bit.
God loves a trier!

She debated on "hearting" the message, just to acknowledge it and end the whole sorry conversation. Then she took
a deep breath and decided against it. She would manage his
expectations and not let him believe she was that sort of
person. She had far too much respect for herself.

She was free. She could move on.

And she decided not to think about the fact she had
possibly turned into a person who broke up with people
via text!

* * *

Ryan had been kept very busy at Wheal Mount in the lead-up
to Christmas. He hadn't had the opportunity to travel up to
Pencradoc to help out with the exhibition prep as such, but he
did intend going up on opening day to support Tegan.

After their trip to London he'd kept in touch with
Tegan much more than he thought he would ever do. And
not just about work, either.

They'd had amusing conversations and normal conversations and friendly conversations. They'd sent each
other silly little memes and gifs, and much more general
things about what they were planning to buy their families
and friends for Christmas. She'd even told him she'd broken things off with Angelo.

He wasn't going to lie — Ryan was pleased she
had done it. From what she'd said, the man wasn't that

interested once she'd left Sicily and had moved onto the next shiny object. She was better off without him, although he kept that thought private and tried not to dwell on why he was so happy she'd ended things . . .

However, it was nice to be so easy in her company now and he really wished they'd taken the time to get to know each other better all those years ago.

Tegan had even met him in Bodmin to help him prepare for his interview at Glasgow. A lady called Allison had agreed to interview him via video-call, as the travel times and prices to Glasgow from Cornwall were ridiculous. He had met Tegan on the Saturday before the interview, just for coffee, but they'd ended up going out for dinner. He'd taken her back to Pencradoc in his van and they'd finished up in the White Lady for a drink afterwards. He'd walked her back to Pencradoc and he'd camped in the car park again.

It had been a good evening; and he thought the interview had, in the end, gone really well. He had felt comfortable chatting to Allison, the work had sounded particularly interesting — she loved his idea of focusing on the Glasgow Girls for International Women's Day as well — and he left the call feeling very positive.

Sybill had been the one going up to Pencradoc to see Coren for exhibition "business" as she'd said darkly, or Coren had been coming down to see her. Between them, they had transported and delivered all the things Ryan had discovered in the archives relating to the wedding. He was certain there would be more if he ever had the time to check everything, but they seemed happy with what he had located.

'Isn't it funny,' Sybill had said, 'how things happen?' Her pregnancy was hugely obvious now and that day, she was wearing an oversized Christmas jumper, black leggings and boots. Tinsel was stuck around her computer screen and Christmas music played out of the speakers. 'This time last year, none of us knew exactly how much we would have found out about Elsie and Louis, and how much we would find out about ourselves as well.'

An enlarged copy of Elsie and Louis' wedding photo was currently propped up on her desk like a family photograph, next to a pen-holder in the shape of a reindeer. 'If Tegan hadn't gone to work at Pencradoc, who's to say we would have had this much information about Viola *or* the wedding?'

'She's certainly found some interesting things out,' said Ryan. Funnily enough, it didn't gall him to praise her now, and Sybill must have noticed as she smiled at the comment and raised her eyebrows.

'You've managed to work together pretty well,' she said. 'I think it's safe to say that Coren and I are happy with how it's worked out. We're really impressed with the winter wedding wonderland display — you'll be amazed when you see the finished article, I promise. But it's so much easier to say Snow Queen, isn't it?' She grinned. 'How did *you* find it anyway? Working so closely with Tegan in the run up to this, I mean.' She steepled her fingers and leaned her chin on them, studying Ryan. It made him feel a little uncomfortable.

'We called a truce,' he said, pathetically.

'Good.' Sybill smiled. 'Anything else? Anything else at *all* happened to you both in the last few months to help that truce?'

Ryan clamped his lips shut, determined not to spill about the Laurie/Viola connection they seemed to have adopted. But Sybill's gimlet eyes and steely silence worked, and he opened his mouth and it all spilled out anyway.

'Um. We found out — a lot — about Laurie and Viola.'

'I thought you might.' Again she was silent and he rushed to fill in gap, cringing at himself for speaking.

'We — think that we look a bit like them and I suppose it's only natural that we've become interested in them.'

'You look a *lot* like them. I could see it, as soon as I saw that group wedding photo. Even more so when I saw the

273

blown-up Halloween photos. I thought at the time "interesting choice". When you had all the family to choose from.'

'It was to link into Laurie going into the army. Merryn wanted the World War thing, remember? I think Tegan felt she owed her one.'

'If you say so.'

'Yes.' This time Ryan was silent. 'We enlarged the picture of Fabian as well,' he eventually said defensively.

'You did.'

'And we didn't see anything of him, floating around in the shadows . . .'

Shit. And there it was, it was out.

Sybill nodded thoughtfully. 'Curious. Let's backtrack.' She waved her hand in a reversing sort of motion. 'You said that you'd become interested in them. Would it be fair to say that they'd become interested in you?' She was guileless and Ryan felt his cheeks heating up.

'I . . . guess.' It was impossible to lie to Sybill. Ryan remembered again that she was named after a witch and at times it seemed she had powers to match.

Did witches celebrate Christmas?

Stupid question. Of course they didn't.

Unless they were Sybill, of course . . .

'Thought as much,' she said.

'Sybill . . .' He took a deep breath and gave up the charade. 'Do you think Wheal Mount is haunted?'

Sybill frowned. 'That's a good question. I'm not sure. I don't think it's as haunted as Pencradoc, if that's what you mean. I believe that the Pencradoc spirits find you if they need to let you know something. They pop up and let you know if you're being a bit — unreasonable about something. Stubborn. That kind of thing.' She nodded, as if her words had satisfied her. 'Maybe we've just had nobody at Wheal Mount who needs to be told something. Everything seems to happen up there.' She sat back in her seat, waved her hand in the direction of Pencradoc and folded her arms across her huge bump. 'Anyway — what are you up to for Christmas?'

'Going to my parents,' Ryan answered, relieved that the interrogation seemed to be over. 'What about you?'

'Pencradoc.' Sybill smiled. 'We've got the whole family this year. Merryn and Kit are coming with Rosie, and Coren's mum and dad are coming too. And Tegan will be there, of course. You should go up there and see the exhibition before it comes down. You've been part of it and I know you've got photos, but it's not the same as the real thing. Is it?'

Ryan flushed again, wondering if that comment had a double meaning. In the same way that Sybill had a photo of Louis and Elsie, he had kept a copy of the group wedding shot, tucked inside a notebook. He looked at it occasionally, but he didn't think Sybill had noticed.

But this was Sybill and perhaps she had.

'No,' he said. 'Photos aren't the same at all. Actually . . .' He thought for a minute. 'Can I ask you something about that? I think I'd like to do something with a picture I've got.'

Sybill sat forward again, her eyes bright and her expression eager. 'Ask away.'

'It's just about making old photos colourised. I've seen some and they are so lifelike . . .' He shook his head, wondering how he could explain what he meant.

'Oh! Yes.' Sybill nodded. 'I know *exactly* what you mean. Is that something you want to look into? And I also know just the person who can help. Let me get the info. I'll email it straight over.'

'Thanks.' He grinned and headed back to his desk, looking forward to getting it sorted. He sat down and opened his emails, a smile still on his face.

Then he saw an email from the Glasgow gallery. From Allison, who had interviewed him.

He read the email. Then he read it again.

Congratulations, it said. *We would like to offer you the job . . .*

CHAPTER THIRTY-TWO

1911

Laurie was pleased his scheme had appeared to work so far. He had watched until he'd seen Fabian pass the note to Viola, and then had slipped away. The last he'd seen of her had been her fair head bent down, as she'd scanned the letter.

Perhaps he should have written something a little more creative and poetical, but once he'd decided on his course of action, he'd felt as if he'd just needed to — *do* it. To grab the moment and go with his heart.

And if it all fell flat . . . well, they could easily avoid one another tomorrow and he was sure she'd head back to America at some point anyway.

So maybe it would cause an awkward moment or two, but they'd both get over it eventually.

But he really didn't want to get over it. He had, for the first time in his life, found someone who he wanted to get to know a whole lot better, and the only way for that to happen was for him to try this. Despite her protestations, he was hopeful that she would accept a grand gesture from him and this was the best he could come up with.

He took a deep breath and sped up. He needed to get to Rose's garden and get there before midnight . . .

* * *

The carriage lurched along and Viola felt the horse go quicker. The snow wasn't enough to stop the wheels from ploughing through it, but she figured that, if it got much deeper, a sleigh would be the best way to travel and that was dreadfully exciting . . .

But for now, she was in a carriage and just up ahead, she could see Pencradoc House, lit up and welcoming everyone back from church. How very odd — was Rose's garden here, then?

'Oh!' She suddenly remembered that a previous duchess had been called Rose. Elsie's real father's first wife. Rose had almost been eradicated from Pencradoc history, but her lasting legacy was the gothic rose garden on the estate.

That, then, was where they were heading!

The carriage veered off to the right, off the main driveway, and Viola peered out of the window, rubbing the condensation off the glass. Gosh, it was *cold*. But the sight that greeted her made her gasp in delight and forget the chill. The pathway to the garden was lit by a string of those jam-jar lights — and, up ahead, was a pool of light — the garden itself was a shimmering winter wonderland and her heart began to pound again.

The carriage drew to a halt and there was more movement as the driver apparently got down. There was a rap on the door and she jumped as his silhouette filled the small windowpane, and then the door opened . . .

And there, standing in just his shirt sleeves, was a very cold and pink-nosed person she recognised so very, very well.

CHAPTER THIRTY-THREE

Present

If someone had told Tegan how successful her midwinter wedding exhibition would be, she would have nodded and agreed and said of course it would.

But if she was honest, she'd had her wobbles over the last three months or so, and, truly, if anyone had told her how much she would ultimately enjoy working with Ryan Jackson, she would have thought them crazy.

However, she had loved it.

He'd made a point of coming up on the opening day — on his day off, apparently — to give her moral support, a bottle of champagne, a lovely box of chocolates and a huge bouquet of flowers. He'd then asked Coren if he could work on Pencradoc's ticket kiosk that day as well, to help out.

'You really don't need to be here,' she'd said, gnawing at the edge of her thumbnail, bobbing around next to him as they'd prepared to open up. 'Nobody will come anyway.'

'Yes, they will.' He grinned at her. 'Trust me. I've been sharing the hell out of it on Wheal Mount's socials as well. I think you underestimate Elsie's fan base. Wait and see. And if

278

not, I'll be here and we can commiserate with each other and get wrecked at the White Lady tonight to forget it all.'

She couldn't help but laugh. 'It's a long time since I got wrecked!' she said. 'But — crap. I didn't arrange any press coverage!' She looked at him in a panic. What a stupid, stupid, rookie mistake!

'Not to worry,' said Ryan. 'I did. And also, it's a while since I got wrecked too. Maybe we've grown up a bit.' He smiled at her, then nodded towards the door. 'Do you want to unlock it? I'm ready for the onslaught.'

The onslaught was a trickle at first and Tegan started to panic, but by about ten o'clock, there was a steady stream of visitors — including a journalist from the local newspaper and someone from *Sunday Stage*, a creative-arts magazine who often reported on the Pencradoc and Wheal Mount events. Tegan could have hugged Ryan — but, obviously, she didn't.

Almost everyone left looking delighted, apparently stunned at the amazing outfit and chattering excitedly about how romantic it was, and how perfectly presented it was. The beautifully illustrated copies of *The Snow Queen*, ordered by Tegan on a whim, flew off the gift-shop shelves, as well as so many postcards, pretty notebooks, sketching and painting sets, guidebooks and reproduction wedding photos — so much so that Tegan found herself called into the gift shop to help out.

When they closed the door on the final visitors of the day, she looked up at Ryan and exhaled.

'Wow.' She shook her head. 'Did *we* do *that*?' She pointed at the closed door, and then at the healthy sum in the till. 'Sorcha radioed through before and said her takings had been much higher today in the tearoom. Actually, she was asking if I could go over and give her a hand, but I couldn't so I had to send Katy over.'

'We *did* do that. Or rather, *you* did. And it was just as well Katy was around, wasn't it?'

'Definitely. But honestly.' She shook her head. 'I couldn't have done any of this without you.'

'Yeah, you could.' He grinned, shrugging his jacket on.

'Well, yeah, I *could*,' she said nonchalantly, teasing him. 'But it was better with your help. It actually was.'

'Better than that sodding catalogue we effed up in Glasgow?'

'Much better.'

'If we'd adulted earlier, the first time we worked together, we would have been unstoppable.' He looked at her, a little sadly perhaps. 'How stupid we were. Never mind.' He blinked, as if trying to stop himself saying something. 'Anyway. Yeah. So, White Lady? Not gonna get wrecked, but I think we can celebrate. My trusty van is ready and waiting for me in the car park, so I'm good for a celebration.'

'I think we can certainly celebrate,' she said.

'Um, yeah.' He looked down for a moment and took a deep breath. 'Also, I have something to tell you. I didn't want to say until after today because I didn't want to take the shine off your exhibition.'

'Oh?' Her heart pounded a little faster.

'Yes. Another — um — cause for celebration.'

'Really? What . . . what's that?'

'I got the job.' He looked up at her, his eyes sadder and more puzzled than they ought to have been considering he had his dream job. 'The Glasgow one.'

'Oh. I mean oh! Brilliant!' She forced a smile on her face and tentatively reached out and patted his arm. 'Well done.' The leather coat felt cool and ridged where the creases were on the arm. That little gesture turned her stomach into a spin-dryer and she felt as if she was going to burst into tears.

This sucked. It really did.

But she was not going to rain on his parade?

'You rocked it, then,' she said, reluctantly removing her hand from his arm.

'Apparently so.' They stood in silence for a moment. 'Thanks to you helping me,' he added eventually.

'Yeah. Any time.'

He half smiled. 'Pub?'

'Pub.'

And so the celebration was a double one, but Tegan's heart was no longer in it, although she tried to laugh and joke and act normally and say all the right things.

But yes. Deep down, it sucked.

The exhibition continued to be a huge success, and the press reports were very complimentary indeed. Even Coren congratulated her in his own quiet way and that meant an awful lot to Tegan. Merryn was a hard act to follow, but she thought she, Tegan, was doing okay, actually.

And now, finally, it was Christmas Eve! The exhibition would stay there for a few more days, and, as one member of the public wrote in the visitors' book, it certainly had "added in an entirely awesome way to this whole, magical time of year!". But Christmas Eve was, in Tegan's opinion, the *most* magical day of the year. Obviously, when she was younger, she'd much preferred Christmas Day, with all the food and the gifts and the music and the company . . .

To be honest, she still loved all of that — and this year was going to be even better and something very special. Her family was coming to Pencradoc and it would be little Rosie's first Christmas. Her niece was a bit more interesting now, being nearly three months old. She would happily lie on a play mat and kick her legs, or raise her head up if she was on her tummy. There were smiles now too — many, many smiles, and some of them were even directed at Tegan. Rosie also seemed to recognise her, which delighted her more than she'd thought possible.

But still — three months! She had to keep reminding herself she had actually only been at Pencradoc for three months, more or less, and look at what she'd achieved.

Just as they were starting to close Pencradoc on Christmas Eve, she told Coren she needed to check something in the ballroom and slipped away to her Snow Queen realm.

The ballroom no longer scared her or felt peculiar. The feeling she'd had that day when Ryan had been here, when they'd looked at Viola's portrait and witnessed that mist coming towards them had, somehow, dissipated with the exhibition going up.

Elsie's dress was still beautiful and sparkly, and Ianthe had been correct that the evergreen headdress and wreath would last well. Tegan would head out to the gardens soon and get some more flowers to scatter around the glass "lake", as the ones she'd put down were looking a little sad now.

Of course, she knew that in a few days the exhibition would be coming down, ready for something else in the New Year, but there was no need to keep tired old flowers here when there was a garden full of stuff. She'd ended up with a guilty conscience after her last botanical expedition, so she'd checked with the gardeners earlier if it was okay with them that she picked some more, and they'd said that was fine, and one of the best places to forage would be Rose's gothic garden because there was a lot of greenery there that wouldn't be missed. So that was her plan.

But for now, she just wanted to sit quietly in the darkened ballroom and look at the dress, and imagine Elsie's wedding, and perhaps that reception in Claridge's . . .

"I swear, if that report goes out and says I'm maid of honour, I'll come back and haunt the fellows who think that!"

Tegan blinked. 'But we didn't *say* you were maid of honour,' she whispered into the air. 'You just came back and haunted us anyway!'

It didn't seem an odd thing to say in that quiet room, surrounded by the scent of evergreens and floor polish.

She could have sworn she heard a laugh. But before she could catch anything else, the scent of evergreens was overlaid with something else. Woodsmoke and tobacco and leather . . .

Ryan.

She would recognise that aftershave anywhere, although she'd never been certain if the leather was anything to do

282

with his boots or his ridiculously long coat, or those thong bracelets he wore on his wrist . . .

Whatever.

She smiled into the empty room. She didn't know why she did it — this was *Ryan*! But she couldn't help herself. She would miss him terribly when he went to Glasgow and she wanted to hang on to every precious moment she could grab with him.

Even if he perhaps didn't think they were *quite* as precious as she did. She didn't know for sure how he felt. She'd never asked him.

But she did wish she could somehow slow down time.

'Hello, Ryan,' she said now, without turning around. 'I wondered how long it would be before I saw you today.'

But there was no answer and she turned around, surprised. Nothing and nobody else was in the room with her. That familiar shiver ran up her spine again and she wondered if Laurie had drifted in, looking for his lover.

She stared at the door, wondering if she should stand up and leave, or just wait here and see what happened. Half of her thought that, actually, she'd enjoy seeing them both, today of all days . . .

There was a movement at the door and she caught her breath as a figure emerged from the darkened corridor beyond.

'Tegan! I thought I might find you in here!' called the person. He walked into the room and she exhaled.

'Ryan. It *was* you.'

'Was me what?' He came over to her, their voices oddly echoing in the long room.

She stood up and brushed the dust off her bottom. 'Was you what came in here a moment ago. I recognised your aftershave.'

'That sentence isn't even English. And, no, I didn't come in before. I just got here.' He smiled down at her. 'I parked the van out front. Going a bit further north, home for

Christmas and all that. Devon.' He nodded approximately north. 'But I brought Sybill up and brought you something too.' He flushed and stuffed his hands in his deep pockets. He was, she saw, sporting the hideous man-bag again.

'Man-bag.' She nodded to the offending article.

'I'm getting quite attached to it,' he said. 'Does that mean I'm now officially an adult, or does it mean I've turned into a hipster.'

Tegan smiled. 'You could never be a hipster.'

'Good.' Ryan grinned. 'An adult I am, then. I still like the Mission, still play their songs *all the time*, so I was hoping not to be hipster. Truth is, the man-bag contains the things I have for you.'

'Oh?' Tegan looked up at him, their eyes fixed on one another, and a weird little charge of electricity seemed to flicker between their gazes. It made her catch her breath and her heart pound just a little faster.

By the look on Ryan's face, she felt that he had experienced something similar.

She cleared her throat. 'Do you — want to talk in here, then? Or go elsewhere.'

'Are we alone in here?'

She slowly shook her head. 'Not certain.'

'Hmm.' He tore his gaze from hers with apparently some effort and looked over her head. 'This is amazing, by the way. Elsie's dress — it's fantastic. I know I've said it before but you've really got the feeling in here. That magical Christmas shizzle. Sorry you couldn't get a real sleigh. But that one looks great.'

'It does, doesn't it?' she said. 'But, yeah — my budget-busting sleigh was not to be.'

'Not to worry.'

'Um, I was just about to go outside.' She pointed to the window. 'I was going to—'

'Rose's garden?' He fixed her with a look that sent a strange combination of static and apprehension throughout her body.

'Exactly there.'

'On Christmas Eve,' he said, almost to himself. 'Could it *be* more perfect?' Then he grinned and nodded. 'Yes. Okay. Let's go. I think what I've got for you would work pretty well there.'

'Cool.' She nodded. 'I've been told I can forage for my flowers there. Just want to refresh the display.'

'Perfect. After you.' He took his hand out of his pocket and gestured for her to go ahead.

And so she did.

* * *

Ryan followed Tegan out of the ballroom, with the weirdest sensation that they were being watched.

It wasn't surprising, considering what he had in that document case.

In fact, when he'd come into the ballroom to find her, she hadn't looked as if she'd been on her own at all. There'd been definite shadows moving behind the dress, but, oddly they hadn't worried him. He could almost see two people, one tall, one petite, walking together hand in hand, heading out of the door at the far end of the room.

But his attention was on Tegan and she was the one he wanted to see. And, yes. He did want to see her. And when she'd said she was going into that garden . . . It just made perfect sense.

They walked past the Grand Staircase, the place no longer feeling eerie or scary or anything negative at all. Since he'd been here last, Pencradoc, like Wheal Mount, had gone all out for the festive season. A huge Christmas tree was in the hallway, and Little Elsie, at the bottom of the stairs, had a cheerful garland around her hair, not unlike the holly and ivy headdress she'd been wearing on her wedding day. Bowls of pinecones were placed on tables and jam jars with lights inside were strung in a zig-zag fashion across the hallway ceiling, interspersed with giant silver stars and baubles, suspended there for good measure. The scent of spices and fir trees was everywhere, and it really did feel like Christmas was eventually here.

Tegan led him outside and along the pathway to Rose's garden. It was actually more eerie out here than it had been in the house and Ryan followed, the lanterns that lit the pathways flickering in the late afternoon twilight.

'Here we are,' said Tegan, almost in a whisper. She hesitated. 'Can you feel it here too? Or is it just me?'

'No, there's definitely something here,' said Ryan, equally quietly. He looked around him and the rose garden had, as well as the house, been treated to some Christmas cheer. There were fairy lights winking out from the plants and strings of them were wrapped around the tree trunks. Sparkling silver baubles hung from the highest tree branches and there was a sort of net above the hollow the garden was situated in, covered in lights and crystals.

He wondered what it had been like all those years ago, when Laurie had . . .

But no.

Before that, he needed to show Tegan the first thing he'd brought with him.

'Do you want to sit down?' he asked, indicating the bench they had shared three months or so ago.

Tegan shook her head slowly. 'No. I think I want to stand, actually.'

Ryan grinned. 'In case we need to make a hasty exit?'

'Something like that.'

He nodded. 'I'll be quick then. Here. I asked Sybill for some advice on photo restoration.' He rummaged in the document bag and brought out an envelope. 'Specifically, colour restoration. Have you ever seen it?'

'Oh! Yes!' Tegan nodded. 'It's where people bring the colour back to black-and-white photos, isn't it? Makes the people really come alive . . .'

She stopped herself from continuing and Ryan laughed. 'Yes. I get it. But this is different. Look.' He opened the envelope and took something out of it.

He handed it to Tegan and she gasped. 'It's the wedding photo! The group shot. Oh, this is fantastic! What a brilliant piece of work.'

'Isn't it?' He was impressed with the thing himself. 'All I had to do was tell the specialist some of the colours I knew were in there. Like red, for Elsie's sash, and the colours of their hair and the headdress and all that. He did the rest.'

'Well, even if it's just clever guesswork,' Tegan said in delight, 'look how *real* they all look!'

Ryan nodded. He'd studied the photo so many times since he'd received it back from the restorer that he knew it off by heart. The girls' dresses were red, green and gold, their faces peaches and cream. The men were all smartly dressed in black, and, to Ryan's surprise, three of the attendants had sported rich, red hair. Sybill had told him their mother Lily Valentine had been famously red-headed, so it was unsurprising in some ways.

He had, of course, studied the figures of Laurie and Viola most. It had given him a shock the first time he'd seen them — they looked even more like himself and Tegan. But Tegan seemed to have bypassed that and was just delighted with the whole thing.

'Thank you. Thank you *so* much!' she said, clutching the photo to her chest. 'This means so much. Honestly, it's like the icing on the Christmas cake.'

'Brilliant.' Ryan smiled. 'But if you like that, then I think you're going to love this one.' His heart pounding, he extracted the second item from the envelope.

It was something that he had never come across before.

In fact, it was something that had been inside his note-book, when he'd gone to take out the wedding photograph. It had fluttered to the floor and he'd leaned down to pick it up, and . . .

But no. He wasn't going to overthink it, he wasn't going to wonder how it had got there.

It was there, that was all that mattered.

He offered it to her and Tegan took the folded piece of paper from him, looking up questioningly.

'Be careful with it,' he said quietly. 'I think this is maybe the most precious thing we've got. But I still don't know what relevance it's got. But — I know it has some.'

'Okay.' Tegan nodded, and turned her attention to the paper.

She carefully unfolded it and read it. Then, her eyes wide, she read it out aloud.

'For the prompt attention of Miss Viola Arthur,' she said. 'Come to Rose's garden at midnight on Christmas Eve. Your carriage awaits.'

'And here,' said Ryan quietly. 'We are.'

CHAPTER THIRTY-FOUR

1911

'You!' Viola said. 'It was *you* driving the carriage!'

Laurie nodded. 'It was. May I?' He held his hand out and prayed desperately that she would take it, and that he wouldn't be left standing here like the last snowman of the season, quietly drooping and disappearing into the soggy earth.

Suddenly she smiled and he felt his heart lift. An unusual sensation, admittedly — but he swore that at that very moment, it genuinely happened.

'You may,' she said,

He was done for. Finally, utterly and completely head over heels in love with this annoying, beautiful, sparky American girl.

He helped her out of the carriage and then guided her through an archway towards the centre of the garden. He was pleased to see that the lanterns and candles he and Fabian had brought out earlier were lit up and shining, and sent a silent prayer of thanks to his partner in crime. He absolutely couldn't have done it without him.

* * *

Viola, her hand safe and warm in Laurie's, allowed herself to be gently guided through the garden. She looked around her in wonderment, seeing the leaves and shrubs gilded with frost; holly and ivy were wound around everything, and, above them, was a bright, shining moon. The snow clouds had passed over and it was enchanting.

'"The moon on the breast of the new-fallen snow, gave a lustre of midday to objects below,"' she whispered, quoting the poem Pearl's children had enjoyed earlier.

'I couldn't have said it better myself,' said Laurie. She realised he had taken hold of her other hand as well and they were standing close, so very close to one another.

And there it was, the scent she would recognise anywhere. Woodsmoke and tobacco and leather . . . How did it now make her go weak at the knees?

'I'm sorry for the subterfuge,' he continued. 'It's not the first time I've crept around under your nose, though.'

'Oh?'

'The tearoom at Bodmin. You were there with Pearl and my sisters. When I found out they were going into the town, I went as well — but about half an hour after they did. I took Jester. Raced across the moor. And then I deliberately walked past the tearoom, just to see if I could see you.'

Jester, for of course it was he who had drawn the carriage, whinnied as if to remind everyone of his part in the charade. Laurie cast a glance in his direction and grinned.

Viola laughed as well. 'I *thought* it was you! I saw you!'

'*Not* my proudest moment.' Laurie smiled. 'I'm not given to general lurking. But this — the grand gesture thing.' He shrugged, suddenly looking embarrassed. 'It's completely new to me. I generally pride myself on my use of words and saying the right thing and all that, but when I'm with you, I can't actually string a decent sentence together without saying absolutely the wrong thing. So a grand gesture of sorts was the only way I could think of to get you alone, away from all our families, and to do this . . .'

And then, as the moon broke fully through and cast its magical light down on them, he leaned in and she closed her eyes and reached up towards him, responding . . . and then he kissed her, so very gently, that at first she thought it was a snowflake brushing her lips. She shivered and he pulled her closer, then he kissed her again and she realised it was no snowflake.

Finally, they drew apart, and she opened her eyes and looked into his.

'I think,' he said slowly, 'I've maybe wanted to do that since the first day I saw you.'

'When I was sitting in a puddle?'

'Exactly then.'

She smiled. 'Maybe I've been wanting to do the same. I'm glad we called a truce.'

'Me too.'

'But can I just ask one thing?'

'What's that?'

She ran her fingers up and down his arms and then placed her own arms around his waist. 'Why just the shirt?'

He grinned and it made her heart stutter. It was an expression she felt he only shared with the people who mattered to him most — this was the Laurie he kept hidden from most of the world.

'Ah. That.' He pulled her closer and laid his forehead against hers for a second, then moved ever so slightly back so he was looking directly in her eyes again. 'At Halloween. When you fell down the stairs and you said you didn't want me to be a romantic hero.' Again, that smile. He reached his hand up and moved a strand of her hair out of her face and behind her ears. 'In *my* experience, if my sisters had reacted like that and said no, quite so vehemently, and went quite so red, it might have meant something different. So, I *figured*,' he emphasised the Americanism and that made her smile again, 'that you might actually want the gallant behaviour and the grand gestures, and a romantic hero or two wouldn't go amiss.' He looked up at the sky ruefully. 'This wasn't my first plan. Had it not snowed, then you would have been delivered here, probably by Fabian, and I was intending to ride a horse across the estate and sweep you up on it. Possibly declaiming some poetry while I did it, possibly not.'

Viola laughed. 'Hence the shirt sleeves.'

'Hence the shirt sleeves. The only way I can look romantic and Byronic. I'm as bad as Medora and that damned dress of hers. And, yes, that was why I had to finally don the overcoat, the scarf and the hat — and become your heroic driver instead.'

'Medora's dress is *beautiful*,' said Viola. 'And your shirt sleeves are just *wunnerful*.' That made his smile even wider. 'But it's damned cold! Here — let's put the coat and scarf back on you!'

But Laurie shook his head. 'Not just yet. Let me be Byronic and heroic just a few minutes more, because, listen . . .' He looked towards the direction of the village, and, sure enough, there was the faint chime of bells striking midnight . . .

'Merry Christmas, Viola Arthur,' Laurie whispered.

'Merry Christmas, Laurie Teague,' Viola whispered back. 'I actually do love you as a romantic hero. Maybe I could kinda be persuaded to love the real Laurie just a little bit too.'

'Then let me try to persuade you on that one, Miss Arthur. It would be my absolute pleasure.'

And then they kissed again and those first few moments of Christmas 1911 were, they agreed many, many years later, the beginning of the most "wunnerful" Christmas morning they'd ever had . . . and absolute proof that secret Christmas wishes did indeed work.

CHAPTER THIRTY-FIVE

Present

> *For the prompt attention of Miss Viola Arthur. Come to Rose's garden at midnight on Christmas Eve. Your carriage awaits.*

It was intriguing, exciting, thrilling . . . all of that and more.

'Why did she need to come here?' Tegan asked. 'And who asked her?'

'I can't answer the first question,' Ryan said. 'But I can make an educated guess as to the second one. I think, for whatever reason, Laurie sent her that note. I compared the handwriting to the story I found and they're the same.'

'Forensic investigation. I like it.' She smiled.

He smiled back. 'Not sure it's part of my job description.'

'Maybe not — but, you know what?' She took a deep breath. 'I'm really pleased we've been working together, Ryan. You've helped me make sense of a lot of things. Like, both here.' She indicated the house. 'And here.' She tapped her heart and was kind of glad that it was maybe a little too dark for him to see her cheeks redden. 'I'll — miss you, when you go to Glasgow. I really will.' And there it was — out in the open. She could have kicked herself. What was it about this sparkling, magical garden that had made her blurt that out?

'I'm glad we worked together too,' he said. His voice seemed somehow softer and gentler, and she felt her shoulders relax. It had taken a lot of courage to admit what she'd just told him, but she was so pleased it hadn't been thrown back in her face.

The old Ryan, the one she'd known at Glasgow, might have done that. He might have scowled and huffed and grumbled and argued. But then again, the old Tegan wouldn't even have given him the time of day, never mind thanked him for anything at all.

'But you won't miss me, Tegan.' He sounded convinced of that fact.

'Wait. What?' She looked up, confused. She would miss him dreadfully, she really would. She was in fact considering looking for something up there herself when her contract came to an end at Pencradoc. She wouldn't be going back to Sicily. She wouldn't be returning to Angelo. She'd be returning — home. Returning, really, to wherever Ryan was . . .

He smiled and pushed his hands into his pockets, embarrassed, almost. 'You won't miss me because I'm not going anywhere.' He looked past her, out of the garden, towards the dark, secret moorlands. 'I decided to stay. This place — here. It's like being home. Do you know what I mean?'

'You turned the job down?' Part of her was shocked. She knew how much that opportunity had meant to him. But a greater part of her wanted to dance and cheer. He was staying! 'But yes — I know *exactly* what you mean. And for what it's worth — I'm really pleased you're staying. Honestly. I am.'

'Yeah.' He shrugged, trying, it seemed, to appear non-chalant, but there was a definite smile in his voice. 'Me too, quite frankly. I — I *hope* I did the right thing. Too late now, I guess.'

'It's perfect.' Her voice was almost a whisper, and she looked at him and got caught in his dark, promise-filled gaze. 'It was a perfect thing to do. I mean it.'

Oh my.

Tegan looked down at the letter again and read it, mainly just to break the eye contact between them, because the eye contact was doing weird, fluttery things to her stomach. Pathetically, she tried to change the subject to move on to things that didn't seem so charged and crackling between them. It was difficult. 'So, this letter.' She pretended to study it a little more. 'I would have loved to have been in that garden — *this* garden, actually — that Christmas Eve. I wonder what happened? I wish I knew.'

Ryan laughed softly. 'Remember where we are. Be careful what you wish for, because it is *highly* likely to happen. Christmas wishes and all that.'

'I guess.' She felt something damp on the back of her neck and reached a hand up. More cold, damp spots appeared on her bare hands and she looked up in surprise. 'Snow! Was that forecast?' White flakes were twirling and whirling silently throughout the garden, tumbling gently out of the sky, fluttering through the tree branches and sparkling against the fairy lights.

'I — I don't think so. God, I hope it doesn't settle. I still have to drive home. Don't fancy spending Christmas Eve stuck in my van in a layby.'

'If it gets bad, you could always stay here?' A part of her desperately hoped it *would* get bad and he *did* get stuck — so stuck that he couldn't get the van out of the Pencradoc grounds and had to spend Christmas Eve and Christmas Day at the very *least*, at Pencradoc.

'What — sleep in the car park? I could do, I guess. Wouldn't be the first time.'

'No. But . . .' She took a deep breath. 'I said nothing about staying in the van, did I?'

'No,' he said slowly. 'You didn't.'

He looked down, then looked at her and reached a hand out. He took her hand in his and pulled her a couple of steps towards him. She moved willingly and he took a couple of steps towards her.

'I could easily be persuaded to stay — like, not in the van — if the weather did turn,' he said quietly.

'That's good to know.'

And then, somehow, they were leaning in to one another and their lips were almost touching and her heart was beating crazily . . .

And a horse whinnied, so loudly it made them both jump.

They sprang apart and both turned to face the gateway to the garden, which gave out onto a branch of the main driveway. There was that misty look about the gateway again, the same sort of mistiness that had swallowed them up in Russell Square. Beyond the gateway, Tegan saw a row of lamps lining the driveway, and, coming up it, the shadowy image of a horse and carriage through the heavily falling snow.

The carriage was decorated for Christmas, the horse trotting happily along, lifting its hooves high and, despite the fact that it should have been terrifying to witness, Tegan felt a smile twitch at the corner of her lips. 'Can you see it, Ryan?' she whispered, turning to him. 'Do you see what I see?'

'I suspect I do.' His voice was filled with awe and his eyes followed the carriage as hers had done. She noticed he still held her hand and she squeezed his hand even tighter and moved a little closer to him.

The horse stopped and the driver dismounted. Discarding his coat and hat, tossing it to one side on a tree stump, tearing his scarf off and throwing it on top of them, a young man in a white shirt strode purposefully to the carriage door and flung it open.

Tegan watched as he reached out and bowed, holding his hand out and waiting for another hand to take it. A young woman, petite and dressed in an old-fashioned winter coat, sporting a warm-looking hat and a hand muff, took his hand and alighted from the carriage. There was a moment where she hesitated for a moment and looked up at him.

The couple walked towards Tegan and Ryan, completely oblivious to them, looking at one another, the snow blanketing the ground and falling steadily around them.

'It's them,' whispered Tegan. 'Laurie and Viola!'

'Definitely.' Ryan was staring at them, wide-eyed. 'Is it them, though, or one of those ghostly memory things, where something happened that left its imprint on the area?'

'You've been doing your research. But yes, I've heard of those too . . .'

The couple came closer and stopped. Then they turned to one other . . .

But whatever happened after that was lost to the mysteries of time and the magic of Pencradoc as the figures faded and became as unsubstantial as the mist and the snowflakes that, even now, were slowing down and melting on the ground around them.

Tegan blinked and the scene settled into her own familiar time and place. The horse and carriage had gone, the paths were only lit by the cheerful jam jars and the ground was just simply wet.

She turned to Ryan and there were still the ghosts of snowflakes glistening in his hair and on his shoulders, but, even as she watched, they melted and disappeared. No snow was evident beyond that, anywhere at all.

'Snow's stopped,' she said.

'That's actually a bit of a shame,' he replied. Then he shrugged. 'Mum and Dad will be happy at least.'

Tegan hid a smile and was just about to make a flip-pant response when the church bells started chiming, and continued chiming until they had rung twelve times.

'Midnight?' she asked, confused. 'But . . .' She checked her watch. It was barely five o'clock in the evening. 'It can't be.'

Ryan shook his head and when he spoke, his voice was low. 'It's not midnight *here*. I think it's midnight on Christmas Eve *somewhere*. Sometime. Like, oh, I don't know, in 1911?'

A chill ran up Tegan's spine. He was right. Midnight on Christmas Eve was the time when Miss Viola Arthur had been requested to visit Rose's garden.

'I'd say it was the witching hour,' she said. 'But it's not.'

'Not at all.'

'It's the magical hour. And I think we just witnessed their magic. Laurie's and Viola's.' She held up the letter. 'I think I can guess the rest and why they kept this. It was special to them. Incredibly special, I'd say.'

'I'd agree.' Ryan nodded. Then he pulled her gently towards him again so they were facing one another. Gosh, he was *tall*!

Or was she just short?

Oh, it didn't matter.

All that mattered was that they were there, together, on Christmas Eve — the most magical day of the year.

'Do you think we could go so far as to say it's incredi-bly special for us as well?' asked Ryan. For the first time, he sounded unsure. He looked, in that enchanted garden, as young and unsure as he had done the first time he'd walked into that gallery in Glasgow.

What had she thought of him then?

If she was honest, and examined her feelings, she hadn't hated him at all, not really. She'd actually felt a little annoyed that yet another man was working in that place and not only that, but a big, tall man with piercings and dark hair and a scowl that could make you scowl back.

But he'd actually tried to look after her and keep her safe. That night in the bar with the drunk who wouldn't give up had scared her, and he'd been willing to wade in and rescue her, even though they'd spent the day arguing over a petty, silly incident.

Things could have been so different if they'd taken the time to get to know each other properly in Glasgow. So very different and so very — nice

What a mess.

And what an utter, utter waste of time.

Because she now had a moment of complete clarity and this man was someone she wanted in her life desperately. Had done for a long, long time — but was afraid to admit it to herself or, God forbid, to him.

She would be completely *stupid* to waste another moment.

'Incredibly special?' she said now. Then she placed her palm on his chest. 'I just wish I'd got to know you properly earlier, so I could have — loved you — longer, and that just about sums it up.' She raised her eyes to his. 'I do actually mean that as well.'

'Really?' His mouth quirked in a smile. 'Even if I have rubbish taste in music?'

'We can work on that,' she said.

Ryan laughed and leaned in towards her again. 'I echo your sentiments,' he said. 'Although I think I have loved you longer than I realised. Longer than we both realised, perhaps. Merry Christmas, Tegan Burton.'

'Merry Christmas, Ryan Jackson.'

And then, finally, they kissed.

And perhaps Ryan wouldn't be spending that particular Christmas Eve at Pencradoc, but Tegan knew without a shadow of a doubt that they would spend Christmas together next year. And the year after that. And the year after that . . .

And that was the most magical feeling of all.

THE END

ACKNOWLEDGEMENTS

It's been wonderful to revisit Pencradoc and create *Mirrors of the Past*, the fifth book in the Cornish Secrets series. I hope that readers will enjoy this book, as it follows almost directly on from *Promises of the Past*, which was largely based in mid-summer. So it made sense for the Christmas story to be based around midwinter. If you know me at all, you'll know that I love the solstices and they fitted this series perfectly.

Once again, I found myself going down the rabbit hole of American socialites — especially the Dollar Princesses who came to England with their wealth to marry into the nobility — and I learned some fascinating facts. Seriously, Google the Alva Vanderbilt Ball from 1883 and look in amazement at the costumes. It's a tale which includes social snubs, "frenemies" and dresses that lit up with electric lights — as well as costumes containing cat headdresses. Truth, as they say, can be stranger than fiction. The parties in this book are a lot less extravagant than that one, but it was a joy to imagine them and write them, regardless.

The story of Viola's acquaintance, Dorothy Arnold, is sadly a true one, and again worth reading about if you wish.

Another true fact is the marriage of the beautiful Flora Davis to Terence John Temple Hamilton-Temple-Blackwood, Second Marquess of Dufferin and Ava.

Thanks must go to my wonderful editors, Radhika Sonagra and Emma Grundy Haigh, and all the team at Joffe Books including Jasmine, Becky, Abbie and Tia, and my amazing cover designer, Alexandra Allden. Also to our fantastic Choc Lit Tasting Panel and the support network of our Choc Lit Family — especially Berni Stevens and Ella Cook, who kept me going when I didn't think I'd crack this one. Thank you!

The biggest thanks of all have to go to my family — to my parents, my husband and my son for various helpful moments including the provision of coffee, biscuits, chocolate and prosecco. And to my dog Robbie, thank you for the soggy chops in my face each day and the warm weight of you on my feet while I'm working — you're much warmer than slippers!

THE CHOC LIT STORY

Established in 2009, Choc Lit is an independent, award-winning publisher dedicated to creating a delicious selection of quality women's fiction.

We have won 18 awards, including Publisher of the Year and the Romantic Novel of the Year, and have been shortlisted for countless others. In 2023, we were shortlisted for Publisher of the Year by the Romantic Novelists' Association.

All our novels are selected by genuine readers. We are proud to publish talented first-time authors, as well as established writers whose books we love introducing to a new generation of readers.

In 2023, we became a Joffe Books company. Best known for publishing a wide range of commercial fiction, Joffe Books has its roots in women's fiction. Today it is one of the largest independent publishers in the UK.

We love to hear from you, so please email us about absolutely anything bookish at choc-lit@joffebooks.com

If you want to hear about all our bargain new releases, join our mailing list: www.choc-lit.com/contact